The Photograph

ALSO BY DEBBIE RIX

The Girl with Emerald Eyes
Daughters of the Silk Road
The Silk Weaver's Wife

The
Photograph

DEBBIE RIX

Bookouture

Published by Bookouture in 2018

An imprint of StoryFire Ltd.

Carmelite House
50 Victoria Embankment
London EC4Y 0DZ

www.bookouture.com

ISBN: 978-1-78681-477-7
eBook ISBN: 978-1-78681-476-0

This book is a work of fiction. Names, characters, businesses,
organizations, places and events other than those clearly in the
public domain, are either the product of the author's imagination
or are used fictitiously. Any resemblance to actual persons, living or
dead, events or locales is entirely coincidental.

For Anthony

PROLOGUE

The crowds in the town swirled and moved and, for a moment, a path opened up between her and Tommaso. He looked up momentarily from his card hand. There was a flash of recognition as he caught sight of her. He stood up, saying something to his friend. She smiled fleetingly at him, and then was gone. Back into her car, reversing down the little road and onto the ring road around the town, heading for the causeway back to Cagliari, onto the ferry to Rome, then back to London – and to everything that was most dear.

PART ONE

I belong to you;
there is really no other way of expressing it,
and that is not strong enough.
Franz Kafka

Chapter 1

Herne Hill, London
March 2016

Sophie closed the door to the little box room as quietly as possible, anxious not to alert her husband, Hamish, who was sleeping in their bedroom across the landing. The box room was filled with dusty packing cases from their last house move five years earlier, and it aggravated her. She wanted the room cleared out, but Hamish refused to help. This niggling disagreement had been going on for several months and was part of a much bigger struggle, a complex combination of simmering tension that festered between husband and wife.

Sophie went downstairs to the kitchen, put the kettle on the range and pottered about, clearing up from the night before. Friends had come for dinner and the sink was still filled with the roasting pans that had been left soaking overnight. They'd had a nice enough evening – sharing jokes, discussing politics and work gossip – but lurking beneath the surface were layers of unspoken resentments between Sophie and Hamish that intermittently bubbled to the surface. Later in the evening, Sophie had filled the sink with hot water and began to wash up the serving dishes. Hamish, fuzzy with red wine and brandy, had stood behind her, his arms wrapped round her waist, nuzzling her neck.

'Don't,' she'd said. 'Help me with this.'

Hamish, hurt at this rejection, had sloped off to bed.

When Sophie had finally followed him upstairs, they'd argued, before climbing into opposite sides of the bed, both bristling with indignation.

As she washed and dried the pans the following morning, putting them away in the bottom of the dresser, Sophie thought about Hamish; about the way his back had been turned away from her the night before. She still felt a glimmer of resentment at his refusal to help, but nevertheless made two cups of tea – a small conciliatory gesture – and took them upstairs. Hamish was sitting up in bed checking emails on his phone when she came in.

'Morning,' he said. 'I'm sorry about last night. I should have been more helpful.'

'Yes… well. The washing-up's all done now.' She put his mug of tea on the bedside table.

'Thanks…' He looked up at her expectantly from beneath his sandy lashes. 'I was just tired,' he explained.

She studied him for a moment with her dark grey-green eyes before wandering over to the chest of drawers and picking up her hairbrush.

'But that's no excuse, is it?' He paused, waiting for her to reply but she seemed intent on vigorously brushing her long dark hair.

'I'm just worried about applying for the new job,' he continued, by way of explanation. 'You know how important it is to me.'

'I do understand, Hamish,' she said, impassively, turning to look at him, 'but I really can't talk about that now. I've got to get off to work.'

'Can we talk later then?' He sipped his tea, admiring the way her loose silk kimono slipped off her shoulder; her dark hair trailing in gleaming tresses down her back. 'Sophie…?'

She didn't reply, but twisted her hair into an instant chignon that she fixed, expertly, with a pair of combs, and selected a black skirt from her wardrobe.

'Why don't you come back to bed?' he asked.

'No, I can't this morning, sorry,' she said from the other side of the room, 'I've got a meeting with my PhD supervisor this morning – I've really got to get going.'

Dressed in the black skirt and a pale blue sweater, she shoved her notes into her bag, leant over the bed and kissed him, fleetingly, on the cheek – the kiss you give a distant relative, not the kiss of a wife for her husband.

'Shouldn't you be off too?' she asked, checking her reflection in the mirror.

'I've got a slightly later start,' he said.

'Time to sort the box room out, then,' she cajoled, slinging her bag over her shoulder.

'Not that again? Can't you just leave it?'

'Fine, fine…' she answered, impatiently, picking up her leather jacket from the chair. 'See you later.'

Sophie was thirty-three, and had been married to Hamish for eight years. They met at a friend's wedding and it had been love at first sight – at least that's how they both remembered it, how they described it to new friends and acquaintances. Sophie was an anthropologist, studying for a PhD at London University, exploring various aspects of Roman burial. Hamish was a registrar at King's College Hospital in south London. They lived in a small terraced house in Herne Hill, South London. Sophie had been brought up in Hampstead and had never really got used to living south of the river. But it was convenient for Hamish's job, and as his hours were more demanding than hers, with weekends on call and frequent late nights, they moved there to suit him.

After nearly four years in the same job, Hamish was on the lookout for a consultant's post. As they prepared dinner for their guests the night before, he and Sophie had squabbled about a job that had recently been advertised in Cheltenham. Hamish was keen to apply, but Sophie was concerned about moving so far out of London.

'How will I complete my PhD from Cheltenham,' she had asked him, as they waited for their guests to arrive. 'I have to be in London at least two or three times a week. I have to meet with my supervisor, I have lectures to give – students who need me. Have you thought about that?'

'Honestly? No,' he'd replied. 'But this is not about you, Sophie; it's about me and our future…'

As she walked down the road towards the station, she smarted with renewed irritation about his assumption that she would just abandon her PhD to suit him. She was annoyed too about the box room. He simply refused to help her clear it out. Why had it become such a battleground? It wasn't that the room really needed clearing. There was no pressing deadline, like a visiting relative, or urgent need for a spare room. But Sophie wanted it cleared; she wanted it to be prepared – cleaned and decorated. She wanted it to be waiting for a time that she hoped would be coming soon, if she could only get pregnant…

If she could just have a baby, she might be more willing to abandon her PhD, move to Gloucestershire and be a consultant's wife. In many ways, it was exactly what she wanted. But the sheer wretchedness of her inability to conceive made her stubborn. The box room, filled with her husband's notes from his student days and the discarded detritus from their previous lives, was a physical manifestation of their impasse. She wanted a baby; her body refused to cooperate. She wanted the room empty for the baby; her husband refused to cooperate. He wanted to move out of London; she refused to cooperate.

As Sophie stood on the platform at Herne Hill station, a cool breeze blew in across the tracks. The station was dirty and, she had to admit, rather depressing.

When her train came in, it was packed as usual, and she stood all the way to London, wedged between a man with appalling body odour and a young woman who spoke loudly into her mobile phone for the entire journey. At Blackfriars station, she took the tube to Tottenham Court Road. From there she walked the final leg of the journey to the British Museum, where one of her supervisors was based. She loved the route – the buildings in that part of London were architecturally all of a piece. Nearing the museum itself, walking past the tourists gathering in eager gaggles, she always got a rush of excitement as she crossed the threshold and entered the vast atrium. This stunning centre of learning – of research, of knowledge – was her playground. She believed, on days like today, that she had the best job in the world.

She took the lift to the first floor where the anthropological library and research centre was based. With ten minutes to spare before her meeting with her supervisor, she wandered into a gallery exhibiting Roman and Greek vessels – intricately designed pots and bowls made of verdigris bronze, and pottery painted with decorative scenes. The idea that something so delicate could survive intact for over two thousand years never failed to impress Sophie. A particular favourite was the Portland Vase. Made early in the first century, this Roman hand-blown dark glass vase was decorated in exquisite detail with a white cameo design of languorous men and women, relaxing by the sea. Discovered in Italy in the seventeenth century, it had been transported from Naples to England, where the Duke of Portland had lent it to Josiah Wedgewood, who created an entire industry based on its stunning designs.

The vase was thought to have been a wedding gift, and as such was a remarkable example of first century workmanship. Any items from this period were of interest to Sophie – not just because they were beautiful but also from a professional perspective. The title of her PhD was *The Rituals and rites associated with burial sites of Ancient Rome, with a particular focus on Pagan, Jewish and Christian traditions in 1st and 2nd century AD.* It was a subject that had long interested her. Her great-grandfather, George Laszlo, had been an expert on classical archaeology and had also

worked at London University. Sophie was proud of this link
with her august antecedent. When she walked into the college
buildings, she often thought of her great-grandfather striding up
the same steps fifty years earlier. After studying for an MA, she
too had taught at the university, and two or three times a year
took groups of students to work on archaeological digs around
the Mediterranean. Her work was challenging and fulfilling,
but time spent away from home for long periods put inevitable
stresses on her marriage and disrupted her attempts at getting
pregnant. To be abroad on a dig at the precise moment she was
ovulating was frustrating to say the least. And, at first, that was
how she reconciled her inability to conceive.

As she sat outside her supervisor's office, she recalled the first
time she and Hamish had discussed starting a family. They had just
moved into the house in Herne Hill; it was in a state of disrepair and
they spent every weekend stripping old woodchip from the walls.

'Do you want children, Hamish?' she'd asked, as she coated the
wallpaper with water.

'What… now?' he had asked, laughing, holding up his hands
covered in glue and bits of paper.

'No… not now,' she'd laughed, 'but, you know… some time.'

'Sure – I'd love kids. But it's your call, Sophie. Whatever you
want really.'

This was not the ringing endorsement she had hoped for. When
she had imagined this moment, she had fantasised that he would
sweep her up in his arms and declare himself excited at the prospect
of fatherhood – like Jimmy Stewart in *It's a Wonderful Life*. Sophie
loved the film, especially the scene when Mary tells George she is
pregnant. Stewart's face goes through the full gamut of emotions,
from disbelief, to joy and excitement. There was no doubting
George's elation at the prospect of becoming a father. By contrast,
Hamish had been about as far from 'elated' as it was possible to
be. On reflection, it was the perfect response and she realised that

he was probably anxious not to put too much pressure on her. He was telling her that whatever happened, he would be happy. If they had a child, then great; if not, then that would be fine too. But, of course, what it meant was that she carried the burden – the desire for a child, the desperation, as each period came and went with lunar regularity – totally alone.

That evening, she sat Hamish down after dinner.

'I'd like to ask you something,' she said. 'Something I've been thinking about for a long time.'

'OK.' He looked momentarily worried and poured himself another glass of wine. 'You're not leaving me, are you? I know we don't always see eye to eye these days…'

'No!' She reached across the table and took his hand. 'Of course not. I realise we've both been rather on edge recently. There are just so many things that are unresolved in our lives…'

'Like my job?'

'Yes… like your job, like my desire to finish my PhD and… perhaps most important – at least as far as I'm concerned – my desire for a baby.'

Hamish flushed slightly. 'A baby…?'

'Yes… You know how much I want a baby – don't you? I'm thirty-three… I've been off the pill for well over two years now – and I'm still not pregnant. I'm worried that there's something wrong.'

'Well, your body needs time to adjust when you've been on the pill.' He reached across the table and took her hand. He squeezed it, comfortingly, but a tiny bead of sweat trickled down his forehead.

'For two and a half years? No, Hamish, there's something wrong, I know it.'

'Maybe it's just not to be.' He wiped the sweat off his forehead with the heel of his hand, pushing his strawberry blond hair away from his face.

She stared at him in disbelief. 'What do you mean? Not to be…
It *has* to be, Hamish. I have to have a child… I thought you knew
that?' She stood up from the table and paced the kitchen, tears
streaming down her face.

'Darling,' he said, putting his arms around her. 'I'm sorry… I…'

'I want to try IVF,' she said, firmly, turning to face him.

'IVF?'

'Yes… is that such a surprise? It's the obvious thing to do. I
made an appointment for Tuesday next week. You'll have to… give
a sample. And take a day off.'

'Well,' said the consultant, staring at his computer screen, 'the
results look good.'

Sophie leaned forward hopefully.

'Good?' she asked, as if she might have become miraculously
pregnant since arriving at the doctor's offices.

'What I mean is, neither of you appears to have anything
wrong. Hamish's motility seems quite normal.' He winked at
Hamish. 'And from what you've told me, Sophie, you appear to
be producing a perfectly healthy egg each month. Your periods
are normal… regular.'

'Pretty much,' said Sophie. 'So why am I not pregnant?'

'Ahh… the million-dollar question. It could be due to several
factors. But the good news is that there is no obvious reason why
you haven't yet conceived. I think I must suggest – given your
relatively young age… you're only thirty or so, aren't you?' he said,
consulting his notes.

'Thirty-three,' Sophie corrected him, firmly.

'That's still quite young. I suggest you just need to just keep
on trying.'

He attempted a sympathetic smile, addressed primarily towards
Hamish.

'Well… thanks.' Hamish stood up, clearly anxious to leave as soon as possible. He hated this medical intrusion into their private lives.

'But there must be something else we can do?' Sophie remained firmly seated.

'Well,' the consultant said, sighing slightly, 'there are techniques we can try, if things don't work out naturally.'

'IVF…' Sophie said, hopefully.

'Yes… that. But it's not a golden bullet… I'm sure your husband, being a doctor himself, would have discussed that with you?' He looked over at Hamish, who nodded.

'Yes,' said Sophie. 'I know there's no guarantee.'

'Look, I really advise you to just relax – if you can. I'm sure things will work out. And if, in a year or so, nothing has happened, come back to see me and we'll see what we can do.'

On their journey home, Hamish sat next to the window in the grubby overground train carriage and read the evening paper. He loathed public transport and chose to lose himself in any kind of reading matter. Sophie, on the other hand, was often content to study the people around her. But that late afternoon, it seemed that every other passenger was a female brandishing her fertility.

The woman sitting opposite was talking to her nanny on the phone.

'I'm nearly home,' she said, 'can you give them tea and I'll do their bath as soon as I get there.'

A small boy, strapped into his pushchair, had been wedged between a pair of grumpy commuters, who were clearly irritated by this contraption banging against their calves as the train lurched round corners.

Further along the carriage, a heavily pregnant woman struggled through the crowded train, hoping for a seat. An older woman on the other side of the carriage stood up for her.

It seemed to Sophie there were reminders of her inadequacy everywhere she looked.

'I think we should go for it,' she said to Hamish as they walked hand in hand down their street.

'What?' he asked, knowing precisely what she meant.

'You know… the IVF.'

'Darling…'

'I know what you're going to say,' she interrupted him. 'There are no guarantees, if we can't get it on the NHS, then it will be expensive, blah, blah… I know. But I want to try – please.'

'It's not just that,' he said as they walked up the narrow brick path to their front door. 'I'm a doctor, Sophie. I understand what it will involve – making love to order, blood tests, hormonal injections – the inevitable highs and lows, have you any idea what kind of Pandora's box you're opening up?'

He unlocked the door, throwing the paper onto the hall table with his keys, and headed for the kitchen. He took a beer out of the fridge, prising the top open, swigging the beer back with relief.

'Hamish… it's four-thirty in the afternoon!' Sophie nodded towards the beer.

'I know, but I'm not at work for once. I think I'm entitled to one beer for heaven's sake.'

He went through to the sitting room and flicked on the television, slumping down in front of a mindless quiz show.

Sophie stood in the kitchen, staring at their well-designed London garden – an anniversary present from Hamish the previous year. They could have had two rounds of IVF at the smart private clinic for what it had cost. The small patch of green lawn was intersected by Yorkstone slabs laid at a trendy diagonal, leading the eye to the summer house painted a fashionable shade somewhere between grey and green. The tiny vegetable patch in the far corner was planted with an artistic display of early salad leaves. In her imagination, Sophie saw a child on a swing on the lawn, a little trampoline in the corner by the summer house. The terrace covered with the detritus of colourful plastic toys. But in reality, there was no swing, no trampoline. There was just a neat new arrangement of elegant architectural plants and a perfect lawn.

She opened the fridge, took out a bottle of white wine, poured herself a large glass and began to cry.

Chapter 2

Budapest
23 October 1956

The handles of Rachael's straw shopping baskets chafed, digging into the soft flesh of her fingers. She stopped on the first-floor landing of her building outside the apartment of her neighbour, Mrs Kovacs, and leant her shopping bags up against the wall. She spat onto the red weals developing on her palms and rubbed them together.

The door of the apartment, scuffed with age, opened a tiny crack.

'Who's there?' asked a querulous voice.

'It's only me, Mrs Kovacs – Rachael from upstairs. My shopping was heavy… I just stopped for a moment…'

The disembodied voice grunted and the door slammed shut.

These were difficult times in Budapest and people were increasingly nervous. You never knew who was listening, or what people might be saying about you to the authorities. Food was short, but that was nothing new. It had been the same since the war. Rachael could not remember a time when she didn't have to queue at the market for meagre rations – a small portion of sausage, or an onion. But today her baskets were filled, almost to overflowing, with turnips. She had arrived at the market on Hold Street just after half past six that morning. If she went any later, most of the stalls would have run out of the basic staples – bread, vegetables and so on. Waiting patiently for her ration of dark rye bread, she'd overheard a couple of women in the queue ahead of her.

'Janos has just had a big delivery of turnips,' whispered one woman to her friend. 'He has a cousin in the countryside – they arrived last night apparently.' Rachael didn't particularly like turnips, and neither did her husband, nor her father; but food was scarce, the air was turning chilly, and a good hot turnip soup would be welcome.

By the time she'd reached Janos's stall there was already a long line of women snaking through the market. She feared there would be nothing left when she arrived at the front of the queue, but she smiled charmingly at the old man as he filled her bags to the brim.

Once inside the flat, she unloaded the turnips and her other groceries into the old pine larder. A slab of grey marble sat atop the centre shelf – a cool place to store cheese, butter or a piece of cold meat. The shelves above were lined with decorated paper, its lacy frieze spilling over the edges, like a petticoat glimpsed beneath a dress. Rachael's mother had always insisted on this lining paper and she continued the tradition. Jars of home-made jam and pickle stood in neat rows, while the cupboards below contained vegetables and tinned food, arranged meticulously in baskets of varying sizes.

The cupboard loaded up to her satisfaction, Rachael set about cleaning the kitchen. She ran a washcloth under the wheezing tap and squeezed it out into an old stained stone sink. From here she had a view of the alley at the back of the house. A tall maple tree grew optimistically out of the bare ground, its branches brushing against the kitchen window. At this time of year, its leaves were evolving from green through yellow and orange. By November they would be scarlet. The tree was one of the joys of autumn for Rachael.

She wiped the surface of the old pine kitchen table free of crumbs – the remnants of their simple breakfast – and retrieved some of the turnips from the larder. She chopped them into small pieces, placing them into a pan of water. József, her husband, and George would be home for lunch soon and she was determined to have a warm meal ready for them.

As the soup simmered on the old gas stove, Rachael tidied the sitting room. She plumped the old velvet cushions on the sofa. She polished the silver-framed photographs of her father, mother and grandparents that were displayed so proudly on top of the walnut boudoir grand piano. The piano had belonged originally to her great-grandparents and the apartment had been in the family for generations – her own father had lived there all his life. It stood on the second floor of an old building on Henszlmann Imre Street and had large bay windows overlooking the park opposite. To live so close to a green space was a luxury and gave the apartment the air of a grand country house – or so Rachael liked to imagine. It was considered one of the most graceful of all the flats in that particular building – with its spacious rooms, high ceilings and elegant proportions. And yet it was conveniently near the centre of town, and just a short walk to the university where her father taught archaeology.

George fretted, from to time, that the spacious apartment might be taken away from them. The communist government had begun to insist that larger houses and flats were split up and shared between families to accommodate the growing influx of workers into the cities. But Rachael was blissfully unaware of these concerns, and as she rubbed beeswax polish onto the piano's surface, her eye fell on a group of children playing in the park. It reminded her of the happy times she had spent with her mother, Irma.

With dark hair and unusual pale green eyes – colouring that Rachael had inherited – Irma had been considered a beauty. She had married George when she was just seventeen. Already a young university lecturer, George was fiercely intelligent, gregarious and energetic. Irma adored him, and he, in turn, was quite devoted to her. She threw herself into domesticity, caring not just for her husband and daughter, but also for both his parents right up until their death. Progressing swiftly up the academic ladder, George became a Professor of Archaeology at Budapest University. He was at the centre of a group of intellectuals who met regularly at the Laszlo's apartment to discuss philosophy, politics and history. They despised the Stalinist regime under which they lived and whilst George had some sympathy with socialist principles, he abhorred totalitarianism. This desire for democracy forced him to live constantly in a state of vigilance; for his political views were considered both dangerous and revolutionary.

This was the world Rachael had been born into. Her mother was a discreet presence in the background, supporting her husband and caring for her family. But the war and its aftermath had taken its toll. She was anxious about George, fearful that he would be arrested for his radical views. She was worried too for their Jewish friends, more of whom were being rounded up and, in some cases, sent out of Budapest. There were rumours of camps where people were being imprisoned, or worse. It seemed unimaginable.

The deprivations of war, the rationing, the bombings and destruction of much of her beloved capital city wore Irma down, and one day, while Rachael was at school, her mother collapsed in the street. A neighbour found her lying on the pavement near the park, her shopping spilled across the road. With a group of passers-by, he managed to carry her into the apartment building and up the stairs. When Rachael arrived home, her father was waiting to give her the news.

'The doctor has been here. Your mother has had a stroke. I must warn you, Rachael; he is not hopeful.'

Together they sat beside her bed for three days and nights, until one morning Irma opened her pale green eyes, made a curious guttural sound in her throat and died.

From that day on Rachael never went back to school. Although only sixteen, she was determined to take care of her father, obsessed with the idea that she had to stay at home in order to keep him safe. The idea of her going out to school each day, living a life separate from his, became impossible. What if *he* too died while she was out? She would be left, abandoned, an orphan.

George was concerned for her.

'You should go back to school, Rachael – you are too young to give up your education.'

'No, Papa – who would look after you? And if anything happened to you… how would I live? How could I go on?'

Her position seemed quite logical to her.

'You staying here won't keep me safe,' he argued. 'And besides, you're a clever girl – you could go to university, become a professional. Aren't you lonely here all day, alone?'

'No…' she had replied honestly. 'I like it. I love this apartment, I love you…'

It was true that she didn't really miss her friends. She missed her mother, certainly, which was why she tried to continue to run the house exactly as her mother had done. In some ways it made her feel that her mother was still there, living with them. As she scrubbed the kitchen, or polished the piano, or stirred pickle on the gas stove, she thought of her mother and liked to imagine that Irma was in the room next door. As for love, Rachael remained quite childlike, and was content to admire handsome men from afar. She read the newspaper each day and was delighted if she found an article about a film star, or a famous sportsman. Ervin Zador who played water polo for his country was a particular favourite. Tall, dark-haired and muscular, she cut photographs of him out of the paper and hid them beneath her pillow.

One evening, George returned home with a young man named Andras. He was good looking, and appeared earnest and intelligent, Rachael thought. The two men sat in the drawing room and talked, and as Rachael wandered in and out with drinks, it seemed obvious that Andras was keen to impress his professor. He looked delighted when George pressed him to remain and share their supper.

As they sat around the kitchen table, George made continual excuses to leave Rachael alone with his student protégé. But the young pair struggled to make conversation. In spite of his good looks, Rachael found nothing in Andras to excite her. And she got the impression that her domestic existence bored him. When the boy had gone, George quizzed Rachael.

'Did you like Andras? I think he is very intelligent.'

'He was all right. Why?'

'Nothing...' said George, lighting his pipe.

'Papa... I know what you are up to... You think I will fall for him because he is handsome... marry him, maybe. Is that it?'

'Well, you have to marry someone. I worry... What if something happens to me? You will be alone. You need a husband. And if you won't go to school and meet someone, I shall bring them to you.'

'Oh, Papa... that poor young man. He had no idea what you were planning. He thought you brought him here because you admired him or were interested in his ideas. And all he got was an introduction to your boring daughter...'

'He should have been grateful,' said George. 'And you are not boring. You are the most intelligent, beautiful daughter any father ever had.'

'Well... I don't think Andras thought so,' said Rachael, laughing. 'Besides, I didn't like him much either.'

Over the following years, a trickle of potential young admirers were invited to the Laszlo's apartment. Rachael was always polite, and the young men clearly confused as to why they were there – momentarily seduced by the idea that their professor had singled them out for special treatment. But one evening, George returned with a young man named József Kelemen. He was a student of archaeology, a couple of years older than Rachael. He was not particularly tall, had dark blond curly hair, wore small tortoiseshell glasses and an engaging grin.

Rachael blushed when the young man first came into the drawing room. Her father, always observant, was encouraged.

József was precisely the sort of young man he hoped his beloved daughter might marry one day – intellectual and quick-witted with an interest in student politics.

After supper József helped Rachael with the washing-up. George had left them to themselves, going to the drawing room to play the piano.

'Your father plays very well,' said József, taking a crystal glass from Rachael, and drying it carefully with the tea towel.

'He does. He does everything well – or hadn't you noticed?' She laughed, handing him another glass.

'He's taught me so much,' said József. 'I feel privileged to have a teacher like him.'

'He's a brilliant man. But you don't have to be so polite. He can be impossible too.'

The washing-up finished, Rachael lingered over the sink, wanting their conversation to continue, but unsure how to proceed.

'Why are you not at the university yourself?' asked József. He was intrigued by Rachael; she was beautiful, certainly – with her long dark hair tucked behind her neat ears, and her large doe-like eyes. But there was something else – a gentleness and sensitivity that he found appealing.

'I… I feel I'm needed here. My mother died a few years ago, and my father needs someone to look after him. He's very busy.'

'But what about your own education? Your own life?'

'I'm quite happy,' said Rachael. 'I read a lot, and I play the piano – not as well as my father, but tolerably. I look after the house – I shop for food, and so on. Not that there is much food to buy these days. Maybe one day I will go to university. But now… my father needs me here.'

When József had gone, she realised she had never opened up so easily to anyone before. Her instinct was always to be reticent, to hold back. In part, it was the world they lived in, where half-truths and lies were advisable to avoid being noticed by the authorities.

*

Over the following days, Rachael found herself daydreaming about József. One morning, as she laid a plate of toast with home-made damson jam in front of her father, she asked if he might bring the young man to supper again.

'So you like this one?' her father said, delightedly.

'I do,' said Rachael, smiling. 'I find myself... interested in him. He was kind, and thoughtful and he made me laugh...'

Their courtship was swift and they married in April 1956. She was just twenty, he was twenty-two. George took the couple to the Astoria Hotel for dinner to celebrate. He ordered champagne – a rare treat, and a new experience for Rachael. She delighted in the bubbles that bounced against her nose, the sweetness, mixed with tartness – like a perfect apple, picked fresh from the orchard.

They ate *paprikás* – a rich stew flavoured with paprika, sprinkled with little dumplings; for dessert there were crêpes stuffed with ground walnuts, flambéed in brandy at the table and served with a rich chocolate sauce. The waiter made rather a show of his culinary skills – holding the pan over the little gas burner, pouring in the alcohol with great aplomb before igniting it. Rachael, who had never seen such flamboyance before, stared open-mouthed as the concoction was laid in front of her.

She could still taste the chocolate as she and her new husband walked back to the apartment building that night to start their new life together.

József slipped effortlessly into the family. He shared domestic chores, and they enjoyed noisy meals together, discussing politics and history. He particularly enjoyed George's social evenings when university colleagues came to supper and their drawing room was filled with intelligent conversation. Rachael was intensely proud of József: his empathy with everyone and his skills in debate. He had a keen intelligence and a maturity that belied his years. Rachael only occasionally ventured an opinion. She lacked the confidence to be truly part of the conversation, preferring her role as hostess, relishing the hubbub, laughter and argument, like the owner of a popular restaurant.

One night, after a successful evening, the guests had gone home and she and József lay peacefully in bed. He was reading through some notes ahead of the following day's lecture and she was trying to concentrate on a novel she had borrowed earlier that day from the library. But her mind kept wandering to a subject she had wanted to broach with József for some time. Finally she laid her book down on the bedside table.

'Would you ever like to have a child?'

'Of course,' he said, casually, not really listening.

'Really? That's good.'

'Why?' He removed his glasses and laid them on top of his notes. 'Are you pregnant?'

'No!' she laughed. 'At least I don't think so. I just meant… if it happened, would you be happy?'

He relaxed visibly and pulled her towards him.

'Darling – of course I would be happy. But you know this is a difficult world in which to bring a child. Our country is not our country anymore… times are hard.'

Rachael had experienced the queues in the market; she had observed the fear on people's faces when the police were inspecting their papers, but beyond that, she had little understanding of the political upheaval in her country.

'But there is never a good time is there?' she asked. 'Even in the war, people had children…'

Over the following weeks, Rachael became aware of her husband's growing disillusionment with both his studies and their country. She often found him together with her father, hunched around the radio in the drawing room, listening intently to Voice of America as it urged the people of Eastern Europe to rise up against their communist overlords. George was excited, obsessed with the opportunities opening up before them.

'Listen... this is the voice of democratic freedom. The time will come, József, you will see, when we will overthrow our undemocratic communist government.'

Unknown to Rachael, József was becoming increasingly involved with a group of radical students who were determined to reinstate a former liberal prime minister – Imre Nagy. A demonstration was planned for later that day. Thousands of students planned to march through Budapest towards the Parliament building. On that morning, as József shaved in the little basin in their bedroom, he declared himself bored by archaeology.

'I should be studying politics,' he said. 'That is what matters now.'

'Don't you enjoy archaeology?' Rachael asked, innocently. 'I always think it sounds so fascinating. When my father talks about people from the past – the Romans, or the Phoenicians – their lives sound so glamorous.'

'You think so...? That shows how little you know. There was glamour, certainly, if you were at the top of the pile; but less so further down. Do you know what archaeology has taught me?'

Rachael knelt on the bed, looking up, eagerly, at her husband.

'That since the beginning of time, life has always been a struggle for most people. There is so much in this world that is unjust, Rachael. While I am studying the buildings and bones of our ancestors, people are suffering around me – *now*. I should be doing something for *them*, not thinking about people who died long ago.'

With two men to feed every day, Rachael had settled into a routine. She would often make soup for lunch, and that morning in October, as the maple tree in the back yard turned from yellow to orange, was no different. After tidying the sitting room, she wandered through to the kitchen and turned up the heat under the soup until it was bubbling merrily. She took three bowls from the shelf and placed them in the oven to warm. She cut the bread she had bought that morning – three slices, buttered carefully. She laid the bread in the centre of the table and arranged the water glasses.

Standing at the old stone sink, she filled a jug with water. The pipes rattled, the tap wheezed; the water spluttered into the crystal jug. Normally these everyday sounds of domesticity were drowned out by the chatter between her husband and father as they flew through the door of the kitchen, bringing their noise and scents from the outside world.

'We only have twenty minutes... Rachael darling. Is lunch ready?' her husband would call out to her.

Then there would be the sound of chairs being pulled away from the table, the thud of boots on the floor and the clatter of spoons against china, as the men hurriedly ate their soup.

But today there was silence.

It was nearing one o'clock when Rachael finally heard the key in the lock. She put the jug of water onto the table and went through to the sitting room. Her father was staring out of the window.

'Papa?' she walked over to him and slid her arm around his waist, feeling the familiar rough tweed of his jacket against her naked forearm.

'Where's József... is he coming later?'

George turned his face to hers and she saw tears cascading down his cheeks.

'Papa!' She was alarmed now. 'What has happened?'

'Sit down, sweetheart...'

'I don't want to sit down. What's happened? Where's József... is he ill? Tell me!'

'He's been shot.'

Rachael collapsed onto a chair by the window.

'Shot...' she repeated, but the word made no sense. She stood up again, her voice calm and decisive. 'Then I must go to him. Which hospital is he in?'

'Rachael... no... you don't understand.'

The terrible story of what had taken place that day – the march József had led down the street towards the Parliament building – seeped out slowly, as day darkened into night. As the turnip soup boiled, and then burned dry, George sat on the sofa in the drawing room trying to explain what had happened.

'Why didn't he tell me he was going to march this morning? I might have stopped him,' said Rachael, agitatedly pacing the room.

'He didn't want to worry you...'

Rachael swung round and glared at George – her face riven with despair, disappointment and fury.

'Well he was right, wasn't he? I would have been worried. I would have forbidden it.' She dissolved into tears and sat down abruptly next to her father, burying her head in his chest.

He said nothing. He could think of nothing to say.

'But I don't understand...' she said at last. 'Why did they shoot at students? They were just marching...'

'There has been a clampdown. The authorities are determined to destroy the movement in this country amongst the young – against Soviet domination, against communism. You know... we've talked about it endlessly.'

But Rachael could not remember any discussion of a march, or any demonstration. Her father and husband often discussed politics, but they discussed so many things in an abstract way. But it was just talk, surely... No one was supposed to act, to get hurt. Is that what József had meant that morning – about doing more to help? And now what help could he be to anyone – lying dead on the street.

'Are you involved too?'

'Yes... I am.' George turned away.

'How? Tell me, Papa!' Rachael almost screamed. 'You have to tell me...'

'It was I who introduced József to the group. I encouraged him. I knew they were marching on Parliament today. He was to lead a group of militants. It was a demonstration, that's all... We discussed it this morning on the way to the university. I'm so sorry, Rachael; truly, I'm so sorry. If I had said nothing to József, if I had not encouraged him, and talked instead of ancient Rome, you might still have a husband.'

The acrid smell of burnt soup filtered through Rachael's grief. She pulled herself up from the sofa and stumbled through to the kitchen. The room was illuminated only by the blue flame of the gas stove. She turned it off, grabbed the red-hot pan with a cloth and threw it in the sink. As she turned on the tap, steam hissed and ballooned up from the black encrusted pan.

When she returned to the sitting room, her father put his arms around her, kissing her head, inhaling the scent of her hair.

'I'm sorry, Rachael. I'm so sorry....'

Forcing its way through her grief came another emotion... shame. While she had been living in a little bubble in her graceful apartment – polishing her piano, fretting over the shopping – in the real world, people – young and old – had been having important conversations, believing in something so much, they were prepared to die for it.

'Why did neither of you tell me... how important it was?'

The drawing room was dark. Neither Rachael nor her father had turned on the light. Neither had eaten or drunk anything. The plate of bread and butter stood untouched on the kitchen table. Rachael had stopped crying; it was as if she could feel nothing – no emotion of any kind – just a pain behind her eyes. They heard a knocking on the door downstairs. George lifted his finger to his lips, suddenly alert.

'Stay quiet…' he whispered.

He stood to one side of the bay window, his body concealed by the heavy damask curtains, and peered outside. One solitary light on the other side of the road illuminated the street below. Three men, dressed in dark overcoats and homburg hats, stood at their door.

'Rachael…' he said in a low voice, moving away from the window, back into the room. 'I want you to do something for me. Go to your bedroom and gather what you need for a few days and put it into a bag. Bring your papers and passport. I will do the same. And don't turn on the light.'

Rachael looked up at her father in confusion. 'Why? Where are we going?'

'We must get out… now. The authorities are outside. They have come – perhaps for you, certainly for me.'

'What is happening, Papa?'

'Please… Rachael, we have very little time. Just do as I ask.'

The police were guarding the main door of their apartment building on Henszlmann Imre Street. But there was a back entrance that led onto a narrow lane. Peering out of the kitchen window in the half-light, Rachael could see that the lane was empty.

Carrying their small suitcases, George closed the apartment door silently behind him. He led his daughter stealthily down the dark staircase. On the first-floor landing, they saw Mrs Kovacs' door opening; she was clearly alert to the slightest noise on the stairs. George pulled his daughter against the wall, so they were invisible to the old woman inside.

'Who's there?' Mrs Kovacs called out.

George put his finger to his mouth and shook his head at Rachael. She said nothing. When the door had slammed shut, they ran as quietly as they could down the last flight of stairs and along the narrow hall. The back door was rarely opened, so the lock was stiff. George fought with the key in the dark, but eventually it yielded and they were outside, their hearts pumping. They walked quickly down the narrow alleyway and onto the main street. They arrived at the train station breathless, but slowed to a walk as they crossed the concourse. Uniformed policemen were patrolling, checking people's papers.

'Papa, I'm frightened,' whispered Rachael, clutching George's arm.

'We are just two people – an old man and his daughter – going on a little trip… stay calm.'

At the ticket office, they bought two tickets for the first train leaving Hungary that evening; it was heading for Austria.

George stopped at a news kiosk and bought a newspaper, affecting an air of relaxation. Then, picking up their suitcases, he guided Rachael casually to their train.

'Papa…' said Rachael, 'why are we going to Austria?'

'Because they are a neutral country,' explained George, handing their luggage to the guard. 'We will be safe there.'

'Are we not coming back… to the apartment? To our home?'

'Not for a while, darling… not for a while.'

Chapter 3

Herne Hill
May 2016

Sophie woke sometime in the middle of the night, still lost in a dream that even now was receding. Damp with sweat and befuddled by sleep, as Hamish snored faintly beside her, she lay half-awake in the darkened room, and struggled to recall the sequence of dream events. The narrative, such as it was, almost evaporated the moment she opened her eyes. All she was left with was the sensation of warmth and the flash of something blue and white; dolphins perhaps, leaping from turquoise water. Where was she…?

She sat up in bed and concentrated, her fingers pressing against her temples, her eyes closed to avoid distraction. In her teens she had spent a whole year writing down her dreams, anxious for some insight into her subconscious self. The moment she woke, she would reach for her notebook and scribble down the snatched glimpses of unfamiliar worlds and conversations that had no meaning, involving people she did not know. But today's dream was different. Massaging her temples with her strong hands, she pieced the dream together. She had been sailing, sitting in the prow of a boat with her brother and her grandmother, who was recounting tales of what she called the 'silken sea' and of the magic 'silk' – woven, she said, by the water women from the beginning of time.

Had she been remembering a real conversation with her grandmother? She had no conscious recollection of this event; neither her mother nor her grandmother had ever described such a sailing trip. And yet... the dream was so vivid. Her grandmother, Rachael, had only died the previous year, and Sophie still missed her. She had fond memories of the stories Rachael had told her – tales from her own childhood, or that had been handed down through the generations.

Rachael often spoke of her father, George Laszlo. An archaeologist, born in Budapest, he had fled his home country in 1956 during the Hungarian uprising.

'You are so like him,' Rachael had told her many times. 'You both have a restless sense of enquiry. He would have been so proud of you.'

Sophie climbed out of bed and felt around in the dark for her slippers. Pulling on a cardigan over her nightdress she went downstairs to the kitchen. She put the kettle onto the range and leant against it, taking comfort in its constant warmth.

Her laptop stood open on the island unit, and as she waited for the kettle to boil, she typed the words her grandmother had spoken in the dream, the only words she could now recall – 'silken sea' – into Google, expecting nothing. It was a meaningless phrase, after all. But surprisingly, there were several references to 'sea silk', which, it seemed, was a delicate woven fabric made from the silky filaments excreted by a giant clam called *Pinna nobilis*. Had her grandmother ever mentioned this to her when she was alive? If so, was her dream really just a memory? And if it was, what was the connection between her grandmother and this unusual and rare fabric? The questions hung – unanswered.

Sophie looked up at the clock in the kitchen. It was already three in the morning. She had an early class that day and needed to get up at seven.

Back in bed, she sipped her cup of herbal tea, before finally falling asleep listening to the gentle wheezing sound as her husband snored.

*

The following Sunday, Sophie and Hamish were invited to her parents' house in Hampstead. It was her mother Angela's birthday as well as her parents' thirty-fifth wedding anniversary and Angela had prepared a party for family and friends. Sixty guests were invited and a small marquee had been erected in the back garden, filled with tables, little gilt chairs and a long serving table to hold the large trays of food which her mother had prepared over the previous week.

As Sophie and Hamish arrived, Angela, her reading glasses perched on the end of her nose, came in from the garden holding a clipboard.

'Oh, Sophie, good, you're here,' her mother said as they came into the long narrow hall of the double-fronted terraced house. 'I've got to arrange the place cards… could you help me? You're so good at who should sit where and all that.'

'Of course, Mum.'

'Oh, and Hamish – be a love and help Alex with the wine and beer, could you? He's supposed to be taking it all out to the marquee and stocking it in huge ice buckets, but he keeps insisting that he can keep it all in the fridge in the basement and serve it from there It will never work. Please organise him for me, will you?'

Angela took Sophie's hand and dragged her along the narrow hall and out through the glass door that led down steep steps to the garden.

Hamish went down the rickety wooden stairs into the basement, where he found Alexander busy choosing wine for the party. This ill-lit space had, at one time, been a functioning kitchen and laundry room. But Angela had moved the kitchen upstairs when she took the house over and the basement was now used as a utility room and wine store. The couple had lacked the money, or perhaps the will, to waterproof or renovate it properly and when it rained heavily in the winter, the old Victorian tiles became slippery and damp. A new American fridge was propped up incongruously on brick piers to protect it from the annual winter deluge. On the walls were wide shelves made of cheap white melamine put up by Alex over twenty years earlier as a temporary measure. These were filled with boxes of unwanted tools and long-abandoned kitchen equipment, all of which were covered with a fine layer of mould. The shelves were too flimsy for the weight they were required to support and sagged alarmingly. It was a constant irritation to Angela that the basement hadn't been made into a proper utility room, which was the cause of many a family row.

'Ah Hamish… good to see you,' said Alex, smiling gently at his son-in-law. 'I'm keeping my head down in here. Angela's in one of her "organising" modes.' He conspiratorially handed Hamish a glass of red wine. 'Try this – I've been saving it for something special. Got a couple of dozen of them stored away down here. Bought them years ago at a rather good little wine shop near Calais. Just checking they've not gone off.'

Hamish gratefully sipped the wine. He swilled it around his mouth, making noises of appreciation before finally swallowing it.

'It's good – a Pinot Noir?'

'Spot on… it is rather good, isn't it? I was worried I'd left it too long and I'd have nothing to serve but two cases of degraded wine. But it will be perfect. Needs decanting though because the labels have all been a bit damaged by the damp…'

'Angela mentioned needing to chill some white wine and beers?' Hamish looked hopefully around the damp basement.

'Oh, I've got those in here,' Alex patted the fridge protectively. 'Easier just to open them as I need them and serve from here really.'

'Oh… OK. If you think so?' Hamish was reluctant to get caught up in a disagreement between his parents-in-law. He had a certain sympathy with Alex, who was an affable, gentle soul. A writer, he had enjoyed some considerable success in his younger days as an investigative journalist, but as he headed towards his seventies he preferred to spend his time in his study, listening to music, well away from the hustle and bustle of the main household. He was tall – well over six feet – and had begun to stoop slightly as he aged. 'Too many years hunched over a typewriter,' was his excuse. His once dark hair was now thinning and grey. He was still handsome, with a high forehead, a straight 'Roman' nose and strong jaw. A devoted father and husband, he was highly intelligent, but also introverted and undemonstrative. Sophie had mentioned several times to Hamish that she and her brother, Simon, had found him difficult to 'read' as they were growing up.

'He's basically in his own little world. Always has been. Happiest with his computer and his abstract ideas...'

Guests were due to arrive about one o'clock. At twelve-thirty, Sophie's younger brother Simon arrived, with his wife, Victoria.

'Oh good,' said Angela, as she opened the door. 'So glad you're a bit early... Go and help Hamish chivvy your father, will you?'

The seating now arranged to Angela's satisfaction, Sophie suggested her mother should go upstairs to change.

'Mum... off you go. Vic and I will just finish tweaking the flowers and make sure everything's perfect. You go up now... Or you won't be ready in time.'

Angela emerged just before the first guests arrived, wearing an attractive pale grey-green linen dress, which emphasised the colour of her eyes and the slightly olive tone to her skin. Her freshly highlighted hair was swept back in a short bob away from her striking face. Her only make-up was mascara and a slick of lip gloss.

'You look lovely, Mum,' said Sophie honestly, kissing her mother.

The guests assembled in the marquee, looking around hopefully for a glass of wine.

'Alex,' hissed Angela, 'we need the wine in here... so we can help ourselves.'

'Don't worry, I'll make sure they all get a drink,' said Alex calmly.

With Hamish's encouragement, he had set up a rickety table as a bar outside the garden entrance to the basement. But guests had to traipse down the old garden steps, slippery with damp moss, to collect their glass of wine, and a queue was beginning to form, snaking back into the marquee.

Sophie caught her brother's eye and together they grabbed four bottles of white wine and a box of hired glasses and set up a separate drinks station next to the serving table.

Soon everyone had been served with a drink and were mingling happily in the garden. Sophie, Simon and Victoria brought large stainless-steel trays of lamb tagine and couscous out from the kitchen and laid them on hot plates arranged down the long serving table at the side of the marquee.

'Lovely grub,' said Sophie's Uncle Tom, approvingly, as she ladled lamb onto his plate. 'Another of my sister's triumphs?'

'Yes… this is one of Mum's stalwart recipes. It's delicious…'

When the main course had been cleared away, Alex stood up and tapped his wine glass. The room fell expectedly silent.

'Well, that's the first time you lot have ever been this quiet.' There was a polite rumble of laughter. 'I wanted to say a few words about the lady at the centre of this gathering today.' He gazed lovingly at his wife. 'Not only has she made the food, arranged the flowers, organised the marquee and the chairs and tables, she has also organised me and her children to do her bidding – once again – which is no mean feat, I can tell you. We're an unruly bunch, but Angela has the ability to persuade and cajole us until we are all her willing slaves.'

The guests laughed and murmured agreement.

'She is, without doubt, the most remarkable, beautiful and intelligent woman I have ever met,' said Alex, glancing at Angela, who blushed. 'I met her first at university. She was studying medicine; I was an inadequate English lecturer. I thought I had no hope. She was constantly surrounded by a gaggle of eager medical students, hoping upon hope that she would grace them with a date. But, for some inexplicable reason, she sat down next to me in the bar one night and asked me if I liked Miles Davis... I did, of course. I'm still not sure if she really does... But, either way, she had me from that day forward wrapped round her little finger. Darling – thank you for sitting next to me all those years ago, thank you for pretending to like Miles Davis. Thank you for marrying me – thirty-five years ago. You are the most wonderful woman I know – to Angela...' He raised his glass.

'To Angela!' the assembled party responded.

Angela smiled, dabbing her eyes with her napkin.

She stood to face the guests. 'I do like Miles Davis – as it happens,' she said, smiling at her husband. 'And I'm so glad that I sat down next to you all those years ago. So I'd like to return the toast... To my darling husband – thank *you* for the last thirty-five years...'

The guests stood and raised their glasses once again.

Angela gently motioned them to sit. 'I'd just like to say a few words more if I may. We have lived a gilded life, here in Hampstead. All these years in the same house – which we could never afford to buy now, by the way...' She looked once again at her husband, who nodded ruefully. The assembled company laughed. 'So, apart from being married to such a clever and thoughtful husband...' the guests cheered, 'we've also been blessed with two glorious children...' Angela raised her glass to Sophie and Simon, accompanied by yet more cheers. 'I've also been privileged to have had my darling mother Rachael with me for so many years – as many of you know, she sadly passed away last year and I do miss her... She'd have been sorry to miss this party too. If you think I'm bossy you clearly never met my mother...'

The guests nodded, murmuring, 'Hear, hear.'

'And apart from my wonderful family, I have been lucky enough to have a worthwhile and satisfying career – to be a GP in this beautiful part of London has been the icing on the cake. As you know, I had the practice here in my house until a few years ago. And even now, I just have to walk five minutes up the road, past the beautiful heath, to our new group practice. I feel so blessed. And finally to be able to call all of you dear people "friends"…' Angela raised her glass to her guests and then, overcome by emotion, mopped her eyes once again and sat down.

The guests erupted into raucous applause and Alex put his arm around his wife's shoulder and kissed her cheek.

Sophie leant back in her gilt chair and perused the marquee. Here were the people her parents had gathered around them over a lifetime: family, old medical acquaintances, grateful patients who had long ago become close friends, people her mother had met at the school gates thirty years earlier when taking Sophie and Simon first to nursery and then to school. Sophie knew all of them; they had been part of her life growing up – here in this happy, ramshackle house with its damp basement and shabby sitting room.

As the afternoon wore on, she managed to speak to most of them. Everyone wanted to know how she was doing, how was the job, when were she and Hamish intending to start a family? These were obvious questions from loving friends who were only showing an interest in a young woman they had known all her life. But she began to find them increasingly intolerable, forcing her to retreat to the kitchen, ostensibly to busy herself with the washing-up.

Uncle Tom appeared at the kitchen door.

'How's it going?' he asked kindly.

'Oh… OK,' she lied, stacking the dishwasher with the first load of dirty plates.

'You look lovely today. I'm sure your mum must be very proud of you.'

'That's kind. But this is her day, isn't it?'

'Your dad gave a good speech,' Tom mused, sticking his dirty pudding plate on the drainer by the sink.

'Yes… he pulled it out of the bag. He always does. He drives Mum mad appearing to be completely uninterested and then goes and delivers a speech like that. Here… pass that plate over.'

Tom handed her the pudding plate, which she squeezed into the back of the rack, then filled the soap dispenser and shut the door of the dishwasher with a satisfying click. It instantly rumbled into action.

'Well,' she said, 'that's that. The first load.'

'You're a good girl,' said Tom. 'You must be fed up with people asking you about starting a family though…' He trailed off, concerned he had said too much.

'Did Mum send you up here?' Sophie asked suspiciously.

'Angela? No. No… I just noticed everyone asking you questions, and thought you looked a bit tearful.'

'Yes… well, it's not for want of trying, you know. I do want a baby.' She felt the tears welling up, her throat constricting as she tried to stop them from coming.

'Oh kitten… come here,' said Tom. He held her to his chest in a bear hug. 'It'll happen,' he said into her hair. 'Just give it time.'

'I've given it time,' she mumbled into his chest.

'Well, give it a bit more then.'

He released her and opened the fridge door, where he found an opened bottle of champagne.

'Here,' he said, pouring them two glasses. 'Let's have a little of this. To you, my little princess.'

'Oh, Uncle Tom, you're so sweet.'

She sipped the glass of champagne and wiped her eyes with the back of her hand.

'I had a dream the other night,' she said at last. 'About Grandma.'

'Did you… dear Mum I do miss her.'

'I do too… she was so special, wasn't she?'

'What was it about… the dream?'

'I can only dimly remember. Just that we were sitting on a boat – a sailboat, I think. Somewhere hot, somewhere with turquoise water and dolphins leaping up beside us.'

'Nice…' said Tom, sipping his champagne.

'Did I ever go sailing with Grandma?'

'I'm not sure…' said Tom. 'Perhaps you did. I have a vague memory of you and your parents sailing somewhere. Alex took you all to the Med – the Greek Islands, I think. He hired a boat. Angela was furious, as he had no real idea how to sail. He'd done a bit of dinghy sailing at school but had never been on a proper yacht. Not sure you could do that now… but in those days apparently you could hire a small yacht and just set off. Maybe you were remembering that?'

'Do you know I have no memory of that at all?' Sophie replied.

'Well – you were only about three and Simon was just a baby. That's why Angela was so cross about it. Neither you nor Simon could swim. She was convinced you'd all be drowned.'

'Oh… well, perhaps that was what I was remembering. I must ask Mum about it sometime…'

'Ask me what?' interrupted Angela, suddenly entering the kitchen carrying a toppling pile of pudding plates.

'Here,' said Tom, putting down his champagne glass, 'let me…'

He took the plates from his sister and put them down on the kitchen table.

'Ask me what?' Angela persisted.

'Oh, it doesn't matter,' said Sophie, 'you're busy.'

Angela stood at the sink, rinsing the pudding plates. 'No go on… I'm listening.'

'I just wondered if I'd ever been sailing – with you and Grandma? When I was a child. Uncle Tom thought perhaps we had…'

'Yes we have,' said Angela. 'We went to a funny little island near Athens… what was it called? Agistri… That's right – when you were very small. We stayed in a weird hotel run by a very odd man, ex-hippy. He lent your father his own boat – it was a positive deathtrap.'

'And was Grandma with us?'

'Mother? Yes, she was. The hotel overlooked a private cove, I seem to remember. No facilities or anything – not like hotels today. But it was rather charming in a basic kind of way. We'd sit in the restaurant overlooking the bay, watching little boats sailing past each day. Alex – who'd last sailed at university, or school – was determined to hire a boat. Somehow he persuaded the owner to lend him one and we all piled on board. It was terrifying. I hadn't the faintest idea what to do, and Alex, for once in his life, was uncharacteristically bossy. He shouted at us all day. It was quite dreadful, and I really thought we'd never see land again.'

'And Grandma?'

'Oh, she was remarkably calm. You children sat with her most of the day and she told you stories – you know what she was like.'

The sound of splintering glass interrupted the story.

Angela and Sophie rushed into the hall to find Alex standing over a pile of broken glass, a flimsy tray hanging uselessly in his hand.

'Oh dear,' said Angela. 'Never mind. They were only cheap and nasty hired glasses. Sophie, get a dustpan, will you?'

Later that evening, back home in Herne Hill, Sophie lay on the sofa, her head in Hamish's lap.

'I thought your dad did rather well today,' said Hamish. 'Your mother's great – but she's quite a handful, trying to organise him all the time. Did I tell you? I found him in the basement hiding from her.'

'I know… she's just used to running things. It's the GP in her, I suppose. But he's spent their whole marriage quietly refusing to be controlled. God knows how they've stayed together all these years.'

'Maybe that's their secret…' suggested Hamish. 'Neither will yield to the other…'

'Are we like that?' asked Sophie.

'No… I'm completely under your spell,' said Hamish, stroking her hair.

'No you're not… you do exactly as you like, you know you do.'

'Ha… I don't think so,' said Hamish smiling. 'I have one word for you… "Cheltenham".'

'Oh, Hamish, not that again…'

She felt him flinch, and instantly regretted her impatient tone. Perhaps it was the champagne and the wine, or simply spending the day with her family, but instead of shutting Hamish down, she softened. 'You really want that job, don't you?'

'Well, it's a great post and a nice hospital in a beautiful part of the world. I mean… darling… do you really want to stay in London, bring up our kids here with our postage-stamp sized garden?'

'It's a beautiful garden…' she said, sitting up. 'And we don't have any kids… yet.'

'I know… Look, I've been thinking. Perhaps we need a compromise.'

'Go on.'

'I apply for the hospital in Gloucestershire, and if I get the job… we start IVF up there. It might be easier to get on the list there – fewer people, less demand than in London.'

'Do you really mean that – about the IVF?' She sat up – excited, elated almost.

'I do… I know what it means to you. Tom said something to me today… before we left. I hadn't realised how upset you are about it all. He said you were in tears this afternoon – apparently people were asking you about when we were going to start a family…'

'He was very sweet to me. Said it would happen eventually. But he doesn't know does he? He was just trying to be positive.'

'Well… it got me thinking. I have been feeling a bit negative about the whole IVF thing, if I'm honest. I spend so much time in the hospital system that somehow it was the last thing I wanted – to medicalise us, our relationship. I kept telling myself, we've only been "trying" properly for a year or so. But I know you've been off the pill for a lot longer than that, and although we didn't take it all that seriously at the beginning – timing when we made love and so on… well, obviously something's not right. And the new thinking, medically speaking, is that we should do something about it while you're still under thirty-five. So let's do it.'

'That's wonderful, Hamish.' Sophie leant over and kissed him. 'Thank you… I know how hard this has been for you – and I'm so grateful. But just one thing… what about my PhD… if we move to Gloucestershire? I guess I'll just have to put that on hold?'

'Not necessarily. I wondered if, perhaps, you could transfer to a university nearby. Cardiff, Bristol… even Oxford? They're not that far away. Perhaps we could find a house halfway between the hospital and whichever university you get into. I'm sure we could make it work, somehow.'

'You really think we could?' She lay back down, her head in his lap. He kissed the top of her head. 'I do…'

'OK then, let me talk to my supervisor tomorrow,' said Sophie, brightly. 'And thank you, darling. We will make it work, won't we?'

Chapter 4

Rachael woke early. As she exhaled, her breath ballooned out of her mouth in a dense fog of condensation. Her hands were icily cold, in spite of the fingerless woollen mittens she had found the previous day in the communal clothes store. She blew onto them, and then tucked her hands underneath the thin blanket, secreting them between her thighs – the warmest part of her body. The sky outside was still dark, but there was a faint glimmer of golden light on the wintry horizon.

She retrieved one hand from its warm place and traced her husband's name on the window. The letters – so sharp at first – became diffuse, as drips of condensation ran down the window. It was not quite eight weeks since József's death and she thought about him from the moment she woke until she was lost once again in the unconsciousness of sleep. They had been together for just nine months. They had loved one another so completely; had lain in one another's arms every night and had shared their every thought. Or so she had believed. And yet, as it turned out, he had kept so much of his political activity from her. Concealed so much. Had he been shielding her? Or had he felt unable to trust her? Sometimes she feared it was because she had been too cocooned in her own world, too lost in domesticity. And he, so involved in the struggle, so energised by the fight, had felt reluctant to shatter her quiet existence, to involve her with the real issues that dominated his thoughts. He had treated her, she saw now, like a child.

She could hear her father's wheezing breath from the bunk below. Their room was in an old army cadet school on the outskirts of Vienna, which had been turned into a refugee camp for the thousands of Hungarians fleeing their country. Previously occupied by the Red Army, it had been left virtually derelict when the Russian army moved out. Once a splendid place of learning, complete with a riding school, swimming pool, gymnasium and mess hall, it was now a hollowed-out building, with broken windows and no running water, electricity or heating.

Rachael and George had been amongst the first to flee from the troubles in Budapest. George knew that an early escape was essential. The policemen waiting for him outside his apartment building would have shown him no mercy. And he was concerned that Rachael – as József's wife – could also have been imprisoned... or worse. Torture, death – both were possibilities. George realised that it was vital for Rachael's sake that they escaped as soon as possible. They had arrived by train in Vienna – one of the few families to do so. Within days of József's death, travelling by train had become all but impossible. And so, when the thousands of ordinary Hungarians – university lecturers, teachers, doctors, bakers – had decided to flee to the west they were forced to take the only route left to them – going on foot across the 'green' border into Austria. Mines and barbed wire had been cleared just months before as a symbol of the thawing relations between Austria and Hungary. Now this land route was a conduit for scared civilians, terrified of the Soviet crackdown and desperate for a new way of life in the democratic West, free of communist rule.

Lying on her prickly straw mattress on the top bunk, staring at the swelling dawn, Rachael had an almost overwhelming desire to be sick. Her mouth filled with saliva, but she was reluctant to climb down the rickety ladder to the floor, and risk disturbing her father, sleeping peacefully on the bunk below. She found the gentle sound of his snoring comforting. It was part of the soundscape of her life – something she had listened to since she was a child.

She swallowed hard and tried to concentrate on the glimmering sky to the east. She had been feeling ill for several weeks, and had been physically sick at least once a day. It was not easy to cope with illness in the camp: the lack of running water, and barely functioning lavatories, made hygiene difficult at the best of times, let alone when ill. Many people in the camp were sick. In spite of the support of the Red Cross who visited the camp regularly, infectious diseases spread like wildfire.

Lying on her bed, resisting the urge to vomit, she made up her mind to brave the queue for the nurse, later that day. It was time she found out what was wrong with her. Besides, she was aware her father was concerned about her deteriorating health.

'I am worried about you, Rachael,' he had told her the evening before. 'You hardly eat. The food is basic, I know. But it's not actually that bad and they are very kind to supply it.' He tried to sound encouraging.

Rachael had smiled faintly, hoping to assuage his anxiety. But although she felt hungry between bouts of queasiness, she found it almost impossible to eat. Even a glimpse of the vast vats of goulash cooked up in the mess hall by kind women volunteers triggered a violent bout of sickness. Just the smell of the meat was enough to send her running from the canteen.

Rachael hauled herself up in bed, positioning the threadbare pillow behind her head, so she could watch the sun rise. New glass had been put into the windows, and although the room was still cold, it did, at least, prevent the wind whistling in from the icy plain to the east. Volunteers were gradually working their way through the camp, replacing broken windows, repairing light fittings and redecorating; the tiny room Rachael shared with her father was to be painted that day. She could hear the clatter of metal painting equipment, and men's chatter outside in the corridor. She climbed down the ladder of her bunk bed and touched her father's shoulder gently. He stirred in his sleep.

'Papa,' she said quietly. 'The decorators are here... I can already hear them outside. We ought to get up... take a shower and have breakfast. Then maybe we could go to the library. They won't be able to do their work if we're in here.'

When Rachael returned a few hours later, she found two young men painting the walls.

'Hi there.' The taller of the two introduced himself. 'I'm Chuck... it's a nickname,' he added, 'my real name is Charles, Charles Bailey, but everyone calls me Chuck. And this guy here...' he indicated a gawky young man with red hair standing on a stepladder, painting above the window, 'this is Heinrich.'

The redhead smiled and nodded to Rachael.

'We're students,' Chuck explained, 'at the University of Vienna... and we've volunteered to make the camp a bit more habitable... I hope you like white paint... that's all we've got.' He'd grinned and held up the large paint pot filled with whitewash. 'We should be out of here soon – we've nearly finished... Heinrich has just got that bit in the corner to do. Oh... and we fixed your window yesterday.' He gestured towards the new pane of glass.

'Thank you,' said Rachael, admiring the freshly painted walls. She was genuinely grateful for their help, but the clawing, sickly smell of new paint brought on a fresh wave of nausea.

'I'm just sorry,' Chuck said, as he'd packed up their painting things, 'that it's not warmer in here. I wish we had some proper heating for you.' He looked helplessly around the tiny room, with its bare walls, straw mattresses and thin blankets.

Rachael smiled sympathetically at him.

'Thank you,' she'd said in faltering English. 'You are very kind. We are happy.'

Rachael did not feel happy. As she had struggled to wash that morning beneath a trickle of lukewarm water in the shower, she had caught sight of herself naked in the cracked mirror. She was almost unrecognisable – her ribs protruding from her hollow chest, her legs and arms stick-thin.

Now, she followed Chuck's eyes, as he took in the ring on her wedding finger. She wondered if he had seen the small photograph frame that she kept beneath her pillow. Perhaps he had come across it as he painted the ceiling above her bed. It was a photograph of her with József, laughing into the camera, in happier days.

'Well… we'd better go,' said Chuck. 'We've got to make a start on the room next door.'

Heinrich clattered out of the room carrying his ladder and bucket of paint, but Chuck lingered in the doorway. Rachael sensed he wanted to stay and talk. Most of the volunteers kept their distance from the refugees, but Chuck seemed different – friendly and respectful. How could she explain to this stranger, especially in a foreign language, what she was really feeling?

'At least you have a ceiling light that works now…' Chuck flicked the light switch and the solitary light bulb flashed on and off. He smiled, encouragingly. 'Good… yes?'

'Good – yes,' she said. 'Thank you.'

Rachael heard George coming down the corridor towards the room. She knew it was him by his gait. He shuffled these days, something he had never done in Budapest. But his time in the camp had obviously exhausted him, even though he tried hard to hide it from her.

'Ah, young man,' George said to Chuck. 'Thank you for helping to make our room so much more comfortable.'

'You're welcome, sir,' said Chuck. Like everyone who met George, he was quickly impressed by the older man's facility with languages, his openness and erudition.

'You are American?' asked George.

'I am, sir. I did my degree at Yale, but at the moment I'm a student at the university here in Vienna. I came to study German – not a popular language in my country... But I like it.'

'Ah... good; all academic study is valuable. I am a professor myself – from Budapest.'

'Oh... well it's good to meet you, sir. What did you teach?'

'Archaeology...'

'Well, that's so interesting. We volunteers were thinking... there must be so many people here with useful skills and knowledge. In the block on the other side – one of your people has just opened up a barber's shop. I got a haircut this morning.'

He ran his hands through his newly shortened blond hair and blushed slightly when he realised Rachael was smiling at him.

'So...' he continued, 'we'd like to organise some classes – teaching different subjects – for the children mainly, but for adults too.'

'I'd be happy to help with any classes,' said George. 'I could teach English... or history – and not just about the ancient Greeks and Romans...' he chuckled.

'That would be great, sir – thank you. I'll put you on the list of teachers.' He turned to leave, but at the door he paused. 'Your daughter, sir... I hope you don't mind me saying... looks a little unwell. Is she OK?'

'I don't know,' answered George. 'She has been sick. We need a doctor.'

'Well, I could ask the Red Cross nurse to take a look. I think a doctor may be coming later, but there are so many people to see.'

'Thank you – we would be very grateful.'

'I'll go and talk to the nurse now...'

The Austrian nurse arrived the following day, just after breakfast. She spoke quietly to Rachael as she examined her, while George waited outside in the corridor. When she had finished, the nurse called George back into the room.

'Your daughter is pregnant. About three months, I would say. She's been quite ill with morning sickness, poor thing. But it should get better any day now. It's unusual for it to carry on much longer. But she must eat a little more – she is very thin. Make sure she goes to the canteen each day – we have good food there. Sardines are often on the menu – they would be excellent for her.'

She smiled sympathetically at Rachael, who lay on the lower bunk, stunned by the news, her mind a whirl of complex emotions.

When the nurse had left, Rachael burst into tears. Her father lay down next to her on the little cot bed and tried to comfort her. He understood why she was crying.

'It must be so hard for you... without József.'

'Yes...' she mumbled through her tears. 'To be alone, without him and yet... to have his child.'

Rachael pondered on her situation. In part, she was excited at the prospect of becoming a mother. At the same time, she was fearful. They had no home, nowhere for her to care for any baby. And the child's presence inside her reminded her constantly of how much she missed József.

Her father tried to comfort her. He spoke of new beginnings, of fresh life... But she could see that he, too, was anxious that she was bringing a child into such an uncertain, chaotic world. She remembered József's words to her a few weeks before he was killed: '*This is a difficult world in which to bring a child. Our country is not our country anymore... times are hard.*' How right he had been. What would he say about her having a child here... in a refugee camp?

She tried to distract herself by reading. A meagre library had been set up in one of the classrooms, and after lunch she wandered down and borrowed a tatty copy of *Anna Karenina*. She had read it before, but, in some way, Anna's tragic tale distracted her from her personal distress. She spent the rest of the day on her bunk bed, absorbed in the story, until she realised it had grown dark. Turning on the light in their room, it occurred to her she was actually quite hungry.

'Papa,' she called down to her father, who was snoozing in the bunk below. 'I am hungry… for the first time. Now I know what is "wrong" with me, I must try to eat more. Shall we go to the dining room?'

'Yes, Rachael… good idea. Let's go.'

As they walked down the corridor, they heard Chuck whistling. He was painting the ceiling of the neighbouring room.

'Hi…' he called out.

He climbed down off his ladder.

'Did you see the nurse? Are you OK?'

Rachael, not quite understanding his accent, smiled and nodded.

'Yes,' said George. 'It turns out… Rachael is pregnant.'

Chuck looked surprised. Although he had noticed her wedding ring, the thought of her being pregnant hadn't crossed his mind.

'Oh… well that's great news,' he said at last. 'Congratulations.' He shook Rachael's hand politely. His grasp was firm and dry – comforting. 'Your husband will be pleased…' he added.

Rachael looked down at the floor, tears welling in her eyes.

'Oh… I'm sorry.' Chuck was momentarily confused.

'Her husband is dead, I'm afraid,' said George flatly. 'He was killed by the authorities in Hungary.' He put his arm round Rachael's shoulder. 'Will you excuse us – we must try to get some food into Rachael. It's important that she eats.'

Chuck stood aside, allowing them to pass.

As they did so, Rachael briefly took his hand and squeezed it. 'It's OK…' she said. 'Thank you.'

A few days before Christmas, Chuck found George and Rachael at one end of the dining hall.

'There you are… I've been looking all over for you.'

'Here we are…' echoed George. 'Rachael has not felt sick today,' he said, proudly. 'She has eaten a whole plate of food and the colour is returning to her cheeks.'

George glowed with pride at his daughter. In the warm dining hall, with the wood-burning stove at one end throwing out heat for several feet around, she looked flushed and pretty, her grey green eyes flickering in the firelight.

'That's good news,' said Chuck.

'Sit… sit.' George shifted his chair to make room for him. He liked Chuck. His concern for Rachael, his quiet enthusiasm for their life in the camp, was infectious.

'It's snowing outside,' said Chuck, settling into a seat. 'It reminds me of home…' He looked wistful suddenly.

'Where are you from?' asked George.

'Vermont – north of New York. It's always snowy in the winter there. It looks a little like here – wooded, little villages. I miss it sometimes – but especially now. I've never been away at Christmastime before… No one does Christmas like we do in Vermont. There are trees and lights everywhere and people have candles in their windows. In the dark evenings, all the houses look so pretty, you know? You feel you could get a welcome anywhere. And when you do call in on a neighbour, they offer you cookies and eggnog.'

'Eggnog?' George looked puzzled.

'Oh yeah… Eggnog. You never had it? It's fantastic. It's a mixture of cream and eggs and brandy and sugar. It's the best… the best thing you've ever had in your life. Really.'

'My goodness,' said George. 'It's been so long since we've had cream… We must try it one day – no?' He looked encouragingly at Rachael.

'Maybe I'll try to get some of the ingredients and make some for you,' suggested Chuck. 'We're organising a Christmas meal and celebration. I don't know if everyone here is a Christian, but we thought it was a nice thing to do… What do *you* think?'

'I think people will appreciate anything to relieve the boredom,' replied George, encouragingly.

'Good – we'll get onto it. We have more time for cultural and academic matters now that the renovations are being done by professionals...'

'Yes, I noticed there are many people here from the Swedish Red Cross,' observed George.

'They've taken over the running of the camp and they're really efficient. The good thing is it's freed up people like me. No one will have to put up with my terrible paintwork anymore.' He winked at Rachael. 'Instead, I've been asked to organise some lessons. Do you remember we talked about it? They want to create a sort of school here. So I'm going to need your help, Professor.'

'Of course – I'd be happy to help.'

'One other thing – after Christmas they're sending teams of immigration people from the States, Great Britain, France, Italy, South Africa to talk to everyone who wants to settle in those countries. So those language classes are going to be more important than ever. I've worked out I need to teach people thirteen languages. I have no idea where to start. I can do English – obviously. But where I'm going to find someone who speaks Afrikaans, I have no idea.' Chuck laughed, and for the first time since they had arrived in the camp, George allowed himself a glimmer of optimism. 'Do you hope to move on soon?' asked Chuck, almost reading George's mind.

'If we can... yes. We can't stay here forever. I need to get back to work, create a home for Rachael and the baby.'

'Sure,' said Chuck. 'Well, I'll make sure you get near the front of the queue.' He smiled at Rachael.

'Don't do anything special for us,' said George firmly. 'We'll take our turn.'

'No... it's OK. I think, given the baby and all... you need to get settled as soon as you can.'

Chapter 5

Gloucestershire
September 2016

Sophie watched the empty removal van backing out of the long gravel drive of their Cotswold stone cottage and sank down, with relief, on a kitchen chair, which had been dumped unceremoniously in the hall. Every room in the house was now crammed with boxes neatly labelled with their final destination – sitting room, kitchen, bedroom and so on – but towards the end of the packing process in London, as Sophie and Hamish grew ever more exhausted, the labelling system had become increasingly erratic. Sophie feared that if she opened any one of the unmarked boxes, she would discover the detritus of her life that had previously been abandoned in their small box room in Herne Hill.

It had been a frenetic summer. One evening in early June, as rain began to fall and the air outside turned damp and unseasonably chilly, Sophie hurried home up their leafy road. She opened the door and threw off her wet coat, hanging it on the banisters, where it dripped water onto the tiled floor. Shivering, she walked through to the kitchen, which was always warm from the range. She put the kettle onto boil, and then took some onions from the fridge to chop up for their supper.

She heard Hamish's key in the lock and, a few seconds later, as the front door slammed shut, he rushed, excitedly, into the kitchen.

'I got it!' he said, picking her up and whirling her around. 'The consultant post in Cheltenham!'

'Careful!' she giggled, as her feet knocked against the kitchen cupboards.

Breathlessly, he ground to a halt, and planted a kiss on her forehead.

'Well done – really, well done.' She was sincere. She knew what it meant to him; what it could mean for both of them. But she also knew that they were facing a summer of disruption.

'When do you start?'

'As soon as we can get organised. Don't worry – they know we've got to sell this place and buy somewhere new – they understand. But they want me to start in September.'

Sophie exhaled sharply. 'September… so just over two months. That's quite a deadline.'

'Yes, but we can do it – can't we?' he asked excitedly, his eyes pleading for a positive response. Sophie had busied herself, sweating onions on the hob. She knew what he wanted her to say, but she was consumed by the implications for herself. *How am I supposed to get pregnant when I'm stressed by moving house?* She knew that the burden of showing people round their house, looking for a new home, packing up their lives, would fall on her shoulders. But, as usual, she repressed her anxieties and tried to be positive.

'Of course we can do it. No problem,' she said cheerfully, opening the fridge. She had a bottle of champagne standing by – just in case he got the job, and she poured them both a glass. He drained his gratefully and refilled it.

'Let's see what's on the market in Gloucestershire.' He flipped open his laptop on the kitchen table. 'Here's one… look at this – huge garden, darling. You'd love that.'

'There's no rush is there, Hamish? I don't even know if I can transfer to somewhere near there yet. I've got no university lined up. We can't settle on where we're going to live until I find a new home for my PhD.'

'I thought you'd spoken to your supervisor already… I thought you had this in hand?'

'I forgot,' she admitted. In her heart, Sophie had hoped he might not get the job and that she might never have to face the disruption of moving. She was so preoccupied with her desire for a child, there was no room for anything else. Her diary was a testament to her reproductive processes: periods were marked in red, her temperature recorded daily, and days when ovulation might be possible were entered in green. If she and Hamish made love that was entered into her diary too. Nothing seemed to matter anymore – apart from getting pregnant. Her work, her friendships, any other part of her life, had begun to suffer. The need to move her PhD to a different university had simply slipped from her list of things 'to do'.

'What do you mean – you forgot?' asked Hamish. 'I thought we'd agreed.'

'I know… I just didn't want to jinx it,' she lied, 'in case you didn't get the job.'

'Thanks for the vote of confidence.' Hamish snapped his laptop shut. 'God, you really know how to kill the mood, don't you?'

Taking the bottle of champagne, he stomped through to the sitting room.

Sophie knew he was right. She should have spoken to her supervisor, and let Hamish have his moment of glory and shared in his excitement. She quickly assembled the casserole and put it in the bottom oven, then, carrying her empty glass into the sitting room, curled up next to him. She held out her glass, inviting him to fill it.

'I'm sorry – I didn't mean to spoil things. I'm really pleased – honestly. There's a lot to do and it will be…' she paused, searching for the right word. 'Exciting!'

'Exciting – yes. Different… certainly.' He kissed her cheek. 'Probably stressful… but we'll cope – won't we?'

'Sure… we always do. I'll get onto my supervisor tomorrow and see what can be arranged.'

Much to Sophie's delight, her supervisor persuaded her that she could carry on with her PhD at London University. She would have to cut down her teaching hours but could continue her research work remotely.

'I'll have to take the train to London at least once a week – perhaps twice, but otherwise I can work from home,' she told Hamish that evening. She felt relieved that her academic work would not be completely abandoned. 'I won't miss the teaching so much, and there will be so much to do when we move.'

The new house was a seventeenth century worker's cottage in the middle of, what the estate agent's particulars described as, 'a chocolate box Cotswold village'. The house had been extended and renovated numerous times and its quaint exterior gave no clue as to the large, contemporary house within. On the other side of their garden wall was the village pub, which – judging by its tiny windows and irregular roof – must have been one of the earliest buildings in the village. The pub faced the village green, which in turn was edged by rows of cottages, built in the local gold-coloured stone, their front gardens filled with a riot of late summer colour. At the edge of the village was a large manor house owned by a family who had farmed the surrounding land for generations. A church stood nearby, which traced its roots back to Norman times. The old rectory next door had a well-proportioned eighteenth century façade concealing its much older origins. This splendid house was no longer inhabited by the local vicar, who lived, instead, in a modern Cotswold-stone bungalow at the other end of the village. The vicarage's current incumbents were a forty-year-old hedge fund manager and his wife, who descended on the village each Friday evening in a gleaming white Range Rover accompanied by their three young children and Daisy, a beige cockapoo. Sophie gleaned this information from the lady who ran the village shop, on the day she and Hamish moved in.

'I just need some fresh milk,' Sophie said, as she leapt out of the car, 'and it will be nice to introduce ourselves.'

'Well, don't be long,' Hamish called after her, 'the removal van is only a few minutes behind us and they can't get in without me – I've got the keys.'

'You go on then,' she said, 'I'll walk down to the house when I'm done.'

'So, you're taking the cottage behind the pub, are you?' said the shopkeeper, as she rang up Sophie's meagre shopping.

'Yes… we're moving in today. I just needed one or two things, and some fresh milk,' said Sophie, looking around the unfamiliar shop. The selection of produce was limited, she noticed, to basic groceries, and a 'not-so-fresh' display of fruit and vegetables.

'Over there in the fridge,' gestured the lady. 'Will you be here… all week?' she asked, as she rang up the milk on her till.

'Oh yes. My husband's a doctor – he starts at Cheltenham General next week.'

'Well, that makes a nice change. So many of the houses round here have gone to weekenders. The place is a ghost town during the week. The old rectory was the last one to go… some posh couple from London who swan down at the weekends pretending to be Lords of the Manor. And there's the poor vicar nearly half a mile from the church in that little bungalow. It's not right. It was lovely when he lived in the proper vicarage. He'd have nice little "do's" down there – the whole village was invited. But money talks now… doesn't it?'

As she walked down to her new house, Sophie could see that most of the houses appeared uninhabited. But here and there were signs of activity. Lawnmowers whirring, washing hanging tidily on the line. The air felt cool and fresh and clean. And whilst she had been anxious at the idea of leaving London, in particular, of leaving her beloved family, the view from the green as she looked across the valley, was breathtakingly beautiful. Perhaps, she thought, she and Hamish could be happy here. Perhaps this was the place where they would finally become a family.

Sophie and Hamish's nearest neighbours presented themselves almost the moment the couple moved in. As the removal van backed away down the gravel drive, Sophie shut the glazed front door with relief. She had just picked up a box of china ready to take it down the long curving hall to the kitchen, when she spied a thin elderly man with sparse grey hair, barely five feet tall, standing on the doorstep, carrying a hen under each arm. He wore a pair of stained twill trousers, a checked shirt and a tweed jacket that had seen better days. Standing behind him was a sturdy grey-haired woman – presumably his wife – carrying a parcel wrapped in tin foil.

'Afternoon, missus,' said the man in a broad Gloucestershire burr, as Sophie opened the door. 'I've come to put the chicks away. I'm Mick... Mick the Chick.'

Sophie stifled a laugh, realising that he was perfectly serious. 'How nice to meet you... Mick. And er... your...' she looked in anticipation at the elderly woman bearing the parcel.

'This is Dorothy – my wife.'

'We've brought you a cake,' explained Dorothy, holding out the tin foil parcel. 'We live in the cottage at the end of your drive,' she explained, gesturing to a tiny stone cottage emitting a faint wisp of smoke from the chimney.

'Oh, that's so kind... really thoughtful. Well, you'd better come in.'

Mick and Dorothy followed Sophie along the curving hall and into the kitchen. As Mick dropped the hens on the floor, they shook their feathers vigorously and meandered contentedly between the packing cases. Mick pulled up the only kitchen chair and sat down, proprietorially, leaving his wife standing. She hovered nervously, surveying the mountain of unopened boxes that had been dumped unceremoniously by the removal men.

'Will the chickens be all right?' asked Sophie anxiously, watching them pecking hopefully at her kitchen floor.

'Oh, they're fine. They're used to coming inside,' said Mick matter-of-factly.

The hens, Mick explained, were part of a flock that lived in a shed in Sophie and Hamish's garden.

'So are they *our* chickens?' asked Sophie, somewhat confused. 'I noticed them when we were looking around, but I thought they belonged to the previous owners – the Standings. I presumed they would take them with them?'

'What's this? Who would take what with them…' asked Hamish, coming into the kitchen carrying two more chairs for their visitors.

'Darling, this is Mick and… I'm so sorry, I've forgotten your name.'

'Dorothy,' said the lady, taking one of the chairs from Hamish and sitting down gingerly at the kitchen table.

'It seems the Standings have left us some chickens,' said Sophie as cheerfully as she could, indicating the two hens.

'I don't think they ever mentioned anything about that when we were buying the place,' said Hamish.

'No… well they wouldn't,' piped up Mick. 'They're mine by rights. I've always looked after them. Since Old Man Trent's days… He used to own this place. Owned most of the village, Old Man Trent did.'

'So they're yours… but they're kept on our land,' said Hamish logically, with just a hint of irritation in his voice. 'Why don't you keep them at your own house?'

Mick-the-Chick gave Hamish a look, as if having to explain a very simple problem to a particularly stupid child. 'Because I don't have enough room for them – that's why. Like I say – I've always kept them here… no one's ever minded before.' He sounded quite affronted at this challenge to his way of life.

'Oh no… we don't mind,' said Sophie hurriedly.

'Well, hold on,' interjected Hamish.

'Let's have a cup of tea,' said Sophie. 'We're in a bit of mess, but I'm sure I can find the electric kettle somewhere.' She unearthed the kettle, along with a knife and three plates from a cardboard box and cut Dorothy's cake into edible slabs. 'I'm afraid the Aga doesn't seem to be working for some reason.'

'Oh, I'll get that going,' said Mick, taking control. 'It'll be the oil intake – it gets clogged up if the oil's a bit low. I suspect they didn't leave a full tank for you – mean buggers.'

'So where did you say the chickens were kept?' asked Sophie, looking askance at the two hens, which were depositing little calling cards on the Yorkstone slabs.

'In the shed – just outside the back door there,' explained Mick, lying prone next to the Aga. 'I come over each morning and let them out into the garden and collect the eggs. I can leave you a box each day if you like – out there on the windowsill. Then, at dusk, I come back and shut them up. Simple… Right, that's working now.' He stood up, patted the Aga, sat back down at the table, ate his slab of cake, drank his tea, and looked quite at home in the kitchen.

Dorothy volunteered her services to clear up the chickens' mess and, as she stooped over the flags, rag in hand, suggested that she would be happy to clean and tidy for the couple. Sophie, who was exhausted from a dawn start and days of packing, heard herself acquiescing. Hamish shot her a dark look.

'I tell you what,' said Sophie, hurriedly backtracking, 'let us get sorted. We'll need a few days and then I'll come and have a chat with you about it… all right?'

The couple left, using the back entrance. Mick put the two hens he'd arrived with into the chicken house and locked the door. From Sophie's position in the doorway, as she waved the couple goodbye, she could hear the chickens clucking contentedly as they settled down for the night. As the tiny scrawny man and his larger, well-upholstered wife, walked away down the drive, Sophie was reminded of the nursery rhyme: 'Jack Sprat could eat no fat…'

A mangy grey cat lay on the drive and rolled over compliantly. Mick-the-Chick knelt down and stroked it under its chin. The cat got up and wandered towards the house. It had only one eye, which gave it a lopsided and frankly hideous appearance. It strolled into the kitchen through the back door and lay languorously in front of the Aga.

'What on earth…?' said Hamish. 'What the hell is this?'

Sophie rushed to the back door and called out to Mick and Dorothy. 'Excuse me… but have you forgotten your cat?'

Mick swung round. 'Not my cat – lives 'ere… always has. He's called Uncle. He's a dirty bugger…'

After they'd gone, Sophie and Hamish looked despairingly at the mangy animal which had taken up residence in their kitchen.

'I don't want a cat…' said Hamish.

'Well… we can't just throw it out,' said Sophie helplessly. 'It's obviously at home here.'

'Well it better not get too comfortable. I shall get onto the Standings straight away and find out what the hell is going on. They'll have to come and collect it.'

He returned to the kitchen twenty minutes later. Sophie had found some tall dark red dahlias growing in the garden and had put them into a vase in the centre of the table

'That looks nice,' said Hamish, pouring her a large glass of wine. 'Something smells good too.'

'It's just a casserole I made yesterday – it's warming up – rather slowly. Think that Aga needs a bit of a service. Did you get hold of the Standings?'

'Ah yes… it appears the old man was right. The cat rather goes with the house. That's how it lost its eye apparently. Someone tried to move it years ago and it ran all the way back – from Devon, incredibly. It seems that we're rather stuck with it.'

'Well,' said Sophie pragmatically, 'I'm sure we'll get used to him.' The cat rolled over onto his other side, so concealing his missing eye. 'He looks quite nice from this angle,' said Sophie hopefully, stroking the cat's flank.

Uncle purred deeply and looked up lovingly at his new mistress. He licked her hand with his scratchy tongue before laying his head contentedly down on the stone slabs, absorbing the warmth from the Aga, inhaling the smell of the casserole.

Sophie smiled up at Hamish. 'And he might have his uses – mice and so on…'

'I'll tell you something,' said Hamish, 'it's not going to be at all like living in Herne Hill.'

Chapter 6

London
March 1957

It was raining as George and Rachael stepped off the boat in Dover – a fine misty drizzle that coated their clothes and hair and seeped into Rachael's bones. Their only possessions were contained in the two suitcases they had brought with them from Budapest. Rachael's dark grey woollen coat, stretched over her swollen stomach, was frayed at the cuffs and had lost two of its buttons. She had no hat to protect her head from the rain. Her brown lace-up shoes were worn through and leaked as she slithered down the slippery rain-sodden gangplank at the docks.

After the inevitable and interminable wait for customs officials to check their passports and papers, the refugees were finally shepherded onto a crowded train heading for London. Father and daughter sat together, holding hands, staring out at the unfamiliar landscape through grimy windows.

While at Traiskirchen, George had been interviewed by both the British and the American immigration teams. Both had expressed an interest in offering the elderly university professor and his daughter sanctuary. In the end, George chose Britain. He had good connections already at several British universities and the authorities were sure they could arrange a suitable post for him. A couple of days before he and his daughter were due to leave the camp, a job at London University was confirmed.

Rachael, who was working in the camp kitchens, ran to find Chuck and tell him their news. She found him walking back from the language block on his way to lunch. He loped along, with his long stride, carrying a sheaf of notes under his arm.

'Oh, Chuck... good, I've found you.'

'Hi Rachael ... how are you today?'

'I'm fine – and happy. My father has got a job – in the department of archaeology at a university in London.'

'That's terrific,' said Chuck. 'Not America then...'

'No,' said Rachael, observing Chuck's obvious disappointment.

'I was hoping we'd end up on the same continent, at least,' he said.

'I'm sorry. My father thought about moving to America, but I think he will be more at home in England. And he knows a professor in London – they collaborated some years ago. He is very happy.'

'Well we must celebrate,' said Chuck.

'Yes... we'd like that,' said Rachael.

As Rachael walked back to the camp kitchens, she turned around and caught Chuck watching her. He raised his hand a little in salute, smiled and turned on his heel.

She had grown very fond of Chuck. They often spent the evenings together. It started as a chance for her to practise her English, but soon they were just chatting. They talked about everything – József, the baby, what she might do if she moved to England, or America. She liked the sound of America, she told him – the snowy landscapes of Vermont, the friendly people, the dance music. Chuck had introduced her to dance music. He'd turned up one evening with an old gramophone and pile of vinyl records. He set the record player up in the canteen after supper and played his favourite tunes – Chuck Berry ('You have to love Chuck Berry,' he told Rachael – 'he's my namesake'), Little Richard and Elvis. Sometimes, he would persuade Rachael to dance with him. He took her in his arms and swung her around the room, holding her carefully, never allowing her to fall, or trip, always mindful of the child she was carrying. Rachael enjoyed these impromptu sessions. She had never danced to modern music before and found it exhilarating. She was fond of Chuck. He was positive and intelligent, and he made her laugh. And although he did not elicit in her the same feelings of love and desire that her husband had done, she did begin to see there could be a life after József and that one day she might find love with someone else.

In the meantime, she had her English language classes to attend, and her duties in the camp kitchen, which was staffed primarily by refugees. She had gained quite a reputation for her jams and desserts among her fellow workers. And she enjoyed the companionship of the other women – women of all ages. They fussed over her, fretting about her pregnancy, insisting she sit to chop vegetables, and were ready with a stream of advice about the baby, as well as bringing her endless cups of tea. It made her realise that by staying at home to care for her father she had missed the companionship of other women. More than that, it made her long for her dead mother.

Their departure from the camp, when it finally came, was swift. Over breakfast, an official came into the room and read out their names from a long list.

'Would all the following people be ready by ten o'clock – waiting with all your belongings in the main hall.'

They packed hurriedly. It was simple enough as they had so little. But Rachael was anxious to find Chuck before they left.

'We must say goodbye to him… he's been so kind.'

'Of course,' said George. 'You go and find him, I'll bring the suitcases.'

Rachael searched all the classrooms, but Chuck was nowhere to be seen. She was just beginning to despair, wondering, if perhaps, he had gone back to Vienna, or out for the day, when she saw him at the other end of the corridor.

'Chuck, Chuck,' she called out.

He turned and ran towards her. 'I just heard… you're leaving today. I was coming to find you.'

'And I you…'

They stood opposite each other in nervous silence, unsure what to say, or how to say it.

'I'll miss you,' she said at last. 'You've been a good friend to us…'

'I'll miss you too,' he said. He gripped her arms; he wanted desperately to tell her how he felt – that he had fallen in love with her. His whole body ached to pull her towards him and kiss her.

'Rachael, Rachael.' George came hurrying down the corridor towards the pair. 'Darling, we must go… the bus is leaving.'

She kissed Chuck fleetingly on the cheek. He held her just a little too long. She felt the bristles of his stubble, his breath against her neck; he whispered something. Had he said, 'I love you?'

Her father called her again: 'Rachael, come now…we must go.'

George and Rachael finally arrived at Charing Cross station. George had been advanced a month's salary and had been given a list of boarding houses in a part of London called Hampstead. At the barrier, as they handed in their tickets, they asked for directions.

'You want to get the underground, mate,' said the ticket inspector.

'Ah, thank you. Yes… of course,' said George.

They walked down the steps into the bowels of the station and were directed to the Northern line. Sitting in the carriage, Rachael had a chance to survey some of the people she would now be calling her fellow citizens. In many ways, they looked no different from men and women in Budapest. They read their newspapers, or books; women sat with children in their laps; men carried briefcases. When the train drew into stations, the passengers jostled for position, but everyone was very polite. Men stood up for women on the train. Young men offered their seats to girls and smiled at them, hoping they might grant them a smile in return. As the train rumbled through the dark tunnels, she wondered about the city above her head. She had seen pictures of Buckingham Palace in books when she was a child. Were they passing beneath it now?

As they got out of the train at Hampstead, they followed the signs to the lift. It was out of order.

'You'll have to take the stairs, I'm afraid,' said a tall man, with jet-black hair and distinguished manner. He carried a briefcase and a rolled-up umbrella. 'It's always breaking down. It's a disgrace really – this is the deepest underground station in London... and they can't even get the lift working. It's quite a climb. Good luck!'

Noticing that Rachael was pregnant, he offered to take her suitcase for her.

'Here... let me carry this. It's a *very* long walk. You'll need your strength.' Turning to her older companion, he asked, 'Are *you* going to be all right?'

'Yes... thank you,' said George. 'We'll follow you.'

Three hundred and twenty steps later, Rachael and George emerged from the emergency staircase. The man handed Rachael's suitcase back to her father.

'Here we are! Heavens – what a welcome to London – what must you think of us...?'

'Not at all,' said George, 'you've been very kind.' He leaned against the tiled wall of the tube station entrance, breathing heavily.

'Do you know where you're going?' asked the man.

'I have an address written here.' George pulled the list of addresses out of his coat pocket and handed it to the man.

'Oh yes... I know the first one on the list. The house is not far. Just a little way up the hill and turn right at the pub on the corner.' Then, seeing the look of bemusement on George and Rachael's face, he added, 'Pub... like a restaurant or cafe, but it only serves drinks. Good luck!'

*

The landlady at the first boarding house stood barring the doorway and looked the pair of foreigners up and down with an air of disdain. She wore curlers in her hair, covered with a thin headscarf.

'I'm sorry – but my regulars wouldn't like it,' she said, nodding towards Rachael's obvious bump, swelling beneath her shabby coat. 'Babies crying in the night… that sort of thing. Sorry.'

She closed the door. They went on to the next house on the list, but it was the same story.

'I've got a lot of theatricals here,' said the landlady, 'they wouldn't like it; sorry.'

When they finally arrived at the third address on the list, Rachael was braced for bad news. The landlady, wearing an apron decorated with a blue and green swirly pattern, stared implacably at Rachael and George.

'When's the baby due?' she asked, her arms crossed over her ample stomach.

'Sometime in May,' Rachael said with a sinking heart.

'Well, you'd better come in,' said the landlady. 'You must be tired. Would you like a cup of tea…? I was just putting on the kettle.'

'Thank you… yes,' said George gratefully.

The landlady returned ten minutes later, carrying a tea tray covered with a lace cloth, and a plate of fruit cake, which she placed on a small mahogany table. After a brief discussion about where they had come from, and the job George had been offered at the university, their rent was agreed.

'There isn't a lot of room up there in the attic, but you can make it cosy, I'm sure. My last gentleman was very happy there, but he had to go back home to Paris. There's a washbasin in the room, and the bathroom is only one floor down, but as for laundry – nappies and so on – you can do them downstairs in my laundry room.'

'Thank you,' said Rachael, grateful for any kindness.

'I'm Mrs Roper, by the way,' said the landlady. 'I hope you'll both be very happy here. I've read a lot about your troubles in Hungary in the newspaper. I'm delighted to help.'

Heath House, Willow Road was a tall double-fronted, early-Victorian house, spread over four floors. There was a large basement, which housed a kitchen and laundry room and was the sole domain of Mrs Roper. The ground floor was dominated by a long narrow hall, with a patterned tiled floor. At the far end was a glass door that led down to the garden. An incongruously grand staircase rose imperiously up to the first floor and beyond. On one side of the hall was the communal sitting room – or parlour, as Mrs Roper referred to it. It had an upright piano against the wall, dark mahogany furniture and stiff, uncomfortable chairs. It was rarely used and smelt faintly of mothballs. Behind the sitting room, and overlooking the garden, was Mrs Roper's bedroom. No one in the house had ever seen inside, as the door was kept permanently locked. Across the hall from the parlour was the dining room, which stretched from the front to the back of the house. Painted in a shade of dingy green, this was where guests took all their meals, at small tables covered with lace cloths. Each table was assigned a number that corresponded to their room number. Rachael and George sat at number five. Mrs Roper was not a talented cook, but she was competent, and the food was nutritious and edible.

Rachael and George had a suite of two rooms in the attic, which comprised a sitting room and a small bedroom. The sitting room contained a single bed at one end of the room, along with two armchairs, a gas fire and a washbasin. The bedroom next door was barely big enough for a single bed and a chest of drawers. George insisted Rachael should have the bedroom and he would sleep in the sitting room. The bathroom was on the floor below and was shared with the four other residents – an Austrian photographer named Max Hass who occupied a room at the front of the house; behind him, overlooking the garden at the back, was a young Norwegian girl called Matta, who worked at the BBC's foreign service in Bush House. Rachael was fairly sure that Max and Matta were involved in a passionate affair – especially after she found negatives of the girl, quite naked, hanging up to dry on a washing line strung over the old tin bath. Across the landing from Max and Matta, lived two gentlemen who worked in a bank in the City. They went off each morning dressed in striped trousers, waistcoats and tailcoats, trailing an air of mystery behind them.

On that first afternoon in March, as Rachael and George surveyed their tiny apartment, they knew they were lucky to have found it. Standing in the sitting room, where George would sleep, they took in the view from the window. The green heath stretched away as far as the eye could see. The tops of the trees fluttered in the breeze. It reminded Rachael of the view from their apartment in Budapest. Rachael felt certain she could make a comfortable home for them both under the eaves of this large ramshackle house. It was not quite the elegant apartment they had left behind in their home country, but it was so much better than a single room in an old army camp in Austria.

Rachael and George soon settled into the attic rooms. Rachael got used to the long climb to the top floor. It was not so different from walking up to their apartment in Budapest, after all. Mrs Roper was friendly and even allowed Rachael to bring one or two small pieces of furniture into their rooms.

Browsing an antique shop on Haverstock Hill one afternoon, Rachael had found a small bookcase. The dealer offered to deliver it later that day. As she signed for it in the hallway, Max was just coming downstairs on his way out for the evening.

'Just as well I was here,' he said to her, 'you shouldn't be carrying anything like that, in your condition.'

'Thank you – that's kind. But I'm quite strong; I'm sure I could have managed.'

'I'm sure you could... but still, it's not a good idea, is it?'

He carried the heavy mahogany piece up to the top floor of the house and deposited it in the attic.

'Here...?' he suggested, placing it against the long wall opposite the window.

'Perfect... thank you, Max.'

Delighted with her purchase, Rachael borrowed some beeswax polish from Mrs Roper, and polished the bookcase until it gleamed. Once her father's books were neatly stacked, she stood back to admire it. The room was gradually beginning to feel like home.

George, who quickly found his feet at the university, helped to create a sense of camaraderie in the house. Most evenings, before dinner, he would sit in the uncomfortable parlour chatting animatedly to the other guests.

'Your father's holding court again,' Mrs Roper would call out to Rachael as she came downstairs for supper.

George would discuss the events of the day with anyone who was prepared to listen. Max, Matta, even the gentlemen who worked in the city were lulled into joining the group by the mellifluous tones of George Laszlo. Conversation rarely strayed into the personal. George, in particular, had no interest in people's personal lives. Instead they discussed the latest news or politics. Mrs Roper, who rather enjoyed this convivial turn of events, bought a bottle of sherry, which she encouraged George to offer to the other residents. Sometimes the conversation became quite animated, and if Rachael closed her eyes, it was just as if they were in their drawing room in Budapest. Except that József was not there.

On a sunny morning in early May, Rachael was walking past the tube station and stopped at the flower stall. Her eye was drawn by a display of tall galvanised buckets filled with scarlet tulips. They would look beautiful in a glass vase on top of the new bookcase, she thought.

Returning home, she was walking towards the kitchen to ask Mrs Roper for a vase, when she felt a sharp stabbing pain in her stomach. She dropped the tulips onto the tiled floor and fell to her knees.

Mrs Roper, hearing the noise, rushed into the hall. She knew instantly what the problem was. 'Right. You've started. Come on, dear… I'll take you to my room. You'll never get upstairs in your condition. Then I'll call the doctor.'

With her arm around Rachael's waist, she unlocked her bedroom door from a large bunch of keys she had attached to her apron.

In spite of her discomfort, Rachael was fascinated to see the inside of this room – a frequent subject of speculation amongst the residents. The glamorous interior came as a complete surprise. A large double bed dominated the room. It was covered with a dusky pink satin bedspread with matching pillows. The French windows overlooking the garden were framed by lace curtains, draped gracefully on either side. There was a mahogany dressing table, covered with silver bottles and dishes, a crystal bowl of face powder, complete with a pale pink powder puff, and numerous bottles of perfume. The room was suffused with the scent of Yardley's 'English Lavender'. It felt more like a boudoir than a bedroom.

'Now, you just lie there,' said Mrs Roper, helping Rachael onto the soft pink bed, 'and I'll go and call the doctor. Do you want me to ring your father too?'

'Yes… Please. Thank you,' said Rachael, panting.

The baby was born with remarkable speed.

'Well,' said Mrs Roper as she bundled up the bloodstained towels to take down to the laundry. 'That was jolly quick for a first-time mum…'

Rachael, who had been just as surprised by her swift but painful delivery, lay back on the lace pillows and beamed.

'I'm sorry about the mess on your beautiful bed…' she said apologetically.

'Oh, don't worry about that. I'll soon get that off.'

The moment George got the message that his daughter was in labour, he rushed out of his lecture theatre and onto the bus back home. When he arrived, Rachael was already sitting up in Mrs Roper's bed, smiling broadly, the baby lying in her arms.

'Here, Papa – here is your granddaughter…'

'Oh… she's so beautiful,' said George, taking the tiny girl in his arms. 'She's like a little angel.'

'That's what we should call her,' suggested Rachael '*Angyalka*…'

'Yes…' said George. 'But I think – in English – Angela. We are in England now and must do things the right way.'

'Angela…. Yes. I like it. It's perfect.'

Over the following weeks, the baby grew happy and fat on her mother's milk. It came so easily to Rachael, she felt she had been born to nurse a child. She would sit in an armchair in the attic, stroking her daughter's head as she suckled, her mind wandering. It gave her space to dream and think as she gazed at the leaves fluttering in the breeze outside, or listened to the radio.

Mrs Roper was keen her young charge should follow the latest medical advice.

'I've bought you something,' she said to Rachael as she came down for breakfast, carrying little Angela. 'It's in the kitchen – baby bottles and some formula. So you won't have to feed the baby yourself.'

'But I like feeding her,' said Rachael. Then, so as not to offend the older woman, she added: 'But thank you… maybe I'll use them later, when she's a little older.'

One afternoon, as Rachael nursed the baby, the scent of newly mown grass wafted up through the window of her small bedroom. It was such an enticing, refreshing smell, and as soon as the baby had been fed, winded and changed, she took her downstairs to sit in the back garden. With a book under one arm and the baby in the crook of the other, she was just walking down the hallway towards the back door, when Mrs Roper appeared.

'Oh hello, Mrs Laszlo.' Rachael never corrected Mrs Roper's assumption that she shared her father's name. Her married name was, of course, Kelemen, but it seemed pointless to mention it. It would necessitate explaining that her husband was dead, and Mrs Roper would naturally want to know why and when it happened. So it was easier to maintain the fiction of being Mrs Laszlo, even though it made no sense. Perhaps, Rachael thought, Mrs Roper believed she was an unmarried mother and it was simply an attempt to conceal her shame. 'Mrs Laszlo... I was wondering if you would like the use of an old pram?'

'A pram...?' It was not a word Rachael was familiar with.

'You know – a perambulator, a sort of bed on wheels – for the baby. It's down in the cellar. Come with me and I'll show you.'

She opened a door under the stairs and led Rachael down a set of rickety wooden steps, to a store room beneath the parlour. There were boxes everywhere and in the far corner was an old black pram – its paintwork dulled with age, atop large wheels, with a sturdy hood to keep out the rain.

'It's a bit dusty,' said Mrs Roper, wiping the raincover with a damp cloth. 'It's been down here for years. I used it for my own son.' She turned away briefly and dabbed her eyes with the corner of her apron.

'Mrs Roper, I did not know you had a son...'

'Well... he was killed in the war. He was in the Navy. I don't talk about it much.' She looked away, feeling in her cardigan sleeve for a clean hankie.

Rachael felt a surge of sympathy for the older woman. She too had a tragedy in her past that she kept concealed. Rachael squeezed Mrs Roper's arm, affectionately. 'I'm so sorry…'

'Yes, dear… thank you. You never get over it, do you? Losing someone. I think you've had your fair share of sadness too… haven't you, dear?'

'Yes… I have.' Rachael felt compelled to continue, to share her story, 'I lost my husband, József. He and my father were part of a movement that wanted democracy in our country. But the authorities tried to suppress it… they shot József. That's why my father and I had to leave Hungary.'

'I thought it had to be something of the sort…' Mrs Roper said, pragmatically. 'Well, that pram should be just the thing for little Angela – don't you think? I can give it a good clean and then you can take her into the garden and let her sleep under the sky. She'll be quite safe out there. Or you can take her shopping with you. And you can leave the pram in the hall when you come in.'

'Won't the other guests mind?'

'No… why should they? That naughty lad Max leaves his bike there all the time. And they'll have me to answer to if they don't like it… Now you go and sit in the garden with the baby and I'll get this pram cleaned up for you.'

As she was leaving the basement, Rachael turned to Mrs Roper. 'You have been so kind to us – I don't know what we would have done without you.'

'Pish… it's my pleasure,' replied Mrs Roper. 'It's just lovely to hear a baby in this house again… it takes me back.'

Chapter 7

It was Guy Fawkes night and the air was hazy with the acrid discharge of fireworks. Heavy drizzle fell from a darkening sky. Waiting for Hamish to get home from work, Sophie loitered anxiously in the hall, hoping he wouldn't be late. As soon as she saw his lights sweeping up the drive, she ran out, her raincoat held over her head, and jumped into the passenger seat.

'Thank goodness,' she said, shaking the raincoat out over the back seat. 'I thought you might have been held up. We're due there in ten minutes.'

This appointment was their first opportunity to meet their GP and assess their suitability for fertility treatment on the NHS.

'Why pay for something straight away when we could get it for free?' Hamish had argued a few days earlier, when he had suggested getting NHS treatment. 'We have to be practical, darling. We've got a huge mortgage, you've cut down your teaching hours, and you and I both know that three private cycles of IVF is upwards of seven grand. I just don't know where we'll get the money from. Besides, we fit the NHS eligibility criteria – you're younger than thirty-five, I'm well under the male age limit of fifty-four... let's at least give it a go.'

'But there might be months to wait – years possibly,' Sophie had protested.

'Let's see what they say – OK? Perhaps my being a doctor might help.'

*

As they sat in the impersonal waiting room of the small group practice, Sophie gazed out of the windows at the night sky. From time to time, it was illuminated with sparkling lights as rockets exploded, filling the drizzly overcast blackness with multicoloured stars. Sophie was reminded of their last Bonfire night. They had spent it, as they always did, with her parents and her brother in the house in Hampstead. After an impressive public fireworks display on Hampstead Heath, the family returned to her parents' house to eat sausages and baked potatoes and light sparklers in the garden. It was a tradition, and one which Sophie had never missed.

Her mother had texted her earlier that day:

*We'll miss you tonight darling. Hope you have fun in Glos…
Mama.*

*I'll miss you too. Nothing much planned here… First time
without you all.*

I know, replied her mother. *It will be odd for us all – the
first year without Grandma too.*

Yes… dear Granny. Hope it's not too sad.

We'll be fine… speak tomorrow.

The GP was called Catherine Boulderstone. Her wavy chin-length hair was brown, streaked with silver. She was handsome rather than beautiful, with an efficient, professional manner, and warmed instantly to Hamish.

'So… anaesthetics,' she said, smiling at him. 'My husband was a surgeon at your hospital.'

'What's his name?' asked Hamish. 'I might know him.'

'I doubt it… he died five years ago.'

'Oh… I'm so sorry.'

This piece of personal information somehow interposed itself into the couple's consultation and neither felt able to say anything remotely light-hearted after that.

'So… you need a little help,' Catherine said briskly.

'Yes,' Sophie replied. 'We've been trying to have a baby… for over two years, nearly three. I've not been on the pill for that long, anyway. But I was busy working and we weren't… you know… timing it all.'

'I understand,' said Catherine. 'Still, even two years does seem a long time. And I gather you've been checked out at a clinic in London?'

'Yes… you should have the notes,' said Hamish. 'They could find nothing wrong.'

'They didn't do an ultrasound on your wife,' Catherine said, studying the couple's notes.

'No… they asked for a medical history – regularity of periods and so on – and decided against.'

'Nevertheless, I think we should arrange that. Do you have any objection?' She began to tap rapidly on her keyboard.

'No… none at all,' said Sophie.

'Good… well, you'll be notified with an appointment. It will be at your hospital, Dr Mitchell – I hope that won't present any problems?' She glanced over at Hamish.

'No… no it's fine.'

'I'm just emailing the department now to arrange the appointment,' she explained, before standing up and extending her hand, indicating the meeting was at an end.

'So…' interjected Sophie, 'are we on the waiting list for IVF…?'

'Not yet. Let's see what the scan reveals, and then we can discuss the results and take it from there. We try to prioritise couples who have minimal issues.'

Sophie sat silently on the way home in the car.

As Hamish unlocked the house and turned on the lights in the hall, the cat lay across the bottom of the stairs and leapt up to greet his new family. He wrapped himself around Sophie's boot-clad calves, purring loudly.

'What did she mean… minimal issues,' asked Sophie as she took off her coat.

'I guess – if you've got totally blocked tubes or something… it would be more of a battle.'

'God… I'd never thought of that. Blocked tubes – so then I'd never get pregnant, would I?'

'Darling… it's not worth thinking about it. It's very unlikely. You have no pain – do you? No history of dodgy periods…?'

'No… well, they were a bit erratic when I was younger. Still are occasionally, if I'm stressed.'

'Look, let's wait till we know what we're up against. Is there anything for supper?'

'No… nothing. I'm sorry.'

'Never mind – let's go to the pub.'

The Black Horse was in a lively mood. A firework display was planned for that evening on the village green and the pub was jam-packed with villagers.

'Have you booked?' asked the waitress, as Hamish enquired about a table.

'No, afraid not.'

'Well – we're very busy, as you can see. You can have a bar snack though – over there.' She indicated an area next to bar, teeming with people frantically ordering drinks from the overworked bar staff.

'There's nowhere to sit,' said Sophie.

'That's fine,' said Hamish to the waitress, 'we'll manage.'

As Sophie stood uncomfortably wedged between a group of strangers, Hamish fought his way to the bar. A couple sitting at a small table suddenly stood up.

'Do you want our table?' they asked Sophie. 'Friends of ours have just arrived – they've got a booking in the restaurant.'

'Thank you, yes.'

Sophie sat down with relief, waiting for Hamish.

The door opened, and along with a cold blast of November air, a large group of people entered the pub amidst raucous laughter. They were ushered straight away to a table laid out for ten. A man wearing jeans and an expensive Barbour jacket took charge of their ordering.

'We'll have two bottles of Merlot, two of Sauvignon Blanc and a couple of menus – thanks,' he said, without even looking up at the waitress.

Within minutes the wine was delivered to the table and poured into glasses.

The man in the Barbour sat next to a woman with long blonde hair. She was dressed in a Tuscan lamb coat of palest grey, her throat muffled with a cream cashmere scarf. She sipped her white wine and smiled enigmatically at Sophie, who was suddenly aware of her untidy dark brown hair held back with tortoiseshell combs, her ancient quilted jacket flecked with mud. She felt dowdy and unattractive by comparison.

Hamish returned from the bar and slammed the drinks down on the table.

'God, what a crush… I only just managed to get served – I've been waiting nearly fifteen minutes.'

'We should have booked,' said Sophie. 'Who knew it was so popular?'

'Well… Friday night, and bonfire night too… I suppose we should have realised.'

'Who are those people, do you think?' said Sophie, sipping her red wine and nodding discreetly at the glamorous couple and their noisy friends.

'God knows – don't look like villagers, do they?'

'I was wondering if they were the legendary hedge fund manager and his gorgeous wife.'

'Is she gorgeous?' asked Hamish, staring at the couple over his pint. 'Mmmm – not bad… if you like that sort of thing,'

'What sort of thing?'

'Ice-maiden. Rich bitch… take your choice…'

They ordered two bar meals: a ploughman's for Hamish and pâté and toast for Sophie.

Sophie was halfway through a piece of toast, when the publican made an announcement.

'Fireworks will be starting in five minutes, ladies and gents, but feel free to take a drink with you…'

People began to push and shove their way towards the door, shouting to one another.

'See you out there…'

'We'll be on the other side of the green.'

The elegant couple and their friends stood up, put on their coats and moved in a crocodile – two by two – towards the door. They appeared oblivious to everyone around them, laughing at their private jokes. They emanated a sense of entitlement, which irritated Sophie. She felt excluded from their jollity, their intimacy. For the first time since moving to Gloucestershire, she realised how much she missed her family.

'Drink up,' Hamish said cheerfully. 'We don't want to miss it.'

There was the sound of a rocket ripping through the night sky.

'Come on, darling – it's started already.'

The pair edged their way through the throng and out of the pub. They took up a position on the drive outside and watched the firework team choreographing a succession of ever more thrilling and colourful explosions. All around them, people were laughing and pointing at the bright lights. Children danced around, waving sparklers, writing their names in the blackness. Sophie recalled all the happy bonfire parties she had been to with her family. Now, she felt she was at the wrong party, with the wrong people.

The blonde with the Tuscan lamb coat sidled up to them.

'Hello…' she said, in her soft, milky voice. 'I'm Flora. Are you the couple who've just moved into the cottage up the lane from us? We live in the vicarage.'

'Yes we are…' said Sophie, surprised by this sudden show of friendliness. 'Nice to meet you. I'm Sophie – and this is Hamish. How clever of you to know who we are.'

'Well, in a place like this,' said Flora, 'any newcomers are *huge* news. It's all round the village – the handsome doctor and his gorgeous wife…' She smiled conspiratorially.

Hamish smirked slightly at this compliment and ran his hands self-consciously through his fair hair.

'You must come over sometime soon,' purred Flora. 'We're always here at the weekends. It's lovely to have a bit of fresh blood in the village. It can get a bit… repetitive – if you know what I mean.' She gestured towards their large group of friends. 'We normally import company… people from London love it down here. All this rustic jollity is frightfully amusing. But they don't have to live here, do they? Take them away from their macchiatos and Pilates and they'd be lost. I'll drop a card in with an invite…'

She sauntered away and took up her position next to her husband, who put his Barbour-clad arm around her possessively.

Sophie observed them whispering together and the man turned round discreetly to look at Sophie and Hamish. He smiled – just an unfriendly slit of a smile – before returning to his boisterous banter with his friends from London.

*

The following morning, as Sophie came down the stairs into the hall, she caught a fleeting glimpse of an arm – clad in a familiar Tuscan lamb coat – as it posted an envelope through the letter box of the glazed front door.

She picked up the envelope from the mat and wandered down the hall to the kitchen. The cat – now officially renamed 'Cat' – lay in front of the Aga on a cheap lambskin rug Sophie had found in a charity shop. Cat had been ecstatic when she brought it home for him and had rolled around on it, rubbing it with his back, dribbling on it, kneading it with his claws as if it were his long-lost mother. He lay now on his 'good side', his missing eye concealed. Sophie knelt down and stroked his long grey flank. He looked up at her lovingly, revealing the damaged side of his face, and licked her hand.

'Morning, Cat. Sleep well?'

She opened the envelope.

A discreet 'at home' card invited her and Hamish to a drinks party later that evening. At the bottom of the elegantly printed card were their hosts' email and mobile details. A brief hand-written note said simply:

Hope to see you later – nothing formal... love Flora.

As they walked up the gravel drive of Flora's house, Sophie had a momentary frisson of panic. Was she wearing the right clothes? What did 'nothing formal' mean exactly? Would Flora's friends all be 'city' types with whom they had nothing in common? She yanked at Hamish's arm.

'Let's go home... I mean... what are we doing here?'

'Oh darling, it will be fun. New people. Come on...'

The elegant pale grey door, flanked by a pair of olive trees, was opened by small girl with long blonde hair. She wore black leggings, suede ankle boots and a fur gilet – a child version of her mother, Sophie thought.

'Hello,' said the girl with a disdainful air. 'I'm Tabatha. The party's in there...'

She took their coats, politely, and laid them on a long high-backed sofa upholstered in bright pink velvet. It was the only splash of colour in an otherwise uniformly white space. The little girl drifted down the classically proportioned Georgian hall, past the grand staircase towards what, Sophie presumed, was the kitchen.

The pair gingerly opened the door to the drawing room and were met with braying laughter. It was the sound made by rich people delighted by their own superiority, Sophie thought, clutching Hamish's arm for reassurance. The women were immaculately dressed, as if for a smart drinks party in London. Sophie looked around the room in dismay, noting the designer 'wrap' dresses and skintight black cigarette pants paired with elegant silk shirts. She looked down at her own 'best' jeans and red T-shirt. She was definitely wearing the wrong clothes.

Flora fought her way across the room and air-kissed them both on the cheek.

'You're here... so glad you could come. Sophie, looking so casual, I love it! Come over here and meet Jimmy. He's so naughty, but you are going to love him. I'll be back for *you* in a moment,' she said knowingly to Hamish.

She guided Sophie towards a middle-aged man in trendy black spectacles, standing next to the fireplace. He wore a dark blue silk shirt and black trousers.

'Jimmy, this is Sophie. She's a neighbour and you must be nice to her or I'll be back and make your life hell.' She grabbed a glass of champagne from a nearby waiter and handed it to Sophie. 'Enjoy!' she commanded.

As Jimmy proceeded to tell Sophie about his job as a government advisor, his role at a merchant bank and his 'far too large' house in Chelsea, Sophie glanced periodically around the room, looking anxiously for Hamish. He had been pinned into a corner of the drawing room by Flora, who wore a slinky silk dress emphasising her lean curves. Her long legs, encased in sheer black stockings, looked toned and slender. It seemed to Sophie that Flora once in a while brushed her breast against Hamish's arm quite deliberately, throwing her head back coquettishly, tossing her long blonde hair.

Sophie was not the only one to notice. She was relieved when their host – Marcus – strode purposefully across the drawing room, dragging a short red-haired woman behind him, whom he interposed between his wife and Hamish. He whispered something into Flora's ear, and she retreated, sulkily, and began to offer round plates of canapés to her guests.

As they walked home later that evening along the silent lane, their way lit only by the moon, Sophie slipped her arm through Hamish's.

'Well… that was… interesting.'

'Yes… it was fun.'

'Was it? I didn't think so. I got stuck with some bore who was determined to convince me that he was the most fascinating man in the world. He failed.'

'Oh darling – you need to lighten up,' said Hamish cheerfully. 'I thought they were all very jolly. Flora's a bit of a surprise. She's rather a laugh, it turns out.'

'Yes. She liked you…'

'Did she?' said Hamish, blushing. 'I didn't notice.'

Chapter 8

One evening in early November, as a full moon rose majestically behind the heath, casting long dramatic shadows of skeleton trees across Willow Road, Rachael put Angela to bed a little earlier than usual. They'd been for a long walk that afternoon, and although it was only half past six in the evening, Angela was tired and fractious.

'I *not* tired,' Angela insisted, as Rachael tucked her up.

'I know…' Rachael soothed, 'but we've had a busy day. Let's read this story together.' She selected a favourite of her daughter's – *Pookie Puts the World Right* – a story about a magic rabbit with wings, but Angela fell asleep before Rachael had finished reading the second page.

Afterwards, as Rachael tidied up her attic room, she glanced out of the window and spotted George hurrying up Willow Road. Although it was dark, she could tell that he was slightly agitated, moving faster than his usual even-paced walk. She heard the front door slam shut and the muffled sound of voices from the hall. She went out onto the attic landing to wait for her father. She could hear Mrs Roper chatting to him. Always polite, George normally stopped and gave his landlady plenty of time; he knew how much she loved these brief conversations. But tonight, he sounded hurried, almost irritated.

'Good evening, Professor Laszlo.'

'Good evening, Mrs Roper. Is my daughter at home, do you know?'

'Yes… she's upstairs, putting Angela to bed. They were out playing on the heath all afternoon. She's such a dear little girl – but quite a handful, isn't she?'

'Yes… yes she is. Most delightful. Well, I must get on – if you'll excuse me.'

Her father ran up the two flights of stairs to the attic. Arriving breathless on the landing, he almost fell into Rachael's arms.

'Ah Rachael – you are here… good.'

He kissed his daughter and ushered her back into the attic.

'Papa! What's going on…?' Rachael sat down expectantly.

Her father stood, his back to the window, flexing his hands. 'I am… excited. I have something to tell you, to ask you…'

'What?'

'I have been offered the chance to go to Italy – to oversee the exploration of a possible archaeological site… in Sardinia. Well, not quite Sardinia, but a tiny island just off the coast, called Sant'Antioco.'

He grinned at his daughter like an impish child, rocking up and down on his heels. His excitement was tangible.

'Oh, that's lovely,' she said, nervously. 'How long will you be away?'

The prospect of being alone, with Angela, without the support and friendship of her father, filled her with understandable anxiety.

'Well… that is the best part. It could be over a year.'

Rachael's stoicism collapsed. Her face fell, and tears began to well up, cascading down her cheeks. 'A whole year… without you.'

'No, darling, no… you don't understand.' He knelt beside her and cradled her face in his hands. 'I could not go without you. I have asked if I may take you and Angela with me. The university has agreed. We are leaving just after Christmas. They will find us a house in a local village and we can live there while I work…'

She gazed into his sparkling eyes. 'Live… In Sardinia…?' Rachael struggled to take it all in. 'Is it nice there…?' It was such a trivial question, and yet it was the only one she could articulate.

'Yes! Of course! The sea is turquoise and the sky is blue. It will be warm. Angela can learn to swim. I will be happy in my work and you will have new and vivid experiences – something to remember for the rest of your life.'

'But we are... happy here. We are safe here.'

Rachael had become used to her life in the little attic, with Mrs Roper always on hand, ready with advice and support. And she liked living in Hampstead. Her English was now fluent, and she had made friends with one or two other mothers with whom she met occasionally in the cafe on the heath. They drank tea and watched their children play together. She enjoyed living in a country where the government seemed benign; where the streets were not policed by men with guns. The thought of leaving this safe, cosy environment terrified her, but she couldn't tell her father that. All she could say was: 'And besides, I don't speak Italian.'

'I will teach you...' said her father pragmatically, 'I speak it quite well. You'll pick it up. And I am taking several students from London with me – they will be company for you. They won't all stay for the whole time – they will come and go, but it will be exciting, Rachael – believe me. It is a great honour for me, to be given this dig to oversee. It's a testament to the faith the department have in me. Sardinia is filled with Roman remains; I've always wanted to go there.'

'Yes, of course,' said Rachael, weakly. 'The Romans are your passion, I know...'

'My darling Rachael, my only passion is for you and Angela.'

As if on cue, the child woke up and began to cry lustily.

'I will get her,' George said enthusiastically, 'she likes her grandpa...'

He returned with Angela on his hip, rubbing her eyes, sleepily. He sat in the armchair with his granddaughter on his lap and jiggled her up and down, singing a little nursery rhyme. At the last line, he pretended to drop the child between his legs, catching her just before she hit the floor. She laughed uproariously – clearly delighted by this familiar game.

'Now… where was I? Oh yes… you're right, of course,' he continued, 'that my professional passion is for Rome and its buildings. I have studied them for over forty-five years. And to find a site that has been hidden away for so long is every classical archaeologist's dream.'

'Give me the baby, Papa; she had her supper an hour or so ago, and all that jiggling won't do her any good at all,' said Rachael, moving the baby onto her own lap. The child snuggled into her mother's chest, her thumb placed firmly in her mouth. 'Now, tell me about the work,' Rachael said.

Her father began to pace the room eagerly.

'It's very exciting… Someone was doing some work on the church in Sant'Antioco – in the crypt – repairs to the drains, or something – and they uncovered what might be a Roman burial chamber. But it needs expert care now. The university has been asked to collaborate with the Italians and I have been given the opportunity to supervise the excavation. This is my chance, Rachael.' He turned to his daughter, his eyes glittering with excitement. 'I enjoy teaching in the classroom. I love to inspire my students with pictures and explanations in textbooks. But nothing… nothing compares with the excitement of lying in the dirt, with a small trowel in your hand, uncovering something that has been hidden from view for two thousand years, or more. *Nothing.*'

He sat down heavily in the armchair by the window. He suddenly looked tired, Rachael thought, as if the excitement of telling her his news had exhausted him, and the adrenalin had finally dissipated.

'Have I ever told you of my first discovery?' he went on, speaking more softly.

'No, Papa.' It was an indulgent white lie, for she was sure she must have heard the story before.

'I was just eighteen; a student at the university in Budapest. I had enrolled in archaeology and had been invited by my professor – a splendid man for whom I had the utmost respect – to attend a dig he was running near a place called Aquincum. Now, this was a sizeable Roman city, you know; maybe fifty thousand people lived there at one time. Nowadays, it is quite famous, but back then – before the First World War – we were making history. I worked there every day through the summer holidays, learning to scrape away the earth, carefully brushing soil from the surface of a fragment of pottery, or metal. It gave me a window into a past world that, until then, I had only understood from reading Roman historians. They left us graphic accounts of the great events of the Roman Empire of course, but to find a little jug, or metal bowl… to see the normal domestic items that people used – to see the workmanship, to understand the level of skill that these people had… well it was so exciting.

'In August we began work on a grave. There were two, in fact, but one had already been destroyed – looted over the years – such a tragedy.' He shook his head sorrowfully, still affected by the memory of this wanton vandalism. 'But the other was untouched. As we removed the limestone cover, we found a carefully preserved corpse wrapped in maybe eight or ten layers of cloth – linen soaked in resin. We carefully unwound the fabric, and there… was the body of a woman.'

Rachael shifted the baby, who, now thoroughly awake, wriggled to be released from her mother's lap. At eighteen months old Angela had developed quite a determined personality. Rachael put her onto the floor, where she sat cross-legged, listening intently to her grandfather as if he were telling her a bedtime story.

'One day – I remember it was baking hot – I found something; a little fragment of brown cloth between the legs of this woman. It looked like nothing, but this little piece of fabric had been there for over a thousand years. My professor took the tiny fragment and examined it very carefully. In the end he declared that it was made of byssus – he was delighted. Have you heard of it?'

Rachael shook her head.

'Byssus. There is much debate about what byssus truly is. There are many references to it in literature and in the Bible. Some scholars say byssus is just another word for linen or cotton cloth. But, the word "byssus" is also used for a fabric made from the thin filaments that attach a giant mollusc to the seabed. These filaments are cut, spun into thread and, over time, people have learnt to weave them, to create clothing, religious artefacts and so on. It is thought that the cloth of gold mentioned in the Bible story was made of byssus. Well, that little fragment that I discovered when I was just a boy, turned out to be the oldest piece of byssus ever found. Can you imagine? It dated from the fourth century AD. And I found it…! And now, I have a chance to go and make fresh discoveries, on a site in Sardinia. I am sixty-four, Rachael; this might be the last chance I ever have.'

He gazed intently at his daughter.

She went over and knelt down beside him and held him in her arms. She inhaled the scent of his skin, the smell of tobacco that permeated his old tweed jacket.

'Then we must go Papa. Of course we will go.'

To say that Rachael was happy about their move would be wrong. She was filled with anxiety at the prospect of leaving everything that had become so dear and familiar to her. But she saw how delighted her father was at the idea of taking charge of another dig – particularly at the end of his illustrious career. He had done so much for her… she felt this was the least she could do for him. Over the following weeks, as she began to imagine life on a Mediterranean island, her apprehension turned to excitement. Her experience of life had been so limited up until then, and the thought of living surrounded by blue sea and sandy beaches... her days filled with sunshine, was, she had to admit, an increasingly appealing prospect, particularly in the middle of a drab, grey British winter.

The family's last Christmas in Hampstead was an understandable mix of anticipation and sadness. The previous year, Angela had been too young to appreciate anything except playing with empty boxes and tissue paper. But this year, Rachael was determined her daughter should experience a Hungarian Christmas, which began, traditionally, with the feast St Nicholas. On this day parents would place a pair of shoes on the windowsill for St Nicholas to fill with presents for their children. Rachael well remembered her own childish excitement as she peered into a pair of dark red velvet evening slippers of her mother's, and found a tiny handmade doll, and perhaps a little 'szaloncukor' – a chocolate fondant sweet, wrapped in brightly coloured paper. Sadly, the velvet shoes had been left behind in Budapest, along with so many other mementoes of her mother. Rachael now owned just a single pair of shoes – a pair of brown brogues that she had polished specially for the occasion. As she carried Angela around the room that morning in her stockinged feet, she encouraged her daughter to peer inside the shoes on the windowsill.

'Look, Angela... look inside Mummy's shoe... what can you see?'

Her daughter looked inside the shoe and then at her mother, seeking reassurance.

'It's for you,' Rachael said, 'a present from St Nicholas... what has he left you?'

The child removed a doll from the shoe, kissed it and held it protectively to her chest. Rachael had made the tiny replica of a girl in Hungarian dress, using old scraps of fabric from Mrs Roper's work basket.

'What do you say?' asked Rachael.

'Thank you, Mama,' said Angela, nursing the doll.

'No… thank you St Nicholas… *he* left it there for you – for being such a good girl.'

The child smiled broadly and kissed the doll again.

Rachael had made a similar doll for Mrs Roper; she would give it to her on Christmas Eve – the traditional day for presents in Hungary.

'I thought we'd put the tree up in the parlour today,' said Mrs Roper one morning as Rachael came downstairs with Angela. 'It will be Christmas Day in a few days time and I normally have it decorated by now.'

'Oh, of course,' said Rachael. 'Can I help you? It was lovely to do it last year. I remember so well. In Hungary, you know, we do it on Christmas Eve. The children are kept out of the room and then a bell is rung and they are allowed in. We tell them the angels have brought them some presents.'

'That's a beautiful idea,' said Mrs Roper. 'Why didn't we do that last year?'

'Well, we hadn't lived here that long and, besides, Angela was just a baby.'

'Well, let's do it the Hungarian way *this* year… Angela will love it, and the tree can wait a few more days.'

'Perhaps we can decorate the room in the meantime.' Rachael knew how sad her landlady was feeling about their imminent departure and some activity might be the distraction she needed. 'We could make paper chains… I've seen them in the shops. The newsagent is selling the paper.'

'That's a lovely idea…'

They sat together in front of the range in the kitchen, sticking the coloured paper chains together, laying it out on the floor as they completed it. When it stretched from one end of the room to the other, Rachael took it upstairs, and attached it to the picture rail in the parlour.

Back downstairs in the kitchen, Mrs Roper was poring over a couple of well-thumbed cookery books and writing out a list of ingredients she still needed to buy. When Rachael came back into the room she sat down next to her landlady and picked up one of the cookery books.

'What's this?' she asked. 'Christmas pudding. Is it nice?'

'Oh yes... I've already made mine – I made it months ago. It's in the larder.'

'Oh... and will it be OK? Not mouldy?'

'No...' scoffed Mrs Roper. 'They can keep for a year or more – all that brandy. What would you traditionally eat in Hungary at Christmas?'

'Well, we normally have fish soup to start,' said Rachael.

Mrs Roper wrinkled her nose slightly in disapproval.

'And then,' continued Rachael, 'chicken or pork and stuffed cabbage, and afterwards pastries and more *szaloncukor* – little sweets.'

'Well... as we're doing the tree your way, I think we'll do the meal my way – if that's all right. Chicken and pork are all very well, but you need something different at Christmas, I always think. When I was young, we always had a goose, but turkey is very fashionable now, so I'm doing turkey this year – as it's a special celebration. We'll make a lovely stuffing and do roast potatoes and chestnuts and sprouts. I've already made the pudding and a lovely dark Christmas cake. But perhaps you and Angela could help me make mince pies this afternoon. I was just checking the recipe to make sure I've got enough currants and so on.'

Angela, delighted to be included, stood on a stool at Mrs Roper's big kitchen table, mixing the currants, raisins, sultanas and brandy with a long wooden spoon. Rachael, meanwhile, rolled out pastry on a cool marble board. While the mince pies cooked, and the house filled with the scents of Christmas, Rachael felt a genuine sadness to be leaving this kind woman who had shown her so much kindness and affection.

On Christmas Eve, while George looked after Angela in the attic, the two women dragged the tree in from the garden and put it up in the parlour. Mrs Roper went down to the basement and brought up the box of decorations.

'Here they are... all the lovely bits and pieces I've collected over the years. There are even decorations my son made as a child.'

She handed Rachael a little robin made of papier mâché, painted inexpertly by a child's hand.

'It's lovely...' said Rachael, climbing on a chair and fixing it to the tree. 'See – he's looking down on us now...'

'Yes dear... that's right. He's always here with me, but especially at Christmas.'

Rachael climbed off the chair and gave Mrs. Roper a hug.

'Thank you, dear,' Mrs. Roper said, wiping her eyes with the edge of her apron. 'Now, we'd better get this tree finished and when we're all assembled, I'll open a bottle of sherry and we can share our gifts.'

Rachael went upstairs and changed into a dark red dress before gathering up her few presents – a leather-bound notebook for her father and a couple of picture books and a simple jigsaw for Angela. For Mrs. Roper, she had made a doll – a six-inch high replica of a girl in Hungarian costume – dressed in a bright blue full skirt, an apron, an embroidered blouse and wearing a little cap over her dark hair.

Once the presents were arranged beneath the tree, Mrs. Roper lit the candles and she and Rachael turned out the lights. Following Hungarian tradition, Rachael shook a little handbell – the cue for George to enter the room with Angela in his arms. She shrieked excitedly as soon as she saw the tree. It was a magical sight in the darkened room – the flicker of candles, their reflections glimmering on the glass baubles and shiny ornaments.

'Look, Angela,' said her mother, handing her a present wrapped in coloured tissue paper. 'See what the angels have left for you.'

George sat the child down on his lap and helped her open the parcel.

Shyly, Rachael picked up the gift she had made for Mrs Roper. 'This is for you,' she said.

Mrs Roper unwrapped the tiny doll, and turned it over in her hands, admiring the workmanship. 'Oh, Rachael – it's beautiful... did you make it?'

'Yes... I thought it would remind you... of us.'

'Well, I'll never forget you – you can be sure of that. I've got something for you too.'

She handed Rachael a small parcel, expertly wrapped up in colourful red and green paper.

'I don't normally give presents to my guests. But... seeing as you're leaving, and we may never meet again...' She took a pressed white handkerchief from the sleeve of her best dress and dabbed at her eyes.

'Oh Mrs Roper... I'm sure we *will* meet again. We'll be back in a year... and maybe live here in the future. If not, I will come and see you – I promise.'

'Yes... well. You open your present, dear.'

Rachael undid the ribbon and removed the wrapping, revealing a bright blue swimsuit. She had never owned a swimsuit before, but recognised what it was from pictures she had seen in magazines. Nestling beside it was a smaller one for Angela - pale yellow edged in white broderie anglaise.

'Oh Mrs Roper... that's so thoughtful. They're beautiful.'

'Well, I've never been to Italy, but I know it's hot there and the sea is lovely. So I thought... it would be wonderful if you could go for a swim. I got them at Derry and Toms. They're good quality. I'm sure if they're the wrong size they'd change them for you.'

'They're perfect… thank you.'

She hugged Mrs Roper, who in turn wrapped her arms around Rachael.

'I shall miss you very much,' she said, running from the room.

PART TWO

'My course is set for an uncharted sea'
Dante Alighieri

Chapter 9

The overnight sea crossing from Rome to Cagliari, the ancient capital of Sardinia, would take over eight hours. George, Rachael and Angela boarded the dilapidated ferry just after sunset, shared a late picnic supper in their cabin and settled themselves in the two narrow bunks – George in one and little Angela and her mother in the other.

The acrid scent of diesel oil caught in Rachael's throat, and the rolling of the craft, as it chugged through the waters of the Mediterranean, triggered waves of nausea as she closed her eyes. Angela slept peacefully on the inside of the bunk, sandwiched between the metal wall of the cabin and her mother, her eyelids fluttering wildly as she dreamed. Rachael lay uncomfortably on the outside, holding onto the edge of the bunk, fearing she would roll out if she lost her grip, and yet reluctant to move in case she disturbed her daughter.

Exhausted, she finally fell into a deep sleep, but woke with a start just before dawn. Peering through the porthole, she saw, with relief, a delicate golden glow on the horizon. A new day had begun.

Still wearing the wool skirt and jumper she had slept in the night before, she swung her legs out of her narrow bunk, laced up her brown shoes and opened the cabin door as silently as she could. Angela stirred slightly, moaned a little in her sleep, and rolled towards the edge of the bunk. Anxious the child would fall onto the floor, Rachael took a towel from her suitcase and, rolling it up, placed it between her daughter and the edge of the bunk. Then, confident that Angela was safe, she slipped out into the corridor.

The engines of the ferry throbbed deep in the bowels of the ship. As she walked along the narrow metal corridor, grabbing the handrails on either side to steady herself, she heard the sound of male voices – sailors, she presumed – shouting instructions to one another. She clambered up a narrow ladder that led to the upper deck. At the end of the corridor, she found a heavy metal door. Yanking it open, she was assailed by a blast of chilly sea air, causing her to stagger backwards.

Out on deck, she walked unsteadily towards the prow of the ship, unnerved by the roll of the ferry as it ploughed through the water. One or two other passengers had clearly had the same idea and she joined a small gaggle of weary but excited people gathering at the front of the ship to watch the sun come up over their destination.

They approached the island from the south-east, its coast shimmering gold in the morning light. Rachael could make out tiny villages dotted along the shores of the isthmus that jutted out into the dark turquoise sea. As the ferry skirted the southern edge of the island, heading for Cagliari, green hills rose up from the sea, sprinkled with the pale yellow and apricot of little hamlets, villages and farms.

As the sun rose, she rushed back to the cabin, hoping to bring her daughter up on deck to share her excitement. She found her wide awake and sitting up in bed next to her grandfather. There were times when Rachael was struck by Angela's extraordinary resemblance to József. Her daughter's mass of unruly curls reminded Rachael so much of her husband's mop of blond hair. Only her grey-green eyes were inherited from her mother. As for her personality, Angela appeared to have the character traits of the male members of her family – in particular, the impish grin and keen intelligence of her grandfather.

'Papa, Angela – good you're awake!'

'We wondered where you'd gone… are you all right?'

'Yes, Papa, I've been watching the sun come up over Sardinia… Come – let's go upstairs.'

The family joined the throng of people now waiting expectantly on deck. Most were Italians: islanders returning home after a visit to the mainland, or people visiting relatives on the island. Many had slept on deck surrounded by their simple possessions – boxes of provisions, and bags of shopping. Some even had livestock – chickens in bamboo cages, and cats and dogs in baskets.

'*Cagliari, venti minuti.* Cagliari, twenty minutes,' the tannoy suddenly announced.

George and Rachael looked out to sea expectantly. The main capital city of the island was visible now. It rose up imperiously from the dark emerald green water – a collection of buildings piled high atop the series of small hills that surrounded the 'Bay of Angels'. Every house or apartment building was painted a subtly different colour; yellow ochre, apricot, pink and peach, all mingling together. These ice-cream-coloured buildings looked so inviting – their windows edged with white coping stones, framed by dark shutters. Protruding from the red rooftops were the silvery grey domes of churches. Even in the chilly winter's air, the sky was a shade of brilliant blue, a startling contrast to the warm tones of the buildings beneath.

As the ferry drew near to the port, George picked his grand-daughter up and swung her onto his shoulders. He pointed at the spiky palm trees that fringed the harbour's edge.

'Look, Angela – now you know you are truly in the Mediterranean.'

From her high vantage point, with her blonde curls blowing in the salt breeze blowing in off the sea, Angela kicked her legs, delightedly. She grinned broadly, and chuckled to herself, her little pudgy hands wrapped around her grandfather's forehead.

'Come on,' said George, setting Angela down on the deck, 'we'd better get back to the cabin and pack up our things.'

*

As the ferry docked, they joined a line of people loaded down with their cargo, heading towards the exits. As they walked down the metal gangplank onto Sardinian soil, there was a shout from the dockside.

'Over here, Professor.'

A young man wearing a dark brown duffle coat and stout hiking boots was calling out to the family.

'Who's that?' asked Rachael.

'It's Giles… one of my students. They came on ahead. They've come to meet us.'

Giles and Pete were two of George's keenest students. In their early twenties, they had been on Sardinia for just over a week, sorting out lodgings for the party of archaeologists who would soon descend on the island of Sant'Antioco. They had hired an old flatbed truck for the duration of their stay, and now they guided the family towards it. As they threw the family's belongings into the back of the truck, they were full of chatter and restrained excitement.

'Not a huge amount of room, I'm afraid, in the old girl,' said Giles, patting the truck affectionately, 'but she goes at quite a lick. If Pete jumps in the back with you, sir?' Giles said, gesturing to a long narrow wooden bench that ran down one side of the open-topped truck, 'there should be room for your daughter and her little girl up front with me… in the cabin. If that's OK?'

Rachael had never met any of her father's British students before. She was impressed by their politeness, but also by their easy charm – so different to József and his friends, who had been such intense, passionate young men.

The drive from Cagliari took them along a winding road through the southern part of the island of Sardinia. They drove across empty plains, through little villages and hamlets, occasionally passing groups of women, carrying wide baskets on their heads, filled with produce. Rachael craned her neck to see what they contained.

'Is that bread they have in there?' she asked Giles.

'Yes probably. Bread, or cakes. They cook them together in one big oven in the smaller villages – once a week, I gather. A bit like my mother and the WI.'

'WI?' Rachael looked mystified.

'Oh… sorry… Women's Institute. It's a sort of meeting place for the ladies back home. They make jam and cakes and that sort of thing. Very important part of village life in Britain!'

Rachael was fascinated by the women she saw on the road. With their long colourful skirts in simple primary colours, headscarves, white blouses and embroidered waistcoats, they reminded her of the dolls in Hungarian national dress she had made for Angela and Mrs Roper. As the truck rumbled slowly past, one woman in particular caught Rachael's eye. She carried a sleeping child – bigger than Angela – in her arms, while at the same time balancing a huge basket of bread on her head.

'Could you stop please…' she asked Giles. 'We should offer them a lift.'

He came to a halt at the side of the road and jumped out of the cabin.

'Just going to see if the ladies need a lift,' he called back to Peter and George.

Minutes later, three women, a sleeping child and their huge baskets of freshly baked bread were installed in the back of the truck, heading for the next village.

George, who spoke good Italian, chatted amiably with them all throughout the journey. When they arrived at their village, the women climbed out, and handed George and the young men a couple of loaves of bread as recompense. As the truck drove away, in a cloud of dust, they waved enthusiastically to their new friends.

The truck ground on, taking the potholes in the road and almost absent cambers in its stride. As the road rose up and over a low mountain ridge, Rachael marvelled at the snow-covered peaks, tinged pink by the sun. From time to time, the truck nearly skidded off the edge of the road, but Giles always managed to haul it back.

'Sorry about that,' he said, smiling. 'The roads here are simply frightful – worse than at my parents' place down in Devon – and that's saying something.'

'It's all right,' said Rachael.

'Your little girl doesn't seem to mind,' said Giles, gesturing towards Angela, still sleeping peacefully in Rachael's arms.

'No... she can sleep through anything.'

Finally, they descended once again onto the plain, heading towards the long winding causeway that crossed the narrow straight to Sant'Antioco. As the truck skirted the edge of the water, Rachael had her first glimpse of the little island that she would call home for the next year.

The town of Sant'Antioco wrapped around the water's edge – a smaller version of the capital, Cagliari. The houses were painted the same ice-cream colours of gold, yellow and apricot, their red roofs standing out against the bright blue sky. Little fishing boats nestled against the harbour walls, rocking gently in the breeze.

'I'll take you to your hotel,' said Giles, as the truck wound its way up the cobbled streets of the little town. 'It's right behind the Basilica di Sant'Antioco, the island's most famous church and the site of our dig, so it's pretty convenient. But we're hoping to get some lodgings in the town in the next week or so. Pete and I have already found a little house to share; we move in tomorrow. And I've also found somewhere more permanent for the professor and yourself. It's a few minutes' drive out of the town, but has a lovely view of the sea...'

As the truck roared into the village square, Rachael got her first view of the basilica, the site of the archeological dig. It was surrounded on three sides by shops, one or two houses, and, on the far side of the square, the hotel.

Although modest, the hotel appeared to be clean and quite comfortable. Rachael and George had been assigned two rooms on the first floor, and a small cot had been assembled in Rachael's room for Angela.

'Rachael,' said George, excitedly, as soon as their bags had been delivered to the room, 'I am desperate to see the site... will you be all right here while I go? It's just on the other side of the square, so you can come across later when Angela wakes up.'

Angela lay fast asleep in the small cot bed.

'Yes... you go. It's fine. I'll unpack and sort things out here... We'll come over later.'

Rachael and Angela emerged from the hotel an hour or so later. Hand in hand, they walked over the cobbles around the side of the basilica. Rachael gazed up at the seventeenth-century façade painted a dark shade of apricot. Angela, refreshed after her long sleep, wriggled her hand out of her mother's grasp and began to run around the town square, laughing. Her mother chased after her and, with her daughter in her arms, sat down at a table at a little café next to the church.

A tall young man with dark curly hair that tumbled over his brown eyes came out holding a notebook.

'*Dica, signora?*'

'I'm sorry,' said Rachael, blushing, 'my Italian is not good.'

The young man looked blank. He clearly spoke no English.

'*Mi scusi,*' she said, eventually, trawling up the little Italian her father had taught her over the last few weeks, '*non parlo Italiano bene... ma... posso... avere un café con... latte? E cioc-colata per la bimba,*' she gestured towards Angela, who beamed at the young man.

'*Benissimo, signora,*' he said, smiling.

He returned a few minutes later with the coffee and hot chocolate. He placed them on the table and left the bill tucked under Angela's cup. He smiled again, revealing large white teeth, and stroked Angela's golden hair, cupping her chin in his hand. It was a gesture of such sweetness that it took Rachael's breath away.

'Ah, Rachael.' It was Giles, walking purposefully towards her. 'The professor sent me to find you… He's going to be quite a while down at the site. He thought you'd prefer to see where you were going to live. Would you like to come with me to the house we've set aside for you?'

'Yes… Thank you.'

The house was, just as Giles had promised, close to the main town. He drove the truck along the coast road, before turning sharply down a bumpy lane. Within minutes the single-storey house came into view. Painted apricot, it sat low in the landscape and was surrounded by scrubby vegetation.

Giles parked the truck in the wide driveway and led Rachael and Angela round to the front door. There was a large veranda, running the length of the house, which overlooked a terrace dominated by an imposing chimney with a wide opening at its base. A metal table and chairs stood invitingly outside.

'Bread oven,' said Giles matter-of-factly, gesturing towards the chimney, 'rather handy, I'd have thought.'

Rachael looked around her. Beyond the terrace was a small garden, encircled by a low fence. A white gate led through to a modest copse of trees, and in the distance Rachael glimpsed the turquoise blue of the sea.

'I can see the sea,' she said delightedly. 'Are we allowed to use it… the beach, I mean?'

'Yes of course… I think the beach is officially public – but because the house owns all the land down to the shore, it's effectively private to this house. We'll go and have a look in a minute, if you like,' said Giles, removing the keys to the front door from beneath a flower pot on the veranda.

The door opened onto the kitchen. There was on old black range against the end wall, a painted dresser arranged with some cracked china, a wooden table in the centre of the room, and set beneath a window overlooking the terrace, an old stone sink.

'Bit of a smell of damp, but I'm sure once you're installed that will go. Just needs the range lighting and the room airing...'

Giles led the way through the kitchen to a sitting room. An elderly sofa stood against one wall and a couple of chairs were arranged companionably on either side of a fireplace.

'Do you want to see the bedrooms?' asked Giles, pointing to the brick staircase in the far corner. Angela ran ahead, scrambling up the stairs. Following her, Rachael was delighted to discover two good-sized bedrooms and a small box room.

'My room,' said Angela, running around the tiny space.

'Oh darling... maybe. Don't you want to sleep with Mummy anymore?'

'My room,' the child repeated, stamping her foot.

'Sorry about that,' Rachael apologised to Giles, 'she'll be two in May and is rather determined about what she wants...'

The young man smiled and shrugged his shoulders.

'Not much in the way of indoor plumbing, I'm afraid,' he apologised, 'the island seems rather behind the times in that regard. But there's a privy out the back, and I gather there's a tin bath somewhere. The old range in the kitchen should produce quite a lot of hot water. I'll make sure you've got enough wood and so on...'

'Thank you; it'll be fine,' said Rachael, uncertainly. 'It would be nice to have a bathroom, but if there are none on the island...'

'Shall we go down to the sea,' proposed Giles. 'It was that which really sold the place to me.'

Angela, rested after her long sleep in the truck and the hotel, was now filled with energy. She toddled ahead of the adults and stood eagerly rattling the gate that divided the garden from the copse and the sea beyond.

'Seaside, seaside,' she chanted.

'Wait, darling,' said Rachael, 'you must not go through the gate without Mummy.'

Giles opened the gate and Angela ran ahead giggling. Rachael ran after her, catching hold of her hand and swung the child up onto her hip. The path led through a little wood, but, within moments, they emerged from the vegetation onto a cove – quite private and secluded. An old boat had been hauled up on the beach and apparently abandoned.

'Oh, how lovely!' said Rachael.

'Pretty spectacular, eh?' said Giles, sitting down on the sand. 'When I saw this, I thought… if I had a child, it would be rather a special place to live. But you'll need to be quite careful with Angela. I presume she can't swim yet?'

'No… but I will be here all the time.'

'It's shallow enough near the shore, but it drops off quite sharply a few yards out.'

Rachael gazed out at the turquoise water nearest the shore. Fifteen or twenty feet out, the colour of the water changed quite suddenly to a deep emerald – almost as if a line had been drawn across the bay.

She sat down on the soft white sand next to Giles and pulled Angela onto her lap.

'You were right. This is a wonderful place. A magical place. I'm sure we can make the house nice. And if we can't have a bath very often – we can always bathe here in the sea, can't we Angela?'

The child grinned at her mother and, wrapping her arms around her neck, kissed her.

Chapter 10

Sophie and Hamish were eating a rushed breakfast at the kitchen table when Dr Boulderstone's receptionist rang to arrange an appointment later that morning.

'If you'd like me to come along, I could try to see if someone could stand in for me?' he said, cramming toast into his mouth. 'But it's a bit last minute – and I've got a long list in surgery.' The cat had wrapped itself around its master's feet and yowled furiously as Hamish struggled to stand up.

'No, don't worry,' said Sophie, 'what's the point? She's just going to tell me the results. What good is it you being there?' She bent down and picked the cat up, which growled at being removed from its comfortable nesting place beneath the table.

'Well... OK, if you're sure,' said Hamish, throwing his jacket over his shoulders, and swilling down the rest of his coffee. 'Text me, obviously... when you know the results.' He pecked Sophie on the cheek, scratched the cat now lying proprietorially in Sophie's arms, under its chin, and was gone. Within minutes Sophie heard the roar of a car engine, as Hamish swept down the drive.

She couldn't help thinking that Hamish was secretly relieved that he couldn't attend the doctor's appointment. She knew that he found this medical intervention into their reproductive lives irritating... distressing even.

At ten o'clock, Sophie sat, anxiously, in the doctor's waiting room.

'Mrs Mitchell…' the receptionist called her name without looking away from her computer screen.

Sophie walked along the corridor to the doctor's office. She felt sick with nerves, as if she was waiting for a diagnosis of cancer… or worse.

'Ah, Mrs Mitchell,' said Dr Boulderstone.

'Sophie please…' said Sophie, sitting down.

'So, how are you?' asked the doctor, with disconcerting friendliness.

'That sounds ominous.' Sophie shifted uneasily in her chair. 'I always think it must be bad news when a doctor asks you how you are…' She smiled weakly.

'No… not at all,' said the doctor, as casually as she could. 'Let's just take a look at these results, shall we?'

The doctor brought the scan up on her computer and turned the screen so that Sophie could see it more easily.

'Now, here is a scan of your womb and fallopian tubes.'

'Is there a problem – a blockage? I knew it,' said Sophie, tears welling.

'No… not at all,' said the doctor, briskly. 'I wanted to show you the scans, because it all looks perfectly healthy. No sign of endometriosis, no blockages… nothing.'

'So that's good – yes?'

'Yes… in many ways it is.'

'So why am I not pregnant? Is it Hamish?'

'No, at least it doesn't appear to be. His sperm count is not massively high – but it's not low either. Motility of the sperm is adequate. It's possible you might be producing antibodies that reject his sperm, but that's unusual. I suspect what we have here… is a case of what we call – rather inadequately in the medical profession – "unexplained infertility". About fifteen per cent of cases are like this. There's no obvious problem. And that's a good thing – it means there is no reason for you *not* to get pregnant. But perhaps you need to consider reducing stress, eating well, drinking less, not smoking…'

'I don't smoke. And I hardly drink at all anymore. I eat like a… health freak. We have just moved house and my husband's changed his job, so stress is a bit inevitable. But short of spending my entire life in bed, hiding under the duvet, I just don't know what else I can do?'

'Well, there are a few options. You could opt for IVF. And… I'm happy to say that, given your age,' the doctor referred to the notes on her desk, 'you're thirty-three aren't you?'

Sophie nodded.

'Good – then I'm happy to say, that I am able to recommend you for one cycle of IVF on the NHS. I'm sorry it can't be more, but that's what the CCG – the Clinical Commissioning Group – here in Gloucestershire allow. Technically, you should have been trying for three years – as in seriously making an effort to have a baby. But I have in my notes that it's more like two?'

She looked up expectantly at Sophie.

Sophie's mind was a blur… she was being offered IVF – at last.

'Yes… two. But I've actually been off the pill for nearly three years now.'

'OK, so we can cross that hurdle,' said the doctor. 'I'll write the report, and you'll be hearing from a consultant soon, I suspect. They will manage the process from here on in – but if you have any worries, or questions, do please give me a call. Or email me…'

She smiled and stood up, indicating the appointment was over.

Sophie, stunned slightly, by the news, remained seated.

'Well…' said the doctor expectantly, 'if I can give you any more advice… do please get in touch.'

Back inside her car, Sophie sat with her fingers hovering over her mobile phone. She wanted to text Hamish. She felt a curious combination of excitement and… something else. What was it? She felt upset. It was so confusing. She knew enough about IVF to realise that it was no magic wand. But at least she had a chance now…

Hi… she typed, *good news. Call me?*

She deleted it. She really wanted to hear his voice, but he wouldn't take a call now; he'd be in the middle of his operating list and up to his ears, almost literally, in blood and gore. Instead, she dialled her mother. It was a Thursday, her mother's day off.

'Hello, Mum…'

She tried to sound cheerful, but Angela could sense something was wrong.

'What's the matter?' she said.

'Nothing,' said Sophie between sobs.

Her mother, always calm in the face of adversity, waited patiently for the sobbing to subside. 'Sweetheart… tell me… Shall I come down?' she asked sweetly.

'Oh Mum… I've just been to the doctor. She says there's no reason why I can't get pregnant,' Sophie wailed down the phone.

'Oh darling… well that's *good* news! Really it is. Why are you crying?'

'I don't know…' sobbed Sophie.

'Is it the relief? Or are you still worried about why it's not happening? I know it's frustrating, but think how much worse if you had blocked tubes. That, at least, is one problem you can cross off your list.'

She paused, hoping for a response, but could hear only sobbing.

'Oh Sophie,' she went on, 'it's so hard, isn't it? *Do* you want me to come? I could jump in the car right now and be with you by mid-afternoon.'

'And what about your patients tomorrow?'

'Yes… well, I could see if one of the others could stand in for me,' Angela said uncertainly.

'No… you mustn't do that. I know how understaffed you are. I'll be fine, Mum. It's good news really. The doctor says I qualify for one round of IVF on the NHS.'

'Well, that *is* good news.'

'But you know as well as I do, that one round is rarely enough…'

'I also know, darling that sometimes it is. You just need to believe and stay calm; go along with the process and don't overthink it. What does Hamish say?'

'He doesn't know yet. He's working today… he couldn't take the morning off to come with me.'

'Well tell him tonight.'

'I will.'

'You don't sound that happy, darling. I'd have thought you would be over the moon.'

'It's just…' Sophie began to cry again, 'up till now I've sort of convinced myself that I was normal… that it would happen anytime soon. But now… it's official; I can't do it on my own. I need intervention. Do you see?'

'Oh sweetie… I do understand. But you must… must stay positive. This is your chance. Do the course, keep the faith.'

'I know… thank you. I love you…'

'Love you too, angel…'

That afternoon, Sophie's sister-in-law Victoria rang to discuss plans for Christmas. Sophie and Hamish had invited her whole family down to spend the holiday at their new house.

'Hi Sophie…' Victoria said cheerily. 'I just thought we ought to touch base about Christmas. Simon and I are so excited to see the new house. So – when do you want us, and what I can do…'

Sophie sniffed on the other end of the phone. It was clear she'd been crying.

'Are you all right?' Victoria asked. 'You sound a bit miserable, sweetie…'

'I'm OK,' said Sophie. 'I've just come back from the doctor…'

'You're not ill, are you?'

'No… I don't know if you knew… but we've been struggling… to get pregnant.'

There was a pause on the other end.

'I didn't know… no,' Victoria replied uncertainly.

'We've been offered IVF – just one round.'

Another silence.

'Well, that's good isn't it?' Victoria said, trying to sound optimistic. 'It can work terribly well these days, I hear…' she trailed off.

'I suppose…' said Sophie, 'it just seems a bit sad to have to resort to medical intervention. Would you do it?'

Victoria took a deep breath. 'Maybe?' she said. 'I think you'd do what you have to.'

When they hung up, Sophie had a curious sense that Victoria had not been her normal bubbly self; perhaps she was simply upset for her sister-in-law, but it was almost as if something had been withheld during their conversation.

When Hamish came home that night, Sophie had supper prepared and a bottle of wine opened on the kitchen table.

'Something smells good,' he said, throwing his jacket over the back of the chair. He picked up the bottle of wine, studying the label. 'That's rather a good one… where was that hiding?'

'I bought it today – in Cirencester. I went there after the… after the doctor.'

'Oh, of course – God, I'm sorry; I'd forgotten. How did it go?'

Sophie pushed aside her disappointment that he had forgotten her appointment and began to tell him about the consultation; she tried to sound upbeat and positive about the course of IVF.

'That's great!' Hamish said, kissing her. 'It's what we wanted... isn't it?'

'Yes,' she said, beginning to cry.

'Darling, what's the matter?'

'I know it's silly – it just makes it all so... real somehow. It just seems so tragic that we need medical treatment to get pregnant. I'm just sorry that I'm so useless.'

'Sophie – you're *not* useless. It's not your fault. It's no one's fault – it's just one of those things. And it will be fine, you'll see. Just try to relax and when we start the whole thing, we'll cope – we always do.'

Chapter 11

As the milky grey skies and cool nights of winter turned to spring, Rachael and the family settled into the cottage on the cove. While Angela napped in the tiny box room upstairs, or played in the kitchen, Rachael scrubbed the house from top to bottom. She learned how to coax the old range into life, riddling it each morning to empty the ashes and filling it with just enough fuel overnight to keep it alight.

Giles was true to his word and regularly chopped wood for her, which he stacked neatly outside the kitchen. He collected her father each morning in the old pickup and took him to the dig. If Rachael needed anything from the shops, she would ride into town with them, and then either wait for Giles to give her a lift back at lunchtime or walk home along the coast road with Angela. It took thirty minutes, but on a sunny day was a good way to give the little girl some exercise.

One morning, she came out of the vegetable shop in town, her basket filled with early spring vegetables – celeriac, artichokes and wild asparagus – and looked around for Giles. Neither he, nor the pickup were anywhere to be seen.

'Come on, sweetie,' she said to Angela. 'We'll walk home.'

She took the little girl's hand and, as she walked out of the square, the dark-haired young man from the cafe roared past on his scooter. He raised his hand in salute, before slowing down and circling back.

'*Vuole un passaggio?*' he asked her, smiling.

'I'm sorry – *mi dispiace, non ho capito…*' she said, blushing with embarrassment at her poor Italian.

She took Angela's hand and set off once again along the road. The young man followed her, his feet dangling on either side of the bike, the engine idling in order to keep pace with her. She looked over at him and smiled quizzically. He held out his hand and pointed towards her basket. She handed it to him and he put it on the footwell of the bike.

'*Grazie,*' she said.

Once more he said something she didn't understand. He patted the seat behind him and pointed at her, his eyes questioning.

Was he offering her a lift? Should she take a lift from a stranger?

He held his arms out for the child. Instinctively, Rachael handed Angela to him and he stood her between his legs, one arm protectively around her waist. The child looked up at her mother grinning broadly, clearly excited at this new experience. The young man shifted forward on the seat, making space for Rachael. She swung one leg across the saddle and sat behind him. With his free hand, he took one of hers and pulled it around his waist so she could also hold onto Angela.

He twisted the controls on the handlebars, and as they accelerated away, the wind streamed through her hair. Involuntarily she began to laugh; she felt exhilarated. She had never been on the back of a motorbike before, and it was a novel experience to be so completely in the hands of this stranger.

After the initial excitement, she began to feel anxious. Where was he taking her? But at the entrance to her lane, he turned confidently off the main road. He slowed down as they drove over the rutted lane that led to the cottage.

When they arrived at the house, he stopped, and steadied the bike while she climbed off. He lifted Angela carefully onto the ground and handed Rachael the basket of shopping.

'*Grazie*,' she said again, fumbling for the house keys in her basket.

Rather than driving off, he leant the scooter against the cottage wall and strode off through the wood towards the sea. He beckoned her to follow him.

On the beach, she was surprised to see him dragging the abandoned boat towards the water.

'My boat,' he said in a thick Sardinian accent.

'Oh… I wondered who it belonged to.'

He grinned, revealing his large white teeth.

'Fish,' he said.

He pushed the boat off the shore, and clambered in. Settling in the stern, he started the outboard engine and roared off out to sea.

Later that afternoon, as Rachael chopped vegetables on the table outside on the terrace, Angela playing around her feet, she heard the 'pop pop' sound of an outboard. Within minutes, the young man emerged from the wood and jumped effortlessly over the garden fence carrying a large basket filled with his catch – lobsters, their pink claws uppermost, clams and mussels. He pulled out two silvery-scaled fish and laid them ceremoniously on the table in front of her.

'For you…' he said, smiling.

'Thank you. *Grazie mille*,' said Rachael.

He bowed politely, and climbing back onto his Lambretta, he placed the basket in the footwell and roared off up the lane.

When Giles brought her father home that evening, Rachael poured them both a glass of wine. They sat together on the veranda, admiring the spring sun setting through the trees.

'Did you manage to walk home earlier today?' asked Giles. 'I had to go to the other side of the town after I'd dropped you off, but when I got back to the square I couldn't find you.'

'That's OK…' said Rachael, uncertain whether she should mention her surprise 'knight in shining armour'. 'I was given a lift actually,' she said coyly, refilling their glasses.

'Oh… who by?' Giles asked suspiciously.

'The young man who works in the cafe. It's his boat on our beach, apparently. He gave me a lift on his scooter, and then he went fishing and brought us two fish; I think they are seabass. We're having them tonight – will you stay and eat with us?'

'Thanks,' Giles said a little too eagerly. 'I'd love to stay for supper.'

As soon as she had invited him, Rachael felt a pang of regret. She had sensed his irritation as she told him about the stranger giving her a lift. As if 'the giving of lifts' was his prerogative. It was true that he had been incredibly helpful to her since they moved to the island. He frequently drove her into town, and chopped wood for the stove. He had even fixed a broken tap in the sink the previous week. And she was grateful – obviously. But she sensed that he was not merely acting out of selfless friendship. That he might expect something in return.

Over the last few months, she noticed that Giles increasingly lingered over their goodbyes, as if hoping for a kiss. When he drove her to town, he had a tendency to lean across her in the truck's passenger seat, helping her to close the door. These could be interpreted as innocent acts of friendship and yet they made her feel uncomfortable. She liked him well enough, but had no romantic interest in him. Instead it was the unnamed Italian who crept uninvited into her thoughts; who preoccupied her, as she lay in bed at night. She tried to ignore these feelings, aware that she was in a vulnerable position. She was a widow with a young child; a visitor on this island. She was also inexperienced. It would be wise, she reflected, to avoid all personal relationships. Caught between the unwelcome advances of her father's student, and her own growing interest in the young Italian, she felt increasingly anxious about how to manage the situation. Her father enjoyed

Giles' company – their glass of wine on the terrace was part of their daily routine, but these evenings spent together, in the candlelight on the terrace, were creating a sense of forced intimacy between the two young people which Rachael was determined to clarify. If she could discreetly explore Giles's feelings for her, then she could head him off and make it clear that she was not interested in a romantic entanglement.

And so, after supper, their seabass eaten, George went inside to put Angela to bed, leaving the two young people alone on the terrace. As the sun began to set behind the wood, casting long shadows across the garden, she asked Giles if he had a girlfriend in England.

'No,' he replied, blushing slightly. 'Most of the girls I know at university are blue stockings... intent on careers, not love.'

'You must know some less serious girls,' she insisted. 'What about girls in your village?'

'In Devon? No... all they want to do is go to parties, play tennis and marry a rich man.'

Rachael had to agree that they didn't sound like the sort of girl Giles would settle happily with.

'Well... I'm sure the right person will come along,' she said, hoping to close the subject.

'Perhaps she already has...' he said, gazing at her across the table.

Rachael knew she ought to force his hand and ask him outright if he had feelings for her. But she lost her nerve. It seemed so needlessly harsh – she didn't want to upset him. And what if she were wrong? What if he denied any feelings for her at all? It would be so humiliating. And so she just smiled and said nothing.

Over the following days, Rachael resolved to give Giles no opportunity to misinterpret her feelings for him. She would be polite, but distant. She also tried to put the young Italian out of her mind. But every time she went into the village, she kept one eye on the cafe, wondering if he would be there. She even sat down at a cafe table with Angela on her lap, hoping he would come and take her order. But instead a young waitress came over to her table. She looked so like him, Rachael wondered if the young man was her brother.

'*Il cameriere – e il suo fratello?*' she asked the girl in pidgin Italian.

'*Si…*' said the girl.

'*Come si chiama?*'

'Tommaso.'

'*E lei?*' asked Rachael, politely.

'*Mi chiamo Maria.*'

So now she knew his name – Tommaso.

His sister Maria smiled shyly and tucked the bill underneath Rachael's cup.

When Giles gave Rachael a lift home that lunchtime, she asked him as casually as she could: 'Why do you think that fisherman leaves his boat on our beach?'

'Tommaso… It's his family's cottage, that's why.'

'Oh… I had no idea.'

'They agreed to rent it out to us while we're here. Bit of extra income, I suppose. I think his mother and sister are living with friends. Not sure about Tommaso. He comes and goes. Bit of wild one I think.' He glanced sideways at Rachael, as if searching her face for a trace of agreement, but she remained impassive.

'Well… that explains him giving me a lift,' she said. 'He seemed to know the cottage very well.'

'He works with the fishing fleet down at the harbour most of the time,' explained Giles. 'The boat at the cove is just for his private use, I think. Does it bother you having it there? I'm sure I could ask him to take it away.'

'No…' said Rachael, calmly, 'don't do that. I don't mind it being there at all – I just wanted to understand the situation.' She didn't want the boat to be removed. It comforted her to think that Tommaso might show up at any time.

'I like your dress,' Giles suddenly blurted out, hesitantly, as the truck bumped over the ruts in the lane leading down to the cottage. She felt his eyes taking her in.

'Oh… thank you.' She wore a simple flowered red dress that day with several buttons down the front. The top button had come undone, revealing a little section of lace from her bra. She fumbled to do it up, pulling the dark red cardigan that was slung over her shoulders around her.

Giles parked the truck and leapt out to open the door for her.

'Let me bring in your shopping,' he offered.

'No… please don't bother,' she replied, 'I can manage… See you tomorrow I expect.'

As April turned to May the weather grew warmer, and Rachael woke to feel the unfamiliar sensation of sweat trickling down her back. She pushed the sheet and the old quilt off her bed and opened the shutters. Her room overlooked the back of the house and the sea beyond. The sun was beating down on the azure blue water; it glinted invitingly.

She put on a new sundress she had bought in the village and padded downstairs to the kitchen, where she riddled the stove, and removed the ash can to empty outside in the garden. As she opened the back door onto the veranda, warm air washed into the room and cicadas struck up their morning song. She shook the ash can onto a flower bed near the veranda and picked up a pile of wood that was stacked outside the back door. After loading the stove, she put a pan of water on to boil; then, kicking off her espadrilles, she wandered barefoot into the garden, feeling the dry sandy soil beneath her feet, the air pulsating around her. Perhaps today she would let Angela put on her swimsuit and have a swimming lesson.

Giles arrived, as usual, at eight-thirty sharp; he knocked casually on the open kitchen door and strode in wearing shorts, sandals and an open-necked shirt. His fair hair was pushed off his high forehead, already glistening with beads of sweat.

'It's jolly hot today,' he said cheerfully, pulling out a kitchen chair and sitting down next to Angela. The table was strewn with egg shells and crusts – the remnants of breakfast. 'For once, that sarcophagus underneath the church is going to be the best place to work… it's nice and chilly down there.'

'I must come down and have a look sometime,' said Rachael. She walked over to the open kitchen door, grateful for the sensation of cool air on her face. 'I can't believe I've been here for three months and haven't seen what you're all up to.'

George joined them in the kitchen.

'What's this… my daughter is showing an interest in the ancient world?'

He sat down at the kitchen table and poured himself a cup of coffee.

'Let's take our coffee outside,' suggested Rachael. 'We can sit on the veranda.'

Angela came toddling out a few minutes later, carrying her swimming costume.

'Seaside,' she said to her mother, 'seaside. Swimshoot'

'Yes… darling. Seaside today. Here… let me help you put the *swimsuit* on.'

She lifted the child's nightdress over her head and guided Angela's legs into the little yellow suit.

'You look so pretty!' said Rachael as the child twirled around, delighted by her new outfit, giggling with excitement.

'Well, we must get off,' said George to Giles. 'Don't let her go too deep in the water,' he warned his daughter.

'Father… of course not. I know she can't swim. I'll be really careful. She knows never to go through the gate without me. She's a good girl.'

'Perhaps we ought to stay,' said Giles. 'Just while she swims…?' He looked enquiringly at George, who was studying his notes.

'Stay?' he said. 'No need,' he said briskly. 'I'm sure Rachael will manage…'

'Yes, of course,' said Giles, hurriedly. 'I just thought we could help… Well… have a lovely day.'

'Thank you… we will.' she replied.

'You can have a swim here when we get back,' said George to Giles. 'And stay for supper – that's all right, isn't it Rachael?'

Rachael, irritated by her father's assumption that she would be happy to entertain Giles once again, nevertheless smiled, politely.

'Yes… of course. I'm going to try to get the outdoor oven to work … I might even make some bread.'

'That sounds wonderful,' said George cheerfully. 'See you later.'

After they'd gone, Rachael busied herself tidying the kitchen, as Angela played happily around her feet.

'Stay here, darling,' said Rachael as she went upstairs. 'I'm just going to put on my swimsuit.'

In her bedroom, she took off her sundress and stepped into the tight-fitting blue suit. She admired herself in the chipped cheval mirror. It fitted her well, showing off her neat waist and long legs. She brushed her hair and swept it up into a tight chignon to keep it out of the water. She gathered up a book from the bedside table, wrapped it in a couple of towels and, headed downstairs.

The house was quiet… unnaturally still. Angela was no longer playing in the kitchen.

'Angela,' Rachael called out. She went back upstairs to look for her. 'Angela… are you hiding? Come out, come out, wherever you are…'

She peered beneath Angela's bed – a favourite hiding place. There was nothing to be seen but a little pair of pink slippers.

'Angela… Angela…' she called out, heading back downstairs, 'come on, we can go to the beach now.' She went out onto the veranda and scanned the garden. Something looked wrong… The gate was open. Her heart lurched.

Her pulse racing, she ran through the woods leading down to the cove. The child was nowhere to be seen. Perhaps she *was* still in the house or hiding in the woods somewhere.

'Angela,' she shouted out urgently. 'This is not funny… Angela! Come here immediately.'

There was no response. She stood scanning the sea, her hand over her eyes, shielding them from the bright light. She heard a scooter engine, somewhere in the distance. Then a man's voice was shouting. Was it Giles or her father returning? Suddenly, she saw a tiny leg emerging from the emerald water, then an arm.

A man rushed past her and ran, fully clothed, into the water and pulled her daughter from the waves. It was Tommaso. He held the child to his chest as he walked back up the beach, stroking her hair and laid her out, quite motionless, like a china doll on the soft sand.

Tommaso looked up at Rachael, his eyes filled with fear, as if imploring Rachael to help. She threw herself down beside her child and touched Angela's forehead, then her hand. The little girl was cold, but not icily so. Rachael held her daughter's tiny wrist and felt the faint thud, thud of a pulse. Overwhelmed with relief that she was still alive, she patted Angela's cheek, crying. 'Angela, Angela, wake up, darling. Angela.'

Moments passed; her daughter remained inert. Rachael remembered something about breathing into the child's mouth – was that what she should do?

And then, quite suddenly, her daughter opened her pale green eyes and smiled.

'Mama…' she said softly.

Rachael cradled her child's face in her hands and sobbed.

Tommaso carried Angela back to the cottage and laid her on the sofa. Rachael wrapped her daughter in a large towel, smoothing the child's hair away from her face.

'OK now, darling? You warm enough?'

Angela nodded, her eyes closing, sleepily.

In the kitchen, Tommaso searched the dresser cupboard and found a bottle of brandy. He poured a large slug into a glass and held it out to Rachael. 'Drink... it's good.'

She sipped the fiery liquid and felt the adrenalin seeping away as the alcohol surged through her bloodstream. He put his arms around her and kissed her forehead, her hair. She inhaled his scent – manly, dark – and rested her head against his chest. She felt safe... and loved.

After checking that Angela was soundly asleep, Tommaso took Rachael by the hand and drew her out onto the veranda. As she sat at the table, feeling her shock subside in the warmth of the sun, he took a piece of rope and tied the gate firmly in place.

'I don't know how to thank you,' she said. 'If you hadn't come along, I dread to think what might have happened.'

She knew he probably wouldn't understand most of what she said, but he smiled, and took her hand and kissed it.

'It's OK...' he said.

'I was going to make bread today,' she said, gesturing to the bread oven. 'I wanted to show Angela...'

'I do it...' he said. He filled the base of the oven with straw and kindling and threw in a match, watching it smoulder and then catch alight. He collected more firewood and added it to the fire until it was burning brightly.

Then he beckoned to Rachael to come back inside.

In the kitchen, he mixed flour and water, and then kneaded it confidently with his strong hands. He smiled as Rachael watched him.

'Mama,' Angela called out; her mother ran to her.

'I'm here, darling...'

The child sat up, shaking off the towel she had been wrapped in. Apparently unaffected by her experience, she ran into the kitchen and jumped onto a chair to stand and watch Tommaso at work.

'Look, Angela... he's making bread.'

Tommaso handed Angela a small piece of the elastic white dough and encouraged her to copy him – patting the dough and kneading it on the floured table. When it was ready, he put it in a large bowl, covered it with a damp towel and took it outside to rise in the sunshine. The fire had begun to die down now and the inside of the oven was white-hot. Tommaso spread the burning embers across the base of the oven to provide an even heat. He took an old broom from the veranda, and after wetting the head in the kitchen sink, he swept the base of the oven. He took the dough and cut it into pieces – making little rolls that he placed on a flat long-handled 'spoon' that he loaded into the oven.

Whilst it baked, he made coffee on the stove, bringing it to Rachael as she read a story to Angela outside on the veranda. When the bread was ready, Tommaso removed it from the oven and broke it into pieces. He dipped it in oil, offering a little piece to Angela, who ate greedily, shovelling the bread into her small rosebud mouth.

Rachael was delighted by his domesticity. She had never known a man who cooked, nor took part in any way with domestic life. Her father had never made a meal – he could scarcely make a pot of coffee; nor had her husband. But this man, who had rescued her child and protected her, was now feeding her – both physically and emotionally, with kindness and gentleness. It was intoxicating.

When it was time for him to leave, Tommaso kissed Rachael gently on each cheek. As he kicked the scooter engine into life, he called out: '*A domani*, Rachael…'

She watched him roar off up the lane and realised some pivotal moment had taken place between them. As if, in the rescuing of her child, an unbreakable bond had been created.

Would she ever tell her father or Giles what had happened that day?

No… she thought not. It would be their secret – hers and Tommaso's.

Chapter 12

Gloucestershire
December 2016

For the first time in three years, Sophie was back on the pill. Each morning, before she brushed her teeth, she swallowed her medication. And as she did so, she said a prayer: 'Please, please, let me have a baby'. She had a renewed sense of optimism about her chances of having a child. She was healthy, there was no physical reason why she was unable to conceive and once her cycle was regularised, she would begin treatment in earnest. In mid-January she would start on a course of fertility drugs. A few weeks later her eggs would be harvested – a phrase she hated. By March, she could be pregnant. She could have a baby by next Christmas.

She exhaled deeply as she studied herself in the mirror. She must not let her imagination run away with her. On the other hand, she must remain positive. The treatment would work; she would have a child – of that she had no doubt. But she worried sometimes that her need for a child, her longing to be pregnant, was verging on the obsessional. Then she would rationalise those anxieties; of course she was obsessional – it was the most important thing in her life right now.

She popped the small white pill out of the foil container and swilled it down with a glass of water. How ironic, she mused, that her road to fertility should begin with taking an oral contraceptive.

'Four weeks on the pill should be enough,' her consultant had said at their first meeting a few weeks earlier. 'We just need to get your menstrual cycle working properly, and the pill's the best way of doing that. Then, you'll start taking fertility medication. This will stimulate the follicles in your ovaries and mature more eggs than would typically take place in a normal cycle. The goal is to produce at least four eggs.'

In spite of the fact that Hamish worked in the same building as the consultant, he had not come with her to that appointment.

'Darling…' he said when she had asked him to check his diary, 'I've got a long list that day. Awkward to get out of it.'

'Don't you want to come?' she asked. She had regretted the question instantly, and felt him withdraw from her.

He crossed the kitchen and turned on the cold water, running it until it was cool. He ducked down and drank from the tap; it was a habit she loathed.

'You don't really need me there, do you?' he said, wiping his mouth with the back of his hand. 'It's not as if either of us is ignorant of what's going on here. I know exactly what he's going to prescribe. It's all quite routine. It's not a problem is it?'

'No… not at all,' she'd replied, untruthfully.

It was a problem, of course. She would have loved to him to be as enthusiastic as she was about the process. Because although, as a doctor, he was familiar with the medical procedure, in this instance, he wasn't just a doctor, he was her husband and the father of her future child. But she knew that he struggled with the medicalisa tion of their situation. Besides, he argued, she didn't require his presence when she had a cervical smear or an inoculation, so why should he attend her IVF appointments?

After taking her pill and brushing her teeth, she pulled on her thick winter dressing gown. It was the middle of December and snow was forecast. Hamish had left for work quite early and the house felt quiet and calm. Down in the kitchen she noticed that Mick-the-Chick had left a box of eggs on the windowsill. The hens were already outside, clucking around the yard, indifferent to the cold weather. She ran outdoors and retrieved the eggs, rushing back inside and leaning up against the Aga for warmth. As she broke two of the fresh eggs into a pan, and whisked them together, she thought about Hamish and tried to recall if he had always been so separate from her – so reluctant to share her experiences. It was true that when they first got together their relationship had been based not just on mutual physical attraction – the strange ephemeral alchemy that takes place between two individuals – but also, an admiration for the other's professional life. Hamish respected Sophie's intelligence, and her academic ability. But he also admired her independence.

'I'm so glad,' he had said after their first few dates, 'that you have a life of your own – a career you believe in. I'm not good at being "needed". Does that bother you?'

'Not at all,' she had replied, honestly. 'I'm independent and happily so…'

As far as Sophie was concerned, going out with a doctor came naturally. With her own mother as a role model, she understood why work had to come first. If Hamish had to cancel a dinner date or a weekend away at the last minute, she was phlegmatic about it. And Hamish was funny; he could always make Sophie laugh and he was a great storyteller – particularly about life in the operating theatre. It was often said that most jokes originate with anaesthetists. They stand at the 'head end' while the surgeon gets on with the business in hand, and their job, apart from keeping the patient sedated and free of pain, is to entertain and amuse the rest of the team. Being gregarious and sociable, Hamish took to this role naturally. And he had a large entourage of mostly medical friends with whom he met once a week to play poker. It was one of his few vices, and she was amused, and rather proud of his poker prowess.

When Hamish decided to specialise in anaesthetics, he was offered a job in Plymouth. Rachael was halfway through an MA at London University, and so they commuted to one another at weekends. For Sophie, that meant a long train journey on a Friday evening. After fighting her way through the commuters at Paddington, she was filled with anticipation as the train chugged through west London. But her sense of exhilaration grew as the train left Exeter station and swept along the perilous stretch of track that bordered the English Channel, the sea spray splashing against the train carriage windows. Hamish would be waiting eagerly at the barrier to meet her. They would rush back to his meagre hospital bachelor flat and make love as if their lives depended on it. Their sex life had always been good. They 'clicked' somehow from the beginning. Hamish had other girlfriends before Sophie – some had been more experienced than her, some more experimental. But with Sophie it had seemed a perfect match.

Sitting now at the kitchen table, listening to the clucking of the hens outside, the cat on her lap, she thought back to their engagement. Hamish had just moved back to London – he'd got a registrar's post at King's College Hospital. He moved initially into Rachael's rented flat near Holborn, but commuting to South London was time-consuming. Eventually, they discussed buying a house together nearer the hospital. They knew it was a momentous decision, and a serious commitment. Sophie was quite content with the idea of simply living with Hamish – she didn't crave marriage; in fact they never even discussed it. But one evening, he slid a tiny jeweller's box shyly towards her across their kitchen table in the flat in Holborn.

'This is for you...'

Inside was a beautiful vintage solitaire diamond ring.

'Oh my God...' said Sophie, taking it out of the box and trying it on, 'is this what I think it is?'

He smiled. 'Marry me?'

'I had no idea you were even thinking about it.' She looked puzzled.

'Really? Why not? Why wouldn't we get married?' he asked logically. 'I've never loved anyone like you. We've survived this long – two years apart when I was in Plymouth… it just feels right. Don't you think?'

'Yes… yes it does. I'm just rather touched by how old-fashioned you are.'

'I didn't drop to my knees,' he said, 'I'm not that romantic.'

'That has been noted,' she laughed.

'But I did ask your dad first…'

'Did you? How traditional and patriarchal of you… what did he say?'

'Rather predictably, he said that it was none of his business and that I'd better ask you…'

'Good old Dad… quite right. Well, as it happens, it is quite all right with me…'

The wedding was a small simple affair in a registry office, followed by a reception in the back garden of her parents' house in Hampstead. They had no honeymoon, but instead put all their money, together with a loan from their parents, towards a deposit. The house they eventually found was a complete wreck. It had been lived in by an old lady for the previous fifty years and needed total renovation. They spent every spare moment stripping wallpaper, sanding floors, even knocking a wall down between the two ground-floor rooms. It had been a shared project – a joint passion. They worked hard, they played hard, they decorated, they made love. They were happy.

Their sex life remained good. Four or five years into their marriage, they still made love spontaneously. He would come up behind her as she cooked and wrap his arms around her and she would turn and kiss him, and sometimes, they would run upstairs and make love before dinner. They once even made love standing up against the kitchen dresser.

But something changed when they began trying to have a child. At the beginning of the process, Sophie suggested they should only make love when she was ovulating, and she bought a special thermometer that indicated which days of the month would prove most fruitful.

'Darling,' she would say last thing at night, 'we should do it now, it's the right time...'

Hamish understood what she meant, of course, but it seemed to him that the right time was when they felt lust for one another, and not when the thermometer told them to 'perform'. The right time, for him, was when something about the curve of her neck, or the way her dark hair fell over one eye, made him long for her. As a relatively normal red-blooded man, the prospect of sex with his wife at any time should have been a turn-on.

'You lucky bugger,' his poker friend Jonno said, when he told his friends he and Sophie were trying for a baby. 'Since we had the third one, my wife doesn't want it at all.'

'I remember those days,' mused Steve, a consultant surgeon Hamish often operated with. '"Come home now", she'd say, "we've got to do it." Happy days...'

Hamish would smile, and laugh along with the others, agreeing that he was lucky, but that was not how he felt. It was as if he was being asked to perform like a circus monkey. For the first time in his life, he developed 'performance anxiety'. A euphemistic phrase that he clung to, in the hope that it would eventually disappear. But, nevertheless, it made him feel a failure, inadequate even.

Sophie was understanding, of course, but also mildly irritated. The first time it happened, she did not handle it well.

'Never mind,' she said, with a false veil of calm which concealed a deeper sense of panic. 'It will still be OK tomorrow – perhaps we can do it in the morning?'

But the following morning, Hamish got up early and went for a run. He was already showered and dressed by the time Sophie woke up. She reached across to him as he sat on the bed putting on his shoes. He flinched.

'Sorry, babe...' he'd said. 'Got to go... long list today.'

And he was gone.

*

As she rinsed her plate under the tap, the cat wrapping himself around her ankles, she pondered how she could address the issue of Hamish and his 'performance anxiety'. What if he simply refused, or couldn't take part. They still did make love occasionally, but she knew that he found the pressure increasingly difficult to handle.

That evening, as small flecks of snow drifted down from a dark overcast sky, she plucked up the courage to discuss it with Hamish.

'Darling… are you really on board with this IVF thing? We've started the treatment – I'm on the pill. Next month, I'll start on the ovulation drugs. It's everything we've been waiting for. And I don't want to…' she cast around for the right phrase, 'put undue pressure on you.'

'It's fine… it's grand,' he said abruptly. 'Don't worry about me. You're the one who's going to be taking all that medication. How hard can it be?' He tried to sound matter-of-fact.

'I mean…' she continued cautiously, 'I'm really nervous. I'm terrified in fact. What if it doesn't work, what if it *does* work… I'm just a mess of nerves, of conflicting emotions.'

He stood up and came round to her side of the table. He sat beside her and wrapped his arms round her. He kissed the top of her head.

She felt a longing for him. She looked up and he kissed her.

'I really want you…' she said quietly.

Afterwards, as they lay in one another's arms, she said, 'I wish it could always just be like this; I hate all the thermometers and timing and all that….'

'Me too,' he said.

The following morning, Sophie was woken by her phone alarm at six o'clock. Groaning she reached out and switched it off. The air in the bedroom was chilly, and as she reluctantly threw off the duvet, she shivered and hauled on her dressing gown. Peering outside into the garden, she was relieved to see that the previous evening's snowfall had not settled.

'You off already?' Hamish asked, sleepily.

'Not yet... shortly,' she said, putting on her slippers. 'I'm leaving about seven. I've got to be in London by nine thirty. I'll be staying with Mum and Dad tonight – hope that's all right?'

He nodded.

'Go back to sleep then?' she suggested.

'Come back for a cuddle,' he said, lovingly.

She smiled at him, slipping the dressing gown off her shoulders. 'I suppose there is time...'

Later, as she dressed and put a few things in an overnight bag, she asked, 'Are you sure you'll be all right – all on your own?'

'Darling – of course! I'll get a poker game together, have a takeaway and go to bed. Besides, it's good that you stay with your folks – gives you a chance to keep up with them. Now bugger off...'

She thought about their lovemaking, as she sat on the train from Kemble to London. Why couldn't it always be like last night, and again this morning, she wondered. Twice in twelve hours – it had been ages since they'd made love like that. Perhaps she'd already be pregnant if they'd always been so enthusiastic. It seemed ironic that he was so keen to make love to her now she was on the pill, but when the 'time was right', he shied away. Perhaps she needed to be subtler with Hamish – to relax more and seduce him. If they could work together, she could have a baby in time for Christmas. She could see it now – a tiny, perfect child, lying in a pram in the hall of their house. A large Christmas tree twinkling with fairy lights in the sitting room. She could imagine her parents giving her presents on Christmas morning – baby clothes and pretty bedlinen and a mobile maybe, to hang over the cot. She could visualise it so powerfully; she could almost smell the warm, clean scent of a tiny baby. And in her fantasies that smell was mixed with the scent of gingerbread men as she took them out of the oven; of a Christmas cake standing on the dresser… just the way Rachael used to make it.

'*Paddington, Paddington station.*' Sophie was jolted out of her reverie by the announcement. *'Please make sure you take all your belongings with you when leaving the train.*'

As she sat on the tube, she focused on the day ahead. She was grateful for the distraction of her work. When she was talking to her supervisor at the university, or visiting the British Museum, researching and writing, she was able to put her yearning for a child out of her mind. She was fortunate that her work was so absorbing. If she had a normal office job, she was sure that she would be even more fixated on her failing fertility.

Sophie had persuaded her supervisor to let her study the connection between byssus silk and first and second century burial practices. She had been intrigued by this rare textile since the dream in which her grandmother Rachael told Sophie about sea silk and the water women. The more she researched it, the more fascinating the subject became. This curious by-product of the giant clam had been used since the time of the ancient Greeks. Many different names had been given to it over the millennia – sea silk, byssus silk, mermaid silk, sea wool. It was called *butz* in Hebrew, *byssos* in Greek and *byssus* in Latin. Academics warned that the word byssus was often confused for *Bombyx mori* silk. Some said that byssus simply meant linen or cotton. And yet… the ancient texts were filled with references to this mysterious cloth. Religious vestments had been made from 'bundles of fibres from the pinna mussel of the eastern Mediterranean coast'. The Bible mentioned 'cloth of gold'. Could that be explained, she mused, by the existence of byssus? As for a link to her own PhD – there were numerous examples of bodies being buried, wrapped in byssus, for thousands of years – as far back as the ancient Egyptians.

The evidence was conflicting and ambiguous, but Sophie was determined to clarify just how widespread the use of this fabric had been. And, at the same time, to understand what her own grandmother knew about it.

She arrived at her parents' house just after six. Since she had moved to Gloucestershire, she had grown to love her Tuesday evenings at home with her family in Hampstead, watching TV, or going through old family photographs. She felt safe and freed from her normal everyday concerns – almost childlike, as if she had never left home. She slept in her childhood bedroom, surrounded by the toys she had left behind when she went to university over a decade before.

'Ma, you really ought to clear out my room,' she said one day as she came downstairs, after dumping her bag.

'Well, you're welcome to make a start,' her mother had replied, 'I'm really too busy. Besides, I rather like it – all those teddies on the bed, and teenage posters of unsuitable pop stars on the walls.'

Her mother made a point of not mentioning Sophie's fertility treatment, unless her daughter first brought it up. Angela felt their weekly meetings should be islands of calm for her daughter. That it was best if Sophie was able to forget her desperate need for a child, at least for one evening a week.

'Remember, Alex,' she said to her husband before Sophie arrived each Tuesday, 'no baby talk. Only if she raises it – OK?'

After supper that evening, her father asked Sophie how her research was going.

'Oh, it's fascinating. I've extended it to encompass the study of sea silk and the part it might have played in burial rituals.'

'Sea silk…' said Angela, 'isn't that the thing you thought Mother had mentioned?'

'I don't know if she mentioned it really,' said Sophie. 'I have no actual memory of a conversation with her about it. But I had this odd dream – I think I told you about it on the day of your party. I dreamt we were on holiday with Grandma, in a boat somewhere hot and she was telling me about sea silk and the water women.

Maybe it was just something my subconscious made up, but perhaps it was a real memory.'

'Oh yes… I do remember now. You were asking me about that holiday, weren't you?'

'Yes – we'd been to some island near Athens, you said.'

'Agistri… Do you remember, Alex? That holiday we had with Mother and the children on that Greek island when they were both very small. And you insisted on taking us sailing in that deathtrap.'

'It wasn't a deathtrap,' said Alex, refilling their glasses, 'it was a lovely old boat… wooden, I seem to remember. None of this fibreglass nonsense you get these days. Quite good wind around there, I seem to remember. She went at a fair lick that little boat.'

'Get the photos, Sophie…' said Angela. 'They're on the shelf behind you in the bookcase. How old would you have been then? Three? Yes… about three. Find the one marked "1987"… they should be in there.'

Sophie brought out the relevant album and laid it on the coffee table. As she turned the pages, there were photos of herself – a serious-looking child with short dark hair – sitting next to her grandmother in the prow of the old wooden boat. Rachael, shading her green eyes with her hand, looking quizzically into the camera.

'Grandma was so beautiful, wasn't she?' said Sophie. 'I'd forgotten how dark her hair was then. It looked lovely swept away from her face like that. And those green eyes… you've inherited them, Mum, and so have I luckily. She was stunning. My real memories of her are of when she was older. Even then she was beautiful. But… oh… she was lovely then. How old would she have been here?'

'In 1987?' said Angela, leaning over to look at the album. 'She would only have been… fifty-one. It's no age at all, is it? Oh look,' said Angela, 'there's the wretched boat. It was a pretty boat though, wasn't it? I don't seem to have taken many shots on board – apart from that one of you and Mum. I was too scared, I should imagine, or busy – winching in ropes, or whatever they're called.'

'Sheets,' said Alex.

'What?' said Angela.

'Ropes on boats… they're called sheets.'

'Anyway…' said Sophie, 'what I don't understand, is how Grandma Rachael knew about sea silk. It's a very rare fabric. Not something that crops up in normal conversation. Did she ever mention it to you?'

'No, I don't think so,' said Angela. 'To be honest, I'd never heard of it until *you* mentioned it. What is it really – do explain.'

'It's an unusual fabric – very rare – made from the beards of the giant clam - the *pinna nobilis*. The beards are cut off from the clam, carded, and twisted together to produce a fine thread that can be spun and woven into a delicate fabric. They treat the thread with lemon juice, and cow urea, and when you hold it up to the sun, it gleams like gold. I'd never heard of it before either, and *I'm* an anthropologist. But when I started looking into it, it's really fascinating. Its use was quite widespread in the ancient world. But hardly any of it is made anymore. There are a few women left on Sardinia who still make it – and that's about it. I imagine it was made quite widely around the Mediterranean at one time. So, Mum… how on earth did Granny know about it?'

'I really don't know,' said Angela, getting up.

'Did Granny ever live in the Mediterranean – in Sardinia perhaps?'

'No… I don't think so. She never mentioned it to me anyway. No, of course not. Oooh… I've just remembered, I left a pudding in the oven; I must go and rescue it…'

As she reached the door of the sitting room she turned back.

'She could be very… private… my mother – secretive almost. Those stories she used to tell… one never knew what was true and what wasn't. I wouldn't be surprised if sea silk was just something she made up. But if it really exists, maybe her father told her about it; he was an archaeologist after all…'

'Do you remember much about him?' Sophie asked her mother when she came back into the room with a dish of apple crumble and three bowls.

'Well, we all lived together, so of course I remember him. But he died just before my sixteenth birthday. I just thought of him as my lovely old grandpa across the landing, who went to work each day at the university and told us funny stories when he came home. I was proud that he was a bit different and slightly exotic. He was Hungarian, after all, and an archaeologist; so few of my school friends had grandfathers who worked, or were so prestigious, but I didn't really understand what he did each day. And sadly he died before I was old enough to have a proper conversation with him about it.'

'I'm sorry I never met him,' said Sophie. 'Grandma used to say I reminded her of him.'

'Yes… perhaps you are like him,' said Angela as she handed out plates of apple crumble and cream.

That night, as she lay in her teenage bed, Sophie opened her laptop, and put the name of her great-grandfather, George Laszlo, with the words 'sea silk' into Google. As she trawled through the various references, she found one that led to an academic paper written a decade or so earlier. It referenced an archaeological dig, which had taken place nearly one hundred years earlier in 1912. A young Hungarian research student named George Laszlo had found a small piece of sea silk in the fourth-century grave of a young woman. The woman had been wrapped in linen cloth, and when the young student had unwrapped the body, he found the tiny fragment nestling between her legs. It turned out to be the oldest piece of 'byssus' silk ever discovered.

Tragically the piece of fabric itself disappeared during the war, but a magnified black and white photograph of the tiny fragment remained – a testament to its existence. As she studied the interlocking warp and weft of the piece of byssus, Sophie was struck by the significance of her great-grandfather making such an important discovery when he was still just a student. The picture seemed familiar, for some reason. Sophie had a sudden memory of herself as a child reading one of George's books on Roman history.

Her grandmother had found her curled up in a large armchair in attic, surrounded by piles of George's precious reference books. 'You remind me of him – your restless intelligence; your sense of enquiry,' she had said then. 'So borrow any book you like; read them and learn… just don't break the backs, and put them back carefully.'

Remembering this exchange, Sophie got out of bed and went up the stairs to her grandmother's bedroom in the attic. Against the wall was a small mahogany bookcase with glass doors. Inside were George Laszlo's precious textbooks – leather-bound with gilded edges. Sophie removed the books one by one flicking through the indexes.

Finally, she found what she was looking for. In a book published just after the First World War was a reference to an archaeological dig in the Roman settlement of Aquincum, and the piece of byssus discovered by a young Hungarian archaeologist named George Laszlo; beside it was a grainy black and white photograph – the same photograph she had found on the Internet.

Was this the entry she had read as a child? Perhaps her grandmother had drawn her attention to it? Rachael had encouraged Sophie's interest in Roman history; she was keen that she follow in George's footsteps. So the knowledge about byssus had been there, locked away in her subconscious all the time.

Was it synchronicity, or destiny that had led her to study something her own ancestor had been instrumental in discovering? Might she, in some small way, continue his work, and uncover new revelations? To tread in his footsteps. She would make him proud of her. She would make her grandmother proud of her too. And if the worst happened – if she could never have a child, if that was not to be her destiny, perhaps she could live on, and be remembered for her academic discoveries.

Chapter 13

Rachael spent a sleepless night, following the incident with little Angela. She kept mulling over what might have happened if Tommaso hadn't arrived... Angela's 'swimming lesson' could have turned into a tragedy.

She sat brooding on the veranda the following morning, nursing a cup of coffee.

'Darling...' George said, pouring her another cup, 'are you all right? You're very quiet.'

'What?' she said, distractedly. 'Yes... I'm fine. I just didn't sleep very well.'

'You need an outing maybe...' he said, cheerfully. 'We talked a few days ago of you coming to see what we are doing under the church; the dig is getting interesting.'

'I'd like that,' Rachael said, weakly, 'but what would I do with Angela?'

'Bring her too!' said George.

'Really... won't she be in the way?'

'Well, Peter or one of the other students could take her for a walk... I'd like you to
see it.'

'I don't think I should...' she said, cautiously. 'The students hardly know her and it's unfair to give them such a responsibility.'

'But she's such a friendly little girl – she'll be fine with one of them,' encouraged George, 'especially Peter. He's very reliable.'

'It's just that she doesn't know Peter very well,' said Rachael, wishing she could tell her father what was really bothering her. 'And what if she runs away? She's quite headstrong.'

'I will tell him to guard her with his life!' George said, laughing. 'He can take her for ice cream at the cafe. She will not run away from there!'

'No... I suppose not,' Rachael finally relented. 'All right – I *will* come, and thank you. I'll go and get us ready.'

Giles arrived in the truck, just after half past eight. Rachael was waiting outside the cottage, dressed in an old pair of slacks and a shirt of her father's.

'Do you need a lift to the market?' he asked her.

'Not today – but I am coming to town; my father wants me to see the dig.'

'That explains the curious outfit...' Giles said, noting her clothes.

'Yes... well, I hear it's rather dirty down there.'

They squeezed into the front seat of the truck – Rachael uncomfortably sandwiched between Giles and her father with Angela on her lap.

When they arrived at the town square, Giles parked the truck in front of the hotel. George's students were gathered together in a huddle waiting for the professor to arrive and give them their orders for the day.

'Ah, Peter,' George said, 'I wonder if I might prevail upon you to do something for me?'

'Of course, sir,' said Peter, helpfully.

'Look after my granddaughter for an hour – would you? Take her to the cafe for ice cream or something. I want my daughter to see the dig.' He pressed some lira notes into the young man's hand. 'Have a coffee yourself.'

Peter looked rather dismayed at this request, but nobly took the little girl by the hand, and headed for the cafe. Rachael watched him leave, nervously.

'Don't lose her,' she called after him.

'I won't,' he called back, over his shoulder. 'I've got four younger brothers and sisters…I've had a lot of practice. See you later.'

The catacombs were entered via a long winding stone staircase that led from the transept of the church. George led the way, followed by Giles and Rachael. A pungent smell of damp rose up from the tomb, overlaid with something else, Rachael thought… a musty, earthy scent.

'The tombs were uncovered a while back during some renovation work,' explained George, holding up an oil lamp to light their way. 'They had, until that day, been quite hidden from view. The workmen were trying to lay some drains and they excavated some of the earth – just here on the left – and realised there was a complete tomb hidden behind this wall. The rest you know… it was decided they warranted further investigation and here we are!' He turned round and grinned impishly at his daughter.

'Come, come,' he said eagerly, crawling through the low opening that led to the tombs.

Her father shuffled forward, squatting on his haunches, making room for her. 'Sit next to me…' he said, patting the earth floor. 'Don't worry about your trousers – they will get dirty. There is nothing you can do about it…'

Giles lit a couple of oil lamps that had been left in the tomb, and the strong acrid smell of oil mingled with the musty earthiness.

Rachael looked around her. It was a low-ceilinged earthen space. At first sight, there appeared to be nothing remarkable about it.

'So what do you see?' asked George.

'Me… nothing,' said Rachael. 'It's just an empty… room?'

'Giles… hold up the lanterns so Rachael can see better…'

As the gloomy light from the oil lamp illuminated the red earthen walls, a design became visible.

'What's that?' asked Rachael.

'It's a menorah,' said George, delightedly. 'In fact, there are two – here and over here.'

Giles adjusted the lamp so its light fell on the second wall painting.

'What's a menorah?' asked Rachael.

'A very important symbol of the Jewish faith,' said George. 'Go on, Giles – you can explain.'

George rocked back on his haunches, clearly delighted at the opportunity for Giles to show off his knowledge.

'Well,' said Giles, equally delighted to be able to reveal his academic prowess to Rachael, 'this island has long been inhabited by people of the Jewish faith. At least four thousand Jews were exiled here, by successive Roman Emperors. When Rome became a Christian Empire, this was a convenient place to send them. They worked in the tin and lead mines on the island and settled well… They were also useful at keeping the local pirates under control, who terrorised the waters around here.'

'Very good,' said George.

'So perhaps these are Jewish tin miners buried here,' suggested Rachael.

'No,' said Giles. 'That's what I thought, but the professor has another theory. You should tell her, sir…'

'Well,' said George, eagerly taking up the tale, 'there are many Jewish burials on this island, but these tombs are special. The people buried here were clearly very important. They are buried as a pair, for a start, which usually indicates a couple who wish to lie together for eternity. And their tombs are marked, which also suggests they were people of high birth.'

'Marked with what?' asked Rachael.

'Well, it's quite a story. One day, as we scraped away the surface layers of mud and dust and filth, Peter called me over. He had found the beginning of a word. It was the letter "B". We brushed very carefully, and it took most of the day, but finally the whole word was revealed.'

'And what was it?' asked Rachael, genuinely excited now.

'Beronice!' declared George. 'Beronice was an unusual name. In fact, the first Berenice, spelt with an 'e' in the middle, was a very important lady indeed – the Jewish Queen, great granddaughter of King Herod, sister of King Agrippa, lover of Titus – the Roman Emperor from 77–79 AD.'

'Could it be her?' asked Rachael. 'Why would she be buried here... on this tiny island?'

'I agree it is odd, but not impossible,' George continued. 'She lived in Palestine, but she followed her lover to Rome when he was appointed emperor. Now, the Romans had had enough of their emperors marrying outside the faith. Caesar and Cleopatra left a terrible legacy, and they were not going to allow another emperor to marry a foreign queen. So his advisors forbade the marriage and poor Berenice left Rome, broken-hearted. It's long been a mystery as to what happened to her. The records show no evidence of where she went after Titus rejected her.'

'But why would she come here?' asked Rachael.

'That is the question. Why would she come here?' George muttered to himself.

'Over the next few days,' Giles continued, taking up the story, 'the rest of the inscription gradually emerged. *In pace iuvenis moritur* was written beneath her name.'

'What does that mean?' asked Rachael.

'"Berenice buried in peace,"' said George.

'And what of the other grave?' asked Rachael.

'Well indeed,' said George. 'That is our next task. We hope that we will discover who is buried there and why the Jewish queen is lying beneath this old church… if indeed it is the lady herself…'

As Rachael sat in the garden of the cottage later that day, playing with Angela, she mulled over what she had seen that morning. It seemed so tragic that the beautiful queen should be torn away from the man she loved. The idea that she might be buried just a few miles from their cottage seemed such a romantic notion. The high-pitched whine of a Lambretta interrupted her thoughts. As the noise grew louder, she knew, instinctively, that it was Tommaso.

He walked towards her, tall and slender, pushing his long dark hair away from his eyes. She felt a surge of physical desire. She had loved József very much but had never before experienced this overwhelming sexual chemistry. It was a mystery; how could she feel so much passion for this man standing before her, when they could scarcely communicate. And yet, they had an understanding. He had saved her child, and she loved him for it.

He kissed her lightly on each cheek and sat down at the table. Angela toddled over to him and he picked her up and sat her on his lap. He made two fists with his hands and asked her to choose one. It was a game she had played before with her grandfather, and she patted one of his large fists with her tiny hand, giggling. Tommaso opened his hand – it was empty. He made two fists again and held them out for her to choose. Once again, she chose the wrong hand. Tears came into her eyes, and she began to cry. He laughed and opened the other hand. Inside was a tiny sweet, which he put into her rosebud mouth; her tears dried instantly.

'You are happy?' he asked Rachael.

'Yes… *si, sono molto contenta*,' she said. She had begun to study an Italian dictionary each morning and was building up a collection of useful words and phrases. 'Happy' was a word she had just learned. '*E tu?*' she asked.

'*Si, sono contento.*'

There was an awkward moment, as neither knew quite what to say next. Finally, Tommaso broke the silence.

'*Vuoi venire a fare la pesca con me?*' he asked.

She looked confused. '*Momento.*' She ran inside the house and emerged a few minutes later with her dictionary.

'*Pescare...?* Fishing?'

'Si – fishing,' he repeated. 'You and me...'

'With Angela... *con* Angela?' She picked the little girl up. 'Is it safe?'

'*Si,*' he said confidently, '*con la bambina – si. Non e pericoloso.* It's OK.'

Her head told her it was madness to take a tiny child who couldn't swim onto a boat. But she wanted to go, and besides, she knew Angela would be safe with him.

With Rachael and Angela installed in the prow of the boat, Tommaso pushed it out to sea and leapt on board. He started up the motor and they roared out of the cove and into the open water. Rachael revelled in the wind in her hair, the salt spray splashing her face. She had her arms wrapped firmly around Angela's waist; the child wriggled, desperate to be free. But Rachael would not release her.

When they were a few hundred metres from the shore, Tommaso took one of the rods that lay along the length of the boat. He cast it into the water and, as he waited for something to bite, took a cigarette out of his top pocket and lit it with a match he struck against the boat. Suddenly the line went taut. He clasped the cigarette between his white teeth and reeled in a large seabass, which he threw into the well of the boat. It thrashed around for a few moments until Tommaso smashed its head against the side of the boat, after which it lay prone, its pale eyes staring blankly into space. Rachael, who had never been fishing before, found the experience unsettling. The destruction of the creature which had moments before been swimming free in the deep blue waters, seemed needlessly cruel – and yet she knew she would enjoy the taste of the fish later. Angela, fascinated, wriggled free of her mother's grasp, and knelt down by the fish, exploring the sensation of its smooth scales beneath her tiny fingers.

Soon there were six fish lying in the well of the boat; Tommaso reeled in his rod, and started up the engine.

As the sun sank over the horizon, the fishing party walked back through the copse towards the cottage, Rachael could see George and Giles sitting companionably on the veranda in the golden early evening light.

'Ah, Rachael,' said George. 'We were just wondering where you had got to.'

'Tommaso came over to get some fish…' Rachael said, 'and offered to take us out in his boat.'

'Well, I'm relieved you're back safely,' said Giles, a hint of disapproval in his voice. 'We were starting to worry – your father and me. It's not for me to say, obviously, but was it such a good idea to take a baby in a fishing boat?'

Rachael flushed with a combination of embarrassment and indignation.

'It's not for you to say… Giles, no. Angela was perfectly safe; Tommaso would never let anything happen to her.'

Giles blushed with embarrassment at this rebuke and looked down at his boots.

'Well,' said George, after an awkward silence, 'no harm has come to either of them, so all is well.' He smiled and stood up. 'Tommaso, please… join us; have a glass of wine.'

'Perhaps I ought to go,' said Giles, standing up, abruptly.

Rachael, for once, did not urge him to stay. But Tommaso sensed the prickly atmosphere and politely declined George's invitation. Instead he laid the two largest seabass from his basket out on the table.

'For you,' he said, bowing respectfully to George. He then stroked Angela's golden hair before turning to Rachael. '*Ciao, bella,*' he said, kissing her on both cheeks. He sauntered out of the garden, climbed onto his Lambretta and roared off up the lane.

After Tommaso left, Giles hovered, uncomfortably, at the edge of the veranda, unsure whether to stay or go. Rachael, who was upset that Tommaso had felt it necessary to leave, hoped that Giles would follow suit. But, to her irritation, George invited his young student to stay and share the fish.

'I'd love to – thank you,' Giles said, anxiously, '… if you're sure?' He looked across the table at Rachael,

'Yes fine,' she replied, crisply. 'I have enough to feed you…' She stood up abruptly and disappeared into the kitchen.

As she gutted and de-scaled the fish, Rachael wondered why her father had placed her in such a difficult position. Had he not noticed how Giles lurked around her, insinuating himself into their lives? As her father's student he was entitled to friendship of course, but did that mean he had to stay for supper quite so often? Slicing into the flesh of the fish, she wondered if George realised that Giles harboured feelings for her. She felt sure that if he did, he would not be quite so friendly with the young man.

As for Tommaso, George had invited him to stay for a glass of wine. Had he sensed her growing affection for the young fisherman? And would he understand why she was falling under his spell? More importantly, would he approve?

As a young widow with a small child, she was keenly aware of the need to preserve her reputation whilst she lived on this tiny island. The last thing her father needed was a scandal. And yet, she reasoned to herself, as she fried the fish on the range, she and Tommaso were both single. They were doing nothing wrong. Why should they not be allowed to find love with one another?

*

To her surprise, Rachael saw nothing of Tommaso for two weeks. He didn't come to the cottage, and when she went into the village to shop at the market, or drink coffee at the cafe, he was nowhere to be seen. She began to worry; had he been offended by Giles at their last meeting, or was he ill? Had he been hurt at sea, or worse... drowned perhaps?

Unable to bear the suspense any longer, Rachael sat down at the cafe one morning and casually asked after him.

'*Suo fratello, Tommaso – sta bene?*' she asked Tomasso's sister, Maria.

'*Si sta bene,*' the girl replied.

As Rachael left, crossing the square towards the grocery shop, she noticed Maria talking to her mother in the cafe and gesturing towards Rachael. They were obviously wondering why the foreign lady was interested in Tommaso.

The following day, Rachael was tidying the kitchen as Angela played at her feet, when she heard the familiar whine of the Lambretta. Within minutes Tommaso was in the kitchen. Rachael hurled herself at him, hugging him to her. He laughed, taking her in his arms and kissing her on both cheeks. They kissed again – this time on the mouth. She responded instinctively, pressing her body to his.

'Hello,' he said, at last, as he pulled away from her.

'Hello,' she replied.

'Hello!' said Angela, pulling herself up onto her feet and reaching up to her mother.

Rachael laughed and picked her child up, who clung, limpet-like, her legs wrapped round her mother's waist.

'I want to take you...' he spoke slowly, anxious not to make any mistakes in his newly acquired English, 'to watch my mother... and my sister. You come?'

Rachael looked bemused.

'*Perché?*' she asked

'Come… come with me… I show you.'

She quickly finished her chores and, together with Angela, climbed onto the scooter. Tommaso drove the Lambretta along the coast road, away from the town. Rachael had never driven so far with him before, but she had learned to put her trust in him and wrapped her arms contentedly round his waist, Angela wedged firmly between his legs. When she had first driven with him on the bike, she had tried to lean in the opposite direction to him, fearful they were going too fast or too low around a bend.

'No!' he had shouted, reaching behind him, and pulling her into line with his own body. 'With me…move with me,' he'd explained, 'or we crash.'

Now, as the sea lapped the shore to their right, she moulded her body against his as he cornered and swerved. It was an act of true intimacy, almost like making love; two bodies learning to work together, in synchrony.

After half an hour or so, he turned the bike down a rough track that led onto a rocky cove.

He parked the bike near the water's edge. 'Come, come…' he said, beckoning to Rachael.

She followed him down to the shore, stumbling slightly over the rocks, carrying Angela in her arms. A group of women were standing near the water. One was singing a curious song.

'*Mia madre,*' Tommaso whispered.

'Your mother?'

'*Sì…*'

'What is she saying?' Rachael quietly asked.

He frowned a little, unsure how to translate.

'I write…' he said, removing a scrap of paper and a stub of pencil from his pocket. As the woman sang, he wrote down the words and then handed Rachael the piece of paper. She would show her father later – he would be able to translate it.

Once their song was finished, the women, wearing simple cotton dresses, walked into the water. They swam a little way and then dived beneath the surface. Rachael gripped Tommaso's arm.

'What are they doing?' she asked.

'Wait…' he said.

From time to time, they emerged onto the surface, before inhaling deeply and plunging back down beneath the water.

Eventually they swam back to the rocky shore and clambered out, dragging a bulging cotton bag behind them. Tommaso went over to the women and said something to his mother. She handed him the cotton bag, and he brought it over to show Rachael.

She peered inside.

'What is it?' she asked, picking out tufts of rough 'hair'.

'Byssus,' he said.

The word struck a chord with Rachael. She remembered her father telling her a story of the grave he had uncovered all those years before in Hungary. Was byssus not the fabric he had found in the Roman grave in Aquincum? The oldest example ever discovered, he'd always told her.

The women sat on the shore and let their clothes dry in the evening sun. They chatted amongst themselves as the sun slipped below the horizon casting a rose pink glow on the surface of the water. From time to time, they looked over at Rachael with curiosity, as she played on the rocks with Angela. Eventually, their clothes dried, the water iridescent with a fiery red glow, the women were ready to leave.

Tommaso kissed his mother, and with Rachael and Angela installed on the scooter, drove back towards the town. But he didn't go straight to the cottage. Instead he drove on, past the entrance to the lane, to a small workshop on the edge of Sant'Antioco. On a sign above the door it said: *Atelier: Italo Diana.*

'Come… come with me,' Tommaso said, pushing open the heavy wooden door.

Inside was a large workroom filled with women. Some were seated at sewing machines, stitching skirts and jackets. Others were pinning fabric to tailors' dummies. They called out to Tommaso as he walked through the workroom.

'*Ciao*, Tommaso.'

'*Come stai*… Tommaso.'

He smiled, and grinned; he shook the odd hand, he kissed one or two women on the cheek, all the while checking Rachael and Angela were following him. He led them to a further room at the back, filled with looms of various kinds. Some were laced up with wool, others with cotton and linen. At the far end, a young woman was carding a pile of stiff fibres; it looked similar to the rough 'hair' Rachael had seen earlier at the cove. The woman held a ball of the fibre out towards Rachael, inviting her to touch it. It felt wiry. Nearby were bowls of the stuff soaking in water. From time to time, an elderly lady, seated in a gloomy corner, staggered to her feet, tipped the water away and replaced it with fresh water from a jug.

Tommaso leant over one of the bowls and sniffed deeply.

'Here,' he said to Rachael, 'smell…'

Rachael breathed deeply through her nose. 'Lemon juice?' she suggested.

'*Si*… *si, limone e cedro*.'

'Cedar?'

He nodded.

The woman who had been carding the fibre now began to spin it. She attached one end of a short piece of thread to a little spinning bobbin. As it whirled round and round, she attached new threads from the pile of fibre at her side until she had yards of long thread which glinted like gold in the shafts of late afternoon sunlight. Angela stared, fascinated…

'*Vieni, vieni qui bambolina*,' the woman said to her.

The child toddled towards her and the woman picked up a little threaded bracelet that was lying on her worktable. She tied it around the child's chubby wrist. Angela stroked the bracelet and held it up to the light, observing how the light caught the gold threads. She looked up, beaming, at the lady who had given it to her.

'It's good luck,' Tommaso whispered to Rachael.

'*Grazie*,' said Rachael, bowing to the lady before kneeling down beside her daughter. 'Angela… you're so lucky,' she said, 'such a pretty bracelet. Say thank you.'

'Thank you…' said Angela, waving her arm around in the early evening light until the bracelet gleamed.

The women laughed amongst themselves, and Tommaso motioned towards the door.

'*Andiamo* – we go now,' he said.

The women smiled and nodded at Rachael; they cupped Angela's little face in their hands as she walked between them. Rachael felt privileged to have been allowed to observe them at their work.

When her father came home that evening, she was bursting with the news.

'Papa! Tommaso took us to visit the atelier in the town. And you won't believe this but they make byssus, Papa. I watched his mother and sister fishing for the clams. They dive down and cut the filaments that hold the clams to the seabed; then bring bags of the raw material to the atelier, who makes it into thread. They made Angela a little bracelet.'

'Byssus… here on Sant'Antioco?'

'Yes, Papa. I knew you would be interested…'

'Of course! How remarkable. I thought no one made it anymore…'

'Tommaso wrote down a song they sing before they go into the water. I have it here. I thought you could translate it for me.'

Her father read aloud, translating as he did so:
'Ponente, Levante, Maestro and Grecale,
Take my soul and cast it to the bottom of the sea
That my life may be for being, praying and weaving
For all the people that may come to me and from me depart
Timeless, nameless, colourless, limitless, penniless
In the name of the Lion of my soul and the eternal spirit, so it will be…'

'What does it mean… Ponente, Levante, Maestro and Grecale…?' asked Rachael. 'What are they?'

'They are winds, I think,' said George. 'She is asking the wind to throw her soul onto the seabed. It is an oath, a prayer, maybe before she gathers up the raw material to make her byssus.'

'Do you think they *have* to pray first?' asked Rachael. 'A shepherd does not pray before he shears a sheep, does he?'

'Maybe they do in Sardinia…' her father said, laughing. 'I should like to discuss it with Tommaso.'

'Shall I ask him to come around one evening perhaps?'

'Yes – do that. He is… someone you like?' her father asked, casually.

'Yes,' said Rachael, 'I like him very much. Do you mind?'

'Mind? Why should I mind? He sounds very interesting.'

'I thought… I thought you might disapprove.'

'Rachael my darling – why would I disapprove?'

'I don't know… he's not an academic. He's just a fisherman. His mother weaves byssus…'

'He is your friend…' said George, taking her hand, 'that is enough for me.'

The following day, Rachael was baking in the kitchen, Angela asleep upstairs. As she kneaded dough on the table, she heard Tommaso's scooter in the lane. She checked her reflection in the little mirror she had hung by the back door. She was a little flushed and her hair was smeared with flour. Quickly, she washed her hands in the sink and ran them through her hair, pushing the long strands away from her face.

She was waiting for him on the veranda when he came round the corner of the cottage. He put his arms out to her and she ran to them, allowing him to embrace her. They kissed, gently at first and then with passion. He ran his hands over her body, feeling her breasts beneath his fingers. She pulled back, nervous suddenly, of getting too close, of going too far. Sensing her slight reluctance, he released her, kissing her lightly on the cheek. She sat down at the table on the veranda, indicating he should sit too.

'A drink?' she asked, her own mouth dry with anticipation, fearful of what she felt, what she wanted from him. Maybe they would just have a drink, she thought, and he would go.

'*Si, grazie.*'

She went into the kitchen and came out with a flask of local white wine and two glasses. He poured the wine and handed her a glass, clinking his against hers.

'*Salute*, Rachael.'

She swallowed, gratefully, feeling the wine relaxing her as it spread through her body. '*Salute.*'

His hand stroked her cheek. She yielded, letting him pull her face towards him. He kissed her again and she kissed him back. She felt her resolve weakening. She wanted him so much. They stood and kissed again. He took her hand and drew her inside the cottage.

'*Dove* Angela?' he whispered, his mouth against her ear.

She put her fingers to her mouth. 'Sshhhh,' she said, 'she is upstairs, sleeping.'

He took her glass and put it on the table, then holding her hand, led her to the sofa. They sat down and began to kiss, exploring one another. She pulled his shirt over his head, and stroked his chest, feeling it cool and smooth beneath her fingers. He undid the buttons of her dress and slipped it off her shoulders. His hands crept up beneath her skirt. She lay back down on the sofa and pulled him towards her.

When it was over, they lay together, his head against her naked breast, their breathing slowing at last.

'Mummy, Mummy.' Angela's voice filtered through from upstairs.

Tommaso pulled himself away from Rachael and stood up, hurriedly fastening his trousers, pulling on his shirt over his head. She sat up, buttoning her dress, smoothing her hair. She looked up at him and grinned.

'Coming,' she called up to Angela.

A few moments later, she came down the stairs carrying the child in her arms. Tommaso was already outside, sitting on the veranda. The child ran to him and he picked her up and twirled her around.

Rachael sat on the large cane chair at the end of the table and observed her lover.

'My father has invited you to supper...'

'When?' he asked.

'Tonight?'

'Thank you,' he said putting Angela down, carefully, on the ground. 'I will come.'

'He says he wants to ask you about byssus...'

'I will tell him what I know.' He grinned at her. 'I should go then...'

'Must you?' She gazed longingly at him.

'Yes,' he said, 'if I am to... eat with your father... I must wear good clothes.' He gestured towards his old jeans. Then, leaning over her, he kissed Rachael tenderly on the mouth. Angela watched them, her green eyes alert to this new relationship that she could not understand.

After he'd gone, Rachael prepared supper, making pasta sauce from beef and tomatoes, and a sweet tart with wild berries she had bought at the market. Afterwards, she took Angela down to play at the cove. They built a sandcastle and paddled in the shallows. Rachael gave Angela a swimming lesson, holding her beneath her tummy as she kicked her legs and flapped her arms in an effort to stay afloat. But Rachael could think of little but Tommaso and how he had held her, and of his scent and the feel of his chest against her naked breast.

Back at the cottage, she laid the table on the veranda and picked some flowers from the myrtle bush in the garden; she arranged them in a little vase in the centre of the table. She and Angela were still salty from their swim, so she heated water on the stove, and filled the old tin bath in the kitchen. She climbed in and pulled Angela in with her. They washed one another, soaping their hair and laughing. Then, wrapped in a towel, Rachael dragged the tin bath outside and emptied it onto the small vegetable garden. The water seeped into the dry soil, feeding the tomato, pepper and aubergine plants she had bought a few weeks before from a lady in the market.

She dressed carefully that evening, choosing a dark green dress that Mrs Roper had helped her to make when they lived together in Hampstead. It was tight-fitting, with a wide boat neck, and suited her slender frame, emphasising her long neck and delicate collarbone. She dressed Angela in a pale yellow cotton dress; it was smocked around the chest and had a little white collar; she wore matching white sandals.

When Giles dropped off her father, he noticed the table laid for three people. He lingered, hoping for a drink, or an invitation to supper. But none was forthcoming and he retreated sulkily to the old pickup, promising to collect George at eight o'clock the following morning.

Tommaso arrived shortly after he'd left, carrying a small bunch of roses.

'For you,' he said to Rachael. As she took the roses with one hand, he brought his lips to the other and kissed it.

George wandered out onto the veranda.

'Ah Tommaso!' he said and held his hand out to the young man.

They chatted easily in Italian, as Rachael poured wine into their glasses and checked on the supper. Her father's easy facility with language was one of his greatest talents. It was as if he had been born with most of the European languages pre-programmed into his brain. He just had to be in a country to be able to slip almost seamlessly into the native tongue of his hosts.

Rachael followed some of what they said. She hoped Tommaso would not mention Angela's accident. But she heard nothing that alarmed her as she served the food and poured the wine. Tommaso watched her as she wandered in and out of the house. And George observed how Tommaso's eyes followed her, how his fingers found every opportunity to touch hers as she laid a plate of food out on the table or filled a glass.

At nine o'clock, she lifted Angela onto her father's lap, for him to kiss goodnight. The child scrambled off and ran over to Tommaso, holding her arms up to him. He picked her up, kissed her head and handed her back to Rachael. Their eyes met. And George saw love there.

But when Rachael came back downstairs half an hour later, Tommaso had gone.

Chapter 14

Gloucestershire
Christmas 2016

Sophie was feeling excited. It was the twenty-first of December, and her family were due to arrive on Christmas Eve and leave the day after Boxing Day. She had been looking forward to the visit for weeks and had tried to persuade her mother that they should stay for longer.

'No thank you, darling. You're very kind, but visitors, like fish, go off after three days,' her mother said firmly. 'We'll come on Christmas Eve and leave on the twenty-seventh. Trust me, darling – you'll be praying for us to go by then…'

'No…!' wailed Sophie. 'I won't. I miss you all so much, and I hardly ever see Simon and Vic anymore. It will be wonderful to just relax and catch up with you all.'

Sophie persuaded Hamish to buy the tallest tree possible. They bought it from a local farmer who had turned part of his land into Christmas tree plantation. The trees could be either chopped down or dug up; either way, the farmer expected customers to do it themselves.

'God this is hard work,' Hamish complained, as he dug round the tree's roots. 'Can't we just chop if off at the base?'

'No!' said Sophie. 'I want to plant it in the garden afterwards. It's our first Christmas tree here… it's special.'

It took over an hour to uproot the tree, and Sophie was delighted when it was finally lifted off the roof of the car and dragged into the sitting room, leaving a trail of pine needles behind it. She pruned its roots so they fitted into a generous pot filled with earth. It was then placed on a large tray to collect any overflow water. But as she tipped the watering can into the earth, it splashed water onto the sitting room carpet.

'Careful, Sophie,' complained Hamish, 'It's going to leave a mark. Surely it would have been simpler to have a fake one?'

'I'm not even going to dignify that remark with a reply,' Sophie said, glaring at Hamish.

Sophie had quite a collection of Christmas decorations. Every year she bought something new – a tiny bird or a sequinned star. When she left home, Angela gave her Rachael's collection too.

'I think you should have some of the family decorations… Most of them were made in the 1950s, so they're quite delicate. But I know you'll appreciate them. You always loved decorating the tree with Granny. They're yours now.'

Nestling amongst the tissue paper, alongside the nineteen-fifties glass balls frosted with glitter, were decorations Rachael had made over the years – little felt stars, embroidered with brightly coloured thread, tiny dolls dressed in scraps of old dress fabric. They were a little tired now, but each year, as Sophie took them out of the tissue paper, she felt her grandmother's presence and recalled what it was like decorating the tree with her at home in Hampstead.

This year, in their new house, it felt special. As she pinned on each ornament, she fantasised about what it would be like to do it with her own child by her side. She never articulated these fantasies to Hamish, of course. He would have thought her foolish – or mad.

Once the tree was decorated, she planned the catering with military precision. A turkey was ordered from a local supplier. Cheese and pâté were bought from a farm shop on the edge of the village. Even the cat had been bought a special Christmas collar made of red tartan.

*

The week before the holiday, Hamish and Sophie received an invitation from Flora and her hedge fund husband.

AT HOME
Flora and Marcus
The Vicarage
Saturday 23 December
7 till late...

Sophie's heart sank. The party was the day before her family arrived and she wanted everything to be perfect for them.

'Let's not go...' she begged Hamish. 'I've got so much to do and the last thing I need is a hangover, or a late night...'

'Oh, for goodness sake,' said Hamish, impatiently, 'it'll be fun. Flora's such a laugh. And we ought to get to know people in the village...'

Reluctantly, Sophie agreed.

Determined not to be 'underdressed' again, she spent an entire afternoon in a chic dress shop in Cirencester, looking for a suitable outfit.

'This is very lovely,' said the attendant, holding out a black sequinned sheath. 'Sequins are very now... it would suit you.'

'Really?' asked Sophie doubtfully.

She tried it on, and it fitted her like a glove.

'Do you think it's a bit over the top for a Christmas party?'

'No,' said the shop assistant firmly, 'it's just the thing round here; perfect in fact.'

Now, as she stood in front of the mirror in their bedroom admiring her reflection, she began to have her doubts.

'Wow!' said Hamish coming in, pulling a jumper over his shirt. 'You look fab!'

'Too much?' asked Sophie, anxiously.

'No…' he said, 'very festive.'

'It's black… how can it be festive?'

'You know what I mean – sparkly. Come on, let's go.'

As they crunched up the gravel drive, past the welcoming colonnade of flares flickering in the darkness, they heard laughter coming from the drawing room. Marcus, wearing a scarlet cashmere sweater, opened the grey front door. He took Sophie's old black coat and laid it on the pink sofa in the hall.

'Very glam…' he said admiringly, taking in Sophie's sparkly dress. She began to relax.

As he led the couple into the drawing room, she saw with alarm that she was the only woman in party dress. Everyone was wearing either jeans or simple day dresses.

Flora bounded up to them.

'You look amazing!' she said, looking past Sophie and pulling Hamish towards her for a kiss. 'Sequins… such fun.'

Flora was dressed almost entirely in white: white jeans, a white silk shirt and a pale grey sheepskin gilet. Her long blonde hair was swept up in a messy chignon. She looked chic, relaxed and elegant, with not a sequin in sight. Sophie was mortified.

'Now,' said Flora decisively, 'drinks. Marcus has insisted on making some mulled wine for the village people,' she grimaced. 'I simply loathe mulled wine. I, on the other hand, have got some wonderful cocktails on the go in the kitchen, for the chosen few.' She smiled conspiratorially at Hamish. 'Come with me.'

She led Hamish and Sophie into the kitchen. It was a temple to modern interior design, with pale limestone floors that merged with grey painted kitchen units, topped with Carrara marble. There was an industrial-sized range and an immense island unit, above which hung a row of six copper lights, gleaming like suns against a white sky. Her four exquisitely dressed children, sat at the long pale oak table making Christmas decorations from coloured paper and sequins. It provided an uncharacteristic island of colour in an otherwise bleached landscape.

'Darlings, say hello to Sophie and Hamish. Sophie ought to be helping you – she's got the perfect dress for it!'

Sophie winced inwardly at this jibe, as the children smiled up at her politely.

Flora drifted across her acreage of kitchen and poured two cocktails into Martini glasses.

'Here you go … cheers!'

Back in the drawing room, Sophie found herself wedged between the vicar – a kind man with gentle blue eyes and thinning hair – and a young man named Jonty, who'd just inherited two thousand acres from his father. Recently graduated from Cirencester agricultural college, it was widely felt that he was not up to the job.

'You look cracking,' Jonty said admiringly, 'lovely to have a bit of glamour about the place.'

'Oh, thank you,' said Sophie doubtfully. 'I wasn't quite sure what to wear.' As she looked around the drawing room, she could tell that the guests were not Flora's usual 'smart' set from London, but locals – villagers mostly – nice, ordinary people who Sophie would have enjoyed meeting, had she not been so inappropriately dressed. Everywhere she looked, she felt the disapproval of other women in the room. She hated to imagine what they were saying: '*Look at her… down from London. Who does she think she is? A celebrity?*'

Conversation with the Vicar and the landowner was increasingly stilted and she found herself yearning for Hamish's company. But he was nowhere to be seen.

Eventually she caught sight of him. He and Flora burst through the drawing room door, carrying the cocktail shaker, giggling conspiratorially. Sophie made her excuses and squeezed through the crowd towards her husband. She slipped her sequinned arm through his.

'Hello,' she said.

'Hello, there,' he said. 'Do you want a top-up?' He tipped the cocktail shaker into Sophie's glass.

She reached up to him, and whispered in his ear, 'I want to go... Please.'

'Already!' he said, with just a hint of annoyance. 'We can't go yet... it would be rude.'

Flora sidled up to him. 'Hamish darling, I want you to meet someone – I'm sure Sophie can spare you. After all... she has you all week...' She pulled Hamish across the room and proceeded to whisper in his ear, causing him to laugh uproariously.

Feeling wretched, Sophie wandered out into the hall, looking for the loo. One of Flora's daughters was walking desultorily towards the stairs.

'Hello,' said Sophie, 'you're Tabatha, aren't you?'

'Yes...' said the child.

'I was just looking for the loo...'

'It's there, next to the kitchen.'

When Sophie came out, having adjusted the sequin sheath, she noticed the child still loitering outside.

'Are you fed up making your Christmas decorations?' Sophie asked.

'Yes,' said the child, sadly, 'they're just for show.'

'I'm sure they'll make a lovely show,' said Sophie encouragingly.

'No... you don't understand. We're not putting them up. Mummy doesn't like them. They're too... gaudy. That's what she says.'

'Oh... that's a shame. Maybe they could go in your playroom? I'm sure you have a playroom.'

'Not in there, either. They don't match the decor.'

The child turned despondently and wandered back to the kitchen, followed by Sophie.

'Hello there,' she said to the other children. 'What are your names?'

'This is Willow,' said Tabatha, pointing at a beautiful blonde child of about three years old. 'And these are my brothers – Noah and Lucas.'

The children looked up from their labours and smiled politely.

'Well, it's very nice to meet you... I like your decorations. I'd love some like that.'

'You can take them home if you like,' said Tabatha.

'No... I couldn't do that. Why don't we put them up now, in here? We could stick them above the cooker. They'd look lovely there...'

Tabatha looked dubious, but there was a hint of a smile playing around her lips.

'Could we?' she asked.

'I don't see why not?'

Sophie rummaged in a drawer and found some drawing pins. Then she took the sequinned paper chains and pinned them in wild swags across the top of the white range cooker. She hung another swag between the copper pendant lights. By the time she had finished, the kitchen was festooned in coloured paper. There was glitter all over the marble worktops and the children were rushing excitedly around the kitchen admiring their handiwork. Thrilled by the obvious delight of the children, Sophie also felt a certain mischievous pleasure in what they had achieved. Flora, she knew, would hate it.

There was a tall Christmas tree in the corner of the room between the pale grey sofas. It was decorated discreetly with white lights and small straw decorations. Sophie picked up a pile of tinsel from the table.

'Who wants to finish decorating this tree?' she asked the children. 'I think Mummy might have forgotten to put this on...'

Noah and Lucas, suddenly animated, ran over to the tree, grabbing handfuls of brightly coloured tinsel. They had just finished draping it around the Christmas tree, when Flora came back into the kitchen in search of more cocktails.

'Oh, here you are,' she said to Sophie. 'Hamish was wondering where you'd got to... What on earth...?' She stood back and stared in disbelief at the multicoloured decorations. 'Children... I thought we'd discussed this...' she said, curtly.

'Aren't they lovely?' Sophie said admiringly. 'Tabatha seemed to think you didn't like them, but I assured her that must be wrong. How could anyone not love such pretty decorations?'

Flora gave Sophie a look of complete contempt. But Sophie, emboldened by the children's happiness and secretly pleased to have scored a minor triumph over her hostess, merely smiled politely.

'Well...' she said, 'Hamish and I really ought to be going... Thanks so much – it was a... lovely party.'

As Hamish and Sophie walked home, he asked her if she had enjoyed herself.

'Yes... in the end, it was quite good fun. I like to think I made it a memorable evening...'

Sophie's family arrived the following day, just in time for lunch.

'I love the house,' said Victoria, her sister-in-law, gazing around at the old kitchen, as Sophie served up some carrot and coriander soup. 'I keep trying to persuade Simon to leave London, but he won't hear of it... Maybe you could make him change his mind.'

'Change my mind about what?' asked Simon, coming in with his father and Hamish. They had been on a 'guided tour' of the property, including the newly restored wine cellar. Hamish opened a bottle of white wine and poured it into six glasses arranged on the table.

'To move out of London, darling,' said Victoria. 'Why can't we live somewhere like this, instead of that shoebox we call home in Cricklewood?'

'Oh Vic... we've been through this...' said Simon, sipping his wine. 'Lovely plonk, by the way, Hamish.'

'Well... we're going to have to move eventually,' Vic continued, 'when the b—' she stopped mid-sentence.

Sophie, who was putting a plate of cheese and biscuits out on the table, looked up.

'When the what…?' she asked.

'Oh nothing… you know – when… if… we ever start a family.' Victoria shrugged her shoulders casually.

'Glass of wine, Vic?' Hamish proffered her a glass.

'No thanks.'

'Why aren't you drinking?' asked Sophie.

'Oh… just that… it's… lunchtime,' said Vic. She was obviously flustered.

'Is there something you haven't told us?' asked Sophie, suspiciously.

Simon and Vic looked at each other.

'Vic…' Simon began.

'They're expecting a baby,' said Angela, gently. 'They weren't going to mention it – I'm sure I don't need to explain why. They didn't want to—'

'What?' asked Sophie. 'Didn't want to… what?' She could feel tears pricking her eyes.

'Upset you, darling,' said Alex, gently.

'Upset me?! So you all know about their baby, but I am not to be trusted with that information. I'm to be treated like a child, or some feeble-minded idiot… is that right?'

'No! Darling, don't overreact,' said Angela, reaching out to take Sophie's hand. 'I'm sure you understand… they just didn't want it to dominate Christmas. They would have told you in January, sometime.'

Sophie, embarrassed and near to tears, rushed from the room.

'Oh God,' said Hamish. 'Sorry about this. Do please sit down and eat… the soup will get cold. And kick the bloody cat off that chair, Alex. Wretched animal. I'll be a few minutes.'

Sophie lay on her bed, her back to the door. Hamish tiptoed into the room, as if visiting a sick relative. He sat down, gingerly, on the edge of the bed.

'Sophie… please.'

'Please what…' she said, her voice thick with tears.

'Don't spoil it for everyone. It's not their fault – is it? They were just trying to be sensitive. They know how much you want a baby. He's your brother for God's sake. Can't you be happy for them?'

Sophie rolled over and looked at Hamish, her eyes red with crying, mascara smeared across her cheeks.

'No,' she whispered. 'No, I can't be happy for them. I'm not happy. I'm jealous. I'm… envious as hell… I didn't even know they were trying. It's so unfair.'

She turned away again.

Hamish sat in silence, uncertain what to say, what to do. Eventually he said: 'Are you coming back down?'

'No,' she said, 'I can't come down – not yet. Tell them I've got a headache.'

As the winter sun dropped low in the sky, casting a rose-coloured glow on the room, Angela tiptoed into the bedroom, walked around the bed and lay down facing Sophie. She held her daughter's face in her hands and wiped away the tears.

'Darling… darling girl. I'm so sorry. They just wanted you to have a lovely Christmas in your new house – which is looking fabulous by the way. The tree, with Rachael's decorations, is a particular triumph. She would have been so proud of you, darling.'

'What… of her barren granddaughter?'

'Don't use that word. You are not barren! You're about to start treatment. In January – it's all going to kick off. You'll see. There will be another baby before you know it… I just know that.'

'Do you?' asked Sophie. 'Really?'

'I do… I really do.'

'I want it so much, Mum… It hurts. In here…' She banged her chest with her fist.

'I know, love.' Angela stroked her cheek.

'Last night, we went to a party,' said Sophie. 'The local rich couple. They have four children – four! And she doesn't even seem to like them. They have everything money could buy, but not their mother's love. It made me so mad.'

'Well not everyone can do parenting... Maybe you can be a friend to those children. Do you want to come downstairs now? Vic and Simon have cleared away and were wondering if you fancied playing cards? Or... watching a movie?'

Sophie blew her nose and sat up. 'What must they think of me?'

'They understand... But let's try and move on – just for the next few days. All right?'

'All right... and thank you... thank you for being my mum.'

Chapter 15

Sant'Antioco
July 1959

It had been several weeks since Tommaso visited Rachael at the cottage. At first she thought little of it, but as the days turned into weeks, she began to feel anxious. She was an innocent, in so many ways – unfamiliar with the games lovers play, uncertain of the rules. Her first and only lover, until Tommaso, had been her husband. The courtship had been supervised, in effect, by her father, and they had slept together for the first time on their wedding night. It had been a nervous, tentative affair. Both were virgins, neither quite sure what to do. In fact, Rachael realised several days into her marriage that they had not actually made love at all that first night.

Tommaso was the first man she had encouraged since József's death. More than that, the first man she had allowed to be so intimate with her – both with her body and her emotions.

She recalled snatches of conversations she overheard when she was living in the camp in Austria. The other women working in the kitchen sometimes spoke of the perils of sleeping with a man before marriage. She remembered Nadia, one of the older women in the camp, as she stirred the large pot of goulash for the inmates, criticising a pretty girl who had arrived a few weeks before and was receiving a lot of attention from the young men in the camp.

'She'd better watch it, that one. She's too free and easy,' Nadia had said. 'They'll all get the wrong idea – you mark my words. She'll regret it.'

Rachael had not quite understood what Nadia had meant at the time. The other women had nodded their heads and muttered, 'Yes. You're quite right,' and Rachael didn't like to ask what they meant by 'free and easy'. And what was 'the wrong idea'?'

Now, as she looked back on that glorious afternoon with Tommaso, making love on the sofa, she wondered if she had been too free and easy. Had Tommaso now got 'the wrong idea' about her? Is that why he had stayed away?

Another comment slipped unannounced into her memory from those days in the camp kitchen: 'When they get what they want, they'll drop her – you'll see.'

Is that what Tommaso had done?

When she visited the town to go shopping, she looked for Tommaso everywhere. She sat in the cafe hoping he might come and take her order for a coffee. But he never came. Disappointed, she wandered down the cobbled streets, with Angela trailing behind her, glancing around, thinking she would bump into him in a shop or side street. But it was as if he had disappeared.

And, to add to her worries, since the evening when Tommaso had been invited to stay for supper, Giles had become distant, even unfriendly.

One market day, when she asked him for a lift into town, he replied sarcastically: 'Can't the fisherman give you a lift today?'

He always referred to Tommaso as 'the fisherman' and it irked her.

'If it's not too much trouble,' she replied, sharply, determined not to be intimidated by him.

He blushed, perhaps sensing he had gone too far.

Her father appeared on the veranda, his briefcase under his arm. 'Are we going?' he asked, a little impatiently.

'Yes, sir – of course.'

Rachael sat by the window, Angela on her lap, gazing desultorily out at the dry summer landscape. Giles also appeared distracted. George, sensing the uncomfortable atmosphere between his daughter and his student, endeavoured to break the silence.

'We have a lot to do today, Giles – I hope you are full of energy.'

'Yes, sir… of course.' Giles sounded lacklustre.

'And what are your plans, Rachael?' George asked.

'Oh… just shopping. It's market day, so I thought I might get some fish…' She looked down at the top of Angela's head, and blushed.

Giles felt unable to resist a retort: 'Has the fisherman not been around – I thought he brought you fish when you needed it?'

Rachael sighed. She should answer – casually. But she understood exactly what he was asking and didn't want to give him the satisfaction of knowing that Tommaso appeared to have deserted her.

'Yes… he's brought us fish,' she lied. 'I just want a little extra and a chance to see the catch for myself. There's so much variety here…'

Giles parked the truck in the square and George went, alone, into the basilica.

'Shall I come back for you in a couple of hours?' Giles asked.

'Thank you,' said Rachael, determined to be civil. 'That would be so kind – yes please.'

Taking Angela by the hand, she walked down to the market near the harbour. There, she pottered among the stalls, picking up vegetables, flour and other provisions. The fish stall, in particular, did not disappoint and she bought two large lobsters and a seabass. The sight of the fish lying on the top of her basket filled her with sadness – as she thought back to the fishing excursion she had with Tommaso.

Angela, bored with the expedition, began to fidget and pull away from her mother. Rachael struggled to carry her basket while at the same time keeping hold of Angela's hand. Suddenly, the basket was whisked away from her. She swung round and Tommaso was standing behind her. He took her free hand and pulled her away from the market, down a small side street, dragging Angela behind her. He looked about him warily, before kissing her passionately on the mouth.

'Oh…' she said, as their lips parted, 'where have you been?'

He blushed; he looked awkward, embarrassed.

'I take you home now,' he said.

'No… someone's coming for me. And you haven't answered my question. Where have you been?'

'I will tell you… but I take you home – please.'

Against her better judgement, she allowed herself to be led by the hand towards his Lambretta. He put the shopping in the footwell and they climbed aboard. It felt so good to have her arms wrapped around him once again, Angela nestling safely between his legs. They drove out of town by a different route – not past the cafe where his sister worked, but by a back road.

When they arrived at the cottage, she took the shopping into the kitchen. Angela was tired and Rachael carried her upstairs and lay her down on her bed, where she fell instantly asleep.

When Rachael came downstairs, Tommaso guided her over to the sofa. He kissed her and embraced her, but she pulled back.

'No… where have you been? It's been weeks since I saw you.'

'I… been working. Much… fishing.'

'I see… but couldn't you come and see me after work?'

'No… your father…'

'My father… what about my father?'

Tommaso got up and paced the room.

'Tell me please,' she urged him. 'Did my father say something to you?'

He turned and looked at her. He sat back down beside her, taking her hand in his and kissing her fingers, one by one.

'Your father ask me… do I love you?'

Rachael felt her stomach flipping. She held her breath.

'And what did you say?'

He kissed her cheek, her forehead, her mouth.

'I say… yes… I love you very much.'

Rachael felt an unadulterated joy. She grinned, a wide happy smile of relief, of happiness. She had known all along that he loved her; she wasn't a fool – like the girls in the camp. He hadn't 'got what he wanted' and deserted her. He loved her, truly loved her.

'I love you too,' she said, kissing him and laying her head upon his shoulder.

She could imagine their life together – living peacefully in the cottage, watching Angela grow, maybe having another child – and they would be happy on this island in the sun.

He kissed her again, his hands reaching beneath her dress, feeling her skin soft and warm beneath his fingers.

'Angela?' he asked as he nuzzled her neck.

'She's asleep,' she whispered in his ear.

After they had made love, and he had gone, she realised he'd never told her why he had stayed away. Why telling her father that he loved her had been such a problem?

When George came back home that evening, he went through to the sitting room to collect something from his desk. Giles, who was staying for a drink as usual, remained on the terrace where Rachael sat at the table, shelling peas. He glared at her.

'I waited for you in the square for ages,' he whispered. 'I even went down the market to look for you. I was worried. Where were you?'

'Oh… I'm sorry. I got a lift. I should have found a way to tell you, but we went out of town a different way. Angela was so tired and the shopping was heavy. It just seemed sensible.'

'Who from,' asked Giles, 'the fisherman?'

'Yes,' said Rachael, defiantly. 'It was from Tommaso, if you must know. He happened to be there and he offered. I'm sorry if it inconvenienced you.'

'Who was inconvenienced?' asked George cheerily, coming back onto the terrace.

'Giles, Papa. He offered to take me home after the market, but I… I got a lift from someone else.'

'Who?' George asked casually, studying his daughter's face.

'From Tommaso.' Her eyes flashed, and her face was flushed in the rosy haze of the setting sun.

'Well, that makes sense,' said George, calmly. 'I'm sure Rachael didn't mean to cause any problem for you, Giles. I think we are all tired tonight. Giles – would you mind if we didn't have a glass of wine this evening? I think Rachael and I need an early night. We'll see you tomorrow.'

It was unusual for George not to offer Giles a glass of wine. Scarcely a day had gone by since they moved to the island when he had not done so. They routine had hardly ever altered – they drank wine, they discussed the dig, they watched the sun go down over the wood and the sea beyond. It was as much a part of their working day as the dig itself. Giles, looking a little hurt and confused at this sudden dismissal, nevertheless took his leave.

'Rachael,' George said quietly, as soon as the young man had left, 'sit down please… I want to talk to you.'

Rachael, feeling uneasy, did as she was told.

'My darling… I think it would be better if you didn't see Tommaso anymore.'

'Why? Why on earth not?'

'Trust me about this. Please.'

'Is it because he's just a fisherman?'

Rachael could feel the indignation rising, her cheeks flushing. Angela, who had been pottering around the garden, saw the pain on her mother's face and began to cry in sympathy.

'Come here, darling, it's all right.' Rachael picked the child up and nursed her on her lap, rocking her to soothe her.

'No… it's not his profession. He's a very interesting young man. But… I don't know how to tell you this Rachael … He is promised.'

'Promised?'

'Elsewhere.'

She was confused.

'He is engaged to someone else.'

Rachael stared at her father in disbelief. 'No… he can't be… he wouldn't… no.'

'He has been promised to a girl in the village most of his life. He cannot break the bond. He does love you, Rachael – I believe him when he says that. But the other day – when he was here, he told me about this other engagement… He didn't mean to, I don't think. But we were chatting about customs on the island and he mentioned, casually, that he had been promised to this girl since he was a young boy.'

'Is that why he left?'

'Yes… I asked him to go. I could see what was happening between you. He will break your heart, Rachael, and I won't allow it.'

She felt a wave of pain, fury and regret at what she had done, what she had felt and given away. She had opened her heart to Tommaso, given him her body. She had trusted him with her child. She could not believe it… He would not use her so, would not humiliate her in this way. It could not be true.

'I don't want to hear this,' she shouted, 'besides, it has nothing to do with you.' She moved Angela off her lap and onto the ground, and ran back into the house. George heard her bedroom door slamming and the sound of her sobbing filtered down from her room above the veranda.

Angela began to cry and ran to her grandfather. He picked her up and pottered into the kitchen holding Angela's hand, soothing the little child.

'There, there… let us see what there is to eat?'

He found some bread and a piece of cheese, which he shared with the little girl. When they had finished he took her upstairs and put her to bed. He knocked on Rachael's door.

'Darling… please can I come in?'

He pushed the door open and found Rachael lying in the dark, her face to the wall. He sat down next to her.

'I don't think he meant to hurt you. I believe he thought he could persuade his family to release him from this bond. But it seems that is not possible. I am sure his feelings for you are sincere. I have watched him with you and I can see how much he loves you. He is a good man, a sensitive man. But we cannot put him in this position, where he must choose. It would make his life so hard, make your life together impossible. The people here would never accept you. You must see that.'

'He could come with me to London,' said Rachael, sitting up, trying to take control of the situation.

'Darling… he's a fisherman. What would he do in London?'

'If he loved me – and he does,' she spat the last phrase out, 'he would find something. We came to London – you and me; it wasn't so hard.'

'I was a university professor – not so hard for me to get a good job.'

'So it's all right for a clever university professor but not for an ordinary man – is that it?'

'Rachael, he would have to leave everything behind… He has no education. He would struggle – think about it. Can you imagine him trying to support you and Angela?'

'We'd manage somehow. I could work.'

'Doing what – baking?'

Rachael's eyes filled with tears. 'Is that all you think I'm good for? Baking…'

'We have to be practical. You have no profession. You have a child. You are so intelligent, but you gave up full-time education…'

Her father was flustered, sweating. Rachael knew in her heart that he would not deliberately hurt her feelings. But, nevertheless, he had. She had always thought her father to be her greatest supporter, her champion. He had always made her feel special for the way she looked after him. Did he, in fact, despise her for her domestic prowess, for her lack of schooling? She felt a wave of regret for her teenage years, when she had chosen a life at home over an education, when she had clung to her domestic sphere, finding solace in the polishing and the tidying and the cooking. She had thought it marked her out; as a homemaker – someone to replace her missing mother. But maybe what she had done wasn't important after all. She couldn't even earn a living, so she was useless. Even her own father thought she was nothing more than a helpless child.

'I don't want to hurt your feelings,' he said – sensitive as ever. 'This is a difficult situation. If he was free to marry, if he was a doctor, or a man with a profession that could transfer to London – it would be fine. But he is not, Rachael, and you must be realistic about what you could achieve. And more importantly perhaps than your own feelings in this matter, we cannot come to someone else's country and impose our views and desires on them. We must respect their customs, Rachael. This man does care for you, but he has another destiny.'

She lay back on the bed, wiping her eyes. The adrenalin of her earlier anger subsiding. She felt exhausted. She knew her father was right.

'Besides,' he went on, 'think... think, Rachael, of the dig.'

She sat up once again, alert, her anger welling up again. 'Is that what this is all about – your beloved dig?'

'No... no,' he protested. 'But there's no doubt the people would be rightly angry; how would I ever be able to come back here, to finish what I've started.'

'I don't care about the dig. I don't care if you ever come back. I only care about him. He loves me!' shouted Rachael. 'I know it... and I love him.'

'Yes... I see that. But sometimes, Rachael, sometimes... love is just not enough.'

Chapter 16

The summer and autumn months were desperately hot. Rachael somehow stumbled through the days of July, August and September in a haze of heat and misery. She stayed indoors in the mornings, hardly troubling to dress herself or Angela properly. She clung to the shade of the veranda, listening constantly for the whine of the Lambretta. But it never came. When she went into town to shop for food, she looked for Tommaso wherever she went. But it seemed he had simply disappeared. In the afternoons, she cooked and she taught Angela to swim. But each time she went down to the cove, the sight of the boat languishing on the beach brought a physical pain to her heart.

George hoped fervently that she would soon recover. He was determined to finalise his work at the dig and get them home to England as soon as possible. The students had finally unearthed the second tomb and its inscription was now visible, but its meaning was ambiguous.

Virus Bonus in Pace Bonus

'It makes no sense, sir' said Giles. 'Do they mean 'Vir Bonus'? In other words... '*Good man in peace, good man*'? Otherwise it's rubbish.'

'Not rubbish exactly – it means something, but I agree that it does not indicate exactly who is buried here... I had thought perhaps...'

'What, sir?'

'Well, an old man must have his dreams,' said George, his thighs aching from sitting too long on his haunches in the cramped space. 'I had thought maybe it was the long-lost burial ground of Emperor Titus. But there is no name here to confirm that. The signs are so ambiguous. Jewish symbols, Latin inscriptions. I must do some more research when we get back to London.'

They had been due to leave Sardinia after Christmas and the students had been eager to experience an Italian festive holiday. But one evening in October, when Giles and Peter dropped George off at the cottage, he invited them in.

'Let's sit on the veranda; the nights are getting cool, but we must enjoy this view as long as we can – we won't be here much longer.'

Together they gathered around the long table and watched as the sun dipped behind the horizon.

'We should be proud of what we have achieved,' George said, as Rachael poured wine into their glasses. 'We've uncovered a pair of tombs of some significance; they are clearly of Roman origin. I suggest we barricade them up again to prevent further damage. I shall write up our notes and we will publish when we get back to England. You'd better to write to your families and tell them you are coming home in time for Christmas.'

Giles glanced across at Rachael, who was sitting silently on the other side of the table.

'How do you feel,' he asked, quietly, 'about going home?'

She merely shrugged her shoulders and went back into the kitchen.

Her silence on the issue, George took as acquiescence. Without discussing it with her, he wrote that evening, to Mrs Roper.

> *My dear Mrs Roper,*
> *I write to give you news of our sojourn in Sardinia. Rachael and Angela are well – Angela is learning to swim, thanks to your beautiful present. My work here is nearly*

*finished and it is time for us to return to London. Might
you have room in your attic for two old friends?*

The reply from Mrs Roper arrived two weeks later. Rachael,
recognising the hand-writing, studied the envelope all day, desperate
to rip it open and find out why Mrs Roper had written to her father.

She handed it to George as soon he arrived home.

'You have a letter – from Mrs Roper... why is she writing to you?'

He tore open the airmail envelope and scanned its contents,
nodding with satisfaction when he had finished.

'She has space for us in the attic – her present tenant is leaving
at the end of the month. So we can return home... She sends
her love...'

He put the letter into the top pocket of his shirt and sat down
at the table on the veranda.

'When did you decide this?' Rachael's cheeks burned with
indignation, angry not to have been consulted.

'You knew that we have to go soon – we've been discussing it...'

'*You* need to go. But I will not go. I shall stay here. You can go
to London without me.'

George looked bemused. 'Go without you...? Don't be ridiculous, Rachael. How will you support yourself and Angela?'

'I will find something to do...'

'How will you pay the rent on this cottage? The university covers
our costs at the moment. You are living in a fantasy if you think
you can afford it. You have no money worries at the moment, but
once the dig is closed, the funding will stop. Do you understand?'

'Of course I understand... I am not stupid.'

'I know, darling... I never said...' George put his head in his
hands and began to weep.

Rachael, who had been pacing the garden throughout their
conversation, ran across and knelt down beside him. He looked
suddenly so old and frail.

'Oh, Papa, Papa… I'm so sorry. I do understand. It's just… I cannot bear to leave him.'

'I know, darling… but he has already left you. You have to accept it.'

He held her face in his hands and kissed the tears away.

'You have a future, Rachael – but it's in London. And who knows who you will meet, where you will go next? But we must leave here soon. Once we are back in England, you will forget… I promise. Love does not hurt forever. I know.'

Rachael spent most of October packing their few belongings into boxes to be sent back to London. The sun was still warm during the day, but a cool breeze blew in from the sea overnight. One afternoon, Angela came down wearing her tiny yellow swimsuit. She had grown tall in the months they had lived on Sardinia and the suit now stretched uncomfortably over her tanned frame.

'Swimming, Mama,' she said, hopefully.

'OK,' said Rachael. 'We'll go swimming – let's hope the sea isn't too cold.'

She removed the rope that bound the gate, and as her fingers worked the knot to untie it, she thought of Tommaso and how he had made it safe that day, after the accident. She held Angela's hand as they walked through the little copse; the sun was filtering through the trees and glinting on the water.

At the cove, she lay a towel on the sand, and they sat together looking out to sea. It was a perfect day – blue sky, the sun high above. But something was missing… the boat; Tommaso's boat was not there. When had he collected it? She began to cry – at the thought that he had removed this last vestige of his presence in her life.

Angela stood up and faced her mother. She wiped the tears away with her chubby little thumbs. 'Don't cry, Mama…'

She threw her arms around her mother's neck and clung to her.

'It's OK,' said Rachael, into her daughter's blonde curls, 'I am just sad that we're leaving this lovely place.'

She kissed her child, stood up and carried her to the water's edge, where she paddled, kicking the water up with her feet, watching the spray catch the light, sparkling like diamonds. As Rachael waded further into the sea, the child wriggled to be allowed to swim.

Rachael put Angela into the water and held her hand beneath her tummy, as she always did. Angela suddenly floated off and began to swim, clumsily, supporting her own weight. Rachael walked next to her anxiously, in case she suddenly sank. But the child swam several feet quite unaided, before she realised she was not being held and began to cry.

Rachael scooped her up out of the water and kissed her.

'You did it! You can swim… my clever, clever girl.'

She carried the child back to the beach and they sat on the towel, eating plums from the tree in the garden. Amidst the sound of the sea lapping the shore, the seagulls screeching overhead came the unmistakeable pulse of the outboard motor. Rachael looked hopefully out to sea and there was the outline of Tommaso's boat with its distinctive pale blue paintwork.

He roared inland and slowed the engine as he approached the shore. He leapt out in the shallows and pulled the boat onto the sand, then ran across to Rachael and Angela.

'You're here,' he said, throwing himself down beside them. He kissed them both, ruffling Angela's hair.

'Where have you been?' said Rachael, her eyes filling with tears. 'I've missed you…'

He put his arms around her and kissed her neck. 'I've missed you too. I'm so sorry.'

Angela picked up a little basket.

'Are you going to get me some shells?' Rachael asked her.

The child nodded and pottered down the beach towards the edge of the cove.

'Why didn't you tell me you were engaged?' Rachael asked Tommaso.

He blushed and looked away, wiping his eyes with the back of his hand.

'Because… I don't love her. Because I hoped that I… not have to marry her. I try to talk to my mother. But she is angry. I love *you*, Rachael.'

'Then don't marry her. Marry me!' said Rachael.

'I cannot. I promised. I… so sorry.'

He got up, stumbling slightly, wiping his eyes.

'Don't leave yet,' begged Rachael, 'please.'

He went over to the boat and came back with a small parcel, tied with a ribbon. He gave it to her…

'For you.'

She untied the ribbon. Inside, nestling in tissue paper, was an intricately woven byssus bracelet. Not a narrow thread like the little one Angela had been given that day at Italo Diana but a beautiful piece, with a little pearl button to tie it in place.

She looked up at him. 'It's lovely…thank you.'

He fixed it in place, kissing the inside of her wrist as he did so. 'Like gold…' he said, lifting her wrist up to the light, so the bracelet glistened.

'Yes… like gold. Thank you,' she said.

'To remember me… good luck for you.'

'It's not good luck if I'm leaving you,' she said through tears. 'How can I ever have good luck again? *You* were my luck. My chance to be happy…'

He held her face in his strong hands and kissed the tears away.

'I'm sorry,' he said, his voice breaking with emotion.

He got up and walked across to the boat, returning with a leather box.

'What's that?' she asked, wiping her eyes.

'Camera...'

He took it out of the case. 'I take photograph... Please.'

He took a photograph of her sitting on the sand in her blue swimsuit. And a second with Angela on her lap.

He offered her the camera – 'You take picture of me?'

He leant against his boat, putting on a false smile. She clicked the shutter and caught his expression forever. She handed him back the camera. He put it carefully back inside the case and into the boat. But when he turned round, she had gone, leaving a trail of footprints behind her in the golden sand.

Chapter 17

As Christmas Day dawned, Sophie woke, her mind buzzing with lists of 'things to do'. Presents needed to be arranged under the tree, breakfast laid out for the family, as well the preparation for the main Christmas meal. But this normally happy sense of activity and anticipation was overlaid with a feeling of shame and embarrassment at how she had reacted to her sister-in-law's 'happy' news.

Climbing out of bed, and pulling on her dressing gown, she made a decision to put the previous day out of her mind, and instead throw herself into her role as hostess. The family drifted down gradually and accepted offers of tea and coffee. Eggs were boiled and poached. Racks of toast laid out on the table alongside home-made marmalade and jam. Hamish even opened a bottle of champagne.

'Fizz, anyone?'

'Not for me,' said Vic, before glancing nervously at Sophie, who smiled encouragingly at her sister-in-law, determined to demonstrate that she had recovered from her outburst.

'None for me either, darling. I've got too much to do,' she said, standing at the sink peeling potatoes. 'Maybe later.'

When the turkey had been put into the Aga, and the vegetables prepared, the family gathered round the tree to open their presents.

'Darling,' said her mother, putting her arm around Sophie's waist, 'it's all perfect – the tree, the house – it looks fabulous. Granny would have been proud to see her decorations looking so beautiful.'

'Thanks, Mum,' said Sophie, trying to take comfort from her mother's words. But she couldn't help feeling just a little nagging regret that if both she *and* Victoria were pregnant, the day would really have been perfect.

The smell of cooking turkey wafted through the house. The cat lay proprietorially in front of the Aga, as if hoping he could somehow prise the door open and eat the contents. Potatoes were basted, bread sauce was stirred, the pudding was put on to steam. Hamish kept up a steady flow of champagne and wine, but each time Vic refused a glass, or Simon patted his wife's stomach affectionately, Sophie struggled to suppress her instinctive feelings of sadness and, if she was honest, envy.

When the meal was over, and the family had played the ubiquitous Christmas games, Sophie retreated to bed, grateful to be alone and able to vent her misery.

She woke on Boxing Day with a renewed sense of shame about her reaction to her sister-in-law's good fortune. It wasn't Victoria's fault after all. After breakfast, she suggested a long walk with Victoria, to clear the air. She was determined to demonstrate that she was pleased for her brother and his wife.

'I'm glad to get you on your own,' she said to Victoria as they trudged across the wide ploughed fields that surrounded the village. 'I wanted to apologise properly for my... frankly outrageous behaviour. It was unforgiveable. I *am* happy for you and Simon – honestly. It was just a bit of a shock.'

'I know,' said Victoria, taking her arm. The ground was frozen solid into brown rutted ripples that stretched away ahead of them.

'It was my idea not to tell you,' said Victoria. 'I didn't want to spoil Christmas for you. I thought it better to wait.'

Sophie squeezed her arm appreciatively.

'Although, 'Victoria continued, 'we *had* been trying for a couple of months; it wasn't exactly instantaneous, you know.'

She felt Sophie's arm stiffen slightly.

'God… I'm sorry,' Victoria said quickly, 'that was tactless. You've been trying for some time, haven't you?'

'Three years, nearly,' said Sophie, gloomily.

'You must hate me.'

'I don't!' said Sophie, stopping abruptly in a deep rut filled with water. It sloshed around her wellington boots, seeping icily through a crack in the sole, soaking her sock. 'I really don't. I can't pretend there isn't a bit of jealousy – it's a horrible thing, and I'm ashamed of it – but you understand that, don't you?'

'Of course. Of course I do.'

They tramped on in silence. Rooks flew, squawking, into the windbreak of trees planted along the edge of the vast tractor-friendly field.

'We'd love you to be godmother,' said Victoria brightly.

Sophie disengaged her arm and walked briskly ahead of her sister-in-law, muttering something about difficult walking conditions.

Victoria ran after her, stumbling in the rutted ground, icy water slopping over the top of her ankle-high walking boots. 'Sophie?' she called out. 'Have I upset you? I didn't mean to…'

Sophie swung round, her face contorted by tears.

'I know you mean well, Vic, and I'm not unaware of the honour you do me… but can we leave that… for now?'

Victoria put her arms out to Sophie, who stood in the biting wind, her shoulders hunched with restrained misery. 'Oh Sophie, I'm sorry. Of course it's all right to wait. Stupid of me to be so insensitive…'

'No,' said Sophie. She relaxed a little and hugged her sister-in-law. 'I am really touched – honestly,' she whispered into Victoria's hair. 'But… just let me get through these next few weeks. I want so desperately to be a mother.'

In the middle of January, the process of IVF was due to begin. Sophie had been on the pill for four weeks and the day finally arrived when she would start to be injected with fertility drugs to increase egg production. She was due at the consultant's office that morning to be given the first of her injections and Hamish, surprisingly, had agreed to come with her.

She woke early, before dawn, and crept out of bed. She was filled with an almost childish excitement. This was the day she would really begin her journey to having a baby. It was happening at last.

Peering through the curtains, the garden was bathed in a cloak of white frost, glistening in the early-morning moonlight. She was relieved that the heavy rain of the previous day had not turned to snow overnight. It would have been the ultimate torture to be unable to reach the hospital because the roads were blocked. She couldn't bear the thought of anything getting in the way of the process that would change their lives.

She climbed back into bed but lay restlessly in the half-light of the gathering dawn, watching Hamish sleep. They had made love the night before. It had been spontaneous and passionate – almost like the old days. How sad, she thought, that their love for one another just wasn't enough to make a baby.

She finally drifted off and was deeply asleep when the alarm went off at seven o'clock.

Hamish rolled over and kissed her. 'Morning, sleepy…'

'Oh…' she mumbled. 'Morning. I've only just dropped back off. I was awake for hours.'

'Oh… why? Fretting?'

She nodded. 'That… and feeling excited. A mix of things really.'

He put his arms around her and pulled her towards him. She lay with her head against his chest, listening to the comforting rhythmic sound of his heart beating.

'I understand,' he said. 'It's a big day, but remember, darling, it's just the start of the journey. We must stay calm and collected… It may work first time, but we need to prepare ourselves for disappointment.'

She pulled away from him and lay propped up on her elbow. 'Are you trying to be negative – to depress me?'

'No… I'm trying to be realistic… to put it into perspective. One step at a time… OK?'

At the clinic, the consultant talked them through the process once again.

'Two weeks of fertility injections to increase egg production – you'll need to do these daily at home. I hope you'll be OK with that?'

Sophie nodded, earnestly.

The doctor looked at Hamish. 'I suppose your husband can help you with that? He's the ideal partner really, isn't he?'

Hamish smiled.

'You'll have to pop in for a few ultrasound checks to monitor how things are going and then, if all is well, there will be another injection to finalise "maturation". Sorry – it's a ghastly word, I know. We'll then retrieve the eggs, mix them with Hamish's sperm and Bob's your uncle. If fertilisation occurs, five days later, we'll then reimplant into the womb. Is that all clear?'

The pair nodded. Hamish reached out and squeezed Sophie's hand.

'The drugs can make you feel a bit rough,' the consultant continued, 'not unlike pregnancy, I'm told. But they're just something you have to get used to. No gain without pain…'

*

The drugs, when Sophie started to take them, did indeed make her feel terrible. Her breasts became painful, and she grew two bra sizes within days – forcing her to buy new underwear. Hamish thought 'the new arrivals', as he irritatingly called them, were rather wonderful. But they were far too painful to touch. On top of that, Sophie had a raging thirst and peed constantly. Her stomach felt bloated as the month wore on and her jeans seemed suddenly a size too small. There were even mental side effects – she became forgetful and absent-minded, but that could have been due to the stress, she reasoned. The process would be so time-consuming that she had arranged to take a few weeks off work. She visited the clinic several times to check the development of the egg follicles.

Finally, when they were declared 'good to go', she was injected with another drug – hCG – which would trigger their final maturation. The eggs would be retrieved under anaesthetic two days later.

Her mother rang to ask if they needed her come down for this stage in the process.

'I could come the night before the eggs are retrieved,' she suggested to Hamish, 'I know you're so busy and she'll need looking after.'

'That's very kind. I am busy, it's true, but I ought to be with her... I want to be with her.'

'Of course!' said Angela. 'But if I come down, I can cook you both dinner and make sure she's comfortable. She's bound to be a bit sore afterwards.'

'Are you sure you can take the time off?'

'Yes – my partner will cover for me. And we can get a locum if necessary.'

On the morning of egg retrieval, Sophie was frantic with nerves.

'You look a bit pale, darling,' Angela said over breakfast, handing her a piece of toast.

'I didn't sleep well,' said Sophie.

The cat leapt onto her lap, poking his nose above the table, in search of a scrap of food. Sophie pushed him off and he skulked away to the Aga, where he lay staring at her, with a sense of righteous indignation.

'Poor old Cat,' said her mother, soothingly. 'He didn't mean anything by it – I haven't fed him yet.'

'He's a filthy old beast,' said Hamish, affectionately, tickling him under the chin. 'But he just wants you to know how much he loves you…'

'He just wanted to eat my breakfast,' said Sophie grumpily, before she relented and knelt down by the cat. 'I'm sorry, Cat,' she said, stroking his long grey flank.

'So,' said Hamish, sitting down at the table, 'you sure you're going to be OK today? I can come along as well, you know…'

'No,' said Sophie, 'Mum's here. She'll look after me. You get off to work – I'll be fine.'

He embraced his wife, pulling her towards him and kissed the top of her head; he made a thumbs up sign to her mother, who nodded discreetly.

The procedure went well enough and, afterwards, when the anaesthetic had worn off, Angela drove Sophie home. She tucked her up on the sofa under a blanket and turned on the television.

'You just lie here, darling. I'll go and get dinner started.'

'What are you making?'

'Controlling as ever…' said her mother, wryly. 'I went into town, while you were having your op. I had a coffee and found a wonderful butcher where I bought some lamb. I thought I'd do my tagine. Is that OK?'

'Delicious – thanks, Mum.'

Hamish had texted throughout the day and arrived home just before seven o'clock with a large bunch of pink roses.

'Oh… these are lovely,' said Sophie. 'What are they for? Guilty conscience?'

'No!' he said indignantly. 'They're just a way of saying well done. Was it painful?'

'No, but it wasn't exactly the most delightful day of my life either.'

'Well, it's over… I'll go and ask your mother to put these in water, shall I?'

'Yes… thank you.' As he turned to go, she called out: 'Hamish – it will be all right, won't it?'

Hamish, reluctant to make false promises, said, 'You've done all you can. Just try to stay calm…onwards and upwards, darling.'

A few days after the procedure, as Sophie and Hamish sat eating breakfast at the kitchen table, the phone rang. As she stood up to take the call, Sophie noted the number on the dial.

'It's the clinic,' she whispered to Hamish. She felt sick with nerves.

Hamish watched her face as she received the news. It went from white-faced anxiety to pure joy.

'OK,' she said to the voice on the other end. 'So I should come back on Friday – yes? OK… see you then.'

She threw her arms around Hamish's neck as he sat at the table.

'One of them has fertilised,' she said. 'We have a baby.'

He leapt to his feet and hugged her. 'That's great… Really great news…'

On the day of implantation, Sophie lay on the bed at the clinic while a catheter loaded with the embryo was inserted through her cervix.

'Does it hurt?' whispered Hamish into her ear. He sat next to her holding her hand as the couple watched the flimsy tube making its way into her uterus on the ultrasound screen beside them.

'No…' said Sophie. 'Not at all.'

The technician palpated the tube and a tiny cellular structure was released.

Sophie grinned, and squeezed Hamish's hand. 'It's going to be OK, isn't it?'

'Yes…' he replied.

The next few days seemed endless. Without work to distract her, Sophie found it hard not to dwell on the progress of the tiny foetus lodged in her womb. She had been injecting herself with progesterone since the day the eggs were retrieved, in order to support the lining of her womb. She had never taken a medication so happily, or so readily. As she injected herself each evening, she said a prayer.

'Keep my baby safe.'

But the fear of losing the baby never left her. She avoided any rigorous exercise. Even digging the garden appeared dangerous. She lay on the sofa or pottered around the kitchen. She wandered up to the village shop to buy groceries – nervous even of driving into Cirencester and visiting the supermarket. She was relieved when, twelve days later, she was able to attend the clinic for her first blood test. This would determine if she was actually pregnant. Hamish agreed to come with her.

'I'm sorry to drag you away from work again,' Sophie had said over breakfast. 'I just don't feel confident driving for some reason.'

'It's fine, Sophie… I understand. I want to come anyway.'

As the nurse took the blood sample, she explained the process.

'You might be wondering why we take blood rather than checking your urine. It's just more accurate. It detects the hormone secreted by the placenta after implantation. The more hormone in your body, the more likely the pregnancy is to "take". We should have the results tomorrow.'

The phone call giving her the results came just after lunch. Sophie was lying down in the sitting room, and as soon as she heard the phone ringing in the kitchen, she leapt up and rushed to answer it, dropping it in her excitement.

'Hello… sorry, Sophie Mitchell here…'

The news was the best she could have hoped for. Hamish was at work, but she rang his mobile and left a message.

'Darling... darling, such wonderful news. It's positive. Come home soon.'

He rang her back half an hour later. 'Oh Sophie, sweetheart... that's wonderful. I'll be back after six...'

'It will be all right, won't it?'

'Of course,' he said. 'Now stop worrying – first hurdle over... see you later.'

She rang her mother and managed to speak to her between patients.

'Sophie – that's fantastic,' said her mother. 'But don't get your hopes up too much.'

'Why do you say that?' asked Sophie.

'Because... sometimes things don't quite work out...' her mother said, regretting ever having brought doubt into the situation. 'But I'm sure it will be fine.'

Sophie was tortured by her mother's reaction and played her words over and over in her mind. She was due to have another blood test a couple of weeks later and again two weeks after that, until the end of the first trimester, or until a foetal heartbeat could be heard. She spent the afternoon googling information about the developing foetus... and discovered that the heartbeat could be audible, as early as six or seven weeks. Determined to remain positive, she pushed any doubts to one side. She was pregnant at last; it was a miracle.

The following two weeks went by achingly slowly. Each night as Sophie climbed into bed, she mentally ticked another day off. 'Just eleven days to go.' 'Ten days.' 'Nine days... until the next test. Hang in there, baby,' she told her child. The second blood test would provide the proof, the definitive evidence – to her mother, to Hamish, to herself – that the baby was all right. That her womb was nourishing it, feeding it. That she could do this.

The second blood test was also positive. Sophie's sense of achieve-
ment was mixed with relief. She was one month pregnant. In just
two weeks' time, she might be able to hear the heartbeat and have
real visceral proof that her baby was there, inside her. In just eight
months she could be holding her child in her arms. This baby for
whom she had yearned for so long; had loved before it was even
created. It was as if her life had been leading up to this moment.
And she would love this child – whether a boy or a girl, whether
dark-haired or blond, clever or stupid… she would take anything.
She would love it forever. She would kill for it. She would love it
more than any child had ever been loved before.

A few days later she woke early.

'Hamish, Hamish…' she said, shaking him awake, 'something's
wrong.'

'What…' he murmured.

'I'm not sure… I can't explain it… I just feel… empty.'

He was instantly alert, the doctor on duty. He sat up in bed.

'Do you have any pain?'

'A little… here.' She pointed to her lower abdomen.

'It might be nothing,' he said calmly, 'it could just be wind, or
bloating, don't panic. Do you want some tea?'

He returned a few minutes later with a tray and two cups of
tea. He opened the curtains. The dawn had come and gone, and
the sun was now twinkling low in the sky at the end of their bed.

'Lovely day,' he said as positively as he could. 'How are you feeling?'

'About the same…'

'OK – well just stay in bed and keep calm. I'll cancel my list
and give the clinic a call. I'll see if they can fit you in for another
test. I can take you in.'

'Who can you find to cover for you at the last minute?' she
asked. 'I'll drive myself. I'll be fine.'

'No, Sophie. John or someone will cover. He had a day off today, anyway. He was only going to play golf. I'll call him.'

The clinic offered them an appointment at two o'clock, and Hamish suggested they spend the morning in the garden. The cat joined them, rolling around in the early spring sunshine, rubbing his back against the rough flagstones. The hens clucked companionably around their feet, scratching in the dirt for worms and insects.

'We should maybe talk to Mick about getting a few more chicks – what do you say?' asked Hamish.

'What?' asked Sophie distractedly.

'More rare breeds. These old girls are fine as egg layers, but I was thinking of a few glamorous ones… Perhaps some Old English game hens – they're really beautiful.'

But Sophie wasn't listening. She could think of nothing but the unfamiliar empty sensation in her womb.

At one o'clock she was already in the hall, with her coat on.

'It's a bit early, darling,' said Hamish, 'our appointment's not till two.'

'Well I'm sure they won't mind. I need to find out what's happening.'

At the clinic, the nurse tried to be as encouraging as possible.

'It could be all sorts of things… try not to worry. You've been doing really well.'

'When will we know?' asked Sophie, holding back her emotions.

'Someone will call tomorrow with the results of this blood test.' The nurse smiled bravely, but Sophie had a sick, sinking feeling.

She began to bleed on the way home. Just a little at first, but she knew what it meant.

As the afternoon wore on, the bleeding became more profuse, and the cramps more severe – like the first day of her period. While she lay in bed, weeping, Hamish called the clinic.

'I'm really sorry,' the doctor told him. 'Just give her some pain relief – we'll be in touch with the results tomorrow, but it's not looking good.'

Hamish lay next to her in bed, as she wept. There was nothing he could say. All he could do was be there…

When the call finally came the following day, they didn't need to be told the results. She had lost the baby.

'I'm so sorry,' said the receptionist. 'If you'd like to come in and see the doctor, I can arrange something as soon as possible.'

Sophie could barely speak through her haze of tears. They choked her, suffocating her. Somehow, somewhere, the baby had gone. But where? The idea of her child disappearing was a form of torture. Had she peed it out on the loo? Had it slipped out in bed, or as she stood in front of the cooker? She was only a few weeks' pregnant - how small had it been? In her mind, she saw it as a complete child, a miniscule version of a human being. A tiny doll that had somehow been mislaid – like one of the figures who had inhabited her doll's house when she was a child.

Hamish encouraged her to stay in bed and rest. He covered her with a blanket, and lay next to her stroking her hair. Remarkably, after a little while, she fell asleep, exhausted by emotion.

She dreamt vividly of the lost baby – a little girl, no bigger than a lentil… like Thumbelina. She imagined her tiny child adrift in the world, wandering alone through the garden, with blades of grass towering above her head, calling for her mother. But she couldn't reach her. Couldn't find her. In her sleep she lashed out.

'Hey…' said Hamish, smoothing Sophie's hair away from her damp forehead. 'Your mother's not here, but I am. You've had a bad dream, that's all. You're too hot, darling… here… drink this.'

He helped her to sit up in bed and handed her a glass of water. Her lips were dry and cracked. Her eyes hot, still stinging from the tears.

'I lost the baby…' was all she could say.

Chapter 18

As the day of the family's departure from the island approached, Rachael's life became a round of domestic tasks – packing up belongings, cleaning the cottage and ensuring their final bills were settled.

She also had to prepare Angela for the family's return to city life – the hustle and bustle of London would be so at odds with their rural existence on the peaceful island. The cottage and the garden beyond were Angela's whole life. At nearly two and a half years of age, she spent many happy hours playing with a friendly lizard or a wriggling worm in the garden.

'That child will be a scientist – or a doctor perhaps,' George often said, as he observed his granddaughter. 'She is obsessed with how things work... have you noticed? Yesterday, she found a worm that didn't move. She brought it inside, put it into a matchbox and insisted that we "took its temperature". The thing was obviously dead, and I didn't really know what to say.'

'What did you do?' asked Rachael, packing a pile of George's books into a cardboard box.

'I held the thermometer against the worm's lifeless body. I was in two minds as to what I should say: to pronounce it miraculously recovered, or to be honest and tell her it had died in spite of the best of care. I chose the latter and she accepted it quite happily. "We did our best," she said, phlegmatically. Can you believe it? Extraordinary.'

Rachael smiled. 'She is extraordinary. I think she is very like her father – don't you? There is so much of József in her. She has passion, a desire to rush in and be involved – just like him. But you're right – she is also very analytical. I think she gets that from you…'

He nodded ruefully. 'Possibly,' he said, a little smugly.

On the surface, Rachael appeared to have accepted her separation from Tommaso. She went about her chores – she cooked, cleaned, shopped and packed. But he was never far from her thoughts. With every box she filled, her mind wandered to their last days together. Whenever she went into the garden to pick tomatoes for lunch or to sit on the veranda soaking up the last rays of autumn sunshine, she was aware of the little gate leading down to the water's edge and the rope Tommaso had put there to protect her child. The rope was a little frayed now, but it remained a constant reminder of his kindness and love to her and her daughter.

One afternoon, she and Angela were sitting on the veranda preparing vegetables for supper when she heard the familiar sound of a scooter winding its way down the lane. Convinced it was Tommaso, she stood up abruptly, knocking the chopped fennel to the ground; she removed her apron and smoothed her hair, in anticipation of him appearing at any moment. He had come to whisk her away, she thought – to tell her he had broken his engagement and defied his family. But it was only a young couple, searching for an accessible beach.

'I'm sorry,' she told them, 'this beach is private – just for the house.'

When they expressed surprise, she shrugged her shoulders.

'There's a public beach further along the coast you can use… just follow the signs to *Spiaggia*.'

She felt relief as she watched them disappearing up the lane. The idea of strangers lying on the beach, gazing at the view, was unbearable. It was the place, after all, where Tommaso had rescued her baby, where he had first kissed her, where they had said their final goodbye. It was his beach... *their* beach.

As the family's final twenty-four hours in the cottage approached, Rachael began to feel a sense of desolation that she would never see Tommaso again. Her spirits were so low, she struggled with even the simplest task.

On their final day, she lay on her bed, the shutters closed, surrounded by boxes of possessions. Angela, bored by her mother's inaction, clambered on top of her.

'Mama... Mama... let's go beach.'

All right,' Rachael said weakly, struggling to her feet. 'Give me a minute to change. You go and put your costume on.'

Downstairs in the kitchen, she filled a basket with towels and made a small picnic with the last of the bread and a couple of plums.

At the cove, they paddled in the warm water and explored the rocks at either end of the beach. But Angela was determined to have one final swim.

'Lesson, Mama,' she said, running into the water. Rachael followed her, and stood guard next to her daughter, as she swam a few strokes of doggy paddle.

'Good Angela,' she said, encouragingly, her hands hovering beneath the child's body, ready to catch her. Suddenly, over the sound of splashing water, she heard the familiar sound of the Lambretta.

'Angela, darling...' she said, urgently, 'come – we must go back to the house... quickly.'

'No, Mama – I'm swimming... look.' The child refused to get out of the water.

Rachael was desperate to get back to the cottage and see if Tommaso had come at last. It would be so like him to want to say goodbye. She tried to drag Angela out of the water, but the child kicked and screamed. Rachael heard the sound of the bike as it roared away again up the lane. When she finally persuaded Angela back to the house, there was no sign of anyone.

Opening the door, she saw an envelope on the kitchen table, addressed to her. As she tore it open, a photograph fell out. It was of Tommaso, leaning against his boat. He was smiling but there was sadness in his eyes. Rachael held the photograph to her breast, before tucking it into a side pocket of her handbag. To have missed him, and this final last chance to say goodbye, seemed so unfair. She began to weep silently, taking some onions from the basket on the dresser and chopping them at the table, to disguise her tears.

'Why you crying, Mama,' asked Angela, kicking her legs against one of the chairs as she ate some bread and butter from the picnic basket.

'It's just the onions,' Rachael answered.

At six o'clock, as Angela concentrated on a jigsaw puzzle at the kitchen table and Rachael stirred a pot of risotto for dinner, she heard the sound of Giles' truck coming down the lane. She should invite him to stay for dinner, she thought – it would be an act of friendship on their last night. She checked inside the pot – there was just enough for four people.

The truck came to a halt outside, and Rachael heard the sound of raucous male laughter. She moved the pot to one side of the range, so it wouldn't catch, wiped her face and hands with her apron, before taking it off, and went out onto the veranda. A group of young men stood excitedly around their professor.

'Ah Rachael,' George said cheerfully, 'I've brought all the students back for a little supper – as it's our last night.'

She looked at the group of cheerful, happy young men and smiled politely, pulling her father into the kitchen.

'What do you expect me to feed them on?' she whispered. 'We have hardly anything left. We are leaving tomorrow. The cupboards are bare. I have a small pot of risotto for supper – nothing else.'

George looked slightly perplexed. 'Can't we make more risotto?' he asked logically.

Giles came into the kitchen, sensing a domestic crisis.

'Is there anything I can do…? I realise things might be tricky – what with you leaving tomorrow. Pete and I have supplies at our place. Let me go and bring what we have. I'm sure we can concoct something edible for them. They're all just so keen to show their appreciation to the professor…' He looked hopefully at Rachael, seeking her approval.

'Of course,' she said, at last, smiling. 'Of course they can stay. I've got a little risotto here. I can perhaps make some more, but I don't have much else – some tomatoes in the garden and a bit of fruit…'

'That's wonderful,' said Giles, enthusiastically. 'I'll bring the rest. Oh, and there's a large bottle of local wine on the table – we picked it up in town before we came over.'

The bottle, wrapped in raffia, was poured into glasses and handed round. Giles roared off up the lane and returned thirty minutes later with a large salami, fresh bread, tomatoes and a hunk of local cheese.

As Rachael lit candles and arranged them down the long table, she observed the young men – laughing together, sharing memories of their experiences on the island and toasting George. In spite of her sadness, she felt pride in her father and what he had achieved. When the meal was finished and the glasses replenished, George rose to speak.

'When we left Hungary – my daughter and I – little did I realise what opportunities awaited me in London, nor that I should have such a remarkable second chapter to my career and be privileged to teach such intelligent and enthusiastic students. But what I really never anticipated was that I would be given the opportunity to lead such an important dig once again in the autumn of my days. So, please raise your glasses: here's to you – my young compatriots, my fellow archaeologists.' He raised his glass, and the group cheered and whooped.

'To us!' the group shouted.

'And we should not forget the lady who brought us all here in the first place. Here's to Queen Berenice and her mystery burial partner...'

'To Queen Berenice,' they chorused.

'I should like to say one more thing,' George continued, when the cheering had died down. 'I would like to thank my daughter Rachael – without whom I would almost certainly be dead – lying starved, like a shrunken corpse, next to my beloved Berenice...' He smiled impishly, and the young men roared with laughter.

'Darling Rachael,' he continued, holding his glass up to her, 'without you, this trip would have been impossible. Thank you for coming with me, for feeding and caring for me, and for the joy you bring to me and everyone who knows you.' As he looked around at the young men gathered at their table, his gaze fell upon Giles, who had tears in his eyes. 'To Rachael,' George said.

'To Rachael,' echoed the students.

The following morning, as Rachael turned the key in the lock for the final time, replacing it beneath the pot of geraniums, she felt as if she was saying goodbye to a dear friend.

As Giles and George loaded the family's luggage into the truck, she wandered one last time down through the copse to the sea. She scanned the cove for signs of Tommaso – but the horizon was clear. Walking back through the garden, she automatically tied the rope around the gate. Passing the veranda table, her fingers trailed across it, reflecting on all the happy times they had spent there.

As they drove through the village, past the shopkeepers she had come to know, past the atelier where women sat outside in the autumn sunshine, carding and spinning, she waved quietly, wiping tears from her eyes. At the cafe in the square, she scanned the area for any sight of Tommaso, her heart beating fast. She wanted so desperately to see him, to embrace him and beg him to allow her to stay. But he was nowhere to be seen.

They drove on down the steep cobbled street that led to the market. As they crossed the causeway back to the mainland of Sardinia, she noticed a fleet of fishing boats leaving the harbour. For a brief moment she thought she saw Tommaso's boat – the familiar outline, the blue paintwork. But she could not be sure. She craned her head, following the fleet out to sea, until the boats disappeared over the horizon.

'You'll be sad to say goodbye to it all, I imagine,' said Giles.

'Yes,' was all she could reply.

They drove back to Cagliari in relative silence – all of them, in their own way, experiencing a sense of anti-climax. For Giles and Peter the adventure was over; they would be back at university the following week. There would be lectures, and homework, student digs and pints of warm beer in the student union. The long hot summer days on an island in the sun were at an end.

When they arrived at the port, Rachael helped Angela out of the truck, while Giles and Peter unloaded the family's luggage. Once assembled on the side of the dock, they stood awkwardly together, uncertain, now the time had finally come, how to say goodbye. George broke the silence.

'Well… goodbye,' he said, shaking the two students vigorously by the hand, 'and well done both of you. I am proud of what we have achieved together. See you back in London.'

'Goodbye, Pete,' said Rachael, kissing him on each cheek. 'Thanks for everything.'

She turned to Giles.

'Thanks—' she began.

'Well…' he interrupted. Then, blushing and shifting uneasily on his feet, he laughed nervously. 'You go first,' he said.

'I hope your packing all goes well.'

'Oh yes – we'll be fine. You have a safe trip. Look after yourself… and perhaps we can meet in London?'

'Yes… and thanks for all you did for us. Finding the house, taking me to town…'

Angela, bored with these formal goodbyes, interrupted, 'Mama, Mama… there's our boat…' she said, pointing at the ferry already docked at the harbour.

'Yes, darling. That's our boat; we'll go back to the mainland to Italy, and then…' she gazed out to sea. This was it; she was leaving, leaving *him* behind; and the dreams she had had of living with Tommaso were ebbing away like the tide edging away from the shore. 'Well,' she said, turning back to Giles, 'we'd better be going.'

'Yes… yes of course. See you then?'

She could hear the hope in his voice. She knew he was waiting for her to say, 'Yes… let's meet up as soon as possible in London.' She wished she could be kind, but what was the point of giving him false hope? It was not Giles she wanted to see; he could not fill the gap that had been left in her heart.

Once on board the ferry, George put his arm around Rachael as they stood on the deck. 'Be brave, darling …' he whispered into her ear, 'this is the start of something – you'll see…'

As the ferry backed away from the harbour, Rachael picked Angela up and they waved at Pete and Giles, now just two tiny stick figures on the harbour wall.

Could she ever be really happy again, she wondered. Was her father right – could she find a new beginning?

The golden buildings of Cagliari retreated in the distance, as the ferry ploughed through the emerald waters of the Mediterranean. Rachael stood on the deck long after George had taken

Angela down below to their cabin. She stood there until the island had disappeared from view and all that was left was a vast empty horizon. For Rachael, this was the end not the beginning. It was the end of her dream of living on this island in the sun with the man she adored. It was the end of love.

PART THREE

If you want to keep a secret,
you must also hide if from yourself.
George Orwell, 1984

CHAPTER 19

London
November 1959

It was early November. Oak leaves blew in great drifts up Willow Road, mixing with the thick mulch of sweet chestnuts that coagulated on the pavements. Rachael and George had been back in England for a month and Rachael still struggled to adjust to the chill wind and the pale grey skies, so at odds with the sparkling turquoise waters of Sant'Antioco.

In the days it had taken for Rachael and George to travel back to England, her father had tried his best to comfort his heartbroken daughter. He reiterated the rational arguments as to why her relationship with Tommaso could never have worked. It would have been impossible for her to stay on Sant'Antioco, he reasoned. Tommaso's family would have rejected him, and the community would have turned their backs on them both. And if Tommaso had returned with Rachael, how would a simple fisherman, however bright and intelligent, cope in a city like London, torn apart from everything he knew? Rachael knew that George was right of course, but these arguments, however rational, did not address the central issue – that she was still hopelessly in love with the young Italian.

Mrs Roper was, predictably, delighted to see them.

'Oh, Rachael… and little Angela – look how you've grown! Oh, professor, it's so good to have you all back. We've missed you. Now… the attics are all ready for you and I've taken the liberty of giving you another room on the floor below. That naughty boy

Max has left finally – moved to America, I think. So there was a room free, and I thought… maybe the professor would like it? Then Angela could have the little room and Rachael could have the room next to her. Would that be in order? The rent will only be a little more…'

'That is most thoughtful,' George had replied. 'Thank you, Mrs Roper.'

The family soon settled back into their routines. George went off to the university each day, while Rachael looked after Angela. The child became bored easily and Rachael began to take her for regular walks on the heath. They fed the ducks, studied the birds and trees and, from time to time, Rachael took her daughter to the playground. There she met other young mothers with whom she formed a sort of bond. They would watch their children play together or drink strong tea in the cafe. These women were friendly enough, perhaps a little curious about the Hungarian woman who had lived in Italy and had no husband. But for Rachael, it was a way of spending the time, a useful distraction which prevented her from dwelling on the past. For she couldn't forget Tommaso – the man who had woken a secret part of her, who had turned her from an innocent girl, albeit a young mother, to a woman capable of great physical passion.

One afternoon, after visiting the heath, she walked down Haverstock Hill with Angela. In the window of a shabby antique shop stood a small painted Victorian bureau.

'Let's go inside,' she said to Angela, 'and look at that pretty desk.'

The piece was retrieved from its place in the shop window and Rachael stood back to admire it. It was painted a delicate shade of pale green. The three drawers at the base would provide useful storage, she thought. But she was most taken by the upper part of the desk, with its six small drawers and secret cubbyhole in the centre that could be locked with a brass key. The top of the bureau was concealed by a flap, which formed a writing surface when opened. The flap was decorated with a motif of red roses, exploding into flower from a dark green trailing stem. Rachael negotiated a good price and the bureau was delivered to the attic the following day. She positioned it in the window, so she could look out at the heath. She filled the three large drawers at the bottom with her clothes, and the small drawers above with keepsakes, writing paper and one or two photographs.

She unlocked the small central cupboard. She felt around with her hand and discovered the back of the cupboard was loose and came away quite easily, revealing a secret compartment. Delighted, she removed the photograph of Tommaso from the side pocket of her handbag and wrote on the back: 'Tommaso, my love... Sant'Antioco 1959' before placing the photograph safely in the compartment, replacing the panel and locking the cupboard. She slid the key into one of the drawers beneath a pile of writing paper.

Over the next few weeks, Rachael took stock of her life, brooding on something her father had said to her when they had been on the island. He had suggested she was incapable of supporting herself financially, and he was right. If anything happened to him, how would she and Angela survive? Angela was two and a half years old; in a year or so, she could go to nursery school. With her child occupied for part of the day, how would Rachael fill her time? Mrs Roper did most of the cooking, and tidying and cleaning the attic rooms hardly took an hour, let alone a day. It was time, Rachael decided, to find some sort of occupation. And in order do that she should first get some qualifications. If she passed her General Certificates of Education, she might even go to university one day. She could become a teacher, or maybe even a doctor. She was still young – only twenty-three, and there was no reason why she could not achieve something with her life. She signed up for a course in mathematics at the local night school, attending two evening sessions a week, while her father watched over Angela. She worked her way assiduously through the syllabus during the day, while her daughter played downstairs with Mrs Roper. Gradually, Rachael began to value the time she had to herself. When she was concentrating on a mathematical problem, she had to give it her full attention. There was no room for heartache, and slowly, over time, her longing for Tommaso began to recede.

One afternoon, as she finished her work, she stood up and caught sight of herself in the mirror that hung above her bed. Her stomach was protruding slightly. She had noticed that morning that her skirt felt tight. Was she eating too much? Her breasts were tender – perhaps her period was due?

She sat down at her desk and opened her diary. Since Angela's birth she had written the letter 'P' on the day she started her period. There had been no entries for several months. How could she have not noticed? Her periods were always a little erratic and at first it had seemed unimportant that she was late. She had been so broken-hearted that it simply didn't cross her mind to think about it. Then – packing up the house, saying goodbye to Giles and Peter, sorting out the attic in London – had taken so much of time, she had, somehow, ignored the absence of her monthly bleed.

Flicking through the pages of her diary, she tried to work out when she had last slept with Tommaso. There was an entry on 25 July that said, simply: 'The end… Papa said it must stop.'

That was the last time she and Tommaso had made love.

It was now 13 November. It would be sixteen weeks tomorrow… She was four months pregnant.

She felt sick with anxiety and sat with her head in her hands. How could she have been so careless? So stupid? Her mind was racing. What could she do? The shame of having a child without a father would be terrible. What would her father say? What would Mrs Roper say? She would certainly throw them all out onto the street. They would be destitute and it would be Rachael's fault.

She thought back to the day she discovered she was pregnant with Angela. That had been a shock too – but in a different way. It had been a miracle of sorts… a part of József that had survived his violent death on the streets of Budapest. She had been frightened then – not of disapproval, but rather of the responsibility of bringing a child into the world without a father, and at a time that was so full of hatred and uncertainty.

Her thoughts were interrupted by the sound of her daughter's voice, chirruping away to Mrs Roper. They were coming up the stairs.

'Ah… there's Mummy,' said Mrs Roper. 'Working hard? I hope we're not interrupting, dear, but Angela's a little tired, and I really need to get on with supper now.'

'Yes… yes of course,' said Rachael, closing her diary and swinging round to face them. 'Thank you so much for looking after her.'

'Oh no trouble, dear. How's it going… the studying? OK is it? I've never been any good at maths – terrible with figures.'

'Yes… it's going well, thank you.' Rachael said, politely.

'Well, see you later.' Mrs Roper clattered back down the stairs.

Rachael settled Angela in bed for a nap and, when she was confident that she was asleep, returned to her own room.

'What can I do… what can I do?' she muttered as she paced up and down.

The following twenty-four hours were spent in emotional turmoil. Rachael tried to convince herself that, perhaps, there was some other explanation for her absent periods. Some illness perhaps – she had heard of such things happening. There were fleeting moments when she was reading a book, or studying a mathematical problem, when she could almost forget it all, but they were rare. Realising she couldn't avoid the issue any longer, she booked an appointment to see the doctor, after first persuading Mrs Roper to look after Angela.

*

The doctor's consulting room was in the front room of his family home – a large double-fronted Edwardian house on a leafy street in Hampstead. As Rachael sat nervously on a stiff upright chair in the panelled waiting room, she could hear the distant sounds of children crying, a mother's voice gently comforting them. The last time Rachael had been to see the doctor she had brought Angela for an inoculation. She remembered he had been good with children.

'Mrs Kelemen…' said the receptionist. 'Dr McLean will see you now.'

The doctor was tall and good-looking. In spite of the cold weather outside, he had removed his jacket and rolled up his shirtsleeves. He stood up politely as Rachael tentatively opened the door to his consulting room.

'Good morning, Mrs Kelemen. Do come in. I don't think I've seen you for some time?'

'No… we've been abroad for a while.'

'I see. Do please sit down. What seems to be the trouble?'

Rachael sat opposite him, blushing, and biting her lip.

'There's nothing to worry about…' he said. 'Would you like my receptionist to come in?'

'No! No… the thing is… I think I might be pregnant.' The sentence came out in a rush.

'I see. And what symptoms do you have?' he asked, dispassionately.

'I haven't had a period for four months.'

'Anything else? Painful breasts, thickening of the waist, morning sickness?'

'Um… no sickness, no. My breasts… maybe, and I've definitely put on a little weight.'

'OK…' he said gently, 'well, slip off your skirt please and jump up on the couch.'

The examination over, Rachael sat back down in the chair opposite the doctor.

'It does appear you are pregnant. But I will do a test to confirm it. If you could leave a urine sample...' he handed her a little pot with a lid. 'There's a lavatory next to the receptionist's office. Hand it to Mary when you've finished, and she'll send it to the lab. We'll have the result in a few days.'

'So... I may not be?'

'Well, the signs are all pointing to a positive test, I have to confess, but let's get the result first.'

She stood up to leave.

'Mrs Kelemen...' Dr MacLean said, glancing up from his notes, 'before you go. Your husband... I thought he was...'

'Yes. My husband is dead... yes.'

'Yes, I have it in your notes. The last time I saw you was a year or so ago – when you brought your daughter, Angela, for an inoculation. I think you mentioned your husband then.'

Rachael sensed his disapproval. He was trying to be kind, but she knew, deep down, he was judging her.

'Well,' she said, backing hesitantly out of his consulting room. 'Thank you.'

'If I can help...' he said gently, 'with any advice, or support... you will let me know?'

As she stood outside the doctor's offices four days later and opened the test results, Rachael's hands were shaking. It was exactly as she had feared.

She walked back to Willow Road, her mind in turmoil. She needed advice desperately. She couldn't confide in her father or Mrs Roper. She remembered a conversation she'd had a few weeks earlier with one of the mothers she had befriended on the heath. Sandy was a tall pretty blonde, with three children under the age of five.

'I simply couldn't cope with another child,' she'd said to Rachael one afternoon, as they drank tea in the cafe. 'I'd literally go mad.

I'm run ragged by them as it is and my husband's never at home. We try to be careful, but every month I'm on edge in case my period doesn't come. To be honest, if I did get pregnant, I think I'd get rid of it...'

'What do you mean?' Rachael had asked, innocently.

'Well... you know.'

'No,' Rachael had replied honestly, 'I don't know.'

'Don't they have abortions in Hungary?'

'Abortions... what is that?'

'Oh, you are green,' said Sandy. 'It's when you have an operation to remove the child... you know... get rid of it,' she'd whispered.

'Kill it?' Rachael had asked, aghast.

'Well... yes. I suppose. You don't have to look so shocked – it's not a real baby, not then. Anyway, that's what I'd do. You'd have to find someone though. It's not easy. Well it's illegal isn't it?' She'd sighed and turned to her eldest child. 'Oh Jonny, do stop doing that... Leave the baby alone.'

The waitress came and took their cups and they said nothing more.

Now, Rachael decided she had to talk to Sandy as soon as possible. What had she meant by 'finding someone'?

The following morning, she asked Mrs Roper if she could watch over Angela for an hour or two.

'Yes, dear. You got to pop out? Studying is it?'

'Yes... something like that. Thank you... I won't be long.'

She ran down Willow Road towards the cafe on the heath, hoping that Sandy would be there. She saw her through the window, sitting with another woman – slighter than Sandy, with auburn hair.

'Hello stranger,' Sandy said, as Rachael approached their table. 'Caroline, this is Rachael – a friend from Hungary. She has a little girl called Angela. Where is she this morning?'

'I... left her at home with the landlady. It's nice to meet you, Caroline.'

'Sit down,' said Sandy, pulling out a chair.

'No... thank you. I'll come back another time. I needed a word, Sandy, but it can wait.'

'No, you sit,' said Caroline, standing up and putting on her coat. 'I was just leaving anyway. Nice to meet you... See you soon, Sandy...'

Caroline backed her pram out of the doorway.

'So,' said Sandy, patting the chair beside her, 'where's the fire?'

'The fire?' said Rachael, sitting down. 'I'm sorry, I don't understand...'

'I mean... what's the problem? You seem all... anxious and flustered.'

The waitress bustled over to their table. 'Can I get you anything?' she asked, licking her pencil.

'Just a cup of tea... thank you,' said Rachael, waiting for the waitress to leave.

'So...?' said Sandy

'I don't know how to say it,' whispered Rachael.

'Just say it...'

'I'm pregnant.'

The waitress returned and put a pot of tea and an extra cup on the table, glancing sideways at Rachael as she did so.

'Do you think she heard me?' whispered Rachael once the waitress was safely back behind the counter.

'So what if she did?' said Sandy, flippantly. 'So – do I detect that you are not altogether delighted?'

'It's just so complicated.'

'I imagine it is... you not being married and all. Can I ask – who's the father?'

'A man I met in Sardinia... on Sant'Antioco. We fell in love. I wanted to stay with him, but it was not possible.'

'Why?'

'It turned out that he was engaged, promised to someone.'

'Ha… why am I not surprised? Bastard.'

'No… it was not like that.'

'Yeah… I know. They're never "like that". But he got you pregnant and wasn't in a position to do the right thing. I'm sorry, Rachael, but he's a bastard… So you need to do something about it?'

'Yes… I must. My father would… he would so angry. So disappointed.' Rachael's eyes filled with tears. She felt a bewildering combination of emotions. Embarrassment that she could have been so foolish, as well as shame. But above all – sadness and loss for the man she loved. Her friend was wrong to condemn him. He wasn't some 'bastard' who had used her. He had loved her. And now she was carrying his child – a child she couldn't keep.

'I understand,' said Sandy, reaching across the table, and taking her hand. 'It's difficult. But I'll help you – we'll get this sorted – all right?'

Rachael, nodded uncertainly; she wiped her eyes and sipped her tea.

'Now, if you've got a lot of money there are doctors in Harley Street who'll take care of it. But you'll need around a hundred pounds.'

'I don't have such money,' said Rachael, aghast. 'And how can I ask my father…?'

'Well, if you don't have the money, there are other people. Not proper doctors, but they know what they're doing. I don't know anyone myself, but I know someone who does. Someone who… had to go through it. How far gone are you?'

'Sixteen weeks.'

'Well that's precise… You're sure?'

'Yes… I had a test done at the doctor's…'

'Oh… so he knows, does he? That might make it complicated.'

'Why?'

'Well… think about it. He knows you're pregnant. If you go ahead and… do what we're talking about,' she had dropped her voice to a whisper, 'questions could be asked.'

'Couldn't I say I'd lost the baby?'

'Yes… I suppose… Well, there's nothing else for it. But you can't hang about. It's much harder the longer you wait. Come back here tomorrow at ten, and I'll have a name for you.'

That evening after Rachael had bathed Angela and dressed her in her pyjamas, she lay with the child – as she often did – comforting her until she fell asleep. She thought back to her first pregnancy. It had been such a shock initially – to find herself pregnant by her dead husband. She'd wondered then how she would cope. But she had, and now she had a beautiful golden-haired child – her bright, funny angel who she loved more than her own life.

She ran her hands down over her swelling stomach. She thought about the child she was carrying. Would this one have Tommaso's dark hair, his dark brown eyes? Could she really rip it out of her body, dispense with it, end it…?

Later, as Rachael and George ate Mrs Roper's shepherd's pie in the dining room, George noticed Rachael pushing her food to the edge of the plate. He reached across the table and took her hand.

'Rachael… is something the matter – are you not hungry?'

'No,' she said weakly.

'Something is bothering you… tell me.'

'It's nothing. Nothing at all, really.'

How could she tell him? How could she disappoint him so?

That night, as she lay in her single bed, the thin curtains glowed in the moonlight. Unable to sleep, she crept out of bed, anxious not to disturb Angela in the little room next door. She opened the desk and unlocked the central cupboard. She removed the false panel at the back and took out the photograph of Tommaso. She studied his face – the strong jaw, the long dark hair. Had Sandy been right? Was he, in fact, just an unreliable young man, seeking pleasure without taking responsibility? Had their relationship been an illusion?

No, she decided, kissing the photograph, that was not true. Had he known she was pregnant, she felt sure he would have supported her. But he didn't know, and she was on her own. This was a decision she must make alone.

She put the photograph back in its hiding place.

'It's just an operation,' she told herself as she climbed back into bed. 'Like an appendicitis, or having your tonsils out...'

She fell asleep finally, just before dawn, and was woken just a couple of hours later by Angela padding through from her bedroom, slipping beneath the eiderdown and lying next to her mother. Holding her daughter close, Rachael wept silently.

After breakfast, she went down to the kitchen in search of Mrs Roper.

'I have to go... to a college today. For an exam.' She hated lying. 'I don't know how long I'll be. Could you take Angela for me – please?'

'Yes, dear, all right. What time will you be back?'

'I don't know... late. After six, maybe.'

'All right. I'll put her to bed for you if you're really late...'

'Oh, thank you so much.'

'Is everything all right?' asked Mrs Roper, taking Angela's hand. 'You look a little pale.'

'I'm fine. See you later.'

She found Sandy waiting in the cafe, as promised.

Her friend slid a piece of paper over the table towards her. 'Here you go... they're good, so I've been told. But you mustn't tell anyone. Do you understand, Rachael? It's illegal; you could go to prison, and probably so could I... for just giving you the name.'

'Don't worry… I will tell no one.'

'Not even your dad?'

'No! Definitely not him. No one… I promise.'

The address on the piece of paper was in East London. It would take over an hour to get there by bus. The street, when she found it, was more like an alley – narrow and dark with piles of rubbish gathering at the edges. There was a sex shop on the corner, advertising erotic dancers. Rachael scurried past, trying to ignore the photographs of women in scanty clothing. Halfway down the alley, a man lay drunkenly in the darkness of doorway. He reached out for Rachael as she passed him, touching her calf with his filthy hand. She recoiled and stumbled on.

Anxiously scanning the piece of paper in hand, she realised she had arrived at her destination. The doorway was unremarkable – a perfectly ordinary, brown scuffed door with a knocker in the middle.

A woman's voice called out as she knocked. 'Who is it?'

'My name is Rachael… I've been given your address by a… friend.'

'What do you want?'

'I need help.'

Locks slid back and the door opened into a dark corridor with peeling wallpaper and ripped lino on the floor. An Alsatian stood guarding the kitchen at the end of the corridor. He growled as Rachael stepped across the threshold.

'Don't mind him,' said the voice, 'come in.'

As the door closed behind her, Rachael came face to face with a world-weary middle-aged woman wearing an apron over her cotton dress, her brown hair flecked with grey, caught up in a hairnet. She had an air of defeat about her.

'Through there…' she said, directing Rachael to the front room. 'Have you got the money?'

'I wasn't sure how much.'

'Ten pounds. That's the price. Take it or leave it.'

Rachael had a little more than ten pounds in her purse. It was all the money she had saved. She had hoped to use it for her education, or for Angela.

'Yes... I have the money.'

'And how far gone are you?'

'Sixteen weeks.'

'Right... well hand over the money and then lie down there.' She pointed to a table, covered in newspaper. An array of sharp-pointed instruments were laid out on a smaller table at the foot. It was an orderly arrangement, consisting of a coat hanger, a knitting needle, a small hook and a long tube with one end soaking in a bowl of liquid. There was an overpowering smell of disinfectant.

Rachael's hand shook as she placed the pile of notes down next to the bowl. She removed her coat and looked around the dingy room for somewhere to put it. She placed it carefully over a chair, anxious it should be uncontaminated by any part of this sordid room. Gingerly, she lay down on the hard table, the newspaper rucking up beneath her, rustling as she tried to make herself comfortable. She looked up at the ceiling, staring at the peeling paintwork, trying to concentrate on a brown nicotine stain at the centre of the telltale marks of an old flood. She wondered fleetingly what might have caused such water damage but the smell of disinfectant suddenly caught in the back of her throat, causing her to wretch. She swallowed hard as waves of nausea washed over her.

'Well, take your pants off first,' said the woman, a tinge of irritation in her voice.

Rachael stood back up clumsily and lifted her dress. As she bent down to remove her underwear, she felt the room spinning around her. Reggae music pulsed through the room from the floor above. The drunk outside was shouting at a passer-by. She thought of Tommaso – beautiful, loving Tommaso – and of what they had meant to each other. She thought of the child inside her... their child.

'Well come on,' said the woman, impatiently, 'I haven't got all day.'

'I... I don't...' Rachael stumbled backwards.

'What is it?' said the woman, glaring at Rachael.

'I'm sorry. I can't do this...' She snatched up the money, and grabbed her coat, knocking the vicious-looking hook off the table as she rushed out of the room.

'Oi, careful,' said the woman, picking the hook up from the floor.

As Rachael yanked open the front door, the Alsatian, sensing danger, rushed forwards, eager to defend his owner. Its teeth connected with Rachael's calf, just as she fell out into the street. She managed to slam the door shut behind her and heard the dog yelping. Wincing with pain, she staggered up the alley, inhaling the sour stench of urine and vomit. The drunk came reeling along the alleyway and collided with Rachael as she ran towards the main road. She felt his stubble against her face, the stench of alcohol on his breath.

She jumped onto the first bus she saw and sat down, her calf throbbing, blood dripping onto her dark brown shoes. She put her head in her hands and sobbed.

Chapter 20

London
March 2017

In the weeks following Sophie's miscarriage, Hamish went out of his way to be kind and caring. But in spite of his love and attention, Sophie sank into a depression. She lost all her enthusiasm for life, showed little interest in her appearance – hardly bothering to wash her hair, or change her clothes. She slept fitfully at night, roaming the house in the early hours, then sleeping deeply on the sofa during the day. Hamish, concerned for her mental health, suggested a possible course of antidepressants.

'I don't need medication,' she snapped. 'I'm entitled to be sad… I've lost our child. Don't you understand?'

He did understand, of course, but in his rational medical world, the loss of a four-week-old foetus was just a setback; it was not the end of their journey towards parenthood. It was certainly not a reason to give up on life.

A few days after Sophie's miscarriage, the consultant who had been in charge of her IVF treatment rang with his condolences.

'Are you keen to have another try?' he asked.

'I don't know,' said Sophie. 'Maybe… In a little while. I just need to…' she'd trailed off, uncertain how to explain her feelings. How could she use the word 'grieve'? It sounded ridiculous. She had only been a few weeks pregnant; it was just a collection of cells. Women miscarried babies all the time at that stage and had no idea it was even happening. Why was she justified in feeling so much grief when parents all over the world were coping with the death of their children from illnesses like cancer? Or losing their young people in the prime of their lives through knife crime, guns or war. That was grief. When you lost a child who was a real, sentient human being, someone you could chat to on the phone, whose hopes and dreams you could share. To lose a child like that would be unimaginable. The grief would never end. And yet she had loved her tiny little 'lentil' child… and now felt utterly bereft.

'To grieve?' suggested the consultant.

'Yes!' she said, surprised by his sensitivity. 'How did you know?'

'You're not the first patient I've had who's lost a baby… We do understand. But when you're ready to start again, get in touch.'

Sophie's birthday fell almost two months to the day after the miscarriage. She would be thirty-four. Hamish tried to persuade her that they should go to a restaurant or see friends.

'Come on, darling… I know you're still sad about the miscarriage. I am too. But we have to get on with our lives, we need to have some fun.'

Sophie could hardly bring herself to respond. She knew Hamish meant well, that he was just trying to be supportive in his own way. But she didn't feel like having fun. And 'sad' was just not adequate to describe her emotions about the baby she had lost. It was so much more than sad. She felt engulfed in grief. Another year had passed and she was still no closer to becoming a mother.

'Please Hamish… just leave it. I'm going to London on my birthday. It's time I got back to work. I'm not celebrating and that's that.'

On the morning of her birthday, she woke early. As she stood in the shower and washed her hair for the first time in over a week, she breathed deeply, visualising her pain spinning away down the plug hole. She dried her hair and put on her clothes in the bedroom

next door, so as not to wake Hamish – who'd come in late the night
before. Dressed and ready to leave, she stood in the doorway of
their bedroom, watching him sleep. She felt a pang of sympathy
for him. It hadn't been easy for him either over the last few weeks.
Tiptoeing across the room, she leant over to the bed and kissed
him on the cheek. He opened his eyes sleepily.

'Morning, sweetheart,' he mumbled. 'Happy birthday.'

'Shhhh…' she whispered, 'speak later.'

On the train to Paddington, she opened her work bag.
Nestling next to her laptop was a small parcel. Judging by the
inadequate wrapping, it was a gift from Hamish. He must have
left it there when he came in the previous night. Self-consciously
she removed the present and laid it on the table in front of her.
The passengers around her smiled and tried not to look as she
ripped open the brown paper. Inside was a beautifully painted
Russian doll. She unscrewed the largest doll, revealing the
smaller one inside. There were seven dolls in all. Hamish must
have bought it one afternoon when they had gone to Cirencester
together. They'd wandered round the market in the Corn Hall
and she had admired the Russian dolls on one of the stalls. He
must have gone back for it while she was in the supermarket. She
remembered him making some excuse – something he needed
to buy. She unscrewed all the dolls and lined them up on the
table. They were dressed in pink and green outfits edged with
gold and had the sweetest faces.

At the sight of all these 'mothers' and 'daughters', going back
seven generations, she felt tears welling up. As she blew her nose,
she thought of her grandmother, her mother, herself, the daughter
she might never have.

She replaced the dolls one by one, wrapped them back in the
brown paper and tucked them into her bag. She opened the card.

'To my darling Sophie…if ever there was a mother in the
making – it's you. Happy Birthday. All my love, Hamish.'

She blew her nose once again and wiped her eyes. The man sitting opposite her smiled sympathetically.

'Nice present,' he said.

'Yes… from my husband.'

He nodded, uncertain what else he could say.

Embarrassed by her public display of emotion, she removed her laptop and flipped it open on the table between them. It would be good to get back to work. She had been so preoccupied with the IVF, she had let her work slide. Her PhD supervisor had been very understanding.

'Just come back when you can, Sophie,' he'd said. 'Take your time.'

But she was glad that her period of inactivity was over.

She arrived at her office just after ten and found Michael, her supervisor, hovering anxiously near her desk.

'Sophie,' he began, 'I just wanted to say…'

'It's OK, Michael. You don't need to say anything. I know everyone is sad for me. And it's very kind. But I'd rather just get on and concentrate on my work… if that's all right. Please don't think I'm not grateful for your concern.'

'Quite… good,' he said, backing away, emanating a strong sense of relief that he was not required to 'empathise'. 'Lunch later? Quick catch-up on where you're heading with everything?'

'Yes… lunch would be good.'

She put the Russian doll onto her desk and opened her laptop. She felt nervous – it had been so long since she had done any serious research. Delaying the vital moment, she went the university canteen and brought a coffee back to her tiny office. Then, shutting the door, she began to read through her notes.

An image of her little 'lentil' child floated uninvited into her mind. She shook her head, as if the physical act could banish her thoughts.

'Concentrate,' she said out loud.

She had collected a number of references to byssus cloth. Various pieces of this fabric had been uncovered since her great-grandfather's original discovery in 1912.

A cap made of sea silk had been found in 1978 in the damp basement of the Basilica in St Denis near Paris. The item, made in the fourteenth century, was now kept in the collection of the Musée d'art et d'histoire in St Denis. It looked a little bit like a beanie, Sophie thought. She studied the little headdress. It was so small, it had surely been made for a child. Her own lost child floated back into her mind, until she pushed it away.

She scrolled down through the articles and discovered that many items of sea silk clothing had ended up in museums of natural history. Travellers on the grand tour in the seventeenth and eighteenth centuries had often brought pieces home from Italy and Greece as souvenirs. They were then displayed in cabinets of 'curiosity' – the items of clothing lying next to the *Pinna nobilis* shell and its beard. A Museum in Rouen and another in Strasbourg both had long sea silk gauntlets on display. But the oldest reference she could find for these 'curious items' came from an English traveller called John Evelyn, whose seventeenth-century diary recorded a visit to the museum of the sixteenth-century pharmacist and naturalist Ferrante Imperato in Naples: *'Among the natural herbals, most remarkable was the Byssus marina and Pinna marina.'*

Sophie recalled a holiday she and Hamish had taken in Naples soon after they had first met. They had only been together for a couple of months, and she was surprised when he suggested it. It seemed a sort of test – would they be able to spend ten days together? In the end, of course, the days had flown by and she had loved the city – with its brightly coloured houses in shades of yellow ochre, turquoise and pink that nestled around the harbour. Not that they had seen much of the harbour. They had spent most of their time locked away in their small hotel bedroom…

She smiled at the memory. They had been so innocent then, so happy. She wrestled herself back to her work and clicked on another link.

A man named Swinburne had encountered byssus on a visit to Apulia on the southwest coast of Italy in 1790. '*The Pinna,*' he wrote, '*is torn off the rocks with hooks, and broken for the sake of its bunch of silk, called Lanapenna, which is sold, in its rude state, for about fifteen carlini a pound, to women that wash it well with soap and fresh water. When it is perfectly cleansed of all its impurities, they dry it in the shade, straighten it with a large comb, cut off the useless root, and card the remainder; by which means they reduce a pound of coarse filaments to about three ounces of fine thread. This they knit into stockings, gloves, caps and waistcoats; but they commonly mix a little silk as a strengthener. This web is of a beautiful yellow-brown, resembling the burnished gold on the back of some flies and beetles.*'

The earliest written evidence Sophie could find for sea-silk production was from 210 AD. The church father Tertullian wrote in De Pallio: '*Nor was it enough to comb and sow the material for a tunic, it was necessary also to fish for one's dress; for fleeces are obtained from the sea, where shells of extraordinary size are furnished with tufts of mossy hair.*'

At this reference Sophie sat up. Here then was evidence that byssus was in use during the timeframe of her PhD – the first and second centuries AD.

One final extract proved enticing. Horatio Nelson, it seemed, had bought some byssus gloves on his travels. He wrote to his lover Emma Hamilton of a pair of gloves he had purchased, '*made only in Sardinia of the beards of mussels*'. In addition to the gloves, he had also ordered a sea silk muff for his lover. More interestingly, it appeared that byssus was still produced in Sardinia; specifically, on an isthmus called Sant'Antioco, that could only be reached via a causeway from the main island. An atelier named Italo Diana had produced byssus in the first half of the twentieth century. Many young women had been apprenticed there, including Efisia Murroni, who frustratingly had only died five years earlier at the impressive age of one hundred. She had been the last apprentice. The reference implied that there were still women on the island working with this remarkable product, keeping the secret of sea silk production alive.

An idea began to form in Sophie's mind. A trip to Sardinia; how wonderful it would be to visit Sant'Antioco and observe the women at work.

Over lunch with her supervisor, she brought him up to speed on her recent discoveries.

'I know it's not precisely what my research ought to be focused on, but there's something there. There is a lot of evidence that byssus was used to wrap bodies both in ancient Egypt and perhaps even in Rome. And I can't pretend that I'm not intrigued by my great-grandfather's involvement with the subject.'

'I can understand that,' said Michael. 'But don't get too side-tracked. Burial practices in the first and second centuries – that's your subject. You need evidence that can be substantiated… Perhaps you can find a way to link the two.'

'That's what I've been trying to do… but most of the references are to much later examples of this sort of cloth – seventeenth and eighteenth century. My great-grandfather's piece was the oldest yet found – early fourth century. I keep thinking… if only I could find someone who'd worked with him… who knew more about his work. Maybe they found more but I just don't know about it.'

'He worked here… didn't he?'

'Yes. After he left Hungary in '56 he spent a year or so in a camp, in Austria, I think. Then he came to the UK. The university gave him a job and he worked here until he died. I keep thinking that after his initial discovery back in 1912, surely he would have gone on – searching for other examples.'

'Well, if he did, there should be something in the records – papers he published and so on. Try the library. If he published while he was here, they ought to have a copy.'

'I'm looking for anything published by Professor George Laszlo,' Sophie asked the librarian. 'Sometime in the late 1950s…He was a Professor of Archaeology here.'

'We haven't digitised everything, I'm afraid – and certainly not that far back, unless it was of some particular significance. I might have to go "old school" and see what I've got on my card system.' Flipping through her alphabetical card index system, the librarian soon exclaimed, 'Ah… here we are. In 1959 Professor G. Laszlo published an article… other contributors: Marshall. P and Moncrieff. G. You'll find it in stack no.158.' The librarian handed Sophie a Post-it with more details of the correct location.

Sophie went down to the basement storeroom and found the appropriate stack. Hundreds of thousands of research papers and journals were stored in this labyrinthine, but efficient, system. Turning the huge circular handle, a narrow corridor opened up between the stack and its neighbour. She wandered between the two long rows of journals, her finger tracing their spines, looking for the correct one.

When she found it, her heart missed a beat. At last she had something in her hand, written by the man who had been such an important and yet almost ephemeral part of her life for so many years. She flicked through the journal until she found the article George had published nearly seventy years before, entitled: 'The mystery of the ancient tombs of Sulci, Sant'Antioco, Sardinia.'

She skimmed the article. It was about an archaeological dig he had conducted beneath the basilica in Sant'Antioco. He had been excavating a pair of Roman tombs. From her cursory reading, she could see no reference to byssus. Had he realised he was on an island where they still produced this remarkable fabric? Surely, with his interest in this subject, he would have discovered the link. She knew from her own research that the Italo Diana workshop had been handling byssus when her grandfather George was on the island. Might he have met the women who made this fabric and was it he who told Rachael about the water women when he returned to England?

She took the article to the photocopier, and once she had her own copy safely in her bag, returned the journal. As she turned the large handle, sealing up the stack once again, she wondered how long it would be before someone searched for that journal.

Back in her office, she read the article more carefully. The focus was on the previously undiscovered tombs that lay beneath the basilica. There, in the catacombs of the ancient church, was a Roman burial chamber. It appeared that a woman named Beronice was buried in one of the tombs. Various engravings and inscriptions had been found on the ceiling of the tomb.

Beronice in pace; iuvenis moritur; in pace.

Beside the inscription was a seven-branched menorah. This symbol of the Jewish people indicated that the person buried there was of the Jewish faith. George's theory was that the Beronice buried in the tomb could be the 'long-lost great-granddaughter of King Herod'. This Jewish Queen had a lengthy affair with the Emperor Titus, George explained. She had travelled to Rome to live as his wife but had been banished. All references to this Queen of the Jews had ceased at that point in the literature, and no evidence had ever been found to explain where she went. It seemed that she had simply disappeared. But could she, in fact, have come to Sardinia? If so, why?

The second tomb was harder to explain, with an enigmatic inscription: '*Virus bonus in pace bonus*', which could mean '*Good man in peace, good man.'* 'Good man' was an oft-used moniker for Emperor Titus, but you could not deduce from this flimsy evidence that the man buried next to the woman named Beronice was the emperor.

The summary of George's paper was inconclusive. He skirted round the subject, explaining that the burial chamber was clearly intended for a 'couple'; that the burial appeared to be planned and not random. Judging by the decorations on the walls and ceilings of the tomb, he deduced that the two people buried there were of some significance. But while George was obviously intrigued by the true identities of those buried in the tomb, clearly there had not been sufficient evidence on site to draw a definitive conclusion.

Whilst the outcome of George's paper was frustrating, Sophie felt a sense of professional excitement – something she had not experienced for many months. Could she return to this tiny island and explore these Roman tombs as part of her own research? Might she find the missing link to who was buried there? She would need the permission of her supervisor, and the agreement of the Italian authorities, but perhaps she could finally be able to identify the remains in the Roman burial chamber – something her great-grandfather had been unable to do.

At five o'clock her phone rang. It was Hamish.

'Hello you,' he said.

'Hi… sorry – I should have called earlier. I've been rather busy.'

'Great… that's good to hear. Interesting stuff?'

'Yes. Very. I've discovered my great-grandfather – you know, the archaeologist – visited Sardinia back in the 1950s. I had no idea. He was in charge of a dig there, apparently. I won't bore you with it now… but I think I'd like to go there, and see if I can…' She paused. 'Oh this sounds a bit ridiculous.'

'Go on,' said Hamish, encouragingly.

'Well… see if I can continue his work. He found a Roman tomb, you see – and no one has ever been able to work out who is really buried there…'

'Well, I agree, it sounds fascinating. So you want to go to Sardinia?' Hamish sounded slightly surprised.

'Yes… I could combine it with a holiday. Would you like to come?'

'I'd love to, although I don't know if I can get the time off work. By the way, did you find something in your bag earlier?'

'Oh… yes. The doll! Yes I did. Thank you so much. It's sitting on my desk – looking very pretty.'

'I hope you don't think it was insensitive. I bought it a while ago – before we lost—'

'It's OK,' she interrupted. 'I can't pretend it didn't make me a bit teary… the man on the train opposite me looked a bit startled when I began blubbing.'

'Oh, Sophie… I'm so sorry.'

'No… don't be. We have to face facts, don't we? And maybe you're right. I have to deal with my grief and move on. Onwards and upwards. Perhaps this trip might help… you know?'

As she sat on the bus heading for her parents' house later that evening, Sophie felt the first glimmer of optimism – something she had not felt for several weeks. She was excited at the idea of following in George's footsteps. Perhaps her parents could even accompany her to Sardinia. It could be a holiday, a family trip to an island in the sun, to put the grief of her lost baby behind her.

Chapter 21

As Christmas approached, Rachael had still not confided in either her father or Mrs Roper about her pregnancy. Only Sandy, her friend at the cafe, knew the truth.

'I can't believe you left there like that...' said Sandy, when Rachael told her she had run away from the abortionist. 'What on earth are you going to do?'

'I don't know... But something will turn up – I'm sure of it.'

'Well, I admire your optimism. But you're going to start showing properly soon. You can't hide it forever. Hasn't your father noticed yet?'

'No... he lives in another world. He probably just thinks I'm getting a bit fat.'

'Well, if you want my advice,' Sandy began.

'No... thank you, Sandy,' Rachael interrupted. 'I know you mean well. But I'll think of something.'

In the days leading up to Christmas, snow began to fall. Angela gazed out of the attic window, fascinated, as the landscape gradually became swathed in white. The weather acted as a magnet to the village children, who began to gather in excited gaggles to play in the snow on the heath, dragging toboggans or old tin trays behind them.

'Can we go out, Mama,' Angela begged.

Rachael, who was tired and distracted, reluctantly agreed. Mrs Roper unearthed an old wooden toboggan from the cellar and, dressed in warm coats and wellington boots, Angela and Rachael went out onto the heath. In spite of her worries, Rachael enjoyed the outing. It reminded her so much of her own childhood and, for the first time in many weeks, she felt a glimmer of hope and happiness. She took huge pleasure in Angela's enjoyment – in her shrieks of delight as she slipped down the shallow slopes – and her rosy cheeks as she staggered back up to the top of the hill. When Angela finally tired of tobogganing, Rachael showed her how to make a snow angel. They lay next to one another in the snow, flapping their arms wildly, and giggling. Several village children had made snowmen on the heath, and Angela studied them, like a visitor to a museum admiring a fine sculpture They returned to Willow Road just before lunch with glowing cheeks and cold hands, and after a welcome bowl of soup in Mrs Roper's kitchen, Angela asked if they could build a snowman of their own in the back garden.

'It needs a hat and coat, Mama,' Angela insisted. 'Or he will get cold. Can we borrow Grandpa's?'

'No,' Rachael replied, stacking the soup bowls in the old stone sink. 'Grandpa needs his coat more than the snowman.'

Angela began to cry but was finally placated by Mrs Roper.

'I know,' she said kindly, 'I've got an old felt hat I never wear – and a coat that's only good for the jumble. Couldn't your snowman be a snowlady?'

Delighted by this compromise, Angela agreed, and when the snowlady was completed, and fully dressed, she stood back to admire her handiwork. As darkness fell, she was reluctant to come indoors.

'I want to look at her,' Angela explained.

'But, darling,' her mother protested, 'you can't stay out here all night. You'll freeze to death. How about sitting inside in the hall? You can look at her through the glass door that leads to the garden?'

Angela was reluctantly persuaded indoors, and a chair was positioned next to the glass door; she stayed there all afternoon and long into the evening.

Overnight, a thaw set in, and the following day, Angela was distraught to find that all that was left of her snowy friend was a pile of greying slush topped by a damp hat and coat.

'I know,' said Mrs Roper, as she mopped slushy water from the hall floor, 'why don't we decorate the Christmas tree – it's outside in the garden. Or should we wait till Christmas Eve like we did last year?'

Rachael, who was distracted and anxious about her secret pregnancy, had scarcely thought about Christmas. She had bought no presents and had even forgotten to celebrate the Feast of St Nicholas. Given her concerns, it seemed trivial to fret about Christmas traditions.

'Oh don't worry,' said Rachael, 'why don't we do it now?'

'Well…' said her landlady, concerned that Rachael seemed so lacklustre, 'if you're sure, dear.'

They dragged the tree into the parlour and the decorations were brought up from the cellar. Once the tree had been decorated, and the previous year's paper chains hung up, Mrs Roper suggested a cup of tea. She had been baking a Christmas cake that morning, and the scents of cinnamon and nutmeg floated up the stairs as they headed down to the kitchen. For the first time in weeks, Rachael felt a stirring of Christmas nostalgia. She had always cooked treats for her father in their kitchen at home at Christmastime.

'Mrs Roper… I know this is your kitchen, but I wondered if I could bake something in here. To remind me and my father… of our home, back in Budapest.'

'What did you have in mind?'

'Gingerbread men. I always made them as a little girl. My mother taught me before she died. I'd like to show Angela.'

'Of course, dear. Go ahead. I think you'll find everything you need in that cupboard there…'

*

As the biscuits cooled, they suffused the whole house with their spicy scent.

'It's time for Angela's bath,' said Rachael. 'Can we leave the biscuits here and decorate them tomorrow?'

'Of course, dear,' said Mrs Roper.

As Rachael came up into the darkened hall with Angela, she heard the front door slam shut. Her father stood, removing his overcoat,

'Ah Rachael,' he said, taking off his hat, and hanging it on the hook by the door, 'what a marvellous smell. Have you been baking?'

'Yes Papa – gingerbread men.'

'Ah… I thought I recognised it. Now, I have a wonderful surprise for you… a friend from the old days.'

Standing behind her father in the gloomy hall stood a tall, angular man wearing a homburg and overcoat.

'Chuck!' Rachael cried out, as he walked forward into the light. She ran towards his open arms, and he swung her around the hall. It brought back memories of their time in the camp, when they had danced together in the dining room. 'What are you doing here?' she asked.

'Well, it's a long story…' he replied, putting her carefully back down on the tiled floor.

'Let the man come in first,' said George. 'Come upstairs, Chuck. We have a little space on the top floor. That's all right, isn't it, Rachael?'

'Yes… yes of course. Come, follow me.'

She ran up the stairs with Angela, leading the way to the attic. She quickly plumped the cushions on the small sofa and tidied her desk.

'Take off your coat and hat,' she said, as he came in. 'Sit down here, please.' She laid his coat on her bed and patted the sofa. 'Would you like a sherry? That's all everyone in England drinks. It's quite nice though.'

She poured a glass of the amber liquid into a crystal glass – one of a set she had recently acquired from a junk shop down the road.

'Thanks… this is nice,' he said, looking around at the small neat room. 'You've made it real homely.'

'Thank you,' said Rachael blushing slightly, pleased that he liked it. 'It's only temporary, we hope to get our own house one day, don't we Papa?'

George smiled indulgently.

'But Mrs Roper the landlady has been very kind,' continued Rachael, sitting down on a chair opposite Chuck.

'And this must be the baby…' said Chuck, looking down at Angela, who sat cross-legged on the floor, wearing a tartan dress, playing with her doll. 'Hi there…' he said. 'My name is Charles.'

Angela giggled and looked at him beneath long dark lashes.

'I last met your mother when you were inside her tummy…' He patted his own stomach.

The child looked quizzically at him and turned her attention back to her doll.

'Her name is Angela,' said Rachael, 'she's two and a half now.'

'Wow…' said Chuck, 'doesn't time fly. Well, it's very nice to meet you, Angela…' He held out his hand to the child, who threw her doll down on the floor and hurled herself into his arms. 'Hey,' said Chuck, hugging her and laughing, 'you're real friendly!'

'OK – Angela, that's enough,' said Rachael, holding out her arms to her child. 'Come to Mummy.'

The child climbed off Chuck's lap and came and sat by her mother.

'So… how did you two find each other?' Rachael asked, settling her daughter by her side.

'Well,' said George, helping himself to another sherry, 'I was coming out of the university this afternoon, and we literally bumped into each other in the Strand. Amazing, no?'

'Well, yes it was amazing,' said Chuck, 'but not exactly a coincidence. As I just told your father, I was hoping to meet with him. I finished my degree in Vienna and I'm on my way home to the US. I decided to stop off in London for a few days and look you both up.'

He gazed across at Rachael. He took in her flushed cheeks, her dark hair – longer than he remembered. She wore a woollen skirt and a pretty Fair Isle sweater. She looked a little plumper, but still very beautiful.

'Well I'm glad you did,' she said. 'Where are you staying?'

'Oh, just a little hotel in town – in Knightsbridge…'

'I hope we can see a lot of you?' she said, meaning it. She was surprised by how delighted she felt at his arrival. He radiated positive energy. He had brought joy to their lives when they lived in the camp, and he was doing the same now – bringing their little attic to life somehow.

'I'd love that…' he said, blushing slightly.

'You could stay here with us if you like…' she said spontaneously.

George looked at her with surprise.

Chuck, who had intended to return to his parents' home in America before Christmas, replied equally spontaneously. 'I'd love to… if you're sure that would be OK?'

The room next to George's was temporarily vacant. The tenant had returned to the country to stay with family for the holidays and so Chuck, or Charles as he now preferred to be known, moved in for a few days.

'It's not quite a hotel in Knightsbridge,' Rachael said apologetically as she showed him round the simply decorated room.

'Oh… it'll do just fine. And way better than an impersonal hotel – let me tell you.'

He collected his luggage straight away and moved in that evening. He sent a telegram to his mother, explaining he intended to stay in London for Christmas and promising to be home in the New Year.

They were a happy party. Chuck and Rachael took Angela to the heath for long walks and watched her playing on the swings. He chatted companionably with George about politics and history in the evenings. As the only remaining residents in Willow Road that Christmas, the family ate with Mrs Roper in the dining room each evening and, charmed by Chuck, the landlady took special effort to produce meals he would enjoy. The night before Christmas Eve he invited Rachael out for dinner.

'I've heard a lot about a new jazz club that's just opened in Soho – it's called Ronnie Scott's. It sounds like the clubs in New York. Would your father babysit, do you think?'

'Yes…' she said, thrilled to be asked. 'I'm sure Papa would be happy to.'

Rachael had never been into the centre of town in the evening and was excited as she dressed for the occasion.

'You look pretty, Mama,' said Angela, admiring her mother's simple dark blue dress and pearl earrings.

The taxi stopped outside an Italian restaurant named Bianchi's in Frith Street.

'I hear it's one of the best in London,' said Chuck, as he paid the driver and guided Rachael into the restaurant.

The manager – a tiny, but impressive lady named Chiara – guided them to a corner table, where they ordered spaghetti vongole and a bottle of red wine. Rachael, who had eaten nothing but Mrs Roper's sensible British fare since arriving back in England, was delighted.

'This is delicious,' she said, 'it reminds me so much of the food we had in Sardinia.'

'Tell me about that,' said Chuck, winding spaghetti onto his fork. 'It must have been fabulous living there…'

'Yes…' she said, dreamily. 'It was wonderful.'

Rachael so desperately wanted to tell him everything. To explain about Tommaso and the baby. But shame, or embarrassment, prevented her from revealing too much. Chuck sensed her reluctance and sensitively changed the subject. They talked about Angela and how she had grown; of her father's professional success, and Rachael's attempts to gain some qualifications.

'I don't know exactly what I will do with them, but I missed out on my education – because of my mother dying, and our troubles in Hungary. It was difficult… you know?'

'I know… But you're bright. You could anything you set your mind to.'

'You think so? It's hard with a child though…'

She stared wistfully into her spaghetti. How could she possibly work, with a toddler *and* a new baby? She looked up at him and smiled. But it was a smile that hid her real worries, a false smile. There was a part of the puzzle missing, and Rachael suspected Chuck knew it.

After dinner, they walked arm in arm to the jazz club in Gerrard Street. As they descended the stairs to the club, loud, vibrant music rose up to meet them. The shabby basement was filled with glamorous women wearing tight cocktail dresses and men casually dressed in sweaters and slacks with cigarettes hanging from their mouths. They looked like movie stars, Rachael thought.

'I love jazz,' said Chuck, looking around the dark smoke-filled space. 'It reminds me of New York… a town that I'm going to live in one day…'

Rachael looked across at Chuck's sweet face, at his blue eyes gleaming in the half-light, at his fingers drumming on the table in time with the music. He was so alive, so happy. He made her feel exhilarated and safe at the same time. She found herself wishing he didn't have to leave and go back to New York.

As they climbed out of the taxi later that night, Chuck took her arm.

'Thank you, Rachael – I've loved this evening.'

'Me too, Chuck. I had a lot of fun. I spend so much time with Angela and see so few adults… I had forgotten what it's like to be with someone…'

He looked at her enquiringly.

'...someone my own age, a good friend. Thank you for taking me.'

She reached up and kissed him on the cheek. His skin felt smooth and soft. He took her hand in his and kissed it.

The following day was Christmas Eve and Mrs Roper planned a special supper for the family.

'I thought we'd do something a bit different. I've made a very nice supper and I've got some candles for the dining room. I thought we'd have a drink in the parlour before dinner and Angela could wear her party dress.'

When Rachael brought Angela downstairs to show off her red Christmas dress, Mrs Roper was busy setting the table.

'Oh – who is the belle of the ball,' declared Mrs Roper, admiring Angela, who twirled around the dining room. 'Why don't you leave her with me,' Mrs Roper suggested to Rachael. 'Go and get yourself ready; and take your time.'

Rachael wore a dark green cocktail dress. It was a little tight, she noticed, as she pulled up the zip. She turned sideways and noticed, with dismay, the slight bump protruding beneath her waistband. She pulled on a black cardigan, leaving it unbuttoned to disguise it a little. She was just brushing her hair, when there was a knock at the door.

'You look wonderful...' said Chuck, coming into the room. He was carrying a record player. 'Look what I found?' he said, putting it down in the corner of the room. He went back out onto the landing and returned with a stack of records. 'You just have to have dancing over Christmas,' he said, laying the records out on the floor. 'Here... you choose one.'

'I don't know,' she said, looking at the records. 'I know nothing about modern music – you know that; you choose something.'

He selected a disc and put it onto the gramophone. Bing Crosby's mellifluous voice filled the attic space.

'It's called "True Love",' said Chuck, holding out his arms to Rachael. 'Dance?'

As he held her to him, she laid her head against his chest. He smelt of clean washing, and aftershave. He felt somehow familiar, and she felt safe for the first time in so long.

'I've missed you so,' he whispered into her hair as he guided her around the room.

'Have you?' she felt her body meld with his, blending with him as they danced.

'I never forgot you,' he said, 'that's why I came to London… to look for you. I had to see you again. To see if…'

'To see what?'

'If there was ever going to be any hope?"

'Hope?'

'Do I need to spell it out?' Chuck spun her around the room.

'Yes,' she said laughing, 'I'd like you to spell it out.'

'All right then…' He stood quite still and took both her hands in his.

The record had finished and the only sound in the attic, apart from the thudding of her heart, was the rhythmic sound of the stylus stuck in the click track at the end of the record.

'Rachael Laszlo,' he began, earnestly. 'I am in love with you. I've been in love with you since we met in Austria…' He spun her round in a little pirouette and when she came to a stop they stood looking at one another. 'There,' he continued. 'I've finally said it. I've been wanting to tell you for so long.'

His eyes were filled with such hope and, at that moment, Rachael realised she felt something for him. Whether it was true love, she couldn't yet say. But it felt good.

'Have I said too much?' he asked, anxiously. 'Do you want me to leave?'

'No!' she said, pulling him towards her, laying her head once more against his chest. 'Don't do that. Don't leave me.'

On Boxing Day, Chuck invited Rachael for a walk. George, smiling at them over his book, offered to watch over Angela.

'You go,' he urged, 'Angela and I will have some fun while you're away.'

Angela clung to her mother's leg as she tried to leave.

'Maybe we should take her with us?' Rachael suggested.

'No,' said George, firmly, taking hold of Angela's hand. 'She can stay here with me. Come Angela. Come to Grandpa.'

'Why was my father so insistent that Angela shouldn't come with us...?' Rachael asked Chuck, as they walked towards the heath.

'Maybe because he knows I want to have a private conversation with you.'

Rachael stopped and looked at him.

'What do you mean... private?'

As the Christmas tree lights twinkled from the windows along Willow Road, and the cold wind blew unforgivingly up the street, stealing into every crevice of clothing, Chuck dropped to his knees.

'Rachael Laszlo... would you do me the honour of becoming my wife?'

'Oh Chuck... I don't know what to say.'

'Just say yes.'

'It's not... that simple.'

'Why?'

'I'd love to say yes.' She flushed and turned away. She could feel tears hovering. She would have to tell him – it was only fair, only right. But she feared that once he knew her secret, he would walk away and she would lose him.

'Tell me, what's the matter?'

'All right. I'll tell you. And if you still want to marry me when I've finished, then I will say yes... I promise.'

The cafe next to the heath was closed for the holiday, but a few metal tables and chairs had been left outside. As they sat together on the abandoned chairs, a chill wind blowing drifts of leaves up against the cafe wall, Rachael told Chuck of her brief love affair in Sardinia, and about the child she was carrying.

'So you see, Chuck... it wouldn't be fair. I'm sure you won't want to marry me now.'

'I fell in love with you when you were pregnant with another man's child,' Chuck said, reaching across the metal table and taking her cold hand in his. 'I feel the same way now.'

'But how can you?' protested Rachael. 'You went on loving me all this time. But I fell in love with someone else. Don't you feel betrayed?'

'No... No I don't. You didn't think you'd ever see me again, and besides, you weren't in love with me back in Austria. I knew that. You'd just lost your husband, your home. You were in a state of shock. And then you met someone else in Sardinia. He was kind, you were lonely – you fell in love. I understand...'

She smiled at him and squeezed his hand.

'And you shouldn't blame yourself for what's happened to you. He was... foolish. He should have taken more care, Rachael. And what he did was wrong, and unfair to you – he was promised elsewhere.'

Rachael knew that Chuck's analysis was right superficially, but she couldn't yet bring herself to blame Tommaso – the truth was much more complicated.

'Look...' Chuck continued, 'I know it's unorthodox. But if you think you could learn to love me... I promise I'll do everything I can to make you and Angela *and* the new baby happy.'

'You are such a good man,' said Rachael, 'I don't deserve you.'

He leant across the table and kissed her cheek. 'Sure you do...'

He removed a little jeweller's box from his pocket and handed it to Rachael.

'So... do I get the answer I want?' he asked, slipping the ring – a perfect diamond flanked by a pair of emeralds – onto her finger. 'I chose emeralds to match your eyes...'

'It's beautiful,' she said, admiring it. 'Are you sure you can afford it?'

'I'm sure. My folks are not exactly rich, but they're not poor either. I have a small income from a trust fund, and I hope to go into business when I get back to the States. We could live in Vermont at first with my parents, and then maybe move to New York... How would that be? I'll take you to all the jazz clubs – you'll love it.'

'Live in America?' said Rachael, slightly alarmed. 'But what about Papa?'

'Well, I guess he could come too...'

'No... I don't think he'd like that. He's so happy here. Did he know you were going to ask me?'

'Of course! I asked his permission first. I've been properly brought up, you know,' he laughed. 'So... what's your answer, Rachael Laszlo?'

Rachael stared at the ring and then back at Chuck's smiling face.

'Yes,' she said. 'If that's what you really want. I can hardly believe it. It's like a dream.'

'No... it's not a dream, sweetie. It's a plan; our plan. We're going to have a great life. You'll see.'

'Papa,' said Rachael, when she and Chuck returned to the attic, 'we're engaged!'

George kissed his daughter and shook Chuck by the hand.

'Congratulations both of you,' he grinned. 'I couldn't be more delighted.'

While Chuck went back to his room to collect a bottle of champagne, George seized the chance to have a private word with his daughter.

'I'm really very happy for you.'

'Thank you, Papa,' Rachael said, kissing him. 'Are you sure you're OK about it? Chuck told me he'd asked your permission. When did he find time to speak to you?'

'Oh – almost the first moment he arrived in London. He said to me... "I've come back to ask Rachael to marry me... If you think I have no chance, I'll leave now".'

'He said that?'

'He did. I said, I didn't know what you felt, but that he had my permission to try... I'm glad it worked out.'

'Oh, Papa... I'm glad you gave him hope.'

'He's a good man,' said her father, 'and he loves you very much...'

Chuck burst back into the room, popping the champagne cork; he filled three small crystal glasses. 'Here's to you, my darling,' he said, raising his glass to Rachael. 'We'll live with my parents at first – they're good people. They're going to love you, Rachael. Then, when I can get a job, I'd like to live in New York. Oh, Rachael, you won't believe New York. It's just fabulous. Tall, tall buildings. Everyone rushing around.'

Rachael found his excitement intoxicating, but a little overwhelming.

Later that night, after she had settled Angela, Rachael, exhausted, sat on her single bed, thinking about how her life was about to change. There was a knock at the door and her father crept back into the attic. He sat next to Rachael and put his arms around her.

'Is this what you really want, darling? Don't marry him if you don't want to.'

'Yes, Papa. I do want to marry him. It's the right thing to do….'

'Because of the baby,' he asked.

'Because of Angela you mean?'

'No… the new baby.'

Rachael stared at her father in disbelief. 'How did you know?'

'Darling… I am your father. I know you think I am a stupid old man, living in the past, completely absorbed in my work, but I observe, and I see more than you think.'

'Are you angry with me; disappointed?'

'What for? For loving someone? No…'

'But Tommaso… you didn't approve.'

'No! That's not right, Rachael. I liked him very much. I just could not see how it would work. He was promised elsewhere. Island people take these things very seriously. In a small close-knit society like that you both would have been outcast.'

'When did you realise that I was pregnant?'

'A month, or two maybe. You had a glow about you.'

'You knew all that time and didn't say.' She began to cry. 'I nearly had an abortion.'

'No!' Her father sounded shocked and hugged her closely. 'Oh, darling… that would have been terrible – for you, for the baby… no. I'm so glad you did not do that.'

'I thought you'd be so angry about it all – I was desperate. But in the end, I couldn't do it.'

'Rachael, my dear child, when have I ever been angry with you?'

She looked up at him, her face wet with tears. 'Never,' she said. 'I told Chuck about the baby – and he says he doesn't mind.'

'Well, he loves you,' said George, logically. 'And when you love someone, truly love them, you can forgive anything. Do you think you will learn to love him?'

Rachael looked into her father's watery grey eyes.

'How do you know I don't love him already?'

'I know you don't. But you care for him. And you can see it's a way out of your… predicament. *I* might not mind if you are pregnant, but society is not so kind.'

'You see everything, don't you?' Rachael kissed her father's cheek. 'I think I could love him very much. Part of my heart, I admit, is still on Sant'Antioco… but that chapter is closed. I must go on and try to be happy. I think Chuck can be part of that journey. But Papa, if we go to America, how will I bear not seeing you each day? You could come too… He told me so.'

'He is a kind boy. But it would not be right. No… I will stay here.'

Rachael began to cry again. 'No… please, Papa. Come with us.'

'No, Rachael… trust me, it's better this way. Mrs Roper will look after me. I will work… I will eat. I will chat to the other residents and I will look forward to receiving letters from my American daughter.'

'But we've never been apart – ever… I don't know if I can bear it.'

He kissed her cheek. 'Of course you can. And you must. Now we must both go to bed. You look tired. Goodnight my darling.'

The wedding was held at Marylebone Registry Office in the second week of January. It was the first slot available in the registrar's diary. Rachael had no time to buy a new outfit, so wore her green dress, which Mrs Roper had kindly taken out a little around the waist.

'I'll fix that for you,' she said, when Rachael tried it on, struggling to do up the zip. 'You've put on a tiny bit of weight. Must be my home cooking!'

Chuck had bought her a new handbag and little black hat in a Regent Street department store, and she carried a pair of white leather gloves that belonged to Mrs Roper. The guests at the simple service included George and Angela, Mrs Roper and Rachael's friend Sandy and her husband. Afterwards, the party went out for lunch at Simpson's in the Strand.

When Rachael and Sandy went to the ladies' room to powder their noses, Sandy said simply: 'So – you were right. Something did turn up. I'm happy for you. He seems a nice fella.'

'Yes… he's very kind. We're going to America later this month… I just hope my father copes.'

'Your father will be fine. He's a rock. And I can pop in on him from to time, and Mrs Roper will spoil him to death.'

Leaving her father a few weeks later was the hardest thing Rachael ever had to do. Charles waited outside in the taxi with the luggage, while Rachael and Angela said their goodbyes in the hall. Mrs Roper sobbed as Rachael hugged her.

'I shall miss you so much,' Mrs Roper said, picking Angela up and kissing her. 'And I promise, I'll look after your father, Rachael – you can count on me.'

As Rachael clung to her father, feeling his rough tweed jacket beneath her fingers, sensing his bony arms wrapped around her, she felt her resolve to leave him weakening. She had never been apart from him before. They had shared so much – and he had been her whole life – for so many years.

'I can't go,' she said, inhaling the familiar scent of tobacco, feeling his skin next to hers.

'You must,' he whispered into her hair. 'I will be fine. I will be here and I will write to you and you will write back. And we will see one another again… soon. I can come to the United States of America – for a holiday.' He pulled away from her and smiled, bravely, but his grey eyes were filled with tears. 'It's time now, Rachael, time for you to grow up and live your life. I love you,' he whispered for the last time.

Chuck came back into the house.

'Rachael, honey, we have to go… we don't want to miss our plane.'

He put his arms around his wife and pulled her gently away from George. He helped her, sobbing, into the taxi and closed the door. As the taxi pulled away from the kerb, Chuck leant out of the taxi window, waving cheerfully.

'Goodbye, George, and thanks for everything. We'll be seeing you…'

Rachael watched the diminishing figure of her father through the small rear window of the taxi. He seemed so alone, standing on the pavement outside the house in Willow Road. It was the first time she had ever left him, and her heart felt as if it would break. She watched him waving goodbye, until their taxi turned the corner and he disappeared from her field of vision forever.

Chapter 22

As spring turned to summer, Sophie was just beginning to feel more optimistic and emotionally stronger, when a shock wave rumbled through the family. Uncle Tom's wife, Cecily, died suddenly of breast cancer. Tom and Cecily had been married for over thirty years and had one son, James, who lived in Canada. Cecily had first felt a lump in her breast the previous summer, but being a private person, reluctant to make a fuss, she kept it to herself, and only went to the doctor just before Christmas. It turned out to be a particularly virulent form of breast cancer and from the time of diagnosis, she survived just four months, dying a month after Sophie's birthday.

'I still can't believe she kept it to herself like that?' said Sophie, speaking to her father one evening on the phone.

'I know…' he replied. 'Angela was particularly upset that Cecily hadn't felt able to confide in her. As a doctor, she felt she was in a position to really help. But Cecily's attitude was that she didn't want to be a burden on anyone. And she knew you were going through IVF and had a lot on your plate.'

'Well, it's just so sad,' said Sophie. 'How's Tom been doing since the funeral? I'm sorry I've not been to see him since then.'

'Oh… you know Tom. We went down to see him last weekend.'

'And?'

'He's coping. He's a man of routine. He just gets his head down and works. That boatyard doesn't run itself. And he's got the dogs.

James stayed with him for a few weeks after the funeral. But he's had to get back to Canada for work.'

'Poor Tom…' said Sophie, 'he must be very lonely. Look, I rang partly to discuss Mum's birthday, but it might involve Tom too. I was wondering if we could all have a holiday together: you, me, Mum, Hamish if he can get the time off, and Uncle Tom too. Maybe even Simon and Vic?'

'I'm not sure about them,' said her father, '… their baby's due next month, isn't it?'

Alex regretted mentioning his son's new baby the moment he opened his mouth.

'I'm sorry…' he said.

'No, Dad, don't be silly.' Sophie felt a familiar flicker of jealousy that she pushed away. 'I must give Vic a ring and find out how she's doing.'

'We saw them a couple of weeks ago,' said Alex, 'she seemed fine.'

'Oh good. Maybe Mum won't want to come away if their baby's due… her first grandchild and all that.'

'I think it would be OK,' said her father. 'Vic was pretty clear when we saw them that *her* mother will be coming to stay. I suspect one mother figure is quite enough for any new mum. There'll be plenty of time for us to get to know the baby.'

'So,' said Sophie, 'do you think we could persuade Tom to come with us?'

'I don't know,' replied Alex. 'He's never been much of a traveller. It takes quite a lot to get him out of Dorset. He just loves being at home, and the sea of course.'

'Well, I was thinking of somewhere near the sea – Sardinia, to be precise. I'm hoping to do some research there for my PhD and thought we could make a holiday of it. You and Tom could hire a boat. Mum wouldn't mind if Tom was there to keep an eye on you.'

'Less of the "keeping an eye", young lady. I'm a perfectly competent sailor.'

'I know, Dad, but Tom is... more experienced.'

'Yes... well you're right about that. I'll talk to Mum this evening...'

'OK,' said Sophie. 'Look, I'd better go, I've to a lot to do before Hamish comes home.'

'Before you do...' said Alex, 'I know I shouldn't ask – but any news?'

The phrase hung in the air.

'By news, I presume you mean – am I pregnant yet?'

'No... no. I just meant...'

'It's all right, Dad. I understand... you mean – are we going ahead with another round of IVF? Hamish and I have discussed it once or twice, but he always focuses on the reasons not to do it. I felt so wretched about losing the first one, I think he worries I can't cope with any more disappointment. And it was hard, of course, but you can't go through life feeling pessimistic – can you? Then there's the financial side – it's a lot of money, as you know and the NHS only pay for one round here in Gloucestershire. The trouble is, you can spend two or three thousand pounds and there's no guarantee of a baby at the end of it. And Hamish is a bit worried about money – we need a new boiler amongst other things. So, although I've decided I'd like to go ahead, I've not told Hamish yet. I've been waiting for the right moment.'

'Well – you might be able to tell him tonight.'

'What do you mean?'

'We might have the solution – in fact, I thought Mum had already had a word with you about it?'

'About what?'

'Well, I know she meant to. She must have forgotten, what with Cecily and all that. We'd like to pay for it.'

'Oh no, Dad. You can't do that.'

'No, we'd like to. We *can* afford it, you know.'

'I don't know what to say.'

'Just say yes,' said her father, 'and don't worry about the money anymore.'

When Hamish got home that evening, the smell of fish pie wafted through the hall. In the kitchen, Sophie had lit some candles and opened a bottle of wine.

'This all looks nice,' Hamish said, picking up the bottle and studying the label. 'What are we celebrating?'

'Have a glass… it's good – I bought it today, from the nice wine shop in Cirencester.'

'Mmmm,' he said, sloshing the wine around his mouth, 'it's delicious. Cheers,' he clinked his glass against hers. 'So, what's going on?'

'Well…' she began, hesitantly. 'Oh, I'll just say it. My parents have offered to pay for the next round of IVF.'

Hamish sipped his wine, reflectively.

'I see,' he said at last, 'and how hard was that? To persuade them, I mean?'

'I didn't persuade them! They offered. In fact, I tried to turn it down. But Dad insisted. I thought you'd be pleased. We've had so many other expenses recently – and there's the boiler – and I know you've been worried about money.'

'Yes. I suppose it is good news.' His voice was flat, non-committal.

'You *suppose*? What do you mean?'

'Well,' said Hamish, pushing the cat off the chair and sitting down at the table, 'I wasn't aware we had finally decided to do it again. I mean, the last round really took it out of you.'

'The process wasn't that bad,' said Sophie defensively. 'It was… losing the baby that was unbearable.'

'Yes, and what if it happens again?'

'It might not! I mean, you can't go into it thinking the worst.'

'I would disagree. I don't think you can go into it without preparing for the worst. That has to be the logical place to start, surely. Assume it's not going to be successful and work out how you will deal with that eventuality. Then… if you think it's worth all the stress and misery, you go ahead.'

Sophie felt the blood rushing to her face. She was filled with a sort of fury, a rage against this negative logic. 'I simply refuse to go through life in such a state of pessimism. The thing is Hamish, if we don't proceed what do we have left?'

'We have each other… isn't that enough?'

She leant against the sink, sipping her wine, considering her response carefully. It was important that she was truthful, accurate.

'No… it's not enough, not for me. I'm sorry, but it's not.'

Hamish stared at her, shocked and uncomprehending.

Sophie, aware suddenly of the implications of what she had just said, burst into tears and rushed out of the room. Upstairs, she lay down on her bed, staring at the ceiling, thinking about what had just happened, trying to analyse what she felt.

A few moments later, Hamish came into their bedroom. He leant against the wall, his hands in his pockets, anxiously jangling his change.

'Are you telling me that you don't want to be married to me anymore?'

'No!' she sat up in bed suddenly, knocking the glass of red wine off her bedside table. It pooled a dark red stain on the cream carpet. 'Damn!' she said, swinging her legs out of bed. 'Get a cloth, could you?'

He went into the bathroom next door and returned with a facecloth, which he threw over the stain.

'I just mean…' she said, kneeling by the wine stain and mopping the carpet furiously, 'I want another try. I want a baby. I'm prepared to put up with the disappointment. I have to do this. It's all that I want. I do love you – but it's not about you, Hamish. It's about me. About the need I have. It never goes away. It just eats away at me – nagging, gnawing. The only time I have any relief is when I'm utterly absorbed in my work.' She looked up at him, the facecloth soaked with wine.

'And how do you think that makes me feel?' he asked bitterly.

'I don't know what you mean. It's not about you. Why are you making this so hard?'

'Because, Sophie, just lately, I feel that you are just… using me… in order to have a child – something, that apparently you want more than you want me.'

He left the room. A few minutes later, she heard the front door slam. Had he walked out on her?

'Shit!' she said under breath. She had started the evening so optimistically. How had everything got so out of control? Where had Hamish gone? Surely this wasn't the end of her marriage?

The smell of burning fish floated up the stairs.

'Shit, shit…' she said, running downstairs and into the kitchen. She opened the Aga door and removed the blackened fish pie, putting it down on the floor.

'Here you go,' she said to the cat. 'Enjoy it.'

Chapter 23

New York
February 1960

As the doors of the BOAC Comet opened at New York's Idlewild airport, a blast of icy air blew into the plane. Rachael, standing at the top of the aeroplane steps, turned up the collar of her warm coat and scooped her daughter up into her arms. The airport had been built in a flat, marshy area on the edge of the city, and the landscape beyond the perimeter was bleak and unremarkable. As she gazed at the long low airport building, Rachael had a strong sense that over the horizon lay a city full of excitement, and a new life filled with possibilities.

The family had been flying for over eleven hours and Rachael was stiff and tired. Angela, who had slept well on the journey, was now full of energy, and wriggled to escape her mother's grasp. Exasperated, Rachael turned to Chuck, who quietly enveloped the child in his capacious cashmere overcoat, where she instantly relaxed, wrapping her arms around his neck, allowing him to carry her into the terminal.

As they drove in the taxi towards New York, crossing the bridge that led to lower Manhattan, Rachael was amazed by the sheer physical presence of the high-rise buildings that surrounded them; they arched upwards, blotting out the sky, so much so that she had to lean out of the cab window and crane her neck upwards, just to catch a glimpse of a sliver of blue between the buildings.

The long straight roads created a sense of order, but everywhere she looked, there was an almost visceral energy – the street vendors calling out to customers, the yellow cabs bumper to bumper on the busier roads. She was mesmerised by the steam billowing from beneath the pavements; it looked as if there was a terrifying dragon hidden beneath the city, she thought. Even the people rushing by looked more energetic than their European counterparts. They appeared less down-trodden, sharper, brighter, better dressed.

At Pennsylvania Station, Chuck unloaded their luggage and paid the cab driver.

'It's a long ride up to Vermont…' he said, leading the family through the magnificent marble entrance hall. 'Let's have something to eat first.'

The restaurant was an impressive high-ceilinged room lit by chandeliers. Tables were laid with white linen, silver and glass. Rachael stared around her, in awe at its splendor and opulence.

'I've never been somewhere so beautiful,' she said, as the waiter pulled her chair out from the table. 'Especially not in a railway station.'

'Well, this is New York, honey,' said Chuck. 'The design is Beaux Arts – the station was inspired by the Gare D'Orsay in Paris. You ever been to Paris?'

'No, never…'

'I'll take you. Now we must eat and have something to drink.'

He called the waiter over and ordered two Manhattans.

'I can't drink alcohol now. It's ten in the morning,' protested Rachael.

'This is America… you can do whatever you like.'

As their train journeyed north-east through the states of Connecticut and Rhode Island, the railway line travelled through snow-covered wooded countryside, broken up by inviting glimpses of wooden houses, with wisps of woodsmoke floating up into the bright blue sky. Passing through towns with romantic names like 'Old Saybrook', Rachael noted how the houses became more sporadic, and the scenery increasingly rural. Sprinkled among the white clapboard houses were old barns painted dark red, green and blue, which stood out against the gleaming white snow.

Finally their train turned north, heading up through Massachusetts and New Hampshire. The snow grew deeper, the houses and barns almost buried up to their window ledges.

Rachael and Angela dozed periodically, they ate snacks from the bar, and, ten hours after leaving Penn Station, they arrived in Burlington, Vermont.

As Chuck and Rachael emerged from the station, a tall man wearing a heavy dark overcoat, his grey hair slicked across his scalp, walked towards them. He put his hand out towards Chuck, who shook it formally.

'Hi Dad... good to see you. Thanks for coming out so late for us.'

'No problem... the car's over here.'

He led the way to a pale blue Studebaker station wagon. As Chuck loaded their luggage into the capacious boot, his father introduced himself to Rachael.

'You must be Rachael,' he said, shaking her hand. 'It's very good to meet you. I'm Eric – Charles' father.'

Installed with Angela, on the wide leather back seat, Rachael, exhausted from their journey, gazed out sleepily at the moonlit landscape. Deep snow was banked up on either side of the wide country road. They crossed an old wooden bridge on the outskirts of a small town and, peering down, she observed a river rushing like a torrent, cascading beneath them. The main street was lined on either side by little wooden fronted shops - a general store, a tack-shop and a drugstore advertising ice cream sodas. Then they were heading out of town once again and into the open countryside. Rachael dozed off for a little while, and when she woke up, the car was pulling into the drive of a large clapboard house, painted a dark colour of some kind – green or blue… she couldn't be sure. The windows were picked out in white, and the wide lawn was covered in deep snow and surrounded by a neat white picket fence. An American flag flew proudly from a sparkling flagpole. It looked, she thought, like a house from a storybook – *Little Women* or *The Little House on the Prairie*.

Chuck lifted Angela, still sleeping, out of the car, as his father set the luggage down on the large covered porch. Rachael followed Eric and Chuck into the house.

Standing at the far end of the dark red hall was a slender woman whose blonde hair appeared to have been neatly permed into a hard helmet that hovered over her pale face. Rachael noted the woman's dark red lipstick – her mouth was set in a predetermined smile. But her cool, watery blue eyes told a different story.

'Oh, there you are…' she said, 'You must be Rachael – I'm Constance, Charles' mother.'

The introductions over, Rachael, who was both tired and disoriented by her twenty-four hours of travel, was invited to sit down in the drawing room. A fire glimmered beneath the wooden fire surround and she sank, gratefully, into one of the large comfortable chintz sofas. Two leather armchairs sat on either side of the fireplace. An upright piano stood against one wall.

'You must be hungry, dear…' Constance was saying. 'I've prepared some supper for you all. Perhaps you'd like to freshen up and then come down to the dining room.'

Slightly mortified at the idea of eating so late, and feeling a little nauseous from the journey, Rachael nevertheless accepted the invitation gracefully.

'I've put you in Charles' room,' Constance said, leading the couple up the stairs. 'And I made up the box room next door for your daughter.'

Chuck's room was at the front of the house overlooking the lawn and the street beyond. The four-poster bed had been draped with filmy white curtains and there was a pale blue bedcover and matching armchair.

'You did the room over, Ma,' Chuck observed.

'Well, I thought your new wife wouldn't appreciate the bachelor room you left behind...' said Constance. 'I'll leave you to settle, and we'll see you downstairs.'

Angela, invigorated by her nap in the car, ran, excitedly around the room. Chuck and Rachael took her next door to the box room, where a cot and a bed stood side by side.

'You can choose,' Chuck said to Angela. 'Do you want the cot or the bed?'

Angela demonstrated her choice by clambering nimbly onto the bed and bouncing noisily.

'Angela no...!' said Rachael. 'Get off there this minute.' She lifted her daughter off the bed, and put her firmly back on the floor.

'You look tired, Rachael...' said Chuck, kindly. 'Would you rather just go to bed?'

'I am tired, yes... but we ought to be polite. Your mother has gone to a lot of trouble, making supper, and we should eat it.'

While Chuck took Angela downstairs, Rachael washed her face and hands in the bathroom across the hall. In her bedroom, she brushed her hair and changed her dress, before going downstairs.

The family was gathered in the dining room. It led directly off the dark red hall and was painted in the same shade. There was a large antique mahogany dining table and eight matching chairs. A glass-fronted chiffonier filled with porcelain, china and silver stood against one wall. Family portraits in gilt frames covered the remaining walls – pictures of frontiers people, sour-faced women wearing black silk dresses and dour men in dark frock coats which matched their stern expressions. Rachael felt their stony gaze as she came into the room.

'Ah good, you're here at last,' said Constance. Rachael couldn't help thinking that even this apparent welcome had an air of criti-

cism about it. 'I thought you could sit here, opposite Charles, and
the baby could sit on this high chair – we've had it in the family
for generations.'

Angela was squeezed, protesting, into the old wooden ladder-
back high chair. She wriggled and squirmed and made her reluctance
quite obvious.

Rachael, desperate to make a good impression, flushed and fretted.

'I'm so sorry... she's not used to a high chair.' She tried to force
the child's legs through the narrow opening. But Angela was rigid,
arching her back, refusing to comply – either physically or mentally.

'Goodness, what a performance...' said Constance. 'So what
does she normally sit in when you eat?'

Her question went unanswered, as Rachael tried to reason with
Angela.

'Oh let the child sit on a chair,' said Eric, impatiently, 'if that's
what she's used to. Or our supper will get cold.' He wore a dark
suit with a waistcoat, a fob watch tucked into the inside pocket.

'Yes, Mom,' said Chuck, 'let Angela sit on a chair.'

'Won't she drop food everywhere?' Constance asked, looking
down with consternation at her fine silk Turkish carpet.

'No...' said Rachael, 'I'll be very careful.'

With Angela installed, triumphantly on an adult chair, Constance served up the supper.

'It's just a pot roast,' she said with mock modesty.

'My mother's pot roast is legendary...' said Chuck cheerfully,
passing a bowl of boiled potatoes to Rachael.

When the family had been served, and Rachael was concentrating hard on spooning little pieces of meat and potato into Angela's
rosebud mouth, Constance asked, 'So ... tell us how you met?'

Rachael looked across at Chuck. Constance observed the panic
in her eyes.

'Oh sure,' said Chuck, calmly. 'We met back in Austria. Rachael
and her father – he's a Professor of Archaeology at London Univer-

sity – top of his field, Dad – well they were getting out of Hungary where there was a bit of trouble. You remember, Dad … you must have read about it over here in *The Times*. I was in Vienna and the university asked for volunteers to go and help in the camp. It seemed a good, *Christian* thing to do.' He emphasised the word 'Christian', paused and looked at his mother, challenging her to disapprove of such a charitable act. She smiled faintly between pursed lips. 'So we met…' Chuck continued, 'and Rachael and I fell in love.'

'But hadn't she just been widowed?' Constance asked her son, a look of disapproval spreading across her powdered features. She looked across the table at Rachael, who flushed slightly.

'Yes…' Rachael interjected. 'I had been widowed and I realise it was quite soon afterwards, but I really liked Charles – he was so kind to me, and my father…' she trailed off, not quite knowing what else to say.

'So,' Chuck continued in his usual cheery manner, 'Rachael and her father went to London. We corresponded. It was a long-distance love affair, wasn't it, honey?' He reached across the table and covered her hand with his. He squeezed it and smiled, encouragingly, at her.

'Yes…' she agreed. 'He's a very good letter writer.'

'So, when was your daughter born?' asked Eric.

'Oh – when my father and I were living in London.'

'And when did you get married?' asked Constance, looking pointedly at the developing bump beneath Rachael's newly acquired maternity dress.

'Oh well,' said Chuck, breezily, 'Rachael came over with Angela and her father last year to visit, during my final year. And we decided to get married. We had a lovely little ceremony in Vienna.'

'I'd love to see some photographs,' said his mother. 'It seems so odd, Charles, that you didn't even mention it at the time. We'd have come over to Europe… you know that.'

'I know, Ma… and I'm sorry. It just all got a little complicated. Anyways… we had a lovely wedding and then Rachael went back to London with her father – he's a great man, you must meet him sometime, a real intellectual. And now… here we are, expecting our first child. It's exciting, isn't it?' he asked, defying them to disagree.

'Yes, dear,' Constance replied, uncertainly.

After supper, while Chuck took Angela upstairs to bed, Rachael offered to help clear up. She followed Constance down the hall, past the staircase and through the swing door to the large well-appointed kitchen that ran along the full width of the house. It bore no resemblance to any kitchen Rachael had ever seen, either in Budapest or in Hampstead. There were glazed cupboards arranged around the walls, filled with glass and china, a large range cooker took pride of place in the old fireplace and, beneath the window, overlooking the garden, was a ceramic sink, where Constance was already washing up.

'I'll wash and you can dry,' she said, handing Rachael a tea towel.

This, at least, seemed familiar. Rachael stacked the dried plates up on the kitchen table.

'Oh, not there…' Constance said to Rachael, 'put them in the unit, dear.'

Rachael looked helplessly around the kitchen.

'Excuse me…' she said, 'but what is a unit?'

'There, dear – the cupboard over there…' she pointed to the glass-fronted cupboard on the wall.

As they washed, dried and tidied, Rachael steered the conversation away from herself and onto Constance – how long they had lived in the house, whether Chuck had been born there and where he had gone to school.

When the washing-up was finished, they returned to the drawing room, where they found Chuck and his father sitting on either side of the fireplace, smoking cigars.

'Oh, for heaven's sake,' complained Constance, irritably. 'I do wish you wouldn't smoke in here, Eric. I have to air the room the next day.'

'Well,' said Chuck, observing his wife's pale complexion and the dark rings round her eyes, 'we ought to be getting to bed anyway… We've not really slept for over twenty-four hours.'

'Oh goodness,' said Constance. 'Well, yes off you go. Sleep well, dear.'

She pecked her son on the cheek. It occurred to Rachael that she had not yet seen Constance hold or hug her son once since they had arrived.

That night, as they lay in the pale blue bed, Rachael whispered her anxieties. 'I know your mother doesn't believe our story, Chuck. I can just see it in her eyes.'

'Relax, honey. It'll be fine.' He kissed his wife, rolled over in bed and turned out the light.

Within minutes, in spite of her concerns, Rachael was fast asleep.

Over the coming weeks, Rachael grew used to the routine at the house in Vermont. She and Chuck took snowy walks in the woods with Angela. They helped around the house – washing up, setting the table. Constance even allowed Rachael to make gingerbread men one morning. Chuck and his father spent time together talking in Eric's study, or in his workshop above the garage. When Constance challenged them about spending so much time together. Eric retorted: 'Can't a man spend time with his only son? It's man's talk, Constance. We have business to discuss.' Rachael was pleased to see Chuck so content with his father. There was bond between them that she had not observed between mother and son. One morning, after a particularly heavy snowfall, the two men cleared the drive together with a wide snow shovels. They came into the kitchen afterwards, cold and hungry, laughing and slapping each other on the back, pleased with their morning's work. The sounds they made – the scraping of chairs, the dipping of spoons into bowls of hot soup – reminded Rachael of her father and József all those years before. The following day Chuck and Rachael built a snowman on the front lawn. Chuck threw himself into the task and when Angela saw it she declared it: 'the best snowman in the world'. Even Eric became involved – kindly donating an old coat and scarf. Constance did her best to make the family welcome. But from time to time, Rachael caught her mother-in-law studying her through the kitchen window, or from the other side of the room. Rachael had the feeling that the Baileys did not quite believe the story Chuck had told them about the baby she was expecting.

They were good, religious people, who attended the white clapboard church on the green each Sunday morning. Every evening the family said grace before dinner, which was always served in the dining room using the second-best china.

Rachael wondered when the best china was used. She asked Chuck about it one night as they lay in bed.

'Oh… high days and holidays,' he replied. 'Christmas, Thanksgiving, christenings.'

'So our baby's christening?'

'Sure… it'll all come out then.'

Rachael hoped that he was only referring to the china.

Chuck appeared to be one of life's inveterate optimists. He had set his sights on a career in finance and within a month of returning to America had landed a job at the German 'Deutsche Bank' in New York as a trainee investment banker.

'I always thought it was a good idea to learn another language. They said my knowledge of German was a real asset. This is it, Rachael. I'm going to earn a lot of money and we can have an apartment in New York, and it's all going to be grand.'

*

Rachael was relieved when they moved out of the house in Vermont and were spared the family meals, the saying of grace and visits to church and, in particular, the nightly inquisitions about their courtship and marriage. Chuck found them a first-floor apartment in an old Brownstone in the Upper East Side. With its large graceful rooms, it reminded Rachael of the apartment in Budapest. There was even a huge plane tree visible from the drawing room window that was reminiscent of their view from the attic in Hampstead.

An elderly lady introduced herself to the couple on the day they moved in. As Charles struggled upstairs with their luggage, she inquisitively opened the door of her ground-floor apartment, reminding Rachael of Mrs Kovacs. But there the resemblance ended. Whereas Mrs Kovacs had been a scruffy, rather lumpy woman, this lady was very tall and erect, with fine pure white hair held back in an elegant bun. She wore an old-fashioned high-necked silk blouse with a stiff lace frill that ended just beneath her perfectly formed chin. She had the most remarkable violet-coloured eyes and it came as no surprise when she introduced herself with a cut-glass English accent, as Violet Dreyfuss.

'You must come and have tea,' she called up after Rachael, 'when you've settled in.'

Rachael discovered a nursery school on the next block where Angela could go four mornings a week. With her baby due in May, Chuck found them a doctor who pronounced that Rachael's pregnancy was proceeding well.

During the day, Rachael got huge pleasure from exploring the city – going in ever-increasing circles from the apartment block, fearful she might otherwise get lost. She found a good local grocery store and a druggist – America's strange word for a chemist shop. She also located a small antique shop nearby and, encouraged by Chuck, bought one or two pieces of furniture:

a dining table and chairs, a dressing table and a small desk. She had a pang of regret that she had left her own pale green bureau back in London. Her engagement and marriage to Chuck had been such a whirlwind that she had quite forgotten to retrieve the photograph of Tommaso, hidden behind the panel in the central cupboard of the desk. She worried that her father might sell the desk, or someone might find the photograph and throw it away. These thoughts filled her, occasionally, with panic – the significance of which did not escape her. She couldn't bear the thought, she realised, of losing the photograph. For while she had grown to love Chuck, she was still in love with Tommaso. When Chuck made love to her – something she did not enjoy but felt unable to refuse him – he did so with such tenderness. She tried to block thoughts of Tommaso from her mind, but he came uninvited, unbidden, on every occasion. She was relieved when her growing pregnancy made love-making complicated. Chuck was very gentlemanly about it. He was so delighted to have finally married the woman he loved that he resented nothing. He lived in blissful ignorance of Rachael's true feelings, and for that she was grateful. She had no wish to hurt him – quite the contrary. She owed him so much.

The trees and bushes in Central Park were bursting energetically into life and banks of tulips formed colourful carpets, as Rachael and Angela approached the pond one afternoon towards the end of May. They had a bag of old bread with them to feed the ducks, and as they sat down on a bench, Rachael felt the familiar cramping sensation of labour.

'Sweetheart,' she said, taking Angela calmly by the hand, 'we have to leave now...'

'But I don't want to leave,' protested Angela.

'Well we have to... Mummy's going to have the new baby.'

Rachael took a yellow cab to the hospital and asked the receptionist to call her husband at work. He came to the hospital within the hour, before rushing home with Angela to collect a small bag of nightclothes for his wife. By the time he returned, she was in theatre, being prepared for an emergency caesarian section. The baby was stuck; its heart was in distress, and try as she might, Rachael could not push the child out.

Chuck sat in the waiting room, with Angela on his lap, as the hours ticked by. He prayed for the safe arrival of the child, but, more than that, he prayed for the woman he had loved so long to be spared. The thought of losing her now was unbearable. Sometime after eight o'clock, as Angela lay sleeping in his arms, a nurse arrived with some news.

'Mr Bailey?'

'Yes – that's me…' He sat upright, his heart jolting with anxiety. 'How's my wife?'

'She's out of theatre, and she's going to be fine.'

He relaxed, visibly relieved, sinking back into the chair.

'You have a son… Do you want to see him?'

He picked the sleeping Angela up in his arms and followed the nurse down the corridor until they reached the nursery.

'You can't go in, but you can look at him from here – do you see the label? Baby Bailey?'

In a Perspex cot next to the glass window lay a tiny child with a mop of dark unruly hair. Chuck gazed at the baby's perfect face and felt a curious, and surprising, sensation – it was love.

'He's a big boy,' said the nurse. 'I'm not surprised she had trouble. Nearly ten pounds. You must be very proud.'

He was proud, he realised. This child, this boy, was his son – whatever the truth of his paternity. And he would cherish him as if he was his own.

'Can I see my wife?' He yearned to see Rachael now. To hold her in his arms, to tell her much he loved her.

'In the morning – she's sleeping now. She's had a hard time.'

Chuck returned the following morning at half-past eight. He carried a huge bunch of pink roses in one hand and held Angela's hand in the other.

Rachael struggled to sit up in bed. She looked pale, her green eyes slightly bloodshot. She winced with pain, as she leant over to kiss her daughter.

'Don't move, honey,' said Chuck, lifting Angela up, so she could kiss her. 'Does it hurt a lot?'

'Yes… quite a lot. But at least I hear the baby's OK. I've not seen him yet. Could you ask them to bring him in?'

When the child was wheeled into Rachael's room, he was placed next to her bed. Angela clung to the edge of the cot and peered at her little brother. She stroked his head, looking at her mother for approval.

'That's right,' said Rachael. 'Be gentle… What do you think?' she asked Angela.

'He's got black hair,' Angela noted with admirable perceptiveness. The baby did indeed have a mop of dark hair. Rachael looked up at Chuck – at his blond crew cut; his bright blue eyes. The baby stirred and gazed at his mother with dark blue eyes – they were like pools of still water. At least his eyes were blue, like Chuck's; although she feared that would change. All babies, after all, had blue eyes.

'Isn't he beautiful?' Chuck said with genuine emotion.

'Yes… he is.' Rachael touched the baby's hand and he gripped her finger tightly. She was so lucky, she thought in that moment, to have this beautiful child and a husband who clearly adored him. 'Could you lift him out and let me hold him?'

He was a well-developed baby. It was as if he was already a month or two old. Lying in her arms, he studied his mother's face, staring intently into her grey-green eyes. His mouth opening and closing like a clam.

'I'll feed him,' said Rachael.

'I can bring a bottle,' said the nurse, who had been hovering in the background. 'He's already had two or three feeds. It would be easier – for you.'

'No,' said Rachael. 'I want to feed him myself.'

The nurse pursed her lips, disapprovingly. 'Well, you can try,' she said and left the room.

Rachael was soon comfortably propped up by three pillows; she opened the front of her nightgown and the child snuffled down onto her breast and latched on as if he had been doing it all his life. He sucked hard and Rachael felt such love, such a wave of adoration for him, that it almost took her breath away. Angela watched her mother keenly from the other side of the room.

'Can you ask them to leave him in here...' Rachael said to Chuck. 'I don't want him in the nursery.'

'But, honey, how will you get any rest?'

'When I had Angela, she was with me all the time. I don't want him taken away. Please Chuck.'

The baby, getting little from her breast, grew tetchy and began to grizzle.

'Look...' said Chuck, anxiously, 'he's hungry – maybe it would be best to do what the nurse says and give him a bottle.'

'No... my milk will come in. Just leave him with me.'

News of the 'foreign' mother who refused to bottle-feed her baby spread around the ward. Numerous nurses and even a doctor arrived to persuade her that she was doing her child harm.

'He's hungry, Mrs Bailey. He's a big child; he really needs a bottle.'

'No,' said Rachael, firmly. 'He's not my first child. I know what I'm doing. It will be fine.'

Early the following morning, her breasts throbbing and swollen, she lifted her baby to her nipple, and the milk flowed into his mouth as if a tap had been turned on. There was so much milk, it leaked out of his mouth, dribbling down his chin, causing his eyes to roll up into his head, in sheer bliss.

*

Rachael was booked into the hospital room for a fortnight, but she discharged herself after just one week. She was desperate to get away from the disapproving glances of the nursing staff and she missed Angela dreadfully. She caused quite a stir when she appeared at the nurses' station, fully dressed, with the baby in her arms, ready to leave the hospital.

'You really can't just leave like that, Mrs Bailey. The doctor hasn't discharged you yet,' said the head nurse.

'I'll be fine,' Rachael said, setting off towards the elevator, the baby in her arms. 'Thanks for everything.'

The taxi driver deposited her at the brownstone just before lunchtime. He carried her bag up the steps and she handed him the key to open the door.

'You going to be all right, lady?', he asked, placing her bag inside the hall.

'I'm fine – thank you,' she said.

Somehow she carried the baby and her bag up the stairs, but once inside the apartment, she lay down on the bed, the baby lying in the crook of her arm, and went to sleep.

When Chuck came home at lunchtime, having collected Angela from nursery school, he was horrified.

'Darling… why didn't you call me? I'd have come to collect you. I worry you've come home too soon,' he said anxiously. 'I have to go back to work any day now – how can I look after you and both children? Should I get a nurse?'

'I'll be fine. I've just had a baby – that's all.'

'But you had an operation and how will you manage with shopping and looking after Angela?'

'I'll be fine,' she repeated.

'I should call my parents.'

'No… don't do that. Please?'

'It's the only responsible thing to do. We have a spare room. My mother will look after you.'

Reluctantly, Rachael agreed. Her stitches were still very sore, and she knew she would struggle even to get downstairs and out to the shops.

'Now, go back to bed, please Rachael,' Chuck insisted.

He had bought a cot – a dainty lace bassinet, which was already almost too small for the huge baby boy – and had placed it, thoughtfully, by their bed. She laid the baby in it after a feed, and the child fell into a deep sleep. She slept too, and woke later that afternoon, the spring sunshine filtering through the grimy window.

'I called my folks…' said Chuck, handing her a cup of tea. 'They're coming tomorrow. I hope that's OK.'

'Yes…' she said, untruthfully. She didn't want Constance and Eric there… She wanted her father. 'I'd like to call my father – do you think that would be possible?'

'Sure… I'll put through a long-distance call.'

He brought her the phone once the connection had been made. 'It's Mrs Roper,' Chuck said, handing her the receiver.

'Mrs Roper…'

'Yes… is that Rachael? Oh goodness, all the way from America… How are you, dear?'

'I'm fine. I wondered if my father was there…'

'No, dear, he's still at work. I have to admit, he is rather late. I seem to remember he mentioned an evening meeting. Oh I'm sorry. Is there anything wrong?'

'Oh… No, not at all. I just wanted to let him know that I've had the baby – a lovely big boy. Everything's OK…'

'Oh, that is good news; I'll be sure to tell him when he gets home. He'll be so sorry to have missed you, but we'll have a glass of sherry to celebrate.'

'Thank you – tell him… maybe we can speak at the weekend…'

*

The following day, Rachael felt more rested. Chuck took Angela to nursery school, and then waited at home with Rachael and the baby until his parents arrived late that afternoon. It was their first visit to the apartment.

Lying on the bed, Rachael could hear them in the hallway.

'Well congratulations!' said Eric. 'Our first grandson. Can we see him?'

Chuck led the way to his wife's room. The baby had just been fed and lay in soporific bliss in his little bassinet.

'Look at all that hair!' Constance said, disapprovingly. 'I've never seen such a thing...'

'He's got Rachael's hair,' Chuck said quickly. 'Beautiful thick dark hair – eh, honey?'

Rachael smiled weakly from her bed.

'Well, we won't disturb him now – as he's sleeping,' said Constance. 'Rachael... I shall prepare some supper, if Charles will show me the way.'

Chuck then returned to his office, leaving Constance and Eric in charge.

When Chuck arrived home, just after seven, Rachael could hear the three of them chatting quietly in the drawing room. Once or twice, she overheard Angela crying – just petulant tears, presumably brought on by her mother-in-law refusing something that Angela had demanded – a cookie before she had finished her main meal, or something similar. Then she heard the bath running and Constance's strict tones: 'Now, Angela, it's time for your bath. Be a good girl.'

Angela was clearly intent on being as disobedient as possible. She began to scream.

Alarmed, Rachael struggled to get out of bed. She almost doubled up at the tearing pain that ripped through her lower abdomen but breathed deeply and stood up, pulling on her dressing gown. She walked unsteadily through into the bathroom.

'Angela, angel, Mummy's here.'

The child stood naked, her fists clenched by her side. Constance was kneeling next to her.

'Oh, Rachael, you really shouldn't have got up,' said Constance, impatiently. 'She's absolutely fine. She just won't get in the bath.'

Rachael reached out for her child, who ran to her, pleading to be picked up.

Chuck wandered in.

'Hey… you're up!' he said delightedly, kissing his wife's neck. 'Now, Angela, what's all this noise about – don't you want a bath?'

Angela stopped crying, and instead held out her arms to him. He picked her up, knelt down by the bath, felt the water with his hand and swished it around.

'Hey… feels good, Angela – not too hot, not too cold – just right! Like Goldilocks… Hey – that's you… little Goldilocks.' The child giggled. 'Want to get in?'

Angela wriggled to get into the water and sat happily splashing, playing with a toy rubber duck.

'I could have done that,' said Constance, curtly.

'I'm sorry…' said Rachael apologetically. 'It's just that she knows Chuck so well. He's so good with her.'

'Seems to me,' said Constance, 'that she's been spoiled. Anyway, I'll go and see to supper. I'll bring you a tray later.'

Rachael was sitting up in bed, holding the baby, when Constance brought in a tray of roast beef and mashed potatoes – not something Rachael would have chosen to eat so soon after an operation.

'Oh… he's awake,' said Constance, laying the tray on the bedside table. 'Can I take a peek?'

The baby opened his dark eyes and studied her.

'His eyes are very dark…' said Constance, peering at him intently, 'they don't look at all like Charles', or yours for that matter.'

'No… he looks more like my… mother,' said Rachael hurriedly. 'She had the same dark brown eyes.' She thought back to her mother's pale grey green eyes and blanched inwardly at the lie she had just told.

'Really, honey?' said Chuck, coming in behind his mother. 'Such a shame I could never meet her.'

'Do you have photographs of your parents?' asked Constance.

'No. We had to leave Budapest in such a hurry. We left with the clothes we stood up in.'

'How awful,' said Constance. 'I can't imagine how terrible that would be.'

'Yes… it was very hard. My father had lived in our apartment all his life. It was filled with beautiful things – a grand piano of my grandmother's, silver framed photographs, beautiful furniture… all gone.'

'You poor thing,' said Constance with genuine sympathy. It was as if the loss of these physical possessions was more distressing than the loss of Rachael's own mother. This was something she could understand and empathise with. 'Just fancy,' Constance said, shaking her head, 'losing a grand piano…'

After a week, Rachael had recovered sufficiently to suggest to Chuck that she could now manage alone.

'I just want it to be us…' she said. 'Just the family; could you ask your parents to go?'

'Just the family – I like the sound of that.' He kissed her. 'But only if you're sure? I do have to work… I can't afford to take any more time off.'

'I'll be fine now. I'm having the stitches out tomorrow and I feel well – honestly.'

'We ought to register the baby,' said Chuck, 'before I go back to work properly. We need a name. My parents have been asking constantly. They want him named after some distant ancestor.'

Rachael looked alarmed.

'Don't worry – I've told them we're going to make a decision once we're alone – unless you already have an idea?'

'I do have an idea… yes. Something I've been thinking about…'

'Well – what is it? Do you want to name him after your father?'

'Maybe…but I was thinking of Thomas.'

'Thomas…?' He paused, coming to terms with the name. 'So … after…'

'Do you mind?' she asked hurriedly.

'No… I don't mind. I understand.' He smiled, encouragingly, but she could tell he was a little hurt.

'You're so kind to me, Chuck. Thank you. It could be the Hungarian spelling. Tomasz… but maybe that would be a bad idea. And we could name him after you too…You're going to be his father after all.'

'Poor kid – he's going to be landed with a heap of names… How about this… he could be Thomas Eric Charles George? The American spellings, he is after all going to be an American child. And you could call him Tom for short.'

Rachael could feel he was trying really hard to accommodate her.

'Or maybe Thomas Charles George Eric…' she suggested, tentatively.

'Well why not…?' he said at last. 'Thomas is a good name. I'm sure there's some "Bailey ancestor" called Thomas. And at least this way neither one of our fathers can be upset. I'll go down to city hall and see to it straight away.'

The following morning Constance and Eric returned to Vermont. As Rachael watched the cab carrying her parents-in-law away from the apartment and back to the station, she breathed deeply and collapsed onto the sofa. The baby grizzled and she picked him up and put him to her breast. He guzzled milk greedily, gulping it down with great gasps of air.

'Slow down, slow down, little Thomas, or you'll have wind, my boy.'

He looked up at her with his dark brown eyes, eyes that reminded her so much of his father, eyes she had grown to love and that said: 'I'll always love you.'

Chapter 24

In the days following their argument, neither Hamish nor Sophie could forget the things that had been said in the heat of the moment. 'You're not enough for me,' Sophie had told Hamish. It had been a cruel thing to say, and she felt guilty about it, but she refused to apologise until Hamish had accepted her basic argument – that having a child was crucial to her happiness. Hamish felt desperately hurt; he became resentful and moody, and began to come home late.

'I'm a bloody doctor,' he said, when she challenged him about it. 'I work in surgery – what do you expect?'

'But your lists used to be quite regular affairs – nine till five or six at the latest. What's changed?'

'Ever heard of the word emergency?' he'd snapped.

Sophie couldn't quite believe that all his late nights were due to medical emergencies, but she was reluctant to argue with him. There were more important things at stake – like persuading him that should have another round of IVF.

In spite of the frosty atmosphere between them, she managed to get him to agree, reluctantly, to another attempt. Buoyed up with the prospect of this new opportunity, she threw herself into pleasing him, hoping that delicious meals and a tidy house would ease the strains on their relationship. She even bought new underwear and, against her better judgement, materialised in their bedroom one night wearing black stockings and suspenders.

'Ta-da!' she said, twirling around for him.

Hamish already had his head hidden beneath the duvet. He peered over the top of the bedding.

'What on earth do you look like?'

'Oh…' said Sophie, crestfallen. 'I thought you might like it.'

'What… you thought I'd like the sight of my wife dressed like a tart.'

'I just thought…' Sophie began.

'I know what you thought,' Hamish interrupted. 'That I'm a bloke and all we think about is sex. And sex with a woman in stockings, even better. And as you happen to need to have sex with me, why not dress up like a hooker… Goodnight.' He pulled the duvet back over his head and turned away from her.

She should have left it there – removed the scratchy underwear and put on her pyjamas; but as she slipped into bed, she said quietly: 'You haven't forgotten you have to provide a sample on Friday?'

He rolled over in bed and regarded her with loathing.

'No! I haven't forgotten.'

She silently turned off the light and closed her eyes. They lay rigidly next to one another, the space between them alive with resentment and unspoken anger.

Somehow they staggered through the next few days in an atmosphere of strained silence. Sophie tried to initiate conversations, but Hamish was monosyllabic and grumpy. On Friday morning, she was relieved when he mentioned at breakfast that he would be going to the clinic to give his sample.

'Thank you, Hamish,' she said, kissing his cheek. 'I know you hate it and I want you to know how grateful I am…'

'It's OK,' he said, looking at her across the kitchen table. 'I'm not such a bad man, you know.'

'I know…' she said, reaching across the table and taking his hand. 'I'm sorry,' she began.

'Don't…' he said. 'I'd better be off – see you later.'

*

When Sophie started the medication to stimulate her egg production, she felt like an old hand, so familiar were the symptoms: sore breasts – tick; bloating – tick; memory loss – tick, tick, tick.

After her eggs were harvested, Sophie spent an agonising weekend, waiting to find out if they had fertilised. Forgetful and distracted, she forgot to pay for the car park in Cirencester, and when she returned from the supermarket found a ticket on her windscreen. Back home, she roamed the house tidying up half-heartedly. At dusk, after Mick had locked up the hens, she absent-mindedly opened the henhouse, in search of a couple of eggs, and forgot to shut it up again when she came back inside. Hamish, who had just returned from another 'emergency', swung the car into the drive to be met by a flock of hens running headlong towards him. He got out of the car and shooed them back up the drive and into their henhouse.

'What's going on?' he asked irritably, coming into the kitchen.

'What do you mean?' said Sophie.

'The bloody hens were out – I nearly ran them all over. Where's Mick the Chick for heaven's sake – they're his bloody responsibility. He should have locked them up by now.'

'Oh, I think that was my fault,' said Sophie. 'I just went in to get a couple of extra eggs – I must have left the shed door open. I'm sorry...'

'Oh, never mind,' he said, flinging his jacket down on a chair.

'Hamish... Are you all right?' asked Sophie, anxiously. 'You seem a bit... on edge.'

'I'm fine,' Hamish replied. 'I've just got a lot on...'

On Monday morning, she woke early, relieved that she would know by the end of that day if this first phase of the IVF had been a success. She was in the garden when the call came. Sitting on the terrace outside the kitchen, she heard the phone and rushed to answer it.

'Mrs Mitchell?'

'Yes, yes,' she said, breathlessly.

'I have good news. Two healthy eggs have fertilised. If you'd like… we can put both back.'

'Yes… yes please,' she said through tears.

The garden was wreathed in May sunshine as she sat back down on the terrace. The apple trees on the boundary fence were in blossom and the borders were filled with the spring green of herbaceous plants pushing up through the soil, mixed with colourful tulips. Sophie had never seen the garden looking so beautiful. She sat, her face looking up at the sun, and relaxed for the first time in weeks. In a few days' time she would have the implantation. This time – it was going to work. She might even have twins.

She rang her mother after supper that evening.

'Sophie – that's wonderful news. Do you want me to come down again and look after you?'

'If you have time… that would be lovely.'

'Are you sure Hamish won't mind?'

Sophie glanced up at Hamish who had been rather muted about Sophie's 'good news'. Now, he sat at the kitchen table, his laptop open in front of him, working his way through a bottle of wine.

'I don't think he'd mind.'

He glanced up at her, and mouthed, 'What?'

'If mum comes down after the implantation.'

He shrugged his shoulders. 'No,' he said, looking back down at his laptop.

The day after the implantation process, Angela and Sophie were preparing supper together in the kitchen.

'Sophie… what's going on with you and Hamish?' asked Angela, as she dropped peeled potatoes into a pan of water.

'Nothing…' Sophie said casually.

'Come on…' said her mother, 'he comes home late and then when he is here he's perfectly polite, but he's just not engaged… Is he all right?'

'Oh Mum, I don't know. I can't get to the bottom of it. I think the truth is, he's just not that keen on the IVF. He seems to resent it. It's as if he sees it as a competition between him and a possible child. As if I've chosen a child over him.'

'That's sad,' her mother said, sympathetically. 'You have to remember that most men have delicate egos. They want their wives to make a fuss of them; to put them first. And having a child inevitably means they fall down the pecking order. Even your father was not mad keen to have children. When I got pregnant with you, he took a bit of adjusting.'

'Well at least you could do it naturally. I need medical intervention, and he *has* to help me.'

'Well, none of us can do it alone,' her mother said, laughing. 'To tell the truth – I needed a bit of intervention too.'

Sophie looked quizzically at her mother.

'I did – I put a hole in the condom.'

'You didn't! Mum, that's awful.' Sophie began to laugh. 'I can't believe you did that!'

'I know…' her mother giggled, 'but he was never going to say, "OK, let's have a baby." So I took the decision away from him. I'm glad you're not shocked.'

'Well, it's too late if I am. Does he know?'

'No…! And don't ever tell him… He'd be fine about it, probably, but it's a secret I intend to take to my grave!'

'How is Tom by the way?' asked Sophie, as she fried chicken pieces on the range.

'Oh… getting there. But it's early days. He's the strong and silent type – he doesn't open up that much. I mentioned the idea of a holiday, though, and surprisingly, he sounded quite keen.'

'Oh, that's great. Well, if things go OK with the… implantation, maybe we can go out in a couple of months' time. I should be able to travel then. Or will you be here looking after Vic and Simon's baby?'

'Darling,' said Angela, 'I will spend time with the new baby, of course I will, but Vic's parents will be around too – and a girl always needs her mother more than her mother-in- law…'

'If you're sure. I hope it goes well for them. I spoke to her the other day and she sounded so excited. It was lovely.'

'She'll be fine,' said Angela. 'It's due in a couple of weeks. But you need to forget that for now. Concentrate on your own babies and that trip – that will be quite enough excitement for you.'

After her mother left, Sophie tried to distract herself by researching their holiday. She made a reservation in a simple but charming hotel in a nature reserve on Sant'Antioco. She contacted the church authorities in Sardinia, explaining her professional interest in the Roman tombs beneath the basilica. But all the while, she was thinking about the eggs and whether they would survive. Experience had taught her to be cautious. Perhaps Hamish had been right all along; she needed to be prepared for the worst, and then, if the best happened, that was a bonus.

So on the day of her blood test, she drove herself to the clinic and waited calmly for the results. They were good; she was pregnant, but she kept her emotions in check.

'One day at a time,' she said to herself as she drove home. She was looking forward to giving Hamish the news. She was sure that, once he knew she was pregnant, he would feel more positive.

In spite of her best efforts, as the time of his return from work grew closer, she struggled to keep her excitement in check. She put a casserole in the oven and set the table. But still there was no sign of him. He was normally home by six thirty, so at eight o'clock she rang his mobile. It went to voicemail. By half past eight she was getting quite anxious. He usually texted her if he was going to be late. She called one of his colleagues.

'I'm sorry to bother you, John,' she said. 'I just wondered if Hamish was still at the hospital.'

'No… he left early today – I thought he was meeting you…'

'Oh!' she said hurriedly, 'we must have missed each other. It's fine. Thanks…'

She sat at the kitchen table, the cat lying contentedly on her lap, musing on where her husband could be. She stepped outside into the garden. The sun was beginning to set over the valley; the wisteria draped across the front of the house was in full bloom and the scent as she walked down the drive was intoxicating. As she reached the lane, she considered turning right and walking up to the pub to check if he'd stopped there, on the way home, for a quick drink. But instead, she turned left, towards the church. The sun hung low in the sky, like a vast red orb.

As she walked passed the row of gold-stone cottages, bathed in rose coloured light, she told herself, 'He'll be meeting someone – that's all. I'll just have a walk around the village, and when I get back, he'll be home.' The old vicarage was normally in darkness during the week, but she noticed an upstairs light was on. It was unusual, but perhaps Flora and Marcus had a housekeeper. To her surprise, she saw Hamish's car parked at the side of the house; it was almost hidden by Flora's white Range Rover. She stopped at the gate, confused. What was he doing there? She walked up the drive, her legs feeling heavy beneath her, her mind whirring with possible explanations. Perhaps he was giving Flora medical advice? Or possibly he was meeting Marcus…

She stopped at the front door and was about to ring the bell, when she noticed light spilling from the kitchen window. As she walked around the side of the house and peered into the large white marble space, she saw Hamish kissing Flora. He was fully dressed – he even had his jacket on – but she was wearing nothing but a little satin slip, revealing her small, neat breasts and flat, toned stomach. She had her arms around his neck and one of her long brown legs was draped around his hips. He was laughing and whispered something to her, before pulling away.

He walked towards the kitchen door, but she ran after him and flung her arms around his neck once again.

'Don't go, Hamish,' she said, 'come back to bed!'

Sophie leant against the wall of the house, her heart thumping. She felt sick. She was tempted to bang on the window or march up to the front door and ring the bell. To confront them. But when she thought of Flora and how she would sneer and laugh at poor, badly dressed Sophie, she couldn't face it. The humiliation would be too terrible.

She heard someone crunching down the drive and ducked down behind a large bushy hydrangea. Hamish was getting into his car, his lights illuminating the side of the house. She prayed she wasn't visible. He manoeuvred around the Range Rover, reversed out into the road and roared off towards their house.

Sophie staggered to her feet, scarcely able to comprehend what she had seen. When she arrived back at home, Hamish was in the hallway looking through the mail.

'Hi there,' he said, casually. 'Good day?'

'Yes…' she said, automatically.

'Where have you been?' he asked.

'Out,' she said, while thinking to herself, *where have I been? Where have you been?*

'You're late…' she said.

'Yes… the list ran on rather – sorry. Is there anything for supper?'

She looked up at him, surprised by the ease with which he lied.

'I had my test results today,' she said, quietly.

'Oh… good news?'

'Do you care?'

'Sophie… don't start this again.'

'What?' Her tone was sullen. Cool. Icy.

He noticed.

'Darling…' he said, gently. 'What's the matter?'

'Well, the good news, Hamish, is that I'm pregnant. The bad news is that you appear to be in love with someone else. And no… there isn't any bloody supper.'

Hamish blanched visibly. She could see his mind feverishly working out what she knew.

'Don't bother denying it,' she said, before he could speak, 'I just saw you together… "Don't go, Hamish; come back to bed,"' she said in a mock whine, imitating Flora. 'You're unbelievable. I hate you.'

She was dry-eyed, determined not to give him the satisfaction of seeing her cry. She turned on her heel and walked upstairs; but in their bedroom she locked the door, lay down on the bed and wept.

Chapter 25

New York
December 1960

Rachael and Chuck had lived in New York for nearly a year and while Rachael had grown to love the convenience and energy of the city, she was struck, daily, by its essential contradictions – it combined form with chaos.

'Go down two blocks and turn left,' people would say when giving instructions; or 'across three blocks and turn right'. There was a pleasing logic to it. But within this strict framework, life teemed with excitement. Staccato bursts of jazz music sprang out of doorways. Noisy vendors sold their food from street corners. Bars and cafes and restaurants tempted you in as you walked by with the scent of freshly baked donuts, or bagels, or long bratwurst – a kind of German sausage – that reminded Rachael of Budapest. In fact, much of New York reminded her of Budapest. In particular, she enjoyed the jumble of different cultures jostling for position. It brought back memories of her parents' salons in the 'old days'; those events had always welcomed a wide variety of participants: elderly Jewish academics mixing with musicians from Eastern Europe and young hot-heated students like József.

Rachael's building was a microcosm of this cultural diversity. A Polish musician lived on the floor above and practised his violin each morning at eleven. On the top floor was a university lecturer from Palermo who specialised in medieval art. But the grande dame of the building was, of course, Violet Dreyfuss. In her large elegant ground-floor apartment she held court, upholding English customs where at all possible, serving tea regularly at four o'clock. It was considered an honour to be invited to one of these afternoon soirees and Rachael had been delighted to receive an invitation a couple of weeks before Christmas. Chuck, who had decided to work from home that afternoon, urged her to go. 'I'll look after the children. You'll enjoy it – you know you're dying to see inside that apartment.'

Well into her eighties, and possessed of a rather overbearing manner, Violet was nevertheless widely considered to be a beauty. Her elegance and cut-glass accent had led those who met her to invent all manner of exotic backstories. Some claimed she was actually a runaway duchess, others that she was the ex-mistress of a royal prince. Whatever the truth of her background, Violet had the ability to draw people out and yet gave them the confidence that their secrets would go no further. It was not people's past behaviour or dubious morals that interested Violet, but rather the circles in which they moved. It was her personal quest to find connections between her new acquaintances and old friends. That, at any rate, was what Rachael had been told about Violet by the other inhabitants of the house. Now, as she checked her appearance in the hall mirror, she feared Violet would find her a disappointment in that regard, for she knew no one of any interest.

'Now,' said Violet to Rachael, pouring lapsang souchong into hand-painted porcelain cups, 'I want to know all about you and Charles.' As she handed the tea cup to Rachael, her fingers sparkled with diamond rings.

'Oh, there's nothing much to tell,' Rachael replied, sidestepping the question.

Sipping her tea, she admired Violet's apartment; it was filled with exquisite baroque furniture – gilded chairs with needlepoint covers and little sofas draped in silk. Every surface was covered with objects – Fabergé eggs, pieces of Dresden china and bronze figurines. Rachael was sure that she recognised one or two Rodins in amongst Violet's collection. The turquoise silk-covered walls were lined with paintings – Dutch 'still lives' jostled for position with Italian religious works. There were even Impressionist pieces and pencil sketches that bore familiar signatures. Rachael was dying to know how this lady had acquired so much art, but as usual Violet was asking the questions.

'Oh, I think there's lots to tell,' Violet knowingly. 'For example, you were brought up in Budapest… how on earth did you meet a young American banker…?'

Since arriving in America, Rachael had become adept at presenting a particular version of the truth that avoided any mention of Sardinia, or her love affair with Tommaso. Large swathes of her 'story' were left out of the conversation. The true paternity of her son depended on the inviolable nature of her secret.

'Chuck and I met in Austria,' she would say when colleagues of her husband's enquired about her background. 'Then we married and came here.' It was a well-rehearsed line – and true in its way – except that it edited out a year or more of her life. But for some reason, as she sat in Violet's beautiful apartment, surrounded by all that famous artwork, and gazed into those remarkable violet eyes, she felt the urge to confide in her interrogator.

'We met originally in a refugee camp – near Vienna. My father and I had fled from Budapest. My first husband, József, had been killed and we had to leave in quite a hurry.'

'I'm sorry to hear that, my dear,' said Violet, offering Rachael a cucumber sandwich. 'But what was Charles doing in a refugee camp…?'

'He was a student at Vienna University who volunteered to help the refugees. He was very kind and I liked him a lot, but I'd just lost my husband and then I discovered I was pregnant…'

'I see,' said Violet, pouring more tea. She was adept, Rachael had discovered, at the art of silence. Of simply pausing and allowing the other person to fill the space.

'My father and I moved to London where he got a job at the university – he's an archaeologist. After that we spent some time in Sardinia where he was in charge of a dig. I don't talk about Sardinia...' Rachael went on, nervously. 'No one in New York seems to know much about it...'

'Oh, I quite understand,' said Violet comfortingly, reaching across and covering Rachael's hand with her own long elegant fingers.

'We lived there for eight months,' Rachael continued. 'I liked it. We lived in a little cottage by the sea. It was very beautiful.'

Violet studied her face intently. 'I too visited Sardinia when I was very young,' she said wistfully. 'The people there are rather intoxicating... didn't you find?'

'Yes,' said Rachael, nervously, looking down at her hands, 'they are very charming... So... you have been there too?'

'Oh yes... although it was a long time ago – well before the first war. I was very naïve and fell wildly in love.'

She gazed across at Rachael, who blushed slightly.

'It was very hot and dusty, I seem to recall...' Violet continued. 'So... what happened after Sardinia?'

Rachael, relieved that her interrogator had moved on, said briskly:

'We came back to England and I married Chuck – and then we came here.'

She paused, thankful that she had once again, skirted the full version of the truth.

'How romantic,' said Violet, wistfully. 'Oh yes... true love. Did you get the chance to look around Vienna at all when you were in Austria? I was there myself between the wars. I recall some magnificent parties; I don't suppose you happened to meet...'

As Violet reeled off a list of important people she had met in Vienna, Rachael, only half-listening, studied the apartment once again. It really was an extraordinary collection of art and furniture. She resolved to pluck up the courage to ask Violet how she had acquired it all. But Violet, adept as ever, sidestepped the question when it came.

'Oh, you know… things one picks up along the way.'

It seemed to Rachael that life in New York made anything possible. People reinvented themselves – losing awkward or embarrassing pasts, gathering in new opportunities and futures on the way. Was that what Violet had done? Was that what she, Rachael, had been given the chance to do?

When she returned to her own apartment a couple of hours later, she found Chuck and the children asleep on the sofa, a storybook open and abandoned on the floor. The baby was lying comatose across his lap, and Angela had snuggled under Chuck's arm. Rachael stood watching them all, sleeping peacefully, her heart filled with joy. Her father had been right after all. She had thought her heart would break when she left Tommaso, but she had been given a chance for a new life, and had found true contentment. She loved her husband, she loved her children and she loved New York. Angela was in a good nursery school. Little Tom, at seven months old, was a happy, healthy baby. Charles had been promoted and was beginning to make his way in the world. He talked of them buying a holiday home – a summer house on Long Island where she could take the children for two or three months and escape the heat of the city. It seemed to Rachael that the years of struggle were finally at an end. Even Chuck's parents had accepted their curious Hungarian daughter-in-law. The family drove up to Vermont periodically – for Tom's christening, for Thanksgiving – but Rachael decided to ask Chuck if they could remain in New York for the Christmas holidays.

'I'd like to do it myself,' she said to Chuck the next day over breakfast. 'My mother taught me all sorts of wonderful things to cook at Christmas and I'd like to do it for you and the children, and your parents. Please Chuck?'

'Well, OK,' he'd relented. 'I'll call my parents and break the news… My mother's always done Christmas, but I'm sure she'll get over it – eventually!'

That evening, he came back home from work and announced that his mother had agreed to spend Christmas in New York. 'She wasn't too pleased, mind… ' he said, standing behind Rachael as she washed up a pan in the sink. He kissed the side of her neck, and she swung round and kissed him back.

'Thank you Chuck! We'll have a wonderful time – I promise.'

'Oh…' he said, as he took a beer from the refrigerator, 'I've got to go to Chicago tomorrow. I'll just be away overnight. '

He left the house the following morning in a cheery mood carrying a small overnight bag carefully packed by Rachael. It contained one clean shirt, a fresh set of underwear, pyjamas, a washbag and, nestling in the middle, a photograph of the family. Chuck always travelled with a photograph of Rachael and the children.

'I'll just be away twenty-four hours,' he said over breakfast, his packed bag standing ready in the hall. 'I've got a couple of meetings in Chicago and I'll be back on the first flight out tomorrow. Why they can't just do the meeting on the phone, I don't know… but that's banking.'

Rachael stood in the bay window of the sitting room holding baby Thomas in her arms, as Chuck walked down the road towards Third Avenue. He turned as he reached the corner, and looked back at Rachael; she flapped Tom's hand up and down, whispering in his ear, 'Wave to Daddy.' Chuck waved back before jumping into a cab.

As soon as Chuck had left, Rachael called a local store, and asked if they could deliver a Christmas tree to the apartment that morning. It would be fun to decorate it while Chuck was away and would be a surprise for him when he returned the following day. After she had dressed the children, she stood excitedly in the window of the sitting room waiting for the delivery truck to arrive.

'Just put the Christmas tree there.' Rachael said, pointing to a place at the centre of the bay window. The delivery man dragged the tall tree through the sitting room and positioned it carefully in its stand. It practically reached the ceiling.

The children were delighted. Tom sat on the sitting room floor rocking back and forward, opening and closing his fists in excitement. Angela walked around the tree studying every angle. 'I'd like to decorate it today, Mommy,' she said. 'They have a tree at nursery school and we all decorated it last week.'

'Then we shall,' declared Rachael. 'I know we used to wait till Christmas Eve, but I thought it would be nice for Daddy to come home to.'

She put the baby into the large pram and bumped it down the steps of the brownstone. Then, holding Angela's hand, she walked several blocks until she reached Bloomingdale's. She took the elevator to the Christmas department. The abundance of Christmas decorations was one of the delights of living in America; even in Vermont she had discovered a store that sold nothing but tinsel, tree decorations and fairy lights throughout the year.

With a basket balanced on top of the pram, Rachael wandered between the aisles picking up Christmas lights and glass baubles.

'You can each choose two things for the tree,' she said to the children.

Angela ran around peering into baskets and returned with a glittering unicorn and a huge tinsel star.

'For the top of the tree, Mommy,' she said eagerly.

Rachael pushed the pram between the displays so Tom could choose something. He grabbed a teddy bear with his little pudgy hands.

'Put that back, Tom, we don't need a teddy bear on the tree.'

The little boy grizzled, but they finally agreed on a chubby-faced Russian doll wearing a bright red coat and a blue muffler, and a pair of straw angels with wings.

When her basket was filled, Rachael paid at the till, went down in the elevator, and walked slowly towards Central Park. She stopped briefly at the children's zoo before heading south to the skating rink at the Rockefeller Center opposite St Patrick's Cathedral. They sat together on a bench and watched the skaters twirling around.

'I wanna go skating, Mommy,' said Angela. 'I'm old enough now… I'm three and a half.'

Angela had developed quite a pronounced New York accent since she'd started nursery school.

'I know, honey,' said Rachael. 'But not today.'

'But you promised,' Angela complained. 'You said when I was old enough…'

'I know I did, but I can't leave little Tom on his own in the pram, while you and I skate. When Daddy's back home, we'll come together, as a family.'

She thought about that word – *family*. She realised that for the first time since her mother had died, she really felt that she was part of a family. Her mother's death, and that of József, had created such a sense of loss. Her own father had done his best to fill the void and was the kindest man she had ever known – until she met Chuck. She *had* learned to love Chuck – her father had been right about that. It wasn't the tempestuous passion of her brief liaison with Tommaso, nor indeed the first, innocent tender love she had felt for József. Instead, it was a relationship based on trust and mutual respect. Each evening she found herself waiting for the sound of his key in the lock, for his cheery voice as he called to her and the children. He adored Angela and Tom, and she loved him for that. He often said he couldn't love them anymore if they were his own.

Her life had taken such a complicated winding path and it was only now that she could look back and see it had all been leading to this point; where she was a happy, much-loved wife and mother, living a good life with two healthy children in New York – the most exciting city on the planet.

'Come on,' she said to Angela, 'we should be getting home.' She looked up at the impressive façade of St Patrick's Cathedral. She had been brought up as a Catholic when her mother was alive. But George was an atheist, and after her mother's death, the ritual of Sunday mornings spent in church had ceased. Now she considered taking her own children to the cathedral. What would her parents-in-law make of it? Stolid Protestants both – they would probably be horrified at the idea of 'their' grandchildren being brought up as Catholics. She'd discuss it with Chuck when he got home.

Rachael and Angela, watched by Tom, spent a happy afternoon decorating the tree. She wrapped up a special present she had bought for Chuck – a vinyl copy of 'True Love' – and placed it beneath the tree. She had loved three men in her short life – all in a slightly different way. But Chuck, she now realised, was her best friend, someone she could rely on, and if that wasn't true love, what was?

That night, once the children were in bed, she sat alone on the sofa as the white lights flickered on the tree and wrote an airmail letter to her father.

> *My darling Papa,*
>
> *It's been weeks since we corresponded. I hope you are well and that Mrs Roper is looking after you. I have just put up our Christmas tree. It reaches almost to the ceiling of our apartment. Can you imagine? Mrs Roper would love it. It is the biggest tree I've ever seen – well, apart from the one at the Rockefeller Center! Do you remember me telling you about it? They skate there and it's so pretty with all the lights. I took Angela and Tom there this afternoon. Angela is so keen to learn to skate and I have promised to teach her.*
>
> *How are you, dear Papa? Is work going well? Do write soon and tell me. Or better still – might you come out and see me? You could fly here, you know. It's expensive, but I'm sure Chuck would pay for a ticket. He is such a generous*

man, and it would be so lovely to see you. I do so want you to
spend some time with the children before they get too much
older. Angela is so grown-up – she is already at nursery school
and little Tom… well, he's not so little anymore. Do say you
will come, Papa. Perhaps when you break up from university.
     I enclose a photograph of myself with the children. It was
taken at Thanksgiving.
     I am thinking of you.
     All my love,
     Rachael

The following morning, Rachael woke to find that it had snowed
in the night. The street outside, normally quite busy with cars and
delivery vans, was silent and still. Looking out of the sitting room
bay window, she observed people tramping past her house, wearing
fur-lined boots and heavy overcoats. The blanket of snow had transformed this frantic place into an urban fairy story. Everything was
peaceful and quiet. She imagined children all over the city excited
at the prospect of a day off school; 'snow days', they called them in
America. It was such a happy-sounding description. They'd be in
their apartments drinking hot chocolate persuading their mothers to
take them to the parks and have snowball fights, instead of boarding
the school bus. It reminded her of the blissful days she had spent
with her mother in the park opposite their apartment in Budapest.
She had a beautiful dark red coat and her mother knitted her a long
red scarf to match. Rachael had loved that scarf.

She rang Angela's nursery and was surprised to discover they
intended to remain open. But Angela was keen to stay at home
and play outside in the snow.

'I don't want to go to school,' Angela complained, her arms
clamped to her sides, as her mother attempted to force them into
her coat. 'I want to stay here with you and Tom.'

'I need to go to the market this morning…' said Rachael. 'You'll be bored. If you go to school, I'll collect you at lunchtime and we can have a lovely afternoon together, playing in the snow. Please, Angela – put on your coat.'

Once Angela was dressed, Rachael fed the baby's arms into his warm woollen jacket and pulled his hood up over his pink ears. She put mittens onto his little fingers and, once he was in the pram, wrapped him up in a warm blanket. After dropping Angela at nursery, she posted the letter to her father, praying, as she did so, that it would get there in time for Christmas.

She bought some beef at the meat counter of the local store, and then wheeled Tom slowly back to the apartment building. A fog was descending over the city, but with luck it would dissipate by lunchtime.

She planned to make a meat loaf for dinner – it was a good warming dish for a winter evening, and one of Chuck's favourites. As she bumped the pram up the brownstone's stairs, she heard a distant rumble. She looked around and saw a plume of smoke rising up. It seemed to be coming from way downtown. A fire, maybe, she thought, or a gas explosion?

Inside the apartment, she put Tom in his cot for a nap, and began to mince the meat. Chuck had bought her a metal mincing machine that she could fix onto her food mixer. As she forced the lump of beef into the tube, spirals of meat twirled out of the mincer into a bowl. She chopped onions and shredded a carrot and some cheese; then made breadcrumbs from an old loaf. After whisking eggs, milk, salt and pepper together, she added the bread, beef, onion, cheese and carrot. She packed it into a loaf tin and then spread the top with a mixture of ketchup and brown sugar. Setting it in the oven to bake she wandered through to the sitting room, where she sat at the desk in the window and began to write her Christmas cards. She was relieved to see that the fog had lifted a little.

At lunchtime, with the meat loaf cooling on a rack in the kitchen, she woke the baby, put him in the pram and, taking her cards, went to collect Angela from nursery school.

On the way back to the apartment, she shoved the pile of cards into the postbox. As she did so, she became aware of the sound of sirens. Several police cars roared past; a fire truck and an ambulance following behind.

She stopped in the drugstore to pick up some cotton wool and asked the lady behind the counter: 'Is there a fire or something...? I noticed the ambulance and police cars.'

'Oh! Haven't you heard? There's been a terrible air accident. Two planes collided this morning just outside Brooklyn.'

Rachael went cold. Chuck was due to fly home that morning from Chicago.

'Do you know where the planes came from?' she asked.

'No... but it's a terrible mess, I hear; one crashed into houses at Park Slope. It's just awful – all those poor people. And just before Christmas too.'

Rachael felt a rising sense of panic. She told herself to calm down. Hundreds of planes flew into New York each day, why should it be his plane? She wanted to go home, to check on her meat loaf, to give the children their lunch. She wanted everything to be just as it always was. For Chuck to come home later, and say in his breezy way: 'Hi honey, I'm home. Gosh what a terrible flight. It's good to be back... Something smells delicious – what's for dinner?'

And she would say, 'Your favourite. Meat loaf.'

'Oh, honey,' he'd say, 'You spoil me...'

But instead she turned the pram towards Brooklyn and, holding Angela firmly by the hand, began to walk fast.

Angela began to whine.

'Mommy, Mommy, you're hurting.'

Rachael couldn't hear her daughter. All she was aware of was the pounding of her heart in her ears. She walked as swiftly as she could, without actually running, but Angela was slowing her down. Finally, Rachael picked her up and put her at one end of the pram, opposite Tom. She hardly noticed traffic, or lights, or other people. She just had to get as close as possible to that accident site and see for herself that it *wasn't* his plane. Then they would go home, and have lunch, and everything would be fine.

The children both began to cry and she soon realised she could never walk all the way to Brooklyn. She hailed a cab and somehow squeezed the children and the pram into the back.

'Brooklyn please…'

'Haven't you heard… there's been an accident. I'm not sure how close I can get. They closed the bridges.'

The driver dropped them south of Little Italy in Canal Street.

'This is as far as I can go, I'm afraid. If you don't need to go there, I'd advise you to get back in the cab and go back uptown. It's chaos down there…'

'Thank you…' she said, putting the children into the pram. 'I'll be fine… I just need to get a little closer.'

There were police cars and ambulances and fire engines filling the road as she approached the Manhattan Bridge. A policeman was barring the way across.

'I need to get over there….' Rachael said. 'I need to see what plane it was.'

'No one can go over there, Mam…'

'But my husband, it might be his plane.'

'I'm sure it's not, Mam… Look, you have to move back. I have to leave the road free for emergency services, I'm sure you understand.'

He pushed her gently along the road, where she stood rooted to the spot, as the icy drizzle fell softly. The children began to cry once more.

'Mommy, Mommy,' said Angela. 'I'm hungry and cold. I wanna go home.'

But Rachael wasn't listening; she'd noticed a man standing nearby, scribbling in a notebook.

'Excuse me…' she said, pushing the pram towards him. 'I was wondering if you knew anything about… the crash. I'm worried that I might know someone on one of the planes.'

'Oh… OK,' he said, putting his notebook in his coat pocket. 'Well, I don't know much. I'm a reporter for the *Daily News* and we're being kept out of the way too. All I know is that two planes collided around ten this morning. One was from Chicago heading for La Guardia. It hit a TWA flight coming into Idlewild.'

Rachael eyes immediately filled with tears.

'Look,' said the reporter gently, 'I'm sure your friend is OK.'

'It's my husband…' she said. '*He* was coming from Chicago.'

'What airline?' asked the reporter, calmly.

'United.'

He looked at his notes and then back at the children.

'It was the United flight, wasn't it?' she asked.

'Yes…' he looked away. 'It was Flight 826… was that your husband's flight?'

'I don't know… I don't know what time he was leaving. Just that he was due back today.'

'Oh… OK,' said the reporter, more cheerfully, 'well, he could be flying in later… there's no way of knowing yet. Have you tried calling his office, or his hotel?'

'No… not yet. I was uptown and heard about it. I just ran down here… it was stupid really. I didn't know what to do.'

She broke down and sobbed.

The reporter put his arm around her.

'Hey… I'm sure he'll be OK. Look… here's my card – call me later and I'll see if I've heard anything. I expect he'll back home by then – all safe and sound – you'll see.'

Somehow Rachael managed to find a cab driving north. The driver dismantled the pram for her and put the children in the back.

'You all right, Mam?' he asked. 'You look a little shaken. Terrible business with those planes. I hate air travel. It's just not natural.'

*

Back home, Rachael turned on the radio and found the public news channel. The reporter had been right: a United flight overshot the runway at La Guardia and collided with the TWA Constellation. As the United flight flew over Prospect Park, a teacher at a nearby school told reporters he was close enough to see the pilot's face as he dipped the wing of his plane in an attempt to avoid the school. The plane crashed into Park Slope on the intersection of Seventh and Sterling Place, scattering wreckage and setting fire to ten brownstone apartment buildings, a church, a funeral parlour, a Chinese laundry and a delicatessen.

Somehow, Rachael fed the children lunch and then she settled them in their room with some books to look at, while she called Chuck's office.

'Do you know which flight he was on?' she asked his secretary.

'No… Mam, but we're checking now. We'll let you know as soon as we hear anything, I promise.'

She heard nothing for two hours. She was frantic with worry. As darkness fell over the city, snow began to drift in from the west. Wild flurries of snowflakes splattered against the windows. Rachael sat in darkness, except for the flashing Christmas lights, watching the snow, her mind blank. When the phone rang, she was so startled, she jumped, as if she'd woken from a bad dream.

'Mrs Bailey,' said a sympathetic voice on the phone, 'this is Marion Roberts from the office. I'm so very sorry to tell you, but Chuck *was* on board the United flight from Chicago. There were no survivors…'

Rachael dropped the phone. She never heard what Marion said next. She dropped on her knees and began to scream. 'No… No… No…'

*

Eric and Constance came down to New York the following day. Rachael didn't want to see them, but her father-in-law had insisted.

'There will be formalities to deal with,' he'd said. His voice was clipped, unnaturally calm. 'I should be there to sort things out.'

Rachael, who was almost helpless with grief, felt unable to disagree. She was sitting at the desk in the sitting room when she saw their cab arrive. Constance, dressed in a black coat and hat, was helped out of the cab by her husband. Eric looked up at the window and raised his hand to Rachael. Once he was indoors, it was clear that he was in organisational mode. He'd fought in the second war; he'd been an army major stationed in Europe and he was used to dealing with tragedy.

Constance, though, was mute; as if she was unable to speak. Her husband helped her into a chair in the drawing room, where she sat staring into space. Angela ran in from the kitchen, followed by Tom, shuffling on his backside. Constance winced visibly, as they clambered onto her lap.

'Angela, please... don't do that,' said Rachael, leaping to her feet and grabbing the baby. 'Grandmother is tired. Please... Angela just go back to the kitchen.' She sat back down, with Tom on her own lap.

'I just wanted to say hello...' said Angela logically.

'I know, darling... but later. OK?'

Angela wandered desultorily towards the kitchen.

'Do they know yet?' asked Eric.

'I've tried to explain, but they don't really understand. Tom... certainly not. Angela maybe a little. But she keeps thinking he'll come home later.'

Constance let out a deep moan, followed by a wail and began to weep.

'Oh Constance,' said Rachael. She put the baby on the floor, where he sat happily playing with the buttons on his cardigan. Rachael knelt down by her mother-in-law. 'I'm so, so sorry. I loved him so much, but I cannot imagine, as his mother, what you must be feeling.' She tried to put her arms around Constance's shoulders, but the older woman pulled away.

'This is your fault,' Constance said, bitterly.

'No, dear,' said Eric. 'That's just not fair.'

'No…' Constance continued. 'If he hadn't married this woman, he'd be living in Vermont now… Nowhere near a plane.'

'You can't think like that… we talked about this,' Eric said, exasperated. He turned to Rachael. 'I'm sorry,' he said, 'she's so distraught, she doesn't know what she's saying.'

Rachael went and sat back on the sofa, pulling Tom back onto her lap; she understood the need to blame someone, anyone. It was normal. Perhaps this was the first time Constance had ever lost anyone. She, on the other hand, had lost so many people, the pain, the sheer agony of grief and loss were almost familiar.

'Now,' said Eric, calmly. 'There are things we need to discuss. To sort out.'

'Yes…' said Rachael, compliantly. 'Would you like coffee, or tea?'

'No… thank you. Maybe later. I've spoken to Chuck's office. He had a life assurance policy – that will go to you. It's a good sum, but not enough to live on forever. The rent on this apartment is eighty-five a month. It's paid up until the end of January. We can go on paying it for a little while but can't really keep it up permanently. I'm sure you understand. I've not seen the will yet, but Chuck had a small trust fund. By rights, it reverts to the family, but he may have changed that when he married you. I just want you to know that there will be some money to take care of you and the children, but not to the same standard, if you understand me. Once the funeral is taken care of, the rest can all be sorted out.'

Rachael felt numb. This talk of money was bewildering. Part of her mind still clung to the idea that he might just walk through that door anytime – that his name on that passenger list had been a mistake. The thought of life without Chuck was almost unimaginable now. And life after Chuck was not something she had ever considered. As far as she was concerned, her whole being was focused on simply coping with the next minute, the next hour.

'I see. I am grateful of course. I ... wasn't expecting anything. I didn't marry Chuck... for his money.'

'No... I know. But once the will's been read, it'll all become clearer. Is your father still alive?'

'My father... yes.'

'Have you spoken to him?'

'Yes, I rang him last night.'

'Good. And I suppose he's keen for you to come home?'

'He wants me to do whatever is right for me and the children...'

'And what *is* right for you?'

Rachael put Tom back on the floor, stood up and walked over to the window.

'I really don't know. I thought I had found the love of my life. We had a home and a family and I thought I would live here forever...'

Eric remained silent and looked down at his shoes.

Constance glared at Rachael's back.

'*You* had a family. Those children had nothing to do with my son,' Constance said, sharply.

'He was their father,' said Rachael, turning to face them both. 'He loved them.'

'That's as maybe,' said Eric. 'But we both know that Tom is not Chuck's son. You just have to look at him. At least be honest about that now, Rachael.'

The funeral took place a week later in Vermont. The organisation was taken out of Rachael's hands. Eric had dealt with the authorities and identified the body, although how much of her husband's body was actually in the smart oak coffin that stood on a dais in the church on the green, Rachael couldn't be sure. The wreckage of the plane had been so terrible, it seemed impossible to imagine any part of her husband surviving. After the ceremony, which was attended by Chuck's work colleagues and old family friends, everyone went back to the Bailey family house. A maid served small glasses of sherry and little canapés – tiny pieces of food that you could put into your mouth in one bite. Rachael had never eaten such a thing. The drawing room gradually filled with smoke from the men's cigars and cigarettes. One or two people came over to Rachael and told her how sorry they were, but most of the sympathy was reserved for Constance, who sat in a tall wing armchair, dressed in a black silk sheath, her dark red mouth set in a thin, mean line.

After the wake, Rachael ordered a cab back to the station. She gathered the children together and was just putting Tom into his little dark coat when Eric came into the hall.

'You leaving?' he asked.

'Yes… I thought I should.'

'Well, let us know what you plan to do…'

'I will,' she said.

'Bye Grandpa,' Angela said cheerfully, reaching up for the old man.

He removed her little hands, and brushed his suit down, as if wiping away something unclean, and went back into the drawing room.

The apartment in New York seemed so empty and dark when Rachael returned. She turned on the Christmas lights and they flashed incongruously – their innate jollity at odds with her pain. The next day would be Christmas Eve and somehow she had to get through it for the sake of the children. But in the New Year she would go home – back to London. She saw that now. She was not welcome in America any longer.

Chapter 26

Gloucestershire
May 2017

Hamish moved out the night Sophie discovered him with Flora. He had tried to argue that it meant nothing, that it was just a fling, nothing more.

He had stood outside their locked bedroom and banged on the door.

'Let me in – please, Sophie. I'm so sorry. I'm not in love with her. I love you. She was just… available. Fun. She wanted nothing from me, except me…'

Sophie lay on her bed and listened to him. She had some sympathy with this view. She understood very well what Flora had offered. No-strings sex. No 'baby' sex. Flora didn't need baby sex. She already had four children.

'I don't think you can love me, Hamish,' she'd called out to him, 'or you couldn't have done what you did.'

'I'm sorry, I'm sorry. I'm an idiot. Please let me in.'

'No. Just go, Hamish… I don't know what to say to you. And, honestly, I just need to stay calm and strong for the babies I'm carrying. I am not going to allow your behaviour to upset me.'

Eventually, she had heard the front door close and his car starting up in the drive. He turned right out of the drive, she noticed, not left towards Flora's house.

She hardly slept that night. She couldn't get the thought of him kissing Flora of her mind. How could he? But even worse than the kissing, worse, even, than the idea of them having sex, was the thought that he might have taken Flora into his confidence. Talked to her about his marriage; shared their intimate secrets with her – in particular, Sophie's desperation for a child.

'Sophie's only interested in having a baby.' Is that what he would have said? And had she leant across the table, or the bed, and taken his hand and replied: 'What a silly girl, when she could have you…'

Exhausted, but unable to sleep, she eventually got up and roamed around the house. She wandered into the second bedroom along the corridor – the room she had chosen for 'the nursery'. It had been painted white by the previous owners, and was clean and tidy, but wasn't suitable for a child. Just that afternoon, after leaving the clinic, she had visited a shop in Cirencester that sold paint and wallpaper. She had discussed paint colours with the assistant and had finally decided on yellow.

'It works brilliantly for a child's room,' the assistant had said. 'And the good thing is that it doesn't matter if it's a boy or a girl.' They had selected a paper decorated with pale yellow unicorns and the assistant had given her a sample to take away; it was still downstairs in her handbag. How ironic, she thought, that while she had been choosing wallpaper for their baby's room, Hamish had been with that woman.

'I'm only just pregnant,' Sophie had said, relishing the words. 'I realise it's rather early to be choosing wallpaper. And I don't want to tempt fate.'

'Oh I know,' said the assistant, 'I know women who won't even buy a babygrow until their child is born. But a nursery is different – it needs to be ready and you won't have time once it's born.'

Sophie had nodded in agreement.

'I mean one has to be practical, after all,' the assistant had declared.

Now, staring at the white walls, Sophie wondered when it would be safe to decorate. When she reached twenty weeks? Twenty-two maybe… the babies would be viable by then surely. But it would be tricky, climbing a ladder with a large belly, especially without Hamish's help.

As she went downstairs in search of the wallpaper sample, she could see the sun coming up through the landing window. It rose over the tops of the trees that ran along the river valley, beyond the edge of the village. Did Flora have the same view? What colour were her children's bedrooms? Remembering the scene in their kitchen at Christmas, when the children had revealed her distaste for colourful decorations, she thought their rooms were probably painted a discreet shade of beige. They would certainly not be bright pink, lilac or deep denim blue. And they would definitely not be yellow.

She found the wallpaper sample and stuck it on the dresser to admire it while she made herself a cup of tea. She fed the cat and then, still holding the piece of wallpaper, went back to bed.

It was odd, she thought, as she settled beneath the duvet, that after her initial shock at what Hamish had done, the whole situation felt surreal, as if Hamish was just away somewhere; as if he was no longer her concern. All that mattered to her now was the health of her unborn children. She thought about what it would be like if he never came back. Whether she wanted him to come back.

If the pregnancy went well and she had two children – could she cope by herself? She thought about Rachael and how admirably she had coped for all those years, bringing up two children alone. But the difference between her and her grandmother was that Rachael had no choice in the matter. Her husband had died. Whereas, if she and Hamish separated, he would still be part of her life and that of her children. He would turn up at weekends to see the children. Worse… he might even be with Flora. That, surely, would be agony.

'Stop now,' she said to herself. There was no point, she realised, in imagining things that might never happen. She sipped her tea,

DEBBIE RIX

turned on the radio and eventually slipped into a deep sleep. She was woken after nine by the ringing of the phone.

'Sophie… it's me, Hamish.'

'Oh… yes,' she said in a befuddled state. 'I was asleep.'

'I'm sorry to wake you. I haven't slept a wink. Can I come and see you?'

She shook herself awake and hauled herself up in bed.

'Aren't you at work?' she asked.

'No, I've called in sick.'

'Oh I see. Well… I don't want to see you.'

'Darling – that's just unreasonable.'

She felt a flare of anger, which she tried to suppress, but it erupted nevertheless.

'Unreasonable!' she shouted. '*I'm* being unreasonable! You've got a nerve.'

Slamming the phone down, she breathed deeply and wandered into the bathroom, where she ran a bath, pouring in some soothing lavender oil. Lying down, she examined her belly and her breasts. The nipples looked different; they appeared to be bigger, but it was hard to tell if things had really changed. It was probably too soon for changes anyway.

Afterwards, wrapped in a bathrobe, she went downstairs and made some scrambled eggs.

She was just finishing eating when she heard someone in the hall. Within minutes Hamish appeared in the kitchen.

'I thought I said I didn't want to see you,' Sophie said, curtly, running her plate under the tap.

'I know. But I need some clothes and I wanted to explain.'

'You did that last night… there's no need to go through it all again. If I recall correctly, you said something along the lines of: you didn't mean it. That *woman* in her slinky nightwear meant nothing – is that right?'

He blushed, and stood awkwardly, nervously fiddling with the back of a kitchen chair.

'How much did you see?' he asked, anxiously.

'Enough… I saw you together in the kitchen. I was going for a walk. I was worried about you – about why you were so late. As I passed the vicarage, I saw your car parked in the drive. I came to look for you.' At the memory, Sophie's eyes filled with tears. She heard her voice wavering.

Hamish took a step towards her.

'Sophie…'

'No… stay there… I went round the side of the house – and there you were. She was practically screwing you in the kitchen.'

Hamish winced and looked away in shame.

'God, Hamish… If you think that's no-strings-attached sex then you're more of a fool than I thought,' Sophie said angrily, drying her eyes on the sleeve of her dressing gown. She was annoyed with herself for crying. 'Flora is not the sort of woman to let you go easily.'

Hamish pulled the chair out and sat down heavily at the table and put his head in his hands. The cat jumped onto his lap and circled proprietorially, before finally settling down, his paws tucked neatly beneath him, purring loudly.

'At least the ugly cat likes me,' said Hamish quietly.

'I LIKE you… you idiot. I loved you – do love you, I think…' Sophie was sobbing now. 'Just because I want a child, doesn't mean I don't love *you*. Why can't you see that?'

Hamish began to cry. 'I don't know. I'm an idiot. I was… jealous. Jealous of the passion you seem to have for this unknown person, this child that doesn't even exist yet.'

'What, and so you thought… I know, I'll go and find someone of my own to feel passionate about… someone who loves only me. Except she doesn't, does she, Hamish? She has four children, who she does a poor job of loving, and a husband who she doesn't seem too fond of either. So don't hold your breath for true love there, Hamish. She's simply not capable of it.'

'You're right – I know. I know exactly what sort of person Flora is. She's pretty hard-bitten. I'm so sorry.'

He looked so pathetic sitting at the table, she felt her anger dissipating, slightly.

'She was just fun, Sophie,' he continued, 'it didn't mean anything.'

The glibness of this comment enraged her.

'How long has it been going on?' she asked, suddenly alert to the possibility that he had been deceiving her for quite a while.

'Just a few weeks.'

'A few weeks! How long, exactly?'

'Oh, I don't know. I bumped into her in Cheltenham one day; she was shopping, or something. We had lunch. We kissed.'

Any hope Hamish might have had that she could forgive him, evaporated.

'So you had no time to come to the clinic with me while I had my eggs harvested,' Sophie said with barely concealed fury, 'but you had time for lunch and kissing in the car park, or wherever it was… How many times have you slept with her? I want the truth…'

'Four… five… Five,' he decided, finally. 'Definitely only five.'

'*Only!* Only five! Oh well, that's OK then. That's fine. If you had said six it might have been a different matter. But five is just fine. Why don't you just leave, Hamish? Go. Get your shirts or whatever you want and just go.'

'Can't we talk about this?'

'We did. We've finished.'

The pain in her abdomen began a week later. It was just a little pain – nothing too bad. But she drove to the clinic with a heavy heart and asked them to test her. The results came back just as she'd feared. She was no longer pregnant with twins. Two more lentil babies had been washed away. When she got home, she rang her mother.

'Oh darling...' said Angela. 'I don't know what to say. I'll come and see you. I can be there in a few hours.'

'No... it's OK.'

'Are you sure? You don't sound OK. What does Hamish say?'

'He doesn't know yet.'

'You shouldn't be alone,' her mother protested.

'I've got to go now...' said Sophie. The thought of explaining what had happened between her and Hamish seemed overwhelming. 'I'm sorry, Mum. I just need to sleep.'

'I'll call you later,' her mother said, her voice filled with concern.

Was this the end? Sophie thought, as she sat at the kitchen table in the gathering gloom. The end of her journey towards children? Was it the end of her marriage?

The cat, lying on her lap, purred loudly, licking her hand with his rough tongue.

There were so many questions, she thought, and no answers. She just knew that she was very, very tired.

Chapter 27

London
January 1961

As the plane touched down at Heathrow, Rachael breathed a sigh of relief – grateful they had arrived safely. Given what had happened to Chuck, Rachael had understandably wrestled with her nerves as they waited to board the plane in New York. Settling the children in their seats, tightening their seat belts and listening to the safety announcements, she tried desperately to stay calm. As the plane taxied down the runway, the engines got louder and louder; when the pilot released the brakes, the plane leapt forward down the runway, causing the passengers to be thrown back into their seats. Once it had lifted off the ground, Rachael was determined not to look out of the window, but the plane banked sharply before turning east. The whole of Brooklyn was laid out below her. She could see the rooftops, the chimney stacks, the tiny squares of garden.

Was this Chuck's last view of New York? What had gone through her husband's mind, as the pilot struggled to keep control? Since his death, she had often wondered what his last thoughts had been. She hoped it was something comforting – perhaps of her and the children? But now, as their plane juddered and roared its way to thirty thousand feet, she understood that his final thoughts would have been fear and it was almost more than she could bear. Once the plane was truly airborne, the children became fractious and irritable. Tom had an ear infection and screamed as the plane gained altitude, clutching the side of his face. The air stewardess, in an attempt to comfort him, gave him a sweet to suck, but he was clearly in so much pain, he finally spat the sweet out, rubbing his ear frantically, his little cheeks scarlet with the added discomfort of teething. He finally fell asleep half an hour or so before they landed.

Back on *terra firma*, as the plane taxied to its parking bay, Rachael felt a combination of exhaustion and relief mingled with a sense of anticlimax – that her time in America, her great happy adventure with wonderful Chuck, was over.

It was drizzling, and the sky was a dense, dull grey. Fog hovered at the edges of the airfield, as Rachael walked unsteadily down the plane's steps, carrying Tom, who was fast asleep and a dead weight. The stewardess followed behind, holding Angela's hand. It was all so different to the last time they had descended aeroplane steps.

Once she had collected her luggage, she walked into the arrivals hall. It was a consolation to see her father standing at the barrier with Mrs Roper.

'Papa,' she said, bursting into tears of relief. Angela, recognising Mrs Roper, ran ahead and threw herself at the older woman, who picked her up and twirled her around.

George put his arms around his daughter and his sleeping grandson. He kissed the top of the boy's head.

'Come, darling… Let's go home.'

Installed in the taxi, Rachael slumped into her seat, almost catatonic with tiredness.

Angela chattered constantly to Mrs Roper, who was clearly delighted to have the little girl back with her again.

'I came on an aeroplane,' the child said, excitedly. 'It was high in the sky and we flew right round the world.'

'Yes, you did, you clever girl.'

'My daddy says we can go on our holiday on an aeroplane. Am I on a holiday now, Mommy?'

'Yes, darling,' said Rachael flatly.

George, who had taken the sleeping Thomas on his lap, smiled at his daughter and squeezed her hand, encouragingly.

When they arrived at the house in Willow Road, Angela ran towards the kitchen.

'Angela… come upstairs, darling,' said Rachael.

'No, I want to do some cooking with Mrs Roper.'

'Not now, darling. Later maybe.'

'Do as Mummy says,' said Mrs Roper, watching Rachael anxiously from the hall, as she pulled herself laboriously up the stairs, holding onto the handrail. She looked like an old woman, Mrs Roper thought. She caught George's eye and smiled sympathetically. 'We can cook later,' Mrs Roper said to Angela, who was dancing energetically around the hall.

Mrs Roper had reorganised her guests so that Rachael and George could have their old configuration back.

'I hope Rachael will be able to squeeze both the children into that little box room,' Mrs Roper fretted to George. 'We might need another room for them. As soon as one becomes available, I'll keep it for you.'

'Thank you, Mrs Roper, you're very kind. Perhaps we ought to find somewhere of our own,' George suggested.

'Oh, you don't want to do that. Not when I can look after you all so well here. No, don't worry.'

'I fear we're becoming an imposition,' said George, his eyes following his daughter as she trudged slowly up the stairs.

'Professor…' Mrs Roper held the old man firmly by the arms and looked intently into his grey eyes. 'You could never be an imposition. You are like family to me.'

Rachael opened the door to the attic. It was just as she had left it. The green desk stood in the window, her bed up against the wall. The crystal glasses and a half-drunk bottle of sherry still stood on the little table. She knelt down next to the record player Chuck had bought and lifted the lid. 'True Love' was still on the turntable. She broke down, sobbing, her head in her hands.

The children, who had been exploring their grandfather's room downstairs, burst excitedly into the attic. Rachael got hurriedly to her feet and wiped her eyes.

Angela ran around the room, pointing to things she remembered. 'This is my bed, this is Mama's desk, this is our sofa…'

Tom, of course, had no memories of the house in Hampstead at all. The only home he had known was three thousand miles away. But he was happy, the pain in his ear had subsided, and as far as he was concerned, home was where his mother was. He happily followed Angela around, shuffling behind her on his backside and giggling.

George, who had followed them in, tried to calm them down.

'Come on, darlings,' he said, taking Angela's hand. 'Let's go to your bedroom, take off your coats and have a little lie-down. You must be tired.'

'I'm not tired,' said Angela defiantly. 'I'm going to do some cooking with Mrs Roper.'

'Not yet, Angela,' said George, firmly. 'Nap first, cooking later.'

The children reluctantly lay down and finally fell asleep.

Rachael was herself lying down when George emerged from the children's room.

'Shall I stay with you?' he asked, sitting on the edge of the bed.

'No… thank you, Papa. I'm tired too. I need to try to sleep. I'll come down in a little while and we'll talk.'

George kissed her and reluctantly left her alone.

Rachael thought back to the day she had danced with Chuck in the attic. How he had proposed to her, accepted her for who she was. How he had loved their children – how he had loved her. The record he had played that day, 'True Love', had been prophetic. That's what he had given her – she knew that now. As exhaustion mingled with pain, her eyes fluttered closed and she was enveloped, at last, by sleep.

*

The following morning, she woke as the sun, coming up over the heath, cast its cool, wintry light around the room. She had fallen asleep wearing her coat and, throwing off the eiderdown, took the coat off and hung it behind the door. She opened her suitcase, removing her washbag, which she put back in its familiar place by the washbasin. Silently she opened the door to the children's room. They both lay still fast asleep, their eyelashes fluttering mid-dream.

She closed the door quietly and went downstairs to her father's room and knocked on the door.

'Papa, Papa…' she whispered through the door.

'Yes…' he responded. 'Come in.'

His bed had been positioned along one wall and faced the window. He woke to a view of a tall horse chestnut that towered over the back garden. She sat on his bed and then, exhausted suddenly, lay down next to him. He wrapped his arms around her.

'My poor child,' he whispered into her hair. 'I don't know what to say. It seems so unfair.'

'I really loved him, you know, Papa. You were right. You said I would learn to love him and I did. Chuck was such… fun – so optimistic, so positive, and so kind. I can't believe what has happened. How could someone so alive, so vibrant, just be… snuffed out like that.'

'How did his parents take it?'

'Ah… my parents-in-law…' She turned her tear-stained to face him.

'They must be devastated,' continued George.

'Yes, of course. But… you know… they were not kind to me…'

'Tell me.'

'They shut me out of the funeral arrangements – it was as if we had never been married. Various people stood up and spoke about him. One of his old university friends, a work colleague, even someone he had been at school with. But there was no mention of me, or the children. Before I left, they told me that they always had suspicions that Tom was not their grandson. I couldn't deny it. I didn't have the energy to fight.'

'Poor Rachael. Were you tempted to stay in New York?'

'Yes… at first. I loved New York – I felt at home there. But the apartment we had was expensive and Chuck's parents made it clear that they wouldn't pay for it.'

'I could have sent you money,' said George.

'No… that wouldn't have been fair. You told me a long time ago that I needed to work, to be independent. You were right. If I'd had a job, maybe I could have stayed, paid the rent. But what could I do – with two small children to look after?'

'Had you no friends who could help you?'

'One or two friends, but no one I could ask for money. An old lady, in my building – Violet… was very kind. She wanted to help, and tried to me persuade to stay. "I'll introduce you to some people," she told me a few days after the funeral. "I know everyone… darling… everyone." But I had no strength left… you know? The idea of meeting new people, of starting again, seemed impossible. Besides, I missed you so much. I wanted to come home.'

'Well… I'm glad you did. I've missed you so much.' He kissed the top of her head, breathing in the scent of her hair that always reminded him of his beloved wife. 'I think you were right to come home, and Mrs Roper was delighted – not about Chuck, you understand, but at the prospect of seeing you and the children; she has been counting the days.'

'She's so kind… but maybe we should think of finding a little house of our own? We can't stay here forever.'

'Give it time, darling. You need to recover.'

*

Later that evening, after supper, when the children were in bed, Rachael sat at her desk in the window. She pulled down the front flap of the bureau and took out the key from beneath the pile of writing paper in the little drawer. She opened the cupboard in the centre and removed the panel at the back. She found the envelope easily enough. Inside, beside the byssus bracelet he had given her on that final day, was the photograph of Tommaso. He stood smiling, leaning so casually against the boat. She tied the bracelet around her wrist and examined the brown threads woven intricately together. It looked like nothing really, and yet, when she held it up to the light, it still glistened like gold – it hadn't lost its sheen. Tommaso had said it was a talisman… a good luck charm. Perhaps if she had taken it with her to America she might have had better luck.

She looked again at Tommaso's picture. She wondered if he had married the woman he was promised to. Had he learned to love again, just as Rachael had learned to love Chuck? She hoped so… And yet there was a little pang of regret. Maybe, if she had stayed in Sardinia, she would be married to Tommaso now, living in the cottage, bringing up her children in the sunshine…

'No!' she said to herself, out loud. 'Don't think that. It's over… you can never go back.'

She replaced the picture and the bracelet in the envelope, returned them to their hiding place and locked the cupboard. She undressed, put on her nightgown and went into the children's room to check they were asleep. They lay, facing one another, on either side of the little room. Angela – her hair a mass of golden curls, her thumb in her mouth. And Tom – his thick dark hair damp with sweat. She removed the quilt from his bed, tidying the sheet. He stirred, opening his dark brown eyes briefly, before turning over. She stepped back, anxious not to disturb them, but stood drinking in the physical presence of her beautiful children. They had been her good luck. Yes, she had known grief – unimaginable grief – but through it all, she had been given these two wonderful gifts, her children, both born of love and affection. And Chuck had loved them both, as if they were his own. Yes… she had known real love and good luck. She had been blessed and somehow she would find a way of being happy again – for them, for her father and for herself. She silently closed their door, crept into her own single bed and fell into a dreamless sleep.

Chapter 28

A few days after Sophie had lost the babies, Hamish rang.

'Your mother called me to tell what had happened... I'm so, so sorry, darling,' he said. It sounded to Rachael, as if he was crying.

'Thank you,' she said flatly. 'I should have told you myself.'

'You have nothing to apologise for,' he said. 'Is there anything I can do?'

'No, nothing.'

'Perhaps I could pop over? We ought to talk. Your mother sounded worried. Apparently you only told her about us a couple of days ago?'

'I couldn't face it when I'd just lost the...' she trailed off. 'There was too much going on – in my head.'

'I understand. But she's your mother – the most logical, sensible woman in the world...'

'I know... well I've told her now, so...' Sophie's voice ground to a halt.

'Well...' said Hamish, 'I need to collect one or two things. How about I come over this evening?'

'Well you can come, but I won't be here.' Her voice was impassive. 'I'm going to London today, and after work, I'll be visiting Vic and Simon.'

'Oh, of course,' he said, 'they must have had their baby... how did it go?'

'Fine. He's called Alastair… and weighed in at eight pounds.'

A silence hung between them as they considered this new addition to the family.

'And are you… all right?' he said, his voice filled with concern.

'I'm fine,' she answered, briskly. 'Come today, or tomorrow to get your stuff – whatever works for you.'

As Sophie sat on the train to London, her overnight bag by her side containing a small teddy bear wrapped in blue paper for her new nephew, she wept, silently. She wore dark sunglasses that protected her from the bright sunshine outside but also obscured her tears from the other passengers. She cried for so many things – the loss of her own babies, the envy she would inevitably feel when she met her brother's son and the thought of her husband removing things from their house, dismantling their marriage piece by piece.

The only positive thing in her life was her work. As she walked through the portals of the university she began to look forward to teaching a class of undergraduates. It was weeks since she had had any contact with students and always found their probing questions and enthusiasm for their subject refreshing. The university was due to break up for the summer in a couple of weeks' time, and the students were in a happy, energetic mood.

After the lecture, she realised she hadn't thought of her personal problems at all. Her work had provided a much-needed respite from the endless emotional wrangling.

At the end of the day, she took the bus to Hampstead. Her brother and his wife were bringing the baby to spend the evening with her parents, and she had to admit she was nervous about it. Concerned that she might be jealous or harbour some negativity.

As she came into the house, she heard the sound of a baby crying. It was like a physical shock to her system. She took a deep breath and went into the kitchen. Her sister-in-law Victoria was rocking the screaming newborn, anxiously, in her arms.

'Sophie!' Victoria said, delightedly. 'So lovely to see you!'

'Lovely to see you too,' Sophie said truthfully. She kissed her sister-in-law and peered at the angry bundle in her arms. 'Look at him…' she said wistfully. 'He's so beautiful, Victoria…'

Sophie meant it. He had gold hair, like her own mother. His eyes were still the inky blue of the newborn child.

'Can I hold him?' she asked, surprising herself. She realised she wanted desperately to cradle her brother's child in her arms.

'Yes, of course,' said Victoria, gratefully. 'He's hungry I think and in a terrible temper…'

She handed the swaddled baby to Sophie, who took him and sat with him on a kitchen chair, stroking his cheek.

'Hello Alastair.'

He looked up at her and his sobs subsided. She unwrapped him from his blanket, settling his head against the crook of her arm. He relaxed, lolling on her lap, his hands forming little fists that he raised towards her in greeting. He gazed, blinking, at her face, studying it intently.

'My goodness,' said Victoria. 'You've got the knack. He's been crying for over half an hour. None of us could do a thing with him.'

'Oh, I'm just someone new, I suppose. I think he was a bit hot… but what do I know?'

When Sophie returned to her house the following evening, she went up to her bedroom and opened the wardrobe to hang up her jacket. The empty hangers where Hamish's shirts and jackets had once been struck her with a force that took her breath away. It felt like another bereavement. And yet, she had been instrumental in his departure; had demanded it.

He'd been gone for several weeks and she couldn't help wondering if she had been too hasty. They had been together so long and were so entwined in one another's lives. She found herself wanting to talk to him about meeting Simon and Vic's baby. She wanted to tell him how easy it had been – that she had surprised herself, and had felt no jealousy or animosity – just affection and love for her brother's little boy. She wanted to tell him how relieved she was. But he wasn't there to tell. So instead, she fed the cat, made herself an omelette and sat down in front of the television until it was time for bed.

The following morning, the clinic rang.

'Hello,' she said, recognising the number.

'Good morning, Mrs Mitchell. We wondered how you were getting on.'

'Oh, that's kind of you. Not too bad, thank you.'

'We're here… if you need to talk. Our counsellors are always available if you feel the need to discuss any aspect of your treatment…'

'Yes,' she said, surprising herself. 'I would like to talk.'

The counsellor was younger than Sophie had expected – no more than thirty, Sophie thought. She had long brown hair and kind pale blue eyes.

'Please… do sit down,' she said to Sophie. 'So… how are things?'

'My husband's moved out,' Sophie said, abruptly.

'Oh, I'm so sorry,' said the young woman, obviously caught off guard.

'Yes… it's only just happened.'

'Do you want to talk about it?'

'I suppose I should.'

'Was it connected to the IVF?'

'I don't know. I suppose so. It was the pressure, I think.'

'That's not uncommon.'

'Really?' Sophie was surprised. 'I imagined everyone else working as… a team, you know? Both in it together.'

'No,' said the woman kindly, 'not always. It's quite common for the man to feel excluded from the process. Sometimes they refuse to cooperate; I've even known some men to have an affair.'

'*He* did that,' said Sophie, relieved to discover she was not alone, '…he had an affair – well, a brief liaison. He tried to tell me it didn't matter.'

'But it mattered to you…'

'Yes. Of course. I felt it was so… disloyal, apart from anything else. There we were trying for a baby and he was with someone else.'

The counsellor slid a box of tissues towards Sophie, who took one and blew her nose.

'And he became increasingly uncooperative about the process,' she continued. 'It was as if… he resented the intrusion, the medicalisation.'

The counsellor nodded.

'Maybe…' said the counsellor, 'you both need to take a little time out from the process? The procedure takes its toll on everyone involved.'

'I just worry that I'm getting older by the day and if I lose my husband, I lose my chance of a baby, too. And that would be just too difficult to bear.'

Sophie broke down and sobbed. The counsellor sat, quietly, making notes. When Sophie finally dried her tears, the counsellor said, 'You still have plenty of time, Sophie. You're only thirty-four. We help people here who are far older than you.'

'But I don't know if my husband and I will ever get back together.'

'Well – one day at a time, eh? I'm not a marriage counsellor, but I'd have thought that if you really love each other you could come back together again.'

'But how can I ever forgive him?'

'That's not for me to say. But… it's a two-way process – forgiveness, isn't it?'

'But I've not done anything wrong...' said Sophie.

'No... But maybe your husband felt unloved or ignored. I'm not saying what he did was right – not at all – but people usually act badly, or out of character for a reason.'

This comment lingered with Sophie, as she showered, or cooked, or tidied the garden. The following Tuesday she was due to travel to London for work, as usual, and stay overnight with her parents. She'd arranged with 'Mick the Chick' to feed the cat in her absence.

'I'll just be away overnight,' she'd said. 'Back tomorrow.'

'Is the Doc not going to be at home?' asked Mick, fishing for gossip.

'No,' said Sophie, firmly. 'He's away at a conference.' She shut the subject down, determined the village rumour mill would get no details of her marriage problems. She couldn't bear the idea that Flora might find out that Sophie and Hamish were having difficulties.

That evening, as her mother prepared dinner in Hampstead, Sophie mentioned the counsellor's advice.

'Do you think she was right? That there was a good reason for him to have an affair? It seems to me, she's just excusing him.'

'Well, I agree,' said Angela, rinsing the rice under the hot tap. 'You didn't *make* him sleep with someone else. But, on the other hand, you had become utterly fixated... you know... on the idea of a baby. I think he obviously found that hard to cope with. He felt excluded, I suppose.'

'I know. I see that now... I was so hurt to begin with I couldn't see past his betrayal.'

'That's to be expected.'

'He texts me you know... Hamish.'

'That's good,' said Angela.

'Is it? I don't know whether to reply.'

'Darling. You've been together for years. You don't just walk away from that overnight. Do you miss him?'

'Sort of... yes. Of course. I miss the man he was – before all of this.'

'Before he met Flora, or before you started IVF?'

'Ouch... If I'm honest, it all began to go wrong when we started IVF,' said Sophie.

'Well, that's honest of you,' said her mother. 'But I don't want you to blame yourself. Just let things process a while... you've got a lot to think about. Just remember this – there is no right and wrong here. Whatever you decide to do – we'll support you.'

'Thank you, Mum...' said Sophie, leaning over and kissing her mother's cheek.

'Now...' said Angela, 'before we start dinner, I wondered if you could help Dad bring Granny's desk down from the attic. It's so pretty and no one gets to see it up there. I'd like it downstairs in the sitting room. It won't be that heavy if we take the drawers out...'

With Angela overseeing the operations, Sophie and her father engineered the desk, now denuded of its contents, down two flights of stairs from the attic.

'Oh... mind that wall,' exclaimed Angela. 'You'll have to turn it a bit on its side if you're going to get round that corner; maybe push it that way?'

Finally, Alex, who was normally very patient with his wife, put the desk down and said firmly: 'Are you doing this, or am I?'

'Sorry...' Angela said. 'I'll go downstairs and finish dinner.'

As Sophie manoeuvred the desk into the alcove into the sitting room, her father went back upstairs for the three large drawers that fitted into the base

Sophie opened the flap of the bureau, admiring the smaller drawers and central cupboard.

'This is a lovely piece, isn't it?' she called through to her mother. 'Is this the original paintwork?'

'Yes, I think so,' said Angela, coming into the sitting room. 'Mum had it for years. It's always just been there somehow. But it will look nice there in the alcove, don't you think?'

'Yes,' said Sophie. 'It's very pretty. Did you know what Granny kept in these little drawers?'

'No,' said Angela. 'What have you found?'

'Lots of photographs, and postcards. We could look through them later.'

Her mother went back to the kitchen to finish preparing dinner, leaving Sophie to inspect the contents of each small drawer. She found a small brass key and was delighted to find it fitted the lock of the central cupboard. To her disappointment, the cupboard was empty, but when she put her hand into the space and felt around inside, the back panel shifted slightly. Intrigued, she tucked her fingers behind the panel and pulled gently. It came away easily. With the panel removed, behind it she spotted an envelope. Sliding it out, she found it was obviously quite old, yellowing at the edges. The flap had not been stuck down, so she felt no hesitation in opening it. Inside she found a photograph of a young man – tall, and athletic, with black hair swept back from his high forehead, and dark eyes. He was leaning against a wooden boat that had been dragged up onto a sandy beach. Turning the photograph over, she found an inscription: Tommaso, my love, Sant'Antioco, 1959.

She looked again at the picture. It reminded her of someone.

'Mum…' she called out to her mother. 'Could you come in here a minute?'

Her mother came into the sitting room, drying her hands.

'Look at this photo – who is this? And look at the inscription on the back – that's Granny's writing isn't it?'

Angela studied the photograph. 'I have no idea…' she said. 'He looks familiar, though.'

'He does, doesn't he? Tommaso – do you know the name?'

'No… I don't know anyone called Tommaso.'

'And she has written: Sant'Antioco. That's where her father discovered those Roman tombs; I've been looking at his research as part of my PhD. He was there in 1959,' said Sophie, 'and she must have gone with him. You would have been about two then. Surely, you'd have gone with her?'

'Oh, I don't think so,' said Angela. 'I have no memory of being in Sardinia, and Mum never mentioned it. I suppose it's possible she went out for a week or so while Grandpa was there, and met this man...'

Sophie put the photograph back in the envelope. As she did so, her fingers touched something else. She pulled out a little narrow bracelet made of brown thread. Instinctively she held it up to the light. It glimmered a little. What was it made of? It reminded her of the photographs she had seen of gloves and gauntlets made of byssus. The material was the same. She tied the bracelet around her wrist. Could George have given it to Rachael? Had he found it when he was working on the dig in Sant'Antioco? She knew from her research that Sardinia was one of the last outposts of byssus production – perhaps he had it made for Rachael when he was there?

What now seemed clear was that her grandmother had known about byssus all along. And the dream Sophie had all those months before in which Rachael talked about the water women diving for sea silk... maybe that wasn't a dream after all. She untied the bracelet, put it back in the envelope with the photograph and placed it into her handbag.

Later that evening, as she lay in her childhood bedroom, she had another text from Hamish – the third that week. With each communication, she felt her resolve to banish him from her life weakening:

Hello there... how are you? Hamish wrote.

I'm fine. How are you? Sophie replied.

Missing you. I love you.

The following day, there was another message from Hamish:

Lunch sometime? I miss you so much.

I'm not sure... Sophie replied.

I'm buying… somewhere different.
Just lunch you understand? she relented.
Yes… this Saturday?

They met in a small pub in a neighbouring village, filled with braying weekenders wearing Barbours and expensive waterproof boots that had clearly never seen mud. Hamish found them a cosy corner to sit in and ordered a bottle of wine.

'I don't really want wine,' Sophie said. 'I've almost given it up… drinking.'

'Really… I seem to drink more and more.'

He poured the Rioja into his glass and drained it.

'So,' she said, 'you're becoming an alcoholic now.' She smiled faintly. 'Just joking. But take it easy – you've got to drive, presumably.'

'I know,' he said, dejectedly. 'It helps to dull the pain a bit.'

They sat in awkward silence, as Hamish nervously fingered the bottle of wine, eyeing his empty glass.

'Oh Sophie,' Hamish said, eventually, reaching across the table and holding her hand. 'I just want us to get back together. I've done a lot of thinking. I'm so, so sorry.'

'I'm sure you are,' she said removing her hand from his. She felt irritated by his apology. Slightly insulted – as if merely saying sorry was enough for her to just forgive him. 'It must be very annoying for you,' she said, 'not to be living in your own house.'

'It's not that… It's *you* I miss. I even miss that awful cat. How can I prove that I'm sorry – what can I do that will make you realise that I mean it?'

'I don't know…'

'I spoke to the clinic yesterday,' he said.

'Really?'

'Yes… I told them that – if you're agreeable, I'd like to go ahead with a third round. I'll pay for it.'

Sophie looked at him, intently. 'It's not a bargaining chip, Hamish.'

'I know… that's not what I meant by it.'

'I don't know how you expect me to respond.'

'Just say what you think. Look… Living without you has demonstrated something very important – that I love you and I want to be with you more than anyone in the world. If having a child is the thing that will make you happy, then *I* want to give you that child. That's the best thing I can do for you – isn't it? It's the best way I can show you how much I love you. Better than a new house, or great holiday. You want a child – so I want a child with you.'

He poured himself another glass of wine but didn't drink it.

'Can I have a little of that?' Sophie asked.

He poured her a glass and she sipped the wine, thoughtfully.

'Do you really mean this?'

'I do.'

'I've been thinking too. I… I think I was guilty of something. The baby… issue… became so huge in my mind, so all-consuming, that I excluded you. I… didn't show my love for you, perhaps, quite as much as I should.'

'Oh Sophie,' Hamish said, taking her hand, and kissing it, 'you've done nothing wrong. Nothing…'

That afternoon they drove back to the house in tandem. They kissed as they entered the hall and Sophie took Hamish by the hand and led him upstairs, where they made love. They lay in one another's arms for the rest of the afternoon. As Sophie rested her head on his chest, she was surprised at how safe he made her feel. It just felt right.

'Hamish…' she said, looking intently at him. 'I can't believe you're back; and I can't believe how much I missed you. I'm still angry about what you did… I don't think I'll ever quite get over that. But one thing I know now… it's not worth losing you over. These last few weeks have been so strange. I tried to pretend I could do without you. Not just because of having a baby – not that at all. But I tried so hard to visualise a life without you. And I couldn't. Not if I was honest. All the time you were away I just mentally put you in a box marked "away for a bit" – not gone forever. I realised, I couldn't bear to lose you.'

'You haven't lost me,' he whispered into her hair. 'You never could have. And I know I've hurt you badly and I promise I will never hurt you again. I will look after you forever.'

'And whatever happens with babies,' she whispered back, 'I will learn to be content. What will be, will be.'

PART FOUR

'No legacy is so rich as honesty'
William Shakespeare

Chapter 29

Hampstead
August 1978

In the summer of '78, a few months after Tom's eighteenth birthday, Rachael found herself quite alone at Willow Road. Angela was travelling through Europe with her boyfriend Alex and would not be back until the end of August. Tom had recently moved down to Dorset to work for a boat builder. The yard was not doing well, financially, and the owner was keen to sell it. If Tom made a success of the job, and could demonstrate enough ability, Rachael planned to buy the yard for him. No one wanted old yards anymore, and it wasn't expensive. Besides, dear kind, thoughtful Chuck, had left a small fund of money to be settled on Tom when he reached twenty-one. There should be enough to buy the yard and give her son a relatively secure future.

Sitting alone at her bureau, listening to the scratching of the branches against the attic window, the rustle of the wind through the trees on the heath, and the purring of her ginger cat, who lay stretched out on the patchwork quilt, Rachael opened the central cupboard and took out the photograph. It had become a little ragged around the edges. Lying next to it in the envelope was the little byssus bracelet Tommaso had given to her that final day. Had it brought either of them luck? On the face of it, Rachael's life had been filled with sadness. She had lost so many people she had loved – her mother, her father, two husbands. And yet... she had also been blessed. Her children were, without doubt, the greatest gift and had brought her so much happiness. But she also had financial security thanks not just to the generosity of both Chuck and Mrs Roper, but also her determination to finally get a career.

When Rachael moved back to London in 1960, the family had decided to remain at Willow Road. Although Rachael sometimes yearned for a house of her own, the big house on the heath felt like home. Mrs Roper was so much more than a landlady. She had become a friend – an unofficial grandmother to the children, a support to Rachael, a companion of sorts to George. As the children grew and started school, Rachael acquired some qualifications and after considering several options, decided to train as a book keeper. She had always found lists of figures strangely comforting. She thought, from time to time, of becoming an accountant, but it would have involved further training and she was reluctant to spend too much of time away from the children. Book-keeping wasn't a glamourous occupation, but she could do it from home, it provided a steady income, and gave her a sense of her own self-worth. 'You see, father,' she told him on the day she passed her book keeping certificate, 'I'm not completely useless and I can do more than baking…'

He smiled and kissed her. 'I have never thought you were useless, my darling girl.'

Life was good, the children were strong and healthy and George was content in his work. But one afternoon, nearly eight years after she moved back to Hampstead, Rachael heard a curious muffled cry from the hall. She ran down several flights of stairs and found Mrs Roper unconscious on the tiled floor. The children were both at school, and George was at work, so, alone and scared for her friend, Rachael frantically called the emergency services. She travelled with Mrs Roper in the back of the ambulance, but when they arrived at the hospital, the old lady was already dead. She had suffered a massive heart attack. Rachael and George were enormously saddened by her death and took charge of her funeral.

They were surprised to discover that she had no relatives and when Rachael received a lawyer's letter a few weeks after Mrs Roper's death she learnt that Willow Road and all its contents had been left to her in Mrs Roper's will.

When the legalities had all been finalised, and the other paying guests had finally left, Rachael wandered around the house, thinking of all the years they had spent with Mrs Roper providing a kind of safety net for their lives. Not quite a mother, nor a grandmother, but a friend – as stalwart and loving a friend as you could hope to have. Standing in Mrs Roper's bedroom, infused with its scent of Yardley's 'English Lavender', Rachael ran her finger over the glass top of the dressing table arranged, as always, with Mrs Roper's silver backed hair brush, the bottle of perfume, the crystal dish filled with face powder. She remembered how thoughtful and generous the older woman had been to her the day Angela had been born, fussing over her like a mother would have done. But it was in the kitchen that most of her happy memories were triggered. Standing together round the big pine table, making mince pies and gingerbread men, teaching Angela to cook.

For several months she felt unable to make any changes to the house, but gradually she set about turning it into the family home she had always wanted. The most urgent task was to give each of the children a room of their own. They had been sharing the tiny attic room since they had returned from America, and had long outgrown it.

'I think they should have a room each on the first floor,' she suggested to George.

'Why not have those rooms yourself?' he asked. 'The children could sleep on the other side of the landing and I could go upstairs to the attic.'

'No...' she said. 'I feel at home in the attic – I'll stay there. I could turn the children's old room into a little bathroom for myself. You stay on the first floor, Papa; and we could turn the bedroom

next to yours into a nice big study – wouldn't you like that? The
children can sleep on the other side of the landing, as you suggest.'

Initially, she felt guilty, removing the belongings of her old landlady. But there seemed no point in keeping Mrs Roper's bedroom
furniture, or her dusky pink bedspread. She kept the silver and
crystal dressing set though – putting it upstairs in her own room.
It meant she could simply open the crystal powder compartment
and inhale the scent of the face powder, to be reminded instantly
of her beloved benefactor. Once the dark furniture had been
removed, she transformed Mrs Roper's bedroom into a playroom
for the children. With the doors leading out to the garden, it was
the perfect space and the children were delighted with it. Over
time, it became a haven of rocking horses and 'tent' houses. The
wooden floors were a jumble of toys and books. Two old sofas,
covered in ethnic throws, became a place to lie on a winter's day
and lose themselves in a book. The large dining room, running the
full length of the house, became the family's drawing room; a space
where they could gather together and entertain. The old parlour
became a formal dining room, but they rarely used it, preferring
to eat in the basement kitchen. Rachael painted the kitchen walls
bright red and acquired some orange casserole dishes that added
a touch of zingy colour.

She loved the house. Its size and high ceilings reminded her
constantly of both the apartment in Budapest and the old brownstone in New York. She bought a boudoir grand piano at auction
and was thrilled when it was delivered and positioned in the bay
window of the sitting room. As she sat on the piano stool, she felt
she had found her physical place in the world at last. The years of
upheaval, of homelessness, were finally at an end.

As the children grew, they developed interests and passions of
their own. For Tom, that meant fishing – and the rack of fishing
rods that covered one wall of hall were testament to his skill, first
perfected while on a family holiday near Winchelsea. Sitting on the

stony beach, protected by a windbreak, Rachael had been delighted to see her children running wild on the beach, catching crabs in rock pools and collecting tiny sea creatures in jam jars. She had bought Tom his first rod on that holiday, and it came as no surprise to see how naturally he took to the sport. As she watched him grow through his teenage years, he reminded her constantly of his father.

Rachael often daydreamed about taking Tom to meet his real father in Sardinia. As each birthday came and went, she rehearsed how she would explain this curious development to her son.

'Tom, there's something I need to explain to you… I know you thought that Charles was your father, but he's actually an Italian fisherman named Tommaso…'

Then what would she say?

'We met, we fell in love, but it wasn't to be…?'

What sort of explanation was that? How could she explain to her son that Tommaso had been promised elsewhere? Tom would feel his father had betrayed her. That he had led her on. But that would be an inaccurate representation of what had taken place. Or Tom might feel that his mother had been foolish to trust the young Italian and reckless not to have taken precautions. It was so hard for young people in the 1970s to understand what life had been like before the pill. Tom would almost certainly conclude that his mother had been stupid not even to realise, before she left Italy, that she was pregnant. No… that wouldn't do… either. Somehow each explanation failed at the first hurdle. By telling him the truth she risked everything: Tom would lose respect for her or despise his natural father. And the flimsy ephemeral memories Tom and Angela both had of Chuck could be damaged. He, after all, had been so good to them all; didn't he deserve to live on in their memories as kind and loving man who had died tragically? The family often looked at photographs of the man Tom believed was his father. The albums from those two brief years were filled with pictures of Chuck beaming proudly at the camera – feeding

Tom in his highchair, bathing him, cuddling 'his son'. How could she take those memories away from Tom? It would seem such a betrayal to both Tom and to Chuck. Her son might even come to hate his own mother, for all the years of deception and for making such a mess of it all. Children, after all, could be the harshest critics.

And so the years came and went. George never revealed her secret either. He took it with him to his grave. He died of pneumonia when Tom was fourteen and his death rocked Rachael to the core. It felt quite different to the earlier loss of her two husbands. Both were young men in the prime of life, and were taken away so suddenly. Their deaths had been shocking. Devastating. But George's death left her with a vast empty cavern of sadness. George was her link with the past. The one person who knew everything about her life, and his passing left her feeling as if she was in free fall… spinning through space, alone and lost. She clung to the children – not physically, but emotionally. She listened for their key in the lock when they came home from school – just as she had done for so many years waiting for her father to return. And it frightened her. For she knew that her children would move away eventually, find partners and lives of their own. And she would then be totally alone rattling around in the house in Willow Road.

And so, that summer of '78, a few months after Tom's eighteenth birthday, finding herself quite alone at Willow Road, she resolved to go back to Sant'Antioco.

'The children need never know,' she said to herself, stroking the cat. 'I shall say that I went to Rome… for a holiday.'

A few days later, Rachael flew to Rome and took the ferry to Sardinia – just as she had done twenty years before. She slept quite well in the little cabin in the bowels of the ship but woke early and was eager to relive her earlier experiences. She pulled on a cardigan and went up on deck to watch the ferry arrive in Cagliari. There were a few more developments along the south-east shore, but the island appeared quite unchanged. As they approached the capital, she observed the same colourful buildings, painted in shades of pink, peach and apricot, rising up from the dark emerald waters.

She hired a car and drove along the coast road towards Sant'Antioco. The layout of the roads was remarkably unaltered and she remembered the route without much recourse to the map laid out on the passenger seat. She arrived at the causeway just before one o'clock. As she drove across the narrow strip of land connecting Sardinia to this tiny island, her stomach lurched, not with hunger, but nerves. Her knuckles turned white, as she gripped the steering wheel. 'What am I doing?' she asked herself. But she drove on, nevertheless.

The town had developed a little. A few more houses had sprung up around the harbour and market area, but not so much that she didn't feel a huge wellspring of recognition. She pulled up near the harbour and watched the fishing boats come and go. There was no sign of the blue and white boat. Perhaps she was too late – had he retired? She had a sudden pang of fear. Perhaps, God forbid, he was dead. Maybe her whole trip would be a fiasco – a pointless waste of time.

She had booked herself into a small hotel on the other side of the town and could have driven there via a new ring road that circumvented the town, but decided, instead, to drive through the centre and get her bearings. She looked left and right as she drove up the cobbled streets, anxious to see what she could recall of the place – what was familiar, what could be recognised. The premises of the atelier, Italo Diana, had disappeared. The building appeared now to be a house. There was no sign of the ladies sitting outside in the sunshine carding and spinning.

She pulled up in the square outside the basilica. She was tired and hungry, and so parked the car and wandered across to the cafe where she had first met Tommaso. It seemed quite unchanged.

Tables and chairs were still arranged outside and she sat down facing the square, the church on her left. If he *was* to come, she would certainly see him.

A middle-aged woman came outside and took her order. The waitress looked quizzically at this elegant dark-haired woman with her unusual grey green eyes, who spoke Italian with a slight Sardinian accent.

Rachael recognised her at once as Tommaso's sister. *So*, she thought to herself, *the family are still here...*

She drank her coffee and ate a sandwich, and then wandered around the shops off the square. The little grocery store she remembered so well had survived, but tourist shops had sprung up here and there, displacing the everyday goods that the villagers needed. There was even a little museum telling the story of byssus. She would go there tomorrow, she decided.

She drove out of town, along the coast road. As she approached the turning to the cottage, she slowed down. Her hotel was a few miles further on. She should go there first and register, unpack, get herself settled, take stock. But she couldn't drive on without taking a look. She pulled over at the side of the road, locked the car and walked gingerly down the lane towards the cottage. After five or six minutes she saw the pale apricot walls and green shutters. It was exactly as she remembered. The garden was still enclosed by the little picket fence, slightly tatty now. She considered turning back. What would she do if he appeared suddenly, or if his wife was there? What would she say if she was recognised? It would be so embarrassing. The whole trip, she now realised, was misconceived; it was a terrible mistake. She had been quite happy in Hampstead. She had so much to be grateful for. What was she doing in this strange land, looking for someone who probably didn't exist anymore, at least not as she had remembered him. No one stayed the same, we all change, move on, adapt. And yet, she carried on walking, compelled by some force. What was it? Curiosity? Love? Or unfinished business?

By now she was on a level with the cottage and she walked past, heading towards the copse and the cove beyond. She would go first to the beach, and then anyone coming from the house might just think her a tourist, lost, off the beaten track.

It was just as she had remembered it. The cove formed into a perfect arc – like a child's drawing of a little beach, bookended by large rocks. And at one end, to her surprise, stood Tommaso's boat – still painted blue and white. She wandered over, noting the rods, lying along the length of the boat, the nets folded carefully, a lobster pot or two, even a discarded pack of smoking tobacco and cigarette papers in the well. It was as if he had just dragged it up onto the shore and gone inside with his catch. She thought back to those happy days when he would bring her seabass for their supper, a cigarette hanging loosely from his lips.

She walked back now, towards the house; the sun filtering through the woods. The gate to the garden was closed, but there was no rope holding it in place. No little child to protect, perhaps. The door to the house was shut and it appeared deserted.

Against her better judgement, she opened the gate and walked through the garden, rehearsing what she would say if Tommaso's wife appeared: 'I'm so sorry – my car has run out of water...' or 'I'm so sorry to intrude, but I'm lost...'

She knocked on the door, her heart pounding, thumping so loud in her chest, the noise filled her ears. There was no reply. She tried the door handle, but it was locked. Feeling instinctively beneath the pot of geraniums, she found the key. Unlocking the door, she turned the handle and the door opened, just as it had always done, onto the kitchen. It was instantly familiar. Perhaps a few more pots and pans on the shelves, but the same sink, the same table, the same painted dresser. The only sign of modernity in the sitting room was the little portable TV sitting atop an old chestnut table, but the furniture was just as she remembered – even the worn sofa where she and Tommaso had made love...

She climbed the stairs to the bedrooms above. Her room… *their* room had a double bed covered with a lace bedspread. Had his wife made that? The other room where George had slept now had a pink coverlet on the bed. There were pictures from magazines of American movie stars stuck on the walls. So… he had a teenage daughter. She scanned the room for a photograph of the girl, but there were none. Would she look like him, Rachael wondered? Or like her mother? The box room next door was now a bathroom. It pleased her to think he had some comfort.

Over the distant sound of the waves rolling on the shore in the cove, she heard the unmistakable sound of a motorbike approaching the house from the lane. Her heart missed a beat – perhaps it was him? Horrified to be found in his house, she ran downstairs, through the kitchen, and out onto the veranda, turning the key in the lock, just as a woman appeared at the gate. She carried a basket of shopping and was accompanied by a teenage girl. Rachael struggled not to stare at the girl, taking in her strong Roman nose and dark hair – she looked exactly like her father. So, she thought, Tom had a sister.

'Ah, *mi dispiace*,' Rachael began, hurriedly. She fell into her well-rehearsed line about running out of water for her car. The woman nodded, and as she opened the garden gate, Rachael ostentatiously dropped her car keys and surreptitiously slid the cottage key back beneath the pot of geraniums.

The woman seemed not to notice the sleight of hand. She took her own key from her bag and unlocked the door, went inside and brought out a jug of water, which she handed to Rachael. As she carried the jug towards her car, Rachael felt the eyes of the woman following her as she walked up the lane. She went through the motions of opening the bonnet, pouring water into the windscreen washer compartment, rather than the engine, closed the bonnet and then ran back to the cottage, thanking them for the water and wishing them a good day.

At her hotel, she felt ashamed. What had she hoped to achieve? To spy on someone, was so awful, so humiliating. And what would she have done if Tommaso had been there? Fall into his arms? Show him the photographs of Tom that she had brought with her? Tell him how their son was so like him, that he would have been so proud of him? And how would Tommaso have felt? Hurt, distressed – to think he had abandoned her, left her with a child. Guilty about his own family? What was the point of it? What good could it do?

Rachael ordered a bottle of wine over dinner and took it upstairs, where she finished it, feeling more alone than ever before.

The following morning, she paid her bill and loaded up the car. She had decided to catch the next ferry back to the mainland, and spend a few days in Rome. But as she drove past the turning to the cottage, her heart lurched. She fought the inclination to turn off and take one last look. Driving on into the town, she found the square and surrounding streets filled with people. Abandoning the car on the outskirts, she enquired of a passer-by what was going on.

'Ferragosto,' the woman told her. 'It's a holiday.'

The townspeople were out in force. Most of the shops were closed and everywhere Rachael looked families were milling about, chatting to one another, enjoying the carnival atmosphere. She went into the grocers' shop – one of the few still open – and bought a little bag of oranges for her journey. As she put them into her straw bag, intending to walk back to the car, her gaze travelled across the square. In the distance, seated at the cafe, she saw him. His dark hair, cut a little shorter now, greying slightly at the temples. Still the same large dark eyes, the strong Roman nose. He wore an open-necked shirt, with the sleeves rolled up. He was playing cards with a friend. His wife was not with him, nor his daughter.

Rachael stood, her heart beating loudly. She felt the familiar jolt of passion, just as she had done nearly twenty years before. What was it between them – chemistry, or a deeper emotional bond? Part of her wanted to march across the square; to speak to him, to kiss him, to find out if that passion was still there for them both. But she didn't. She remained on the edge of the square, concealed by a crowd of at least thirty or forty people. He looked content, she thought, as if he has a good life. A man at peace with himself – respected by his friends and the community. He had a role, a home, a wife, a child. She should not disturb his life. What purpose would it serve? Her heart slowed to its normal rhythm and she felt a sort of inner calm. As if a chapter in her life could, at last, be closed. They had both survived. More importantly, their child had survived. His birth had been difficult, he might have died. But he didn't and had grown into a fine strong young man. In so many ways, they had both been blessed. They had been lucky.

The crowds in the town swirled and moved and, for a moment, a path opened up between her and Tommaso. He looked up momentarily from his card hand. There was a flash of recognition as he caught sight of her. He stood up, saying something to his friend. She smiled fleetingly at him, and then was gone. Back into her car, reversing down the little road and onto the ring road around the town, heading for the causeway back to Cagliari, onto the ferry to Rome, then back to London – and to everything that was most dear.

Chapter Thirty

Sardinia
July 2017

Alex drove the hire car from Cagliari Airport to Sant'Antioco, with Angela sitting beside him. Sophie and her Uncle Tom sat in the back seat.

'How are you doing?' asked Angela, peering over her shoulder at her daughter. 'Not car sick I hope?'

'No… I'm fine,' said Sophie, 'as long as I watch the road.'

'I can swap if you'd like…?'

'No, Mum, it's OK.'

It was a sweltering hot day and the road wound over dry, dusty red hills. The turquoise sea came into view from time to time – inviting glimpses of refreshing blue that appeared suddenly and then retreated just as swiftly.

As they drove onto the long causeway that led from the mainland of Sardinia to the island, Sophie felt a growing sense of excitement. To be following in her great-grandfather's footsteps, to be in a place he had known so many years before. The town of Sant'Antioco nestled at the foot of a low hill – its apricot buildings in contrast to the bright blue of the sky above and the sea below. Little boats bobbed up and down in the harbour.

'Oh look… that must be Sant'Antioco! How pretty!'

'Yes, isn't it?' said Angela.

They drove up through the little town and stopped next to the basilica on the main square.

'The tombs are underneath the basilica,' said Sophie. 'Can we park over there – I'd love to just take a quick look.'

'You don't want to start work straight away, do you?' asked her mother.

'No… I just wanted to get my bearings. It's only three o'clock. I'll just pop in for a moment – OK? Why don't you go and have a coffee at the cafe over there?'

Inside, the church smelt powerfully of damp. There were several lurid statues of the martyr after whom the island was named – Saint Antioco. To one side of the transept was a wrought-iron barrier, behind which was the entrance to the catacombs. The gate was locked, so Sophie couldn't go down, but she had arranged to meet the curator the following day and it was useful to see the layout. A sour smell rose up from the deep underground tombs; a mixture of damp cool earth and stale air. It smelt of archaeological possibilities, Sophie thought.

She emerged from the church, squinting in the bright sunshine, and joined her family in the cafe.

'Coffee?' asked her mother.

'No… thanks. I've given it up. Along with pretty much everything else.'

Afterwards, they headed towards their hotel, out of the town, following the satnav on Sophie's phone.

'Keep going along this road,' she said to her father. 'It winds along the coast for quite a way.'

The island was neither lush nor green. The ground appeared sandy and there were rugged grasses sprouting up along the sides of the road. Road signs encouraged visitors to turn off towards the 'spiaggia'.

'Looks like there are lots of little beaches to visit,' said Sophie.

Their hotel was in the middle of a promontory that jutted out into the sea. A lighthouse stood a hundred metres or so from the shore – its revolving light warning boats to beware the outcrop of rocks that surrounded it.

The hotel, painted a shade of dark terracotta, seemed to rise up incongruously from the pale sandy dunes. It had turrets at one end, giving it the air of a Moroccan castle, and bright blue shutters on all the windows.

'Well, it's certainly colourful,' said Angela, doubtfully, as they unloaded their luggage into the drive.

Sophie's room overlooked the scrubland and the lighthouse. She had a balcony onto which were squeezed two chairs and a table. Once she'd unpacked, she sat down admiring the sun setting over the horizon, watching the waves crash over the rocks surrounding the lighthouse. She had a momentary frisson of sadness that Hamish hadn't come with her. Since he had moved back, he had been thoughtful and loving and had even begun to talk enthusiastically about another course of IVF. It felt like a new beginning and she was keen that he should join the family on holiday.

'It will be like a little honeymoon,' she had pleaded.

'What? With your parents and Uncle Tom… I don't think so,' he'd laughed.

'Besides,' he continued, 'you don't need me there; you'll be working.'

'It's a holiday too…' she had pleaded. 'Please come.'

'I can't get the time off – we're already short-staffed over the summer. You'll have a good time with your parents. And later in the year, we can go somewhere together.' He'd kissed her.

But now, looking at the dark navy blue waters against the turquoise sky, she wished she had persuaded him.

Her mobile rang.

'Hello Mum'.

'We're downstairs,' said Angela, 'we thought we'd go for a little walk and explore?'

*

'The water's pretty rough here,' said Sophie, as they approached the rocky outcrop that bordered the sea. 'That lighthouse earns its keep – look at the waves, they're smashing right up to the building itself. No good for swimming round here, I think.'

'Well, there's a pool at the hotel,' said Angela. 'It looks quite nice.'

'And there are other beaches, Ma… we saw them from the car.'

'Yes of course,' said her mother. 'It's odd, you know, it all seems rather familiar. It reminds me of Agistri near Athens – don't you think, Alex?'

'Oh… Agistri was more wooded,' he said, 'all those wonderful pines. But it has the same quality of being slightly deserted, I agree.'

After dinner, Sophie was delighted when Hamish rang her.

'Hello there,' he said, 'how's it going?'

'It's all rather lovely. A bit like… what did Dad say over dinner – oh yes, "Camber Sands in the sun…" We've just had a lovely meal, and I had two glasses of wine. I'm feeling a little bit tipsy.'

'Good…' said Hamish. 'You deserve it. You'll be glad to know the cat and I have bonded. He now sleeps on our bed.'

'Oh Hamish… no – that's not good at all. We don't want him getting into bad habits.'

'You're right. I'll put him back in the kitchen tonight, I promise. I was just lonely.'

'Why don't you come out and join us?'

'I told you… I can't take the time off. Anyway – only six more days and you'll be back.'

'Are you counting?'

'I am, darling… I am.'

Angela smiled as Sophie put away her phone.

'Hamish?'

'Yep…'

'How is he?'

'Fine... missing me.'

'That's good then. Things going well there...?'

'Yes, Mum... It's going really well actually. It's as if we've turned a corner.'

'I'm glad, darling... really glad.'

'So am I...'

The following afternoon Sophie went alone into the town to meet the curator at the basilica.

'It's so good of you to find the time to meet me,' Sophie said. 'I'm writing a PhD thesis on the burial practices of the first and second centuries AD – so these tombs are precisely the sort of thing I'm interested in. Also, I have something of a private connection with them.'

'Really?' said the curator, a slight, handsome woman, her brown hair threaded with silver.

'Yes... my great-grandfather – George Laszlo, who was the Professor of Archaeology at London University in the 1950s – was the person who originally excavated the tombs.'

Impressed, the curator led Sophie down into the catacombs. She pointed out the dark earthen walls smoothed over the millennia, by the hands and feet of thousands of visitors. Protected from the rest by a flimsy metal chain were the Roman tombs.

'Please – do go in,' said the curator, unlocking the padlock. 'I have another appointment – will you be all right alone?'

'Yes... of course. I just want to take some photographs, make some notes. I promise to be very careful.'

The roof of the tomb was only a few feet high and Sophie had to squat on her haunches. Shining her bright torch around the space, a barrel-vaulted tomb opened up before her. On closer inspection, she discovered it was divided into two smaller rooms, one of which contained parallel burial mounds – both covered with a fine dust of some kind. Sophie ran her fingers through it; she would take a sample, but it appeared, from the smell at least, to be fine limestone mortar. Her torch picked out a number of inscriptions – some in Latin, and others clearly in Hebrew. Sophie was not a Hebrew scholar but recorded the inscriptions for later translation. The Hebrew epitaph was enclosed at either end by two menorahs – the seven-branched candelabra of the Jewish faith. Above one of the tombs, painted in a rich shade of purple – a colour which in classical antiquity was a symbol of royalty – was the Latin text: *Beronice in pace ivenis moritur*, meaning 'Beronice buried in peace'.

The second tomb also carried a purple inscription: *Virus bonus in pace Bonus*. And to one side – a second inscription – *Bonus in pace Bonus*. Sophie wondered if this was perhaps not a funeral exclamation: 'good man in peace, good man', but rather the name of the person buried there.

The layout of the chamber had been planned meticulously, and from Sophie's previous experience this suggested a married couple had been buried here together. If so, who were they? Was this the grave – as her great-grandfather had originally suggested over seventy years earlier – of the lost queen of the Jews – Berenice? The spelling of the name was different – Beronice was written on the tomb wall and not Berenice. Was this a simple mistake, or did it suggest that the person buried here was not the Berenice of antiquity? And who was the man who lay next to her? If the first tomb did contain the lost Queen, then the most obvious contender for her burial partner was the man Berenice had lived with for over a decade; the man she had loved and been prepared to leave her country for; the man who had been forced to give her up when he became Emperor of Rome – Titus. Sophie's mind buzzed with ideas and theories. No one had ever found Titus's burial chamber in Rome. It was rumoured that he had been murdered by his envious younger brother Domitian, who then succeeded him as emperor. If that was true, how had his body ended up here? Had Berenice, upon hearing of her beloved's murder in Rome, had his body brought to her on this tiny island? More romantically, had she then committed suicide in order to lie by his side for eternity? Were Berenice and Titus just as tragic a union as Cleopatra and Anthony over a hundred years earlier? There were more questions than answers.

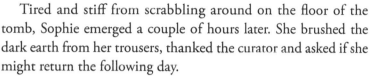

Tired and stiff from scrabbling around on the floor of the tomb, Sophie emerged a couple of hours later. She brushed the dark earth from her trousers, thanked the curator and asked if she might return the following day.

'I would also like to look at some of the other burial chambers around the island. I know that Sant'Antioco was a significant Jewish settlement in the first century and there are many graves dotted around. It will help to set this extraordinary tomb in context.'

Her work took her three further days. She drew a detailed plan of the tomb beneath the basilica. Each piece of evidence was meticulously recorded in notes and photographs. She visited other Roman sites on the edge of Sant'Antioco, and studied other graves on the island – taking photographs and measurements. When she returned to England, she would be able to assess more accurately what she had discovered.

Her parents and uncle had spent a few days getting to know the island. They met with Sophie each evening over dinner and were pleased to see her thriving and so interested in her work.

'You seem so much more settled, darling,' her mother said one evening after dinner.

'Yes... well I love my work. It's important to me. And I'd forgotten how enjoyable it is being in the field. So much of what I do happens in the lecture theatre, or the library – and that's all interesting too, but nothing beats lying on your stomach on a dusty floor trying to piece some evidence together.' She grinned.

'Your great-grandfather used to say that,' said her mother. 'And what about Hamish – have you heard from him today?'

'Oh yes… he rang this morning. He's OK. Eating rubbish food and getting the cat into bad habits.' Sophie laughed.

'Have you been able to…' Angela paused, looking for the right words, 'move on?'

'From the Flora episode, do you mean?'

'Yes…'

'Well, surprisingly… I have. I don't think I'll ever forget it. But I can forgive it – perhaps I forgive too easily, but I don't think it's worth destroying everything we've built together. And he is so very sorry, so contrite. I think our marriage is worth another try, don't you?'

'Only you can really answer that, darling… but for what it's worth – I think it is. I've always thought you were good together.'

'Yes… we are.'

'And what about the other thing…'

'Babies, you mean?'

'Yes… if you don't mind me asking?'

'No… not at all. He's keen to try again – the IVF.'

'Really? I thought the IVF was the problem.'

'It was… But he realises now just how important it is for me to have a child. He's prepared to have another go. He wanted to start before I came away, but that wouldn't have worked – there are too many hospital appointments involved, and so on. So we'll start in a few weeks' time – once I'm back and have written up my notes. I need to progress the work a bit before we have another go. IVF is so all-consuming – it's really all you can think about. And my supervisor's been so patient, but there's a limit to how long I can take to finish my PhD.'

With just two days left of their holiday, the family was determined to spend some time exploring the island.

'I'd like to see if anyone is still making byssus,' Sophie said over breakfast. 'George was interested in it, and I found something in Grandma's things... when we tidied her desk.'

'The photograph you mean?' said Angela.

'Not just that... there was a little byssus bracelet – quite intricately made that was in the same envelope. I've got it here. Look...'

She removed the bracelet and showed it to her mother.

'Are you sure that was with Mother's things?' asked Angela. 'I've never seen it before.

'Yes... it was in the envelope in her desk.'

'How odd,' said Angela.

'Well – I'm just keen to find out a little more... how it's made and so on. I noticed there's a byssus museum near the church – maybe we could pop in there this morning?'

The small museum was filled with all manner of examples of byssus. A giant clam shell stood in the window, next to an arrangement of fake 'undersea' flora. A loom, made of long parallel canes, dominated one side of the space. The walls were covered with examples of embroidery all done with byssus thread. Many featured the Madonna, some a lion – clearly an important symbol – others were of the seven-branched menorah. At one end of the room sat a dark-haired lady, who introduced herself, in a strong Sardinian accent, as the curator of the museum and last 'Master' of byssus. Seated in front of her and listening intently, were a young couple and their little boy. They watched, captivated, as the lady carded a clump of byssus, twisting it into a fine thread. Sophie found it hard to follow her Italian, but she watched and observed, fascinated, nevertheless.

As the woman spoke, her fingers were constantly moving – twisting, winding the thread, holding it up in the light so it glistened – just like the bracelet Sophie had in her handbag. Satisfied at last with her work, the woman tied a length of thread around the child's wrist.

'*Per lei...* for you; it is good luck,' she said.

The little boy leapt up in delight, running round the museum, holding his arm up in the sunlight. The lady began to explain how the thread was produced. She picked up handfuls of rough unprocessed byssus soaking in bowls filled with liquid. Sophie couldn't follow everything she said but she got the impression the bowls contained lemon juice and other herbs that added colour.

The curator held up a jar of byssus soaking in purple water and displayed it proudly to her audience.

'*Uve,*' she said, holding up a bunch of purple grapes.

The woman leapt up, animated now, and moved swiftly around the museum pointing at various embroideries she had made over the years – a golden lion, the menorah, the Holy Family.

On the far side of the museum was a tall chest of drawers. She opened the top drawer and removed a pair of gloves made of byssus, and a tie.

Catching Sophie's eye, the curator smiled, pulling a piece of twisted byssus silk thread from her pocket. Cupping Sophie's chin in her hand, affectionately, she tied it around Sophie's wrist.

'For luck,' she said in English.

Emboldened, Sophie removed the byssus bracelet from her handbag and held it up to the woman. 'This belonged to my grandmother,' she said.

The woman studied it, examined the six rows of twisted thread joined together to form a whole. It was as if she recognised it.

She looked intently at Sophie.

'*Tua Nonna? Come si chiama?*'

'*Si chiamava* Rachael,' replied Sophie.

'*Era fatto qui...*' she said, 'In Sant'Antioco...'

'Made here?' Sophie replied.

The woman nodded.

The little boy who had been given the byssus bracelet, rushed back to his parents chattering excitedly and grabbled the jar of byssus soaking in purple water. As he did so, he knocked a second bowl filled with liquid onto the floor. The curator anxiously bustled back to her station to prevent any further damage.

On their way back to the car, Sophie wandered into a little bookshop a few shops down from the museum, where she bought a book about the history of byssus. Over lunch at the hotel, she flicked through its pages.

'It says here that the skill of spinning byssus was brought to the island by Berenice and her ladies... They acquired the skills in the lands of the Middle East... I had no idea. How extraordinary. And that lady – who was running the museum – is possibly the last person with the skills to make byssus. She is the Last Master. I suppose that's how she knew the bracelet was made here. But if George bought it in 1959, it couldn't have been made by her – she would only have been a baby then. Perhaps it was made by her mother, or grandmother?'

As she studied the pictures of byssus embroidery, she found an almost exact copy of her own bracelet.

'Look, Mum – this looks like the one we've got. It says here that sea silk can never be bought or sold, only received as a gift. Someone must have given it to George...'

'I suppose you must be right...' said Angela.

'So,' said Alex, 'are we going to the beach this afternoon or do you want to stay here and flop round the pool?'

'I don't mind...' said Sophie, putting the book away. 'You all came with me this morning, so it's your choice. Tom... what do you fancy doing?'

'Never been one for swimming pools, really,' Tom said. 'I'd rather be near the sea, if I'm honest.'

'Well, let's go to the coast, then,' suggested Sophie. 'We passed several signs to various beaches when we first arrived. Let's go back along the coast road, and just take pot luck. We should take some towels and perhaps we can hire an umbrella from reception.'

Alex and Tom packed up the car with two hired umbrellas, numerous towels, a bag of books, and the party set off.

The first beach they came to charged five euros for one hour's parking.

'Five euros!' Alex muttered, darkly, to Tom. 'It's a bloody rip-off.'

The family wandered down to the beach but discovered it was a sub-let to a nearby hotel, which provided sunbeds and a cafe for a fee.

'Twenty-five euros for a sunbed!' Alex complained to his wife, 'and we can't use our own umbrellas – they insist we hire one of theirs for ten euros! I'm not paying that'.

'But it looks nice here,' bleated Angela.

'No way,' her husband insisted. 'Come on, back in the car – we'll find somewhere else.'

The next beach along was free, but rocky. There was hardly anywhere to put their towels. Once again, they climbed back in the car.

As they drove towards the town, Angela suddenly said: 'Turn left here…'

'But there's no sign to a beach,' argued Alex.

'I know…' said Angela, 'but I'm sure there's a beach down there. It makes sense – the whole coastline is beach after all.'

Alex turned the car onto the single track and they drove down the bumpy unmade road for five minutes before coming to a stop outside a small dilapidated-looking cottage.

'Oh, this is no good,' said Alex, trying to turn the car around. 'It's a private drive, for goodness sake.'

'No… I'm sure it's OK,' said Angela, firmly, from the back seat. 'Look, they've got a fence round their garden. That's their land.

The sea must be over there, behind that wood – surely it's open to the public. No one owns the beaches, do they?'

'That guy up the road did – cheeky bugger. Thirty-five euros for a sunbed and an umbrella.' He looked knowingly at Tom, who chuckled in agreement.

'Oh Alex, stop moaning,' said Angela impatiently. 'Come on, Sophie – bring your towel, darling…'

Mother and daughter walked past the cottage. The pale green shutters were drawn. The garden overgrown. There was a little veranda overlooking a terrace on which stood a table and chairs.

'What's that?' asked Sophie, pointing to a large concrete structure.

'It's some sort of oven, isn't it?' said Angela. 'Maybe it's someone's holiday home. It all looks deserted anyway.'

They wound their way through the scrubby woodland before coming out onto a private cove.

'Oh!' said Angela. 'How delightful. There's no one here… it's just fabulous. Run back and tell your father and Tom to bring the umbrellas and the picnic. This will be perfect.'

The family set up camp on the beach. They erected umbrellas to keep the afternoon sun at bay. Sophie wandered up and down the cove collecting shells and picking up interesting stones. She strolled back towards the wood. It felt magical somehow, completely untainted by humanity. She caught glimpses of the cottage through the trees, but, frustratingly, the shutters remained stubbornly closed. The owners must surely be away.

At five o'clock, Alex declared it was time to get back to the hotel.

'Oh must we go?' said Sophie. 'It's so beautiful here.'

'Well I'm going to start packing the car – you coming, Tom?'

The two men walked back to the car with the umbrellas.

'I'm just going for one more swim,' said Angela, wading into the water.

'Be careful, Mum… I noticed there's a sort of shelf a little out to sea and then a big drop. Don't get out of your depth.'

'I won't… you know I'm bit of a nervous swimmer.'

Sophie sat on the beach watching the sun going down over the horizon. Her mother swam back and forth across the bay – breaststroke, backstroke – until suddenly she disappeared from view. Sophie scanned the horizon. She saw no sign of her, until an arm flew up in the water, and then another, and then a strangled cry from her mother.

Sophie screamed: 'Dad, Dad… come quick… it's Mum.'

She ran towards the water and threw herself in. But there was a strong undertow and as she swam towards her mother she made little headway. She was aware of a man's voice shouting behind her, but she hadn't the strength to turn around.

A young man, dark-haired, swam swiftly past her with a strong front crawl. He grabbed her mother, holding her expertly beneath the chin and swam back towards the shore. He carried her up onto the beach and laid her down carefully on the sand.

Angela lay, quite still and pale. Alex and Tom, who'd heard Sophie's shrieks and had rushed back from the car, stood helplessly looking on.

'Oh God, Oh God… Mum,' said Sophie.

The stranger leant over and patted Angela's cheek. She didn't respond. He pressed his mouth over hers, giving her the kiss of life. He pounded her chest, before breathing into her mouth once again.

Within moments, Angela rolled over and spewed water from her mouth, gasping for air.

'Oh Angela, darling,' said Alex, dropping to his knees and holding his wife to his chest. 'Are you all right? You gave me such a fright.'

'I'm fine,' Angela panted, spluttering, 'no harm done.'

The young man looked up at Sophie and smiled. 'She's OK… You should bring her inside…'

'Oh, thank you. Thank you so much. That's a good idea…'

He helped Angela to her feet and, supported by Alex, she was led towards the cottage.

The young man opened the little gate to the garden and invited Angela to sit down at the table on the terrace.

Alex wrapped a large towel around his wife and sat down next to her.

'You live here?' Sophie asked the young man.

'My grandfather… it's his house.'

'Oh… I'm sorry,' apologised Sophie, 'we shouldn't have been here at all. We didn't realise the beach was private. Forgive us?'

'It's no problem. I will get my grandfather…' he said.

'Oh, is he here?' said Sophie, embarrassed. 'We thought the house was closed up. Don't disturb him. I'm sure my mother will be fine a moment. Perhaps if she could have just a glass of water?'

'It's no trouble. My grandfather would want to help. And yes… of course, some water.' He went into the house, calling out, '*Nonno, Nonno, vieni qui… subito.*'

He opened the ground-floor shutters, allowing evening light to flood the rooms inside, before returning with a jug of water and some glasses.

'Please… help yourself. My grandfather is coming. Now, *mi dispiace*… forgive me… I should go inside and change.' He gestured to his wet jeans and t-shirt.

'Yes, of course,' said Sophie. 'It's a miracle you were there at the right time.'

'I had just come back from work… I heard you shouting. Ah… my grandfather is coming.'

A tall man emerged from the house. He looked very like his grandson, but with a shock of white hair. He stooped, leaning heavily on his stick.

'*Buona sera,*' he said to the group. 'My grandson – Tommaso – he tell me… *mi dispiace*… my English, not good.'

'Tommaso?' said Sophie. 'That's the name of your grandson?'

'*Si…*' said the old man.

She thought of the inscription on the back of the photograph: 'Tommaso, my love…'

How could there be any connection, she mused.

'I was saying,' Sophie continued, 'that we're sorry we were using your beach.'

'*Non fa niente. Non e privato…* It's not private,' said the old man.

'Thank you, you're very kind. Your wonderful grandson rescued my mother – she's not a strong swimmer. She nearly drowned as a little girl and has been nervous ever since.'

The old man smiled and looked towards the cove wistfully, then back at Angela.

'Yes, thank you,' said Angela, pulling the towel around her. 'I'm so grateful. I don't quite understand what happened, I just lost my footing and the current is very strong out there. We should introduce ourselves – my name is Angela by the way, and this is my husband Alex, my brother Tom and my daughter – Sophie.'

The old man studied her face.

'You come to Sardinia before?' he asked her.

'Me…?' said Angela, sipping her water and drying her hair on the towel. 'No… never.'

'I think… maybe yes. You come here… as child?'

'No,' said Angela firmly.

'Although her grandfather was here,' offered Sophie. 'Back in the fifties – Professor Laszlo, George Laszlo.'

The old man nodded, thoughtfully, and smiled. He looked from Angela to Alex and then Sophie and lastly to Uncle Tom, who stood awkwardly behind his sister, his hand resting protectively on her shoulder. He gazed quizzically at Uncle Tom.

'Stay, please. We will have a glass of wine,' he said hospitably.

'Well – thanks very much,' said Alex.

'Oh… we shouldn't intrude anymore,' said Angela, politely, 'we've been enough of a nuisance.'

'No,' said the old man. 'You stay – please.'

'Perhaps I can help you,' said Sophie, intrigued to see inside this little ramshackle cottage. She followed him inside, where his grandson, now dressed in dry shorts and a t-shirt, was at the kitchen sink, peeling onions.

'Tommaso,' said the old man to his grandson, *'vai a prendere un po' di vino per i nostri ospiti.'*

'*Va bene, Nonno,*' said the young man.

'May I use your bathroom?' asked Sophie.

The young man pointed towards the stairs.

She walked through the little sitting room, past the elderly sofa and two armchairs facing an incongruously large modern television. As she climbed the stairs, she passed a bedroom. A delicate lace bedspread covered the small double bed; it appeared to be the only feminine influence in the house. Perhaps this handsome old man was a widower, she thought. A dressing table stood at the end of the bed. Tucked into the corner of the mirror was a black and white photograph. Intrigued, Sophie crept across the room and took a look. She gasped when she realised who it was. The image was quite unmistakable... It was her grandmother Rachael, holding a little girl with golden hair.

She heard the shuffling of feet on the landing outside and turned around to find the old man standing in the doorway.

'I'm so sorry... I shouldn't have come in... It was very rude. But this photograph... here... I recognised it... it's my grandmother Rachael with my mother as a little girl...'

'Ah!' he said. 'Rachael yes. I knew she would come back... one day.'

'So you knew Rachael?' Sophie asked.

'I knew when I saw you... you are... very like her. And your mother, when she told her name – I realise who you are.'

He sat down, heavily on the edge of the bed. Sophie sat beside him, holding the photograph.

'I have something to show you,' she said.

Sophie fumbled in the side pocket of her shoulder bag and removed the envelope she had taken from her grandmother's desk.

'This... is you, isn't it? My grandmother kept it always...'

The old man took the photo in his hands and his eyes spilled over with tears that ran down his lined brown cheeks.

'*Si* – it's me....'

He turned the photograph over and traced the words Rachael had written sixty years before.

'Tommaso, my love,' he said out loud.

'It was taken at the same time – as this one?' Sophie asked, holding out the other photograph.

He took it from her and held them up together.

'*Si* – before she left.'

Questions poured in Sophie's mind. She hardly knew where to start. Her mother had insisted that neither she nor her grandmother had ever been to Sardinia. Why had there been this secrecy?

'My mother... says she has never lived here, never visited before...'

'Rachael came here... with her father. They lived here in this house... not with me... they rent – understand?'

'Yes... I understand – they rented it from you.'

'From my mother... I was young man – twenty years only. Your grandmother – we...'

'You fell in love?' suggested Sophie.

'*Si*... I loved her.' He gazed wistfully at the pair of photographs, his finger tracing the outline of Rachael and Angela. 'Your mother was... a little girl. She nearly drown – in the cove. Dangerous water here...'

'So *this* was where the accident happened,' said Sophie. 'Rachael often told us about it, but we thought it was somewhere else – in England perhaps. My grandmother never mentioned Sardinia or Sant'Antioco... Why was that? Why did she keep it a secret?'

The old man's eyes filled with tears. Sophie put her arm around his broad shoulders.

'I'm sorry. I didn't mean to upset you...'

She heard her mother's footsteps on the stairs.

'Sophie, love... we really ought to be going... come on now –
these good people have been kind enough.'

'Coming...' shouted Sophie. 'May I come back tomorrow?' she
asked Tommaso, eagerly. 'There's so much I need to understand...'

'*Si*... tomorrow, *si*.'

Sophie leant over and kissed the old man's cheek. It was soft
and damp.

He put his large hands on either side of her face. 'So like Rachael.
So beautiful. Until tomorrow.'

Chapter 31

The following morning, Sophie got up early, and as she ate a solitary breakfast in the almost deserted dining room, texted her mother.

> *Just popping out – something I forgot to do. Won't be long – back before lunchtime. Hope you don't mind but I borrowed the car. Sophie.*

She drove fast along the coast road, desperate to get back to the cottage; she needed to understand what had happened between her grandmother and Tommaso. If she had been alone the previous day, she would happily have stayed all night talking to him, but she was concerned that her mother might be distressed or upset in some way by his revelations. It was important to understand the implications of what had happened all those years ago, to find out why Rachael had never told them that she had lived on Sant'Antioco. Only when she understood that, would Sophie be in a position to discuss it with her mother and uncle.

She was filled with anticipation, as she drove down the long bumpy road towards the cottage. She parked the car and was relieved to find old Tommaso sitting on the veranda.

'Come… come in,' he said, opening the garden gate. 'I was waiting for you.'

'Is your grandson here?' Sophie asked.

'No... at work. He... fisherman.'

He pulled out a chair at the table, inviting her to sit down, and poured her a cup of dark viscous coffee from a rusted steel coffee pot.

'Thank you,' she said, sipping the coffee. 'So... your grandson – he is a fisherman?'

The old man nodded. 'I too... was fisherman.'

Sophie studied his face. The height of his forehead, the square-ness of the jaw, the set of the eyes, the long elegant Roman nose. They were so familiar, she now realised.

'My uncle – Uncle Tom – who was here yesterday – *he's* a fisherman and boat builder...'

Tommaso nodded and tears came into his eyes.

'I didn't know,' he said. 'That she was...' He stopped, searching for the right word.

Suddenly the pieces of the jigsaw slotted into place.

'Of course,' Sophie said, 'how could I be so stupid? Tom is your son...'

'*Si, si*. I didn't know. She leave... *improvvisamente*.'

'Suddenly... quickly,' suggested Sophie.

'*Si, si*. Quickly. I was *fidanzato*... understand?'

Sophie shook her head. 'No, sorry... *fidanzato*...?'

'To my wife...'

'Oh... engaged...?'

'Si, to another... a woman in the village; my cousin – Elena. All my life – yes...*ho fatto una promessa.*'

'You made a promise?' suggested Sophie, trying to understand.

'*Si* – promise. But I didn't love her. I love Rachael – always. But my mother... she refuse. Not possible, she say... And Rachael – she go away. I didn't know... about the baby. When I see your mother and her brother I know... he my son.'

The old man wiped tears from his cheeks with his large, calloused hands. Hands she now realised were identical to those of her uncle.

'Tom, your son, my uncle – he was born in 1960,' said Sophie. 'We always thought – the family – that he was the son of an American called Charles. My grandmother, Rachael, met him in 1957 in a refugee camp in Hungary – do you understand?'

The old man nodded.

'Charles came to London to find her and they married and they moved to New York in 1960. Tom was born in America. But Charles was killed… in an aeroplane accident. *Capito*?'

The old man nodded gravely.

'It was terrible for Rachael. She was alone in New York with two very small children. She came back to England… back to Hampstead, where she lived for the rest of her life.'

Tommaso sat fingering his small coffee cup.

'I so sorry her husband died. I loved her… always. I should have left here… married her… Is she with you – now, here?'

Sophie looked into his dark eyes, full of hope. He was alive and he hoped Rachael was too – of course he did.

'I'm so, so sorry,' she said, holding his hand, 'she died two years ago.'

He wept then – great sobs of pain that made his shoulders heave. She stroked his back, and let him cry. Finally he stopped, all tears spent, and wiped his face roughly with an old handkerchief.

'I have something,' Sophie said, 'that she kept always with her – it was obviously important to her.' She felt in the pocket of her handbag and brought out the little byssus bracelet.

'Ah…' he said, taking it in his large hands. 'I give to her, for luck. Maybe not so good – for her.'

'No – you mustn't think that. She *did* have luck. She *was* happy, Tommaso – you must believe that. She had a hard start in life, but she *was* happy. We all lived together in a lovely house in Hampstead – in Willow Road. It looks over a beautiful wood – like this one. She had a lovely life, in the end. Your bracelet – it did bring her luck… honestly.'

'And you?' he said. 'You keep it now – yes? My mother…' he patted his chest, 'she made the bracelet.'

'Your mother? Was she a byssus weaver?'

'*Sì*… my mother… she was master. Here… on Sant'Antioco. Come… I show you something.'

He led her upstairs to his bedroom. He opened a drawer in the dressing table. There, wrapped in tissue paper, was a man's tie made entirely of byssus thread.

'Oh,' said Sophie, 'that's amazing. I saw one like it in the museum…'

'For my wedding… I wore,' he said. 'But here, look…'

He removed another tissue parcel from the bottom of the drawer and laid it on the bed. He undid the pink ribbon and there, nestling on the paper, was a christening gown; white cotton, edged in lace, embroidered on the yoke with fine golden byssus thread.

'For baby – yes? For my daughter, and for my Tommaso… Good luck. Yes?'

'Yes… I see – the family christening gown. It's beautiful. Your wife, Elena… is she still alive?'

'No… she died… many years ago. And my daughter, Giulia also – last year.'

'I'm so sorry,' said Sophie, squeezing his hand.

He smiled at her.

'But I have my little Tommaso – he is good boy. Here… give me your arm?'

Sophie held her arm out and he tied the bracelet onto it.

'You have something you wish for, I think… maybe this will help.'

Back downstairs, on the veranda, Tommaso made a fresh pot of coffee as Sophie wandered around the little garden.

'Shall I tell my mother – about you and Rachael?' she asked him, as he poured her another cup. 'And my uncle too… should I bring him here to meet you again?'

The old man nodded.

'Your grandson, Tommaso – will he be upset?'

'No… he will be OK. I will tell… He is young, happy. You bring my son to me… I would like very much.'

Sophie drove back to the hotel in a thoughtful mood. It was a huge responsibility – and yet, she felt certain that it was vital she told her uncle about the existence of his real father. He was so alone now, in need of support. Surely it would be better to know that he had a father on this island; a father who, like him, was an expert fisherman – a man of the sea.

The family were seated around the swimming pool when she arrived.

'Hello darling,' said her mother. 'Work finished? We've only one afternoon left – back home tomorrow.'

'Yes… works all done. Mum… Uncle Tom – I've got something important to tell you…'

Angela had initially refused to countenance Tommaso's significance in Rachael's life.

'My mother wouldn't have lied about such an important thing. She never mentioned meeting anyone. Never even mentioned coming here.'

'But, Mum… I've seen the photographs. He has a photo of her and you taken on their last day together. It matches the photo I found in her desk.'

'But how could *he* be Tom's father!' Angela exploded. 'Tom's father was an American called Charles Bailey. Charles left money in trust for Tom. That's how she bought him the boatyard. *Charles* was Tom's father.'

'Angie love,' interposed Tom. 'Let the girl speak… I want to hear what she has to say.'

'Thank you, Tom,' said Sophie softly, 'think about it, Mum – the timings don't really work. She was here in 1959, we know that now – that's the date on the photograph. It was obviously summertime. Tom was born in May 1960. When did she and Chuck marry?'

'I don't know!' said Angela defensively, 'I don't have their wedding certificate. She never mentioned it…'

'Aren't there photographs of the wedding?'

'No… it was all a bit rushed. I don't know. Things were so different in those days.'

'Tom,' said Sophie turning to her uncle. 'I'm sorry if this is a terrible shock for you. I don't want to make your life more complicated, especially after all you've been through recently.'

'No…' he said calmly, 'in an odd way, it makes sense. I always felt a bit different, if you understand me. Your mother, my darling sister,' he said, putting his arm around Angela's shoulders, 'was so brilliant, so academic, and I was a bit useless at school and all of that.' He kissed the top of Angela's head. 'My big sister here, she got all the brains.'

'Oh, don't be so silly, Tom,' protested Angela, pulling away slightly, 'you run that wonderful boatyard – that takes lots of intelligence.'

'Yes, I know… but I'm happiest out on the water, fishing. Chuck was a New York banker, wasn't he? I guess I was only a baby when he died… But I don't seem to have any of his skills. I'm hopeless at maths. And, to be honest, I don't look anything like him – do I? I just thought I looked more like Mum, with her dark hair and so on. But if this man *is* my father – it all begins to make sense, doesn't it?'

'But why would she lie… for all those years?' said Angela, through tears. 'Mother never lied. Not to me.'

'Well,' said Alex, gently, 'different times, Angie love. Think about it. Girl falls in love, gets pregnant, not married – in those days it would have been a disgrace. Perhaps she didn't even know she *was* pregnant for a while. She came back to England when Tommaso's mother dug her heels in about him marrying his old cousin and then found she was up the duff.'

'Oh Alex! Don't use such language,' said Angela.

'Seems to me,' Alex continued, 'it was all a bit of a tragedy, and old Chuck was something of a hero, marrying her like that.'

They sat silently for a while absorbing what they had discovered.

'So,' Sophie to Tom, 'will you come back and talk to him?'

Tom nodded.

'And you, Mum – I know he's desperate to see both of you.'

'Is that where you went this morning?' said Angela.

'Yes… I needed to find out as much as I could. I didn't want to raise any false hopes. They really loved each other, Mum. And he remembers you very well as a little girl. He was the one who rescued you from the sea. This is where you nearly drowned. Grandma covered up where it was, pretending it was somewhere in England. But it was here… in his cove – where you nearly drowned yesterday.'

Angela blew her nose and wiped her eyes. 'I still can't understand why she never told me…'

'Perhaps she was ashamed,' suggested Sophie. 'As Dad says – the 1950s were so different. Abortion wasn't legal, there was no pill. It would have been so difficult. And once you start a lie, when do you end it? She created a version of the truth that worked for her and for both of you. But from what I've heard, she and Tommaso loved each other so much. And he feels so guilty now – he had no idea she was pregnant. His wife, Elena, died years ago and his daughter Giulia died last year too. He's all alone, apart from his grandson. What do you say? Shall we go and meet him?'

'I say,' said Tom firmly, standing up, 'that I'd like to go and meet my father.'

Old Tommaso was watching a football match on the television as Sophie pushed open the door from the veranda.

'Tommaso… we're here,' she called out.

He stood up, stumbling slightly, feeling for his stick. She rushed over to help him, and as she took his arm, felt him shaking beneath her fingers. She took his hand and squeezed it, reassuring him. He leant down and turned off the television and then, holding Sophie's arm, he walked towards his new family, beaming broadly.

Uncle Tom stood in the doorway framed by sunlight; his dark hair backlit with a halo of golden light. The old man walked towards him and held the younger man's face in his hands. There were only twenty years between them, but they could have been brothers, Sophie thought – so alike were they. Both men sobbed, as Uncle Tom put his arms around his father and hugged him. And Angela cried too, watching her little brother, holding his father.

Tommaso had laid the table on the veranda with a bottle of wine and some glasses. Little pieces of cheese had been cut up and placed on an old plate.

'Please…' he said. 'Drink, eat.'

He sat down heavily in his chair at the end of the table and gazed, enraptured, at his son.

Alex poured the wine and handed round the plate of cheese.

'You are fisherman?' Tommaso said to Tom.

'Yes… Yes I am. I love it. Always have. I grew up in London and used to fish on the pond… um… not sure of the word for that … in Italian.' He looked around helplessly at his family. Sophie shrugged her shoulders. 'I caught little tiddlers – small fish, you know? Always loved the sea. My mother, Rachael, she gave me some money when I was twenty-one to buy a little boatyard. Built it up over the years – mending boats. Been there ever since.'

Tommaso nodded, proudly. 'Si… good… boats good.'

'Wooden boats,' offered Alex. 'Beautiful wooden boats.'

He took his mobile phone out of his pocket and logged onto Uncle Tom's website. There were photographs of all the boats he had mended over the years – ketches, schooners, yachts and dinghies in various states of repair.

'See?' Alex said, handing the phone to the old man. 'Lovely boats.' He slapped his brother-in-law on the back. 'Very talented guy, my brother-in-law.'

Tom blushed and grinned.

Tommaso looked up at his son and smiled. 'Beautiful boats. Good boy.'

They talked until the sun began to drift down towards the sea, turning the light from golden to scarlet. Until the shadows of the trees in the copse lengthened across the garden.

The sound of a motorbike engine spluttering down the lane, interrupted the silence.

'He's home,' Angela said.

'Who is Mum?' asked Sophie.

'Tommaso. I remember it now… that sound, well the sound of a scooter, anyway.' Her eyes widened. It was as if a key had been turned unlocking a part of her memory. 'Mum used to light up when she heard it. I'd forgotten all about it – until now.'

Old Tommaso looked across Angela and smiled. '*Si*… I had a motorbike many years ago.'

He struggled to his feet and walked unsteadily out of the garden and around the side of the house to greet his grandson.

'Do you think he's gone to explain who we are?' suggested Sophie.

'I should imagine so,' said Alex. 'Or maybe he already has. Seems a sensible sort of chap. He probably told him this morning. Otherwise we're going to be a bit of a shock for the poor boy.'

'That was odd, Mum,' said Sophie to Angela, '… were you really remembering something when we heard the motorbike?'

'Yes… I was. Definitely. I remember that sound so well. Mum would rush to the door. "He's home," she'd say. Sitting here, I keep getting little flashes of memory – odd things. That gate leading to the beach; it makes me... scared for some reason. This table is familiar. So is that old oven over there. I think we used to cook in it perhaps.'

'We'll ask Tommaso,' said Sophie kindly, 'he'll remember.'

Much later, as they were preparing to leave, Tommaso brought down a parcel wrapped in tissue paper.

'For you...' he said, handing it to Sophie.

Opening it, she found the christening gown.

'No... no, I can't take this,' she protested, 'it's for your grandson – for young Tommaso and his children.'

'You send it back, if we need... You need it first. For family,' said the old man.

Sophie began to cry.

He cupped her face in his hands and wiped her tears away with his thumbs. 'You need it... soon I think.' He kissed her on both cheeks.

As they drove back towards the hotel, all lost in their individual thoughts, Angela asked her daughter: 'What's in the tissue paper. What did he give you?'

Sophie unwrapped it and showed it to her mother.

'I tried to tell him... that I didn't want it... that I didn't need it. But how could I explain? He was so insistent.'

Angela held her daughter's hand. 'Well, darling – who knows...? Maybe you will... one day.'

Chapter 32

Gloucestershire
September 2017

The early morning light glinted through a gap in the curtains, waking Sophie from a deep sleep. As she lay in bed, cursing the daylight, she felt nauseous, a fine layer of perspiration spreading across her forehead. She'd had terrible heartburn the night before and had only managed to get to sleep sometime after two o'clock. She was due to start IVF in two weeks time, and was worried that any illness might delay her treatment. Reluctantly, she hauled herself out of bed.

Hamish stirred sleepily and turned over.

Pulling on an old cardigan, she padded through to the bathroom, and as she looked at herself in the mirror, realised she was going to be sick and wretched violently into the basin. When she stood back up, Hamish was behind her, holding her hair away from her face.

'Darling…' he said, 'you poor thing. Have you eaten something dodgy?'

'I don't know,' she said, rinsing her mouth.

'When did this start?'

'Just now… I had heartburn last night. And now this.'

'Well, come back to bed and I'll get you a cup of something.'

'Not tea. I can't face that.'

'A little hot water and lemon, maybe,' he suggested.

He returned ten minutes later carrying a tray with two cups, the cat at his heels. The cat jumped onto the bed and purred loudly, wrapping himself around Sophie's head, pawing the pillow, nuzzling her ear.

'Oh Cat,' she said, stroking his lopsided head. 'Good boy – go and sleep down there.'

Hamish picked him up and put him firmly on the rug at the bottom of the bed. But the cat had other ideas, and snaked his way up the duvet, towards the object of his devotion.

Sophie sipped her water and lay back against the pillows.

'I've got to get up soon… I'm due to visit Oxford today.'

'You're not going anywhere…' said Hamish.

'I'll be fine. My appointment isn't until this afternoon. I'll have a little sleep now and leave just before lunch.' She closed her eyes.

'Who are you meeting?' asked Hamish.

'One of my great-grandfather's research students,' she said sleepily. 'He's a Professor Emeritus now… at Magdalen College. I wrote to him ages ago and he's only just responded. He was away for most of the summer, I think.'

'What's his name?

'Professor Moncrieff… Giles Moncrieff.'

Sophie arrived in Oxford just after one o'clock. Feeling tired, she had ignored the car park signs on the outskirts of the city and instead drove straight to Magdalen College. She was delighted to find a space right outside and, as she was early for her appointment, decided to explore the college gardens before her meeting.

The Michaelmas term had not yet begun and the college was relatively deserted. She strolled around the quad, enjoying the peace, comparing it to the hustle and bustle of her own university in London. She crossed an immaculate lawn edged by colourful late summer borders. A small bridge led her across the River Cherwell, from where she admired the ancient deer park and spectacular college buildings.

At five minutes to two she headed back towards the quad. As she began to ascend the curving staircase leading to Professor Moncrieff's rooms, a pair of young students rushed past her.

DEBBIE RIX

'Sorry!' they called out cheerfully, as she flattened herself against the wall, allowing them to pass.

'Come!' the Professor called out when she knocked.

It was large room – comfortably furnished with a sofa and two armchairs arranged companionably around a fireplace. The professor was seated at his desk facing the door. He stood as she entered.

'Ah… you must be Sophie Mitchell – yes?' he said, referring to his diary.

'Yes, Professor. Thank you so much for agreeing to see me.'

'I'm just sorry I didn't get back to you sooner. I've been away for a couple of months over the summer… Sit, please.'

He directed her to one of the chairs in front of the fireplace.

'Now,' he said, when she was settled. 'You said in your letter you were interested in the work I did as a student – with a… Professor Laszlo.'

'Yes… I should explain, George Laszlo was my great-grandfather.'

'Oh… I see.' He sat down in the armchair opposite and studied her intently.

'I'm an anthropologist,' she continued, 'and I'm studying for my PhD – the burial practices of the first and second centuries AD, with a particular reference to Roman practices.'

'Ah! I begin to understand.'

'Yes… you contributed to a paper George Laszlo wrote sixty years ago – about the Roman tombs on Sant'Antioco. George died many years ago now – before I was even born – and I was interested to know what you thought you'd discovered back then. I've just come back from Sant'Antioco recently, but there are still many unanswered questions about the tomb – in particular, who was buried there.'

'Sant'Antioco… yes indeed,' he said, gazing wistfully out of the window. 'All a long time ago now. I'm sorry, I'm being very rude – may I offer you something – tea or coffee?'

'No… I'm fine – thank you.'

'So, your great-grandfather was George Laszlo, eh?'

'Yes.'

'Are you – by any chance – also the daughter, or granddaughter, I suppose, of Rachael?'

'Yes, I'm her granddaughter.'

'Ah… I thought I saw a likeness.'

'You knew her?'

'Oh yes… yes. She lived on the island you know, with… your mother I presume? What was her name… the child?'

'Angela.'

'Yes. Yes, of course, Angela. Sweet little thing. What became of her?'

'She's a doctor now. Working in Hampstead – a GP.'

'Ah… Good. I'm not surprised. She was very bright, even as a tiny child. I remember that. Very strong-willed…'

Sophie smiled. 'So you remember them… on the island?'

'Yes. I do, yes. All a long time ago now, though.'

'Can I ask…? I'm sorry – this was not why I came – we should discuss the dig, but do you remember a young man, an Italian named Tommaso?'

Professor Moncrieff flinched; his face fell, momentarily, before he regained his composure.

'Yes. I do remember him.'

'Can you tell me anything about him and… my grandmother, Rachael.'

'None of my business,' he replied curtly.

'You disapproved?' she asked.

'Look – I thought you wanted to discuss the tomb?'

'I do… sorry. Let's do that now.'

The professor told her what he could remember of their discoveries. Of the pair of tombs, and of George's assertion that the first tomb probably contained the remains of the Jewish queen Berenice – but that it had been impossible to verify it.

'And the other tomb?'

'Oh… he had a number of theories. I think it's certainly possible that it was her husband. Or at least someone she thought of as a husband.'

'That's what I thought… the arrangement all suggests a married couple. A planned burial – a deliberate attempt to arrange their affairs, to end their lives lying side by side.'

'Yes… I would have to agree.'

'So could it be Titus, perhaps – the lost emperor?' Sophie suggested, tentatively.

'That's a huge leap of faith,' said the Professor. 'It's a romantic idea, certainly, and one which George posited. But we have no way of knowing. What was the inscription again – I can't quite recall.'

'There were two above the second grave,' said Sophie. '*Virus in pace Bonus*' and '*Bonus in pace Bonus*'… It's odd. Bonus obviously means "good". Virus, at a pinch, could mean "man". But I've been wondering… was "Bonus" in fact a name? Not "good man", but a nickname. Could Bonus have been another way of saying "Titus"?'

'Well, if you know your Roman history,' said Professor Moncrieff, 'you will know that Titus was referred to as "the darling of the human race", by the historian Suetonius. Titus was a good-looking man, affable, cultivated, an excellent rider and swordsman, a wise man. And for the brief period he was emperor, he was considered a fine and kind leader of men. He was most affected by the tragedy of Pompeii and Herculaneum after the eruption and took great trouble to help the people. He was called "the Delight of Mankind" and it's said that if he got to the end of any day without doing a good service for someone, he would cry out "I have lost a day".'

'How remarkable,' said Sophie.

'So – he was, without doubt, in the eyes of many of his contemporaries, a "good man". I agree that it is tempting to assume he might have travelled to visit the woman he loved, against the advice of all his senators. If he died on the journey, or after he arrived, it would be logical to assume he had been buried on the island, and it would have been prudent to leave his grave unmarked. How could they do anything else? It would have been unthinkable for a Roman Emperor to lie for eternity next to a Jewish Queen. So if it is him lying there, it was done without any formal sanction. The combination of Latin and Hebrew inscriptions alone indicates that. The Romans would never have allowed it.'

'So you think, Bonus... could be a secret code for Titus?'

'That's not what I said. It's possible, of course. But we are not interested in possibilities – are we, my dear? We are concerned, only, with evidence. And unless you have discovered something else that we missed, I fear we are still lacking that crucial piece of evidence.'

As Sophie was leaving the professor's rooms that afternoon, she turned at the doorway.

'I hope I didn't upset you earlier, by talking about my grand-mother?'

Moncrieff looked at her with his pale, watery grey eyes. 'I will tell you something, my dear. I loved her... I was only a young man myself, a mere year or two older than she. She was a bewitching girl – your grandmother; a great beauty. I can see her now, in her red dress, laughing as I drove her around the island. We knew one another for six months or so; I cared for her very much. But she never loved me, sadly. She loved another – the young Italian who stole her from me.'

'I'm so sorry,' said Sophie.

'So am I,' said the professor, shaking her hand.

As she drove home that evening, Sophie thought about her grand-mother. The old lady she had known growing up in Hampstead, with her dark hair greying. Her simple, unfashionable clothes. She never wore make-up or dressed in a glamorous fashion. She had seemed so content, and Sophie had thought of her, merely, as the source of comfort and happiness – a steadying influence on the family; always in the kitchen, baking, or cooking, always ready with a funny story, or a piece of advice. But somehow they had all missed something – something desperately important. That her grandmother had the ability to make men fall in her path. Bewitching, Moncrieff had called her...

Like Berenice, perhaps... a queen amongst women. A woman who had the power to entice an Emperor to cross the seas from his power base in Rome and lie next to her for eternity.

Chapter 33

The christening took place in London. The party afterwards was held in the garden of the house at Willow Road. The baby, named Rachael Giulia, wore the christening gown from Sant'Antioco. Uncle Tom stood as godfather, cradling the child proudly in his arms. Next to him, stood his own father – Tommaso. Sophie had booked his flight, arranging for a car to drive him from Sant'Antioco to Cagliari, where he would catch the plane to London. It was the first aeroplane he had ever been on and Sophie and Hamish had gone to the airport to meet him. He looked so out of place standing near the barrier at Heathrow – looking about him, mystified, terrified almost, of the crowds and the noise and the bustle.

But now, here in the garden, as he stood shoulder-to-shoulder with his son, he gazed down at the baby, and his eyes filled with tears.

As the guests arrived from the church, they filled the garden with their chatter, serving themselves with champagne from Alex's outdoor bar.

'So he was right…' said Sophie, as she sat surveying the scene with her mother. 'Old Tommaso… I did need that gown after all.'

She fingered the byssus bracelet around her wrist.

'I wonder how he knew?' asked Angela.

'I don't know… but he seemed quite certain.'

'Do you know when you got pregnant – I've never liked to ask…'

'Well, I think it must have been when Hamish and I got back to together…'

'You don't need to tell me anymore…'

'It just seems so odd… all that effort, all that agonising about IVF and then it just happened – quite naturally.'

'It's not as unusual as you might think…' said her mother, taking her hand. 'And you and Hamish – you're all right?'

'Yes… we're good. Just loving the baby. Look at him, showing her off to everyone.'

'He's completely happy isn't he,' said Angela, watching her son-in-law mingling with the guests, his baby daughter in his arms.

'He's besotted – he won't let me take her out of our room yet. He says he worries she'll be lonely. But the nursery's all ready.'

'Yellow?' asked her mother.

'Yes… all yellow and white. It's very pretty.'

'And is all well in the village,' asked Angela.

'You mean… have I seen Flora?'

'Well, I did wonder.'

'There's news about her, as it happens.'

'Oh really – what?'

'They're moving… It seems she'd been… dallying with one or two village gentlemen. Marcus, her husband, is divorcing her. The house is on the market and she's already gone back to London. I saw the removal vans leaving the village a few weeks back.'

'Gosh – that's rather sudden.'

'Yes… but I'm glad she's gone. I just hope she learns to be a bit nicer to those children of hers.'

'How does Hamish feel about it?'

'Relieved I think. It was a bit awkward her living so close by. He dreaded bumping into her.'

'So the end of one chapter then?' said her mother.

'Yes… and the start of a new one.'

Sophie looked around the garden filled with people she loved. Hamish, proudly displaying his beloved daughter. Tommaso and Tom standing companionably together in the corner of the garden.

'It's good to see old Tommaso,' said Angela, following her gaze. 'Tom is thrilled that he's coming to stay with him. He's been looking up Italian boat terms so they can communicate properly!'

'That's lovely. They look right together – don't they?'

'They do, darling. They do…'

The following day, as the family said its goodbyes, Sophie kissed her Uncle Tom.

'Goodbye Tom – thank you for being godfather.'

'I'm honoured,' he said.

'I hope you have a wonderful time with Tommaso. Will you be all right, do you think?'

'Oh yes…' said Tom. 'In spite of the language barrier, I think we'll be fine. Men and boats – we don't need to say much. Besides, there's just an understanding between us – you know?'

'I know… I can see that,' said Sophie. 'Tom… before we go, there's something I'd like to show you'.

'Yes, darling, what is it?'

'I've been saving it… I wasn't sure whether to give it to you, or Tommaso, but I feel I must.'

'What?'

'It's a letter – a letter I found recently in Rachael's desk. The photograph was hidden in a little cupboard. This was in another larger envelope in one of the drawers. I took all the papers home ages ago to sort them out but didn't get round to it until recently. It's a letter she wrote to Tommaso but never sent. I thought you should have it.'

She opened her bag and handed him the envelope.

'Read it – it's your call whether you ever show it to Tommaso.'

Heath House,
Willow Road,
Hampstead,
London

20th May 1978

My dearest Tommaso,

*I wonder if you know how often I have wanted to write
to you. How often I <u>have</u> written to you. I never sent the
letters of course – not wishing to upset you, or your wife.
What, after all, was the point in writing – we both know
how much we meant to the other; and we both know that,
in the end, it was not to be. You were promised elsewhere
and it would have been wrong to break that bond. But I
am writing today because I think there is something that
you ought to know, something you have a right to know…*

*You have a son… We have a son. His name is Tom – and
today is his eighteenth birthday. I'm sorry if this is a shock. I had
no idea when I left the island that I was carrying your child.
I only found out a couple of months after I returned home. I
thought then of writing, of begging you to take me back. But
it wouldn't have been fair. You may have been married already
by then and what, after all, could you have done?*

*So much has happened since I left you. Where to begin,
my dear?*

*After I left the island, I thought I would never be happy
again. Our love had been so special – there was a tenderness
and passion about it that I had never felt before, or since.
To have that snatched away seemed so unjust at the time.
But I want you to know that I did find love again – with
an American named Charles. We lived very happily in
New York for a year or so, but he was killed in a terrible air*

accident when Tom was just a baby. I came back to England and returned to the house where my father and I lived in Hampstead. I felt so lost, but I did, at least, have the children.

My father, Angela, Tom and I stayed in the house – renting some rooms in the attic. And then one very sad day the landlady, Mrs Roper, died suddenly. It was so very sad. She loved us all and made us all so welcome. When her will was read, I discovered she had left the house to me. I was amazed, and delighted – I cannot conceal it. We have lived here ever since.

My darling father died a few years later. That broke my heart. But he lived long enough to see his grandchildren growing strong and healthy. And he was a good age and, although he had endured much suffering in his life, was content, I believe, at the last. But it was hard to be left, finally alone. I thought then of writing to you... but you had your life in Sant'Antioco, and mine was here...

Our boy grows more and more like you. Even though we live on the edge of a huge city, his favourite pastime is fishing. My husband Charles left a little money to be settled on Tom when he is twenty-one. He wants to repair boats and we have found an old derelict boatyard on the coast in Dorset. If he gets on well there, I shall buy it for him. He will be happy there, I know.

We cannot ever go back, Tommaso. The past, after all, is over and done with. The future is what matters now. So write to me? Tell me about your life. Are you happy with your wife – I never knew her name. Did you have children? I think of you so often in the cottage near the cove. I think of how you saved my child from the waters. Of how you comforted me and loved me...

I think of you...

A Letter from Debbie Rix

I want to say a huge thank you for choosing to read *The Photograph*. If you did enjoy it, and want to keep up-to-date with all my latest releases, just sign up at the following link. Your email address will never be shared and you can unsubscribe at any time.

www.bookouture.com/debbie-rix

I hope you enjoyed *The Photograph,* and if you did, I would be very grateful if you could write a review. I'd love to hear what you think, as it helps new readers discover my books for the first time.

I'm always happy to hear from my readers. You can get in touch through my Facebook page, Twitter, Goodreads, or my website.

Thanks,
Debbie Rix

@debbierix

DebbieRixAuthor

www.debbierix.com

Historical Note

I first became interested in the process of producing sea-silk whilst researching my previous book *The Silk Weaver's Wife*. I came across a reference to this mysterious fabric and began to explore it. I knew instantly that it would form the basis of a novel.

In 2017, I visited the little island of Sant'Antioco, which is linked to the main island of Sardinia by a man-made causeway. This delightful island is now one of the last places in the world where byssus or 'sea-silk' is still produced. At one time, this fabric was widely manufactured by people on the shores of the Mediterranean. There are references to it for at least two thousand years and it is thought to be the explanation for many of the biblical references to 'cloth of gold' – for when you hold up this remarkable fabric in the sunlight, it does indeed glisten like gold.

Italo Diano (1890–1969) founded a weaving atelier in the 1930s on Sant'Antioco, and one or two of her ex-students still work with sea silk on a small scale – but only to demonstrate the process; it is no longer a viable manufactured product. I visited the museum in the town, where I was shown how to spin and weave this remarkable thread and was given a slender byssus bracelet that inspired me as I wrote this novel.

The other 'thread' to this story was inspired by the life and death of the Jewish queen Berenice and her lover Emperor Titus. Berenice met Titus when he came to the Holy Land on behalf of the Roman Empire and suppressed the Jewish revolt. He fell in love with the beautiful Berenice and they conducted a long love affair. She finally followed him back to Rome and lived with him as his wife, but when he was made emperor – on the death of his father – it was considered impossible for him to marry the Jewish queen. Consequently, she was banished, but there are no records of where she may have gone. She simply disappears from the historical record. One possibility is that she went to Sant'Antioco – then an outpost of the Roman Empire and widely settled by people of the Jewish faith. And if she did go to Sant'Antioco, did she also bring with her the skill of weaving byssus – something that was widespread along the shores of the Holy Land?

This theory is given substance by the discovery of a pair of tombs beneath the cathedral in Sant'Antioco. Hidden behind centuries of dirt and dust were the inscriptions that indicate that a woman named Beronice (note a slightly different spelling of the name) is buried in one of the graves, and her husband 'a good man' in the other. They have been the subject of research since their discovery in 1885. Who is the 'Berenice' who is buried there? And could it be that it is Queen Berenice and her lover? Theories abound, obviously; some researchers insist that the graves are not, in fact, Roman, but date from the fourth century and that the woman buried there is not a queen, but another Jewish woman named Beronice. But the mystery around the graves persists, and the idea that this burial site is the final resting place of the Jewish queen remains as intoxicating as ever.

My novels tend to mix historical fact with fiction and this one is no different. The historical facts in this novel include the discovery in 1912 of a piece of byssus fabric dating from the fourth century. It was found by an archaeologist in the grave of a woman at Aquincum – the Roman city near modern-day Budapest. The person who found it was Hungarian, but he was not called George Laszlo – that is my invention.

George's character was loosely based upon the Head of Talks and Documentaries at the BBC – George Fischer – who escaped the Hungarian uprising of 1956 and came to London. I worked for him for a few brief months in the 1970s when I began my career at the BBC and he was one of the kindest and most intelligent men I have ever met. My character is a complete fiction, but I hope the 'real' George won't mind me 'stealing' his Christian name for the purposes of this novel.

Acknowledgements

I am grateful to the following people for their help with the writing of this book:

My family – as always – for putting up with me as I lock myself away for months on end in 'the shed'.

My editor Natasha Harding for her encouragement and insight.

To Kim Nash and all the team at Bookouture for their unwavering support.

My friend Vanessa Nicolson for her invaluable help translating dense Italian archaeological research papers as well as with colloquial Italian.

I was inspired by watching Chiara Vigo – 'the last Master of marine byssus' – at work at the museum of byssus in Sant'Antioco. Susanna Lavazza's book about Chiara and the history of byssus was also a useful resource.

Robert Conard's account of his time working as a young student in the refugee camp in Traiskirchen in 1956 provided a wonderful insight into that period of history.